Baby for the Billionaire

MAXINE
SULLIVAN

DAY
LECLAIRE

TESSA
RADLEY

Mills & Boon, an imprint of Harlequin (UK) Limited, Eton House, 18-24 Paradise Road, Richmond, Surrey TW9 1SR

BABY FOR THE BILLIONAIRE
© Harlequin Enterprises II B.V./S.à.r.l 2013

Valente Must Marry © Maxine Sullivan 2009
Inherited: One Child © Day Totton Smith 2009
Billion-Dollar Baby Bargain © Tessa Radley 2009

ISBN: 978 0 263 90611 0

011-0513

Harlequin (UK) policy is to use papers that are natural, renewable and recyclable products and made from wood grown in sustainable forests. The logging and manufacturing processes conform to the legal environmental regulations of the country of origin.

Printed and bound in Spain
by Blackprint CPI, Barcelona

VALENTE
MUST MARRY

MAXINE
SULLIVAN

THE BABY COLLECTION

May 2013

June 2013

July 2013

August 2013

Maxine Sullivan credits her mother for her lifelong love of romance novels, so it was a natural extension for Maxine to want to write her own romances. She thinks there's nothing better than being a writer and is thrilled to be one of the few Australians to write for the Desire™ line. Maxine lives in Melbourne, Australia, but over the years has travelled to New Zealand, the UK and the USA. In her own backyard, her husband's job ensured they saw the diversity of the countryside, from the tropics to the Outback, country towns to the cities. She is married to Geoff, who has proven his hero status many times over the years. They have two handsome sons and an assortment of much loved, previously abandoned animals. Maxine would love to hear from you and can be contacted through her website at www.maxinesullivan.com.

One

"What are you saying, Dad?" Nick Valente asked his father, Cesare, as they sat on one of the terraced courtyards on the Valente estate.

"I'm saying I've been retired over six months now and while I've loved it here, this place is getting too big for us. Isabel and I have decided to move into an apartment in town."

The statement sucked the wind out of Nick. This place was *home*. He'd grown up on this estate in the Hawkesbury district of Sydney. His own mother had given birth to him here before taking off for greener pastures, leaving his father to meet Isabel six months later.

"The estate is yours," Cesare continued. "If you want it."

Something leaped inside him. Did his father even have to ask? Of course he wanted it. He wanted it so badly he had to turn his head away and look down over the cultivated lawns, lest his father see how *much* he wanted it.

And there was the crux of the matter.

He didn't trust his father.

Cesare was a crafty old devil who'd had a long reign as founder of The House of Valente, an Australian perfume dynasty now branching out in the rest of the world under the control of the eldest son, Alex, with their new perfume, "Valente's Woman." Cesare was used to getting his own way.

"And if I don't want it?" he said, playing it cool, just like he did every day in his job as Chief Operating Officer for the family business.

"Then I'll give it to Matt."

Damn.

He was close to Matt, but his younger brother liked living in the center of the city, and this place would end up neglected. Matt would die out here on the far outskirts of Sydney, no matter that he could commute.

He, on the other hand, would appreciate the break away from his city apartment and from the constant round of hard work and equally hard play.

He casually turned his head to look at his father. "Matt's never liked this place much," he pointed out coolly.

Cesare inclined his gray head. "I know that."

"So why give it to him?"

"I haven't…yet. It all depends on you."

His misgivings were increasing by the moment. "What's the catch, Dad?"

Cesare's lips twisted wryly. "You know me well." A calculating expression took over the older man's face. "You can have the estate on one condition. You have to get married."

Nick straightened in his chair. "What the hell!"

"This place needs a young family again."

"So I'm supposed to get married *and* have a family, too?" he said, sarcastically.

"That's usually the way it goes."

Nick shook his head. He had no plans to get married just yet. No woman was going to tie him down, and he'd be damned if he'd bring a child into the world whose parents didn't love each other.

"What about Alex and Olivia?" It was the most acceptable option to him. At least they would give this place the care it deserved.

"No, they have their own house now and wouldn't want to move. It would unsettle little Scott."

Yes, that was true. Alex and Olivia had adopted

eight-year-old Scott at Christmas. They wouldn't want to move again so soon, if at all.

Suddenly something clicked in Nick's brain as he looked at his father. "Tell me you didn't have anything to do with Alex marrying Olivia."

Cesare didn't even flinch. "I'd be lying if I said I hadn't."

Nick's mouth tightened. "Does Mum know what you've been up to?"

He'd always considered Isabel his mother. She was elegant, charming, loving, and quite formidable when riled. She'd been the only mother he'd known—until his real mother had started turning up during his childhood, causing havoc.

"Isabel and I have agreed to disagree. She knows my feelings on this, and I'm not about to change my mind. It's too important to me."

Nick swore. "Dammit, I'm not marrying some woman just to satisfy your perverted sense of power."

"Then Matt gets the estate."

His stomach tightened. "Matt won't want it once I tell him what game you're playing."

Cesare took a sip of his coffee before putting the cup down on the table. "Then I'll have to sell, won't I?"

Nick swallowed hard. His father thought he had it all figured out, did he?

"Just who the hell am I supposed to marry anyway? Should I just pick a woman from my Rolodex?"

"Sasha Blake."

Nick's brain stumbled. He hadn't thought about that name in years…hadn't thought about *her* in years…hadn't thought about that kiss.

Well, rarely.

"She isn't in my Rolodex," he snapped, not wanting to think about her at all. That kiss had been a minor lapse in judgment.

"She's perfect for you."

"I'm glad you think so."

Displeasure furrowed Cesare's brow, then cleared. "You'll see. Once you marry her you'll—"

"I'm *not* marrying her, Dad." If he was getting married—and he wasn't saying he would—*he'd* choose the woman. "Besides, isn't she in England?"

"No, she's back. She's an interior designer now, and I've asked her to redecorate this house."

The surprises just kept on coming, didn't they?

"This place is fine the way it is."

Cesare considered him. "You've always loved it here."

Nick shrugged. "It's home."

"And that's why I'm offering it to you."

"But only if I marry Sasha Blake, right?"

"It'll be good to join the two families. Porter and Sally Blake have been our friends for years."

"I've never trusted Porter." Sally was a nice enough woman, if a little too submissive.

"Forget Porter Blake. It's his daughter you're marrying."

"I'm not marrying anyone. Period."

There was a small pause. "Sasha will be here tomorrow morning checking things while we're in the city. It might be a good time to talk to her."

"No."

His father went very still. Then, "I think Matt will be more than happy to change the whole look of this place, don't you? And Sasha must have some innovative ideas she's picked up from living in London."

Nick swore. "Why are you doing this, Dad?"

Cesare looked at him, a hint of vulnerability in his eyes. "I've had one heart attack already. I want to see you married before I die."

"It was a mild heart attack," Nick rasped, remembering.

"And the next one may be fatal, *figlio mio*," *son of mine*, he said, lapsing into Italian.

Nick felt an inward shudder at the thought and knew his father had him right where he wanted him. He could fight Cesare on everything but this. That heart attack had really shaken up the whole family, and *he* wasn't about to be responsible for any further attacks.

Marrying to please his father may sound ridiculous in this day and age, but he'd been raised with strong family values. He'd do what was necessary.

But did it have to be Sasha Blake of all people he had to marry?

A shapely female bottom and matching long legs in white trousers greeted Nick when he opened the front door to his parents' house the next morning. They belonged to a gorgeous female figure standing in strappy sandals on a chair near the staircase.

At least they were until the woman turned, saw him and gave a squeal of fright, then started to topple off. He raced forward and caught her as she fell back into his arms.

For a moment she stared up at him. "Nick?" she whispered, almost as if his name was a secret.

He looked down at the beautiful blonde and wanted to lie and say no, he wasn't Nick. And he'd never kissed her either. Nor did he want to again.

She was Trouble.

And he had to ask her to marry him.

"Hello, Sasha."

She continued to stare up at him with eyes good at robbing a man of his thoughts. He'd forgotten the impact of those long sweeping lashes featuring eyes the color of green satin. Even when she was growing up there was something about them that tried to pierce his defenses. It had taken a constant and concentrated effort not to let her succeed.

Their kiss had come close.

"What on earth were you doing up there?" he growled, setting her on her feet, fascinated despite himself at the visible pulse beating at her throat and a faint blush dusting her cheeks. She'd been a pretty teenager before, but now she'd grown into a very beautiful woman.

She pushed against him and stepped back. "I thought I saw a crack in the wall, so I was checking it out."

The impact of her touch lingered. And so did the scent of her perfume—Valente's Woman. Somehow he was glad she wore his family's perfume.

"I hear you're an interior designer now," he said for something to say.

"Yes, I am." She seemed to pull herself together, and an excited light entered her eyes. "And I'm so happy your father chose me to redecorate this place."

Remembering, he shot her a dark look. "I don't want this house redecorated. It's fine how it is."

Disappointment crossed her face before she gave a tiny smile that held a touch of defiance. "Then it's as well this isn't your house, or I wouldn't have a job."

Tension rocked his stomach. "Look, let's go into the salon. I'll get Iris to make us some coffee."

Her expression grew wary. "I'm supposed to be working."

"Then add an extra hour's wages to the bill. My father can afford it."

She tipped her head to one side, her straight blond hair swaying like a sheen of silk over her shoulders. "You're very generous with your father's money."

"He wants me to talk to you."

She tensed. "Oh. I see. He's firing me, is he?"

"No, it's not that at all." But she was going to wish it was.

Relief fluttered across her face. "Then what can you possibly say to me that he can't himself?"

Marry me.

He opened his mouth to say it but realized it would be a bit too much all in the space of a minute. No need to break a record with this.

He gestured toward the salon. "The coffee first." He waited for her to precede him, then used the intercom to ask Iris to bring in some coffee.

When he turned to look at Sasha she was standing by the fireplace. Suddenly he couldn't take his eyes off her. It was crazy but she looked so right standing there in tailored white pants and a soft-knit green top, slim and refined and such a contrast amongst all this heavy, ornate furniture.

"It's not polite to stare."

Her words broke through his thoughts. "You're

different from what I remember." It was more than a physical difference, but he wasn't sure what it was yet.

Her eyelids flickered. "What do you remember, Nick?"

"Our kiss."

She gave a soft gasp. "It's not gentlemanly of you to bring that up."

"I was only being honest."

"Ever heard of being too honest?"

"I don't work like that."

"True. You were nothing less than honest after that kiss, weren't you?" she said, a wry twist coating her lips.

"If you mean that I didn't profess everlasting love, then you're right. I'd prefer not to sugarcoat things." It had been a kiss—a stunner of a kiss—but that's all it was. "Why, did I hurt your ego?"

"What? No way," she said quickly, perhaps too quickly. "It was my first kiss by a man, that's all. Up until then they'd all been boys."

"No doubt you've been plenty kissed since then."

"I'm not naive."

"Yes, I remember Randall. You had a fling with him, didn't you?"

Strangely, the thought of her with other men—with Randall Tremaine—had always unsettled him, but he forced himself to ignore it. She could kiss whomever she liked, make love to whomever she liked. And she had. It had nothing to do with him.

Until now.

She gave a shaky sigh. "I can't believe the first thing we talk about after seven years is kissing."

"I can."

A blush rose up her cheeks but just then Iris appeared in the doorway with the tray of coffee, interrupting the moment. They exchanged a few pleasantries, then Iris put the tray down on the coffee table and left the room.

"Shall I pour?" Sasha said, taking a seat on the sofa.

"Thanks." He sat down opposite, watching as she poured with an elegance that was innate. Once again he had the feeling she looked right in this setting. He grimaced to himself. Or perhaps it was just because his father had implanted the idea in him.

"So how long has it been since you left for London?" he asked as she passed him the cup and saucer.

"Five years."

"You were twenty when you left. That's young to be in a big city by yourself."

"I wasn't by myself," she said, and just for a moment his breath stopped at the thought of her living with another man. "I have an aunt who lives there, so I stayed with her for a few years. Then I got my own place." She picked up her own cup and saucer but didn't drink from it. "Our fathers are friends. I'm sure your father would have told you all this."

"He probably did," he said without thinking, angry at himself for caring even for a moment that she may have lived with some guy.

"But you didn't bother to listen, right?"

He didn't like being put on the spot like that. *He* was usually the one putting people on the spot. "It's been five years. I'd probably forgotten it long ago."

She held his gaze for a moment. "I'm sure." Her tone made him stiffen but before he could analyze her response, she put her coffee cup down on the table. "Now. Please give me the message from your father. I need to get back to work."

Fine. So did he.

He placed his own cup on the table, then leaned back on the sofa, giving himself a full view of her face. He needed to see her reaction. "It's not a message exactly. It's more a request."

Her smooth brow crinkled in a frown. "He wants me to do something?"

"Yes." He paused, trying to find the words that had been going over and over in his head all night. "Did he tell you he and my mother are moving into a smaller place in the city?"

She blinked in surprise. "No, he didn't." Her forehead cleared. "So *that's* why he wants me to re-decorate. He's planning on selling."

"No, he's not selling. He wants to keep it in the family. He wants *me* to have it."

Her eyes lit up, making her look even more beautiful. "Oh, that's wonderful, Nick. This place is gorgeous. I've always loved coming here."

Something wavered inside him. "Then perhaps you'd like to stay."

Her enthusiasm paused. "What do you mean? Rent it from you or something?"

"I mean share it with me."

"Sh…share it with you?" she all but squeaked.

"He wants me to marry you, Sasha."

She sucked in a sharp breath, then slowly let it out. "Good Lord."

His sentiments exactly. His father's ultimatum had been one of the few times in his life he'd had the rug pulled out from under him. He didn't like the feeling. Not one bit.

"Why?" she said in amazement after a moment or two.

"He wants to give me this house to carry on the Valente name but he knows I don't want to settle down so he's blackmailing me. If I don't marry you he'll give the house to Matt."

She shook her head. "No, this place doesn't suit Matt. It suits *you*."

He warmed to her.

"But Nick, I don't understand why he's chosen me for your wife."

He shrugged. "For some reason he thinks you're perfect for me."

Her eyes softened. "He does?" Then she stiffened and began to shift uneasily. "That's sweet of him, but we both know that's ridiculous. I've just come along at the right time, that's all."

"It seems that way," he agreed, happy to see she had a clear head on her shoulders. This was going to be easier than he'd expected. They wouldn't have to get mixed up with all the emotional trappings other married couples had to worry about.

"So what are you going to do, Nick?"

"Marry you."

The blood drained from her face but she soon gathered herself together. "Oh, really?"

He'd made up his mind to do this, and he didn't expect any resistance to the idea. "He's dead serious, Sasha. He wants a Valente to live in this house, and he wants our families to be joined."

She shook her head. "No, Nick."

"I don't like it any more than you do. Frankly, marriage was never in my cards. I like being single."

"So do I."

That surprised him. Career women or not, most of his lady friends had wanted more than a sexual relationship. Most had wanted marriage, despite their declarations that they didn't.

"You may not know this, but my father had a heart attack six months ago. It was only a mild one," he assured her, seeing her slight alarm, "but he's worried he'll have a major one and won't see me married before then. That's why he's come up with this plan."

"Nick, I'm sorry about his heart attack, but I can't do this."

His mouth tightened. "Then this place will go to Matt. I suggest you get ready for some heavy modernization when you redecorate."

She winced. "Talk to your father, Nick. He may let you marry someone else."

All at once he didn't want any other woman. "I know my father. He won't want anyone but you. He can be stubborn."

"So can I."

"Sasha, look—"

She sprang to her feet. "Nick, stop it." Then she straightened her shoulders, her eyes showing a spirit only hinted at while growing up. "Now, if you don't mind, I need to get on with the job, no matter whom the redecoration is for."

She hurried out the door, her high heels clicking on the timber floor as she headed down the hallway toward the kitchen.

Nick sat back on the sofa and contemplated what had just happened. There weren't many women who would actually refuse to marry him. Hell, he didn't think there were any.

But if he was getting married then so was Sasha Blake.

To him.

He just had to find a way to make it happen.

He smiled grimly. Making things happen was one thing a Valente did extremely well.

Two

Sasha finished taking measurements at the Valente mansion, then left as soon as she could. She kept expecting to turn around and find Nick there, ready to pressure her into marriage.

A marriage he didn't want.

And neither did she.

So why was she worried? With his father giving his stamp of approval she was just a convenience, that's all. Nick would go find someone else to marry, and Cesare wouldn't really care as long as it was someone suitable.

Of course if Nick *did* marry then she'd have to

work with Nick and his new wife to redecorate the house. Could she do it, knowing how much she'd been in love with him all those years ago?

Not that she was in any danger of loving him now.

No, it would be a matter of pride.

Unable to concentrate on any real plans for the re-decorating until she knew what would happen to the estate, she spent the rest of the afternoon helping her mother around the house. She was preparing dinner around seven when her father walked into the kitchen earlier than usual.

In all the years she'd lived here previously, her father rarely got home before eight. Sasha suspected back then he hadn't always been working late, and that feeling hadn't abated since her return from London. She didn't know how her mother coped with it all.

"I never thought a daughter of mine would be so selfish," Porter Blake snapped with an accusing glare at her.

Sasha's forehead creased as she glanced across at her mother, then back to her father. "What do you mean, Dad?"

"Nick Valente. He asked you to marry him, didn't he?"

Her heart sank. Had Nick gone running to her father? "How did you know that?"

"Cesare told me. And you said *no*. For the love of God, why?"

She tried not to let him make her feel guilty. "I have that right."

"No, you don't. Your mother and I have given you everything, and you can't even do this one thing for us."

Sally Blake started toward him. "Porter, what are—"

"Be quiet, Sally," he all but growled.

Sasha hated the way he talked to her mother in private. In company, butter wouldn't melt in his mouth.

"Dad, don't speak to Mum that way."

Porter made a dismissive gesture. "This isn't about your mother and me. This is about you and Nick. Dammit, girl. It's not like Nick isn't a good-looking young man."

Sasha could only stare at him in dismay. "I don't understand why you want me to marry at all."

Her father's eyes darted away, then back again. "The Valentes are our closest friends. It would be nice to join the two families."

That was a crazy reason to get married. Nobody did that sort of thing anymore, or if they did *she* wasn't about to do it.

"Dad, I'm not going to marry a man I don't love just to bring two families together."

The wind seemed to leave Porter and he sat down

heavily on a chair, looking defeated. "If you don't, then say goodbye to this house and everything we have."

"What are you talking about?"

"If I don't close a deal with the Valentes soon, I'll lose my shipping business. If that happens we lose everything."

Sasha ignored her mother's gasp. "But Cesare's your friend. He'll give you the deal."

"He's a businessman first. If anyone undercuts my offer he'll go with them." He paused. "Unless you're his daughter-in-law and then he'll want to keep it in the family."

"You don't know what you're asking," she whispered.

Her father sighed heavily. "You're right, but it's the only chance we've got."

Sasha shook her head. No, she couldn't do it. It was too much to ask of her.

Then she caught her mother's pleading eyes. "Sasha, darling," Sally began. "Do you think it would be so terrible to marry Nick?"

She drew a painful breath. "Oh, Mum, no. Don't ask this of me."

"Darling, I have to. If not for your father's sake, then mine."

Sasha hated seeing how her mother always put her husband first, and no amount of talking on her part could change her mind. It was part of the reason she'd gone to London. She'd had to get away from her parents.

And from the memory of Nick Valente.

She sighed with defeat. "Do you have Nick's address?"

Her father's face lit up and so did her mother's. "No, but I can get it right now." He jumped to his feet, then hesitated. "Thank you, Sasha," he muttered, then strode out of the kitchen.

Sasha looked at her mother, who was blinking back tears of happiness. "Darling, I'm sorry. I know—"

"Mum, please don't say anything right now."

Her mother flushed. "Okay. If that's what you want."

"It is."

Sasha went to get her purse when her father came back with Nick's address. It was small comfort to know she could help her parents.

At what cost to herself she wasn't sure.

An hour later she stood in front of Nick's apartment and rang the doorbell. Right now the cost seemed much too high a price to pay.

Oh God, if only this had been seven years ago. She'd have given anything for him to ask her to marry him back then.

She remembered that kiss in the gazebo in the summer rain. It had just happened and she'd almost melted in a puddle at his feet. He'd surely felt everything she'd felt, she'd told herself as it ended and she'd moved in closer for another one. He'd realize he loved her and couldn't live without her and any moment he'd tell her so.

Instead he'd held her back from him, obviously appalled he'd kissed her. She'd seen it in his blue eyes that had turned from light blue to dark in a matter of seconds.

And then he'd left her there, gone back up to the main house to the party and casually taken another woman home, just like he'd been exchanging his Ferrari for another model. It had devastated her, but she'd never let him know it.

Right at that moment the door opened and Nick stood there, devastatingly handsome and undeniably male, and nothing on his handsome face giving away any of his thoughts.

He moved back to let her enter the apartment. "My father said you'd be stopping by."

"Word gets around fast."

She stepped through the doorway, trying to shake her feelings of the past. It was the present…now… that should concern her.

He gestured to the leather couch. "Make yourself comfortable. Would you like a drink?"

"No, I'm fine." She couldn't sit, and if she tried to drink anything she'd probably choke. Her throat ached with pure defeat.

His blue eyes rested on her. "So what made you change your mind?"

"My parents." She didn't want him to think it had been for any other reason. "I'm their only child and they really want our families to be joined." She swallowed hard. "I can't deny them that."

Cynicism twisted the corners of his mouth. "I'm sure your father's delighted."

Her heart thudded inside her chest. Could Nick know that her father's shipping business needed this deal?

Then she realized he didn't know. If he did, he'd have certainly blackmailed her into marriage. Nick wouldn't hesitate to use any leverage he could to get her to do what he wanted.

Still, she felt the need to defend her father.

She angled her chin. "Why do you say it like that?"

"Your mother's a nice woman. I'm sure she wouldn't pressure you into a marriage you don't want."

She realized he didn't know her mother that well. If her father wanted something, then her mother was usually the go-between.

He held her gaze. "I don't think I can say the same for your father."

"And that's so different from *your* father?"

Surprise flickered in his eyes. "True."

She briefly appreciated her feeling of triumph. "*Both* my parents are happy about this marriage, Nick."

He scrutinized her. "Why do I believe you?"

"Because it's the truth." She couldn't confess her mother was happy for Porter's sake, or Nick might get suspicious.

"Okay, let's get down to business. First, I want to assure you that if things don't work out we can always get a divorce later on."

She winced inwardly at his insensitivity, or his honesty, as he liked to call it. It was the same this morning when he'd asked if his rejection had hurt her ego in the gazebo that night.

Could a man be so hard-hearted to a young woman in love with him?

Hadn't he been able to tell she'd put her heart and soul into that kiss?

Of course he hadn't.

"Are you reassuring me or yourself?" she asked cynically.

He scowled. "I just don't want either of us to feel totally trapped."

"How nice."

He shot her a hard look, then, "Do you want children?"

Her heart skipped a beat and all her cynicism disappeared. "Do you?"

"One day. Not yet."

"Me, too." She hadn't thought about children. They were a lifetime commitment, and one that connected her to Nick for the rest of her life.

She wasn't sure she could do that.

Wasn't sure she *wanted* that.

He started toward a small table where there were a bunch of papers. "Right. Looks like we have a wedding to plan."

She took a quick breath. "Hold on. I have one condition of my own before we settle this."

He stopped to look at her, his eyebrow winging upward. "And that is?"

"You remain faithful to me," she said without hesitation. "I won't accept the humiliation of you having affairs. If you can't do it, tell me now."

Something shifted in his expression. "It's not that I can't do it. The question is whether I *want* to remain faithful."

She tensed. "I'd suggest you've probably had enough affairs to last a lifetime anyway."

"You know me so well," he drawled.

She raised her chin. "I'll accept nothing less, Nick."

There was a lengthy silence as their eyes held and locked. This was the one thing she wouldn't relent on, it was too important to her.

Then he expelled a breath. "You may be surprised

to know this but I do take marriage vows seriously, and mine especially. I can assure you I will remain faithful."

She let out a quiet sigh, but wasn't sure if it was relief or despair. Her only chance to refuse to marry him had just dissolved into thin air.

On the other hand, at least she could do this one thing for her mother. She had to keep remembering that.

"The wedding will be in three weeks."

She swallowed past her dry throat. "That soon?"

"The sooner we get this over and done with the better."

"Yes," she said, giving in to the inevitable.

She felt the same as Nick, but probably for different reasons. She suspected Cesare wouldn't let his sons sign the deal for her father until after their marriage vows had been taken. Cesare wasn't a fool.

If only he was.

Nick was pleased with himself after Sasha left his apartment. He'd known he wouldn't have to do a thing except tell his father she had refused his offer. Cesare had immediately got on the phone to Porter and offered regrets that they wouldn't be in-laws.

And that's all that was needed. Porter knew what side his bread was buttered, and the last thing he would want was to offend Cesare.

Nick gave a snort of derision. Porter Blake was a

wimp. If the Valente family didn't have money, the other man wouldn't be hanging around being Cesare's friend. No, Porter would be out with his latest lady friend. The man was a rake of the worst kind, his affairs the worst-kept secret.

No wonder Sasha was insisting on fidelity in their marriage. She had to know about her father's numerous affairs.

Or did she?

He hadn't asked her straight out in case she didn't know. Not that he was protecting Porter. It was merely that if Sasha didn't know, then he wasn't about to tell her.

He only hoped he didn't live to regret giving his word. Women were notorious for having an angle for everything, and he suspected Sasha did, too.

Was she marrying him for reasons other than her family?

More prestige?

More money?

Better contacts for her work?

Time would tell, but he'd be ready for her if that happened. No one pulled the wool over his eyes. If they did, it didn't happen a second time.

Three

At eighteen Sasha had dreamed about a white wedding to Nick in a beautiful church in Sydney—the perfect setting for their perfect love for each other.

Now at twenty-five, a stylish ceremony on the sun-drenched lawn of the massive Valente estate was more than lovely, but a marriage of convenience to a man who'd never given her a moment's thought wasn't quite the same.

And that was never more prominent than on her wedding day. She'd been nervous in her responses throughout the ceremony but Nick hadn't missed a beat. Obviously she still didn't affect him in the slightest, least of all by marrying him.

"I now pronounce you man and wife."

Oh God. Sasha's knees threatened to wobble, making her grateful for her white wedding gown hiding them from view.

"You may now kiss the bride."

She swallowed hard as she turned to fully face Nick, looking so handsome in his black tuxedo. She'd melted the last time he'd kissed her all those years ago but until his lips were on hers again she wouldn't know for sure how she'd react.

His blue eyes gave nothing away as he lowered his head. Their lips touched and Sasha nervously held her breath, waiting for something…anything… to kick in. It was pleasant, but she didn't melt.

Thank God!

He broke off the kiss and they stared at each other. She was so relieved that she broke into a small smile. His eyes narrowed, making her wonder what he was thinking.

Everyone started to clap, bringing the world back into focus. She turned toward their beaming guests seated on the largest of the private courtyards surrounding the main house. Everyone loved a wedding, it seemed.

Everyone but the bride and groom.

People surrounded them with congratulations

and before too long a string quartet began playing music and waiters started circulating with glasses of champagne.

"You've made your mother and me very happy, Sasha," her father said, kissing her cheek, pride shining from his eyes. It was silly but despite everything, Sasha felt teary that she'd done something to make her father proud of her.

"We're so glad," Nick responded, his voice holding a touch of sarcasm.

His words spoiled the moment for Sasha and she blinked the moisture out of her eyes in time to see Cesare send Nick a warning glance. She wondered again why Nick didn't like her father.

Cesare leaned forward and kissed her on the cheek. "Isabel and I are very happy, too," he said, speaking for his wife, who was seeing to their guests. Then he slapped Porter on the back. "We're all one big happy family now, *amico mio.*"

And Porter beamed. "Yes, our two families have been joined together at last, my friend."

Sasha swallowed back a hysterical comment that perhaps her father should have married Nick, but then she saw her mother's happy face and forced herself to relax.

She had done this for her mother.

After that the late afternoon rolled into evening, drawing the hours closer to when she and Nick would be alone. Thankfully their two hundred guests kept her occupied and stopped her thinking about it too much.

"Everything's gone very smoothly, don't you think?" Isabel asked, rescuing Sasha from an older relative and leading her over to the tables laden with wedding gifts beside the open French doors.

Sasha really liked her new mother-in-law. Isabel had always been one of her favorite people. "You've done wonders, Isabel. Thank you so much. I know it took a lot to get it all done in time, especially when you had to move into your new apartment, as well."

Isabel looked pleased. "Anything for you, Sasha. And Nick, of course." Then as quickly she frowned. "I still don't condone what Cesare has done, but after his heart attack I don't want to upset him too much. I've tried all I can, but he's a law unto himself."

Sasha had appreciated it when Isabel had taken her aside two weeks ago and asked her if she knew what she was doing. The other woman had known her husband was blackmailing Nick into marrying her and for a while she'd been very vocal about it.

Knowing she had to do this, Sasha had hurriedly assured her it was okay, and things had proceeded with alarming speed.

"Being a law unto themselves seems to be a trait of the Valente men," Sasha said.

"Yes. And Nick has assured me he knows what

he's doing." She squeezed Sasha's arm. "I'm so happy to have you in the family."

"Thank you," Sasha said huskily. It was lovely to be welcomed so warmly. If she and Nick were truly in love…

"And you know," Isabel's voice cut through Sasha's thoughts, "when I see how happy Alex and Olivia are now, it appears that Cesare knows what he's doing."

Sasha regarded Nick's older brother across the courtyard. Alex was here today with his wife and their adopted eight-year-old son, Scott. Olivia was the daughter of movie legend, Felicia Cannington, and was just as beautiful as her famous mother, and more than gracious. The love between Alex and Olivia made Sasha catch her breath.

Yet just because last year Cesare had black-mailed Alex into marrying Olivia and somehow the two had fallen in love didn't mean it would work for her and Nick.

It wouldn't.

For love to grow there had to be a basic need for love within that person. Nick had no need for love from any woman, and especially not *her.*

"They certainly look very happy," Sasha agreed, keeping quiet about her thoughts. Isabel loved Nick and only wanted the best for her second stepson she'd raised since he was a baby.

Isabel nodded. "You know, I don't think Nick got

any sympathy from Alex about it all." She gave a wry smile. "Especially when he's marrying *you.*"

Sasha forced herself to smile back. She didn't think of herself as a beauty, but she knew her looks were probably the only thing she had going for her with Nick.

"Matt must be getting worried that he's next," Sasha said, trying to take the focus off herself.

A worried gleam entered Isabel's eyes. "He says he's not. He told his father he wouldn't be coerced into anything. Of course, when Cesare wants something…" she trailed off, just as Nick came strolling up to them.

"Somebody wants something, Mum?" Nick said, coming up next to them with a smile that must be more for Isabel, Sasha decided. If he ever smiled at her like that…

"Me. I need a drink," Isabel quipped, shooting her new daughter-in-law a look that said it was time to move on. Sasha wanted to beg her not to leave, but that would look foolish.

"I'll do that for you," Nick offered, about to turn away.

"No, honey, that's fine. I want to see your father anyway. I need to make sure he's taken his medication."

The line of Nick's mouth tightened at the mention

of his father. It was easy to see he hadn't forgiven Cesare for all this.

And rightly so. *Both* their fathers had a lot to answer for, Sasha knew. It was the one bond they had in common.

Nick turned the charm on for some of their guests who had come up to say they were leaving. A charm that wasn't false but neither was it for her benefit.

Still, she gratefully accepted the distraction to say goodbye, fielding more questions about not having a honeymoon. No one had dared ask about the haste of their marriage, but if they thought she was pregnant they'd soon find out she wasn't.

And if they wondered about the lack of affection between her and Nick? Maybe then they would guess the hasty marriage was for convenience. She didn't want anyone thinking it was for love.

Certainly not Nick.

Once all their guests had departed, Sasha left Nick talking to Matt beside his Aston Martin, but not before she saw the scowl on Nick's face and suspected he was probably warning his younger brother to watch out for their father. Though by the confident set of his head, Matt wasn't too concerned for his future.

She almost felt sorry for Matt. Just as no doubt Nick was feeling sorry for *himself* right now for having to marry *her.* She felt an instant's hurt but quickly dismissed it.

She had to keep busy.

Walking into one of the smaller dining rooms, she began tidying up, gathering the few remaining glasses and stacking them at one end of the table for the caterers to collect. It had been a good idea of Isabel's to use the room for some elderly relatives as a quiet place to get away from all the commotion and noise of the wedding.

And didn't she know exactly how they felt? If only she could have hidden in here permanently, away from Nick, away from the night ahead.

"Leave it."

Her head shot up to find Nick standing in the doorway. Panic stirred inside her chest. "But—"

"The catering crew will clean up."

"I know but—"

"You'll get that beautiful dress dirty," he pointed out, his enigmatic gaze pausing over her.

"Oh." She glanced down at the smooth white satin of her simply styled wedding dress. She'd been so anxious she'd totally forgotten she was wearing it. Any other bride would be horrified at the treatment.

Of course, who could call her a typical bride?

"Come on," he said brusquely, interrupting her thoughts. "Let's go upstairs. Iris will see everything is put right here."

Swallowing hard, she placed the glass down on

the table and started to walk toward him. "Has Matt gone?" she said for something to say.

His jaw clenched. "Yes."

Then he cupped her elbow and led her up the sweeping staircase, his touch sending a shiver through her that she tried to ignore. There would be more touching soon, more exploring, molding her softer curves to his hard body.

"Relax. You look like you're going to the guillotine."

"Maybe I've already lost my head," she quipped.

His eyes narrowed as he glanced sideways at her. "What does that mean?"

She blinked. Oh heavens. He surely didn't think she was talking about love?

"Nothing, except that I'd have to be crazy to marry you, that's all."

A moment crept by while they continued up the stairs and she held her breath but he said nothing further.

Soon they came to one of the large bedrooms they would use until she could renovate the master bedroom. The bed had already been turned back for them.

Suddenly she felt overwhelmed and she hung back in the doorway. Part of her wanted to know what making love with Nick would be like. Another part of her wanted to run for the hills.

Nick walked over to the large windows and stood looking out for a few seconds, his back to her. "Come here."

Her breath stopped. This was it.

Not wanting to appear childish or afraid, she started across the plush carpet but when she got close he didn't reach for her as expected.

He stood looking out over the estate's magnificent lawns and gardens deeply shadowed by the setting sun.

"Thank you for helping me keep all this," he murmured, the rough edge of emotion in his voice.

Oh.

Pleasure swept through her. "You belong here, Nick."

He turned and put his hand under her chin, lifting her face up to him. "That's the nicest thing anyone has ever said to me."

And then his lips descended.

She wasn't expecting it right then and she didn't have time to prepare. All at once he was there and the second his mouth touched hers she slid into his kiss. It was soft and slow and she melted for him like a frost in the morning sun.

Just as unexpectedly, he took the kiss deeper, pulling her with him into a world she'd dipped into only once before, many years ago. It was a world that tilted on its axis and began to spin out of control.

His tongue gave her strokes of pleasure, his hands sliding down to her hips and pulling her up against him, his body telling her he was a man who wanted, and that she was the woman to give.

And then he eased back.

And the world righted itself…slightly.

He lifted a strand of hair off her cheek. "Want to take a shower?" he asked huskily, his blue eyes holding a dark glitter.

"Er…together?"

He eased into a smile. "Is that an offer?"

She felt her cheeks wash with pink. "No."

He leaned back further, his eyes softening with understanding. "You're shy?"

She swallowed past her dry throat. "Only the first time," she whispered, hoping he'd take the hint so she wouldn't have to say it in words.

"And after that?" he teased.

"I don't—"

He chuckled and stepped back before she could finish. "Don't worry. I'll shower in my old room so that you can have some privacy." He strode away but stopped at the door and looked over his shoulder, his eyes no longer teasing. "This time."

Sasha stood there until she no longer heard his muffled footfall on the carpet along the landing.

She slowly exhaled. Oh God. How could she

know if she would be shy after she made love with him? She'd never made love with any man.

She was a virgin.

And a virgin who'd never felt anything for any man what she had felt for Nick all those years ago.

Nick whose kiss had blown her away just now. How could their wedding kiss earlier today have felt so different…so mild…yet this one be so mind-blowing?

This was like the kiss in the gazebo.

And unlike the episode after the gazebo, Nick wouldn't be going off with another woman. *She* would be the woman in his bed tonight. And all the nights ahead.

For now.

With a shaky hand she managed to unzip her dress and step out of it, carefully placing it over a chair. Then she headed for the shower, aware she was leaving behind more than her wedding dress. Tonight she was going to be a married woman in every sense of the word.

But would Nick even notice?

Or care?

Thankfully, when Sasha came out of the bathroom Nick was nowhere to be seen. Feeling awkward, she took off her silk robe and slipped beneath the covers in her nightgown, pulling the sheet up to her chin.

In the lamplight she lay there for a few seconds

looking like she'd been mummified, then gave a nervous laugh. Make that *petrified*.

Of Nick?

No, she was being absurd. Nick would never physically hurt her. Realizing she was letting her nerves get the better of her, she sat up against the pillows, only just managing to cover herself with the sheet a moment before Nick opened the door.

His gaze flashed over her. "I see you're already in bed."

She blinked, suddenly confused. Should she have sat on the brocade chair instead? Or stood by the window? What was the protocol on one's wedding night of a marriage of convenience?

"I thought this was where you'd want me."

"Oh, it is." An intense look filled his eyes. "I'd want you anywhere, Sasha."

"That wasn't what I meant."

"It's *exactly* what I meant."

"Nick—" She stopped speaking as he came toward her carrying a bottle of champagne and two glasses. He wore a navy bathrobe, his long legs bare and masculine. She could feel herself grow hot.

"I like the way you're looking at me," he said huskily.

Her gaze darted away, then back as she tried to get some sort of mental balance. "It feels strange being here like this with you," she said, her excuse lame but all she had.

"Why?"

She should tell him now.

She took a deep breath. "Perhaps because I—"

"Hell, you don't think of me like a brother, do you?"

His question took the wind from her sails. She blinked. "No." That was the last way she'd ever think of him. Hadn't those two mind-blowing kisses told him that, if seven years between?

"That's a relief." He was joking but she knew the question had been partly serious.

He held out a glass of champagne toward her. "Here, this should help you relax a little."

Grateful for something to do, she accepted it and took a sip, letting the bubbles slide down her dry throat. Perhaps drunk was the way to go, she mused, then dismissed the thought. If she were drunk she might say too much.

He sat down beside her on the bed, a sudden predatory gleam in his expression. "Why did you look shocked after I kissed you before?"

So he'd noticed she'd been taken aback by the power of that kiss.

"Um…at the wedding?" she said, deliberately misunderstanding him.

"No, not that placid little kiss I gave you at the

wedding ceremony. I mean the one just before by the window over there."

She cleared her throat, then decided on the truth. "I guess I didn't expect to…enjoy it so much."

"I did."

"Nick, I—"

"Have the most delectable looking mouth I've ever seen," he murmured, then put his glass down on the table beside the bed and did the same with hers. He leaned toward her. "I want to taste it again."

She moistened her lips, wanting to tell him about being a virgin but a mere second later his mouth settled on hers and she forgot everything but him. He nibbled on her lips until she sighed with delight, then took advantage by slipping his tongue inside.

In one swoop he was a part of her.

She shuddered. The kiss deepened and stole the breath from her lungs, sending excitement zinging to every pore in her body. She'd never known a kiss to be so all-inclusive.

And then he slowed the kiss and edged back a little to stare into her eyes, probing even. "There's something very unusual about you, Sasha."

She held her breath. Had he guessed?

"You haven't slept with many men, have you?"

"Um…no." She swallowed. "Does it make a difference?"

"Oh, yes," he rasped.

She couldn't read his expression and suddenly she was terrified he *wouldn't* make love to her if he knew she was a virgin. And that would be the biggest waste of her life. She was married to him, yes. And they would make love eventually, yes. But she'd missed out on her dream wedding. She didn't want to miss out on her honeymoon, too.

Not tonight.

"Kiss me, Nick."

A light flared in the back of his darkened eyes. Without hesitation, his mouth found hers again and he kissed her with a hunger that filled her with new awe. This kiss took her to places she'd never been before. She didn't want it to end.

She held her breath, her heart tilting with relief as he feathered kisses along her chin and down her throat. She couldn't bear him to leave her now.

He placed his lips at the center of her cleavage and murmured, "I've always thought your name suited you. Soft, sexy Sasha."

She shivered, never expecting this man would say something like that to her. It was the talk of a lover…a soon-to-be-lover.

He moved back and slid the thin strap of her nightgown off her shoulder, exposing one of her breasts to him. His hot gaze lingered on her for a long moment. She gasped when he began tracing her nipple with his fingertip, then held it between his fingers for his mouth to take over.

He suckled, and she almost came apart. She'd never realized her breasts were so sensitive to touch…to Nick. Oh God, this was *Nick* making love to her. *Nick* drawing on her nipple with his mouth. *Nick* who was sending such delicious sensations rippling through her. Everything he did, every move he made, was overshadowing everything else in the world.

The suckling continued, and she felt an odd sort of curl start at her toes and run its way upward. It tightened as it climbed higher through her thighs…higher and tighter still as it reached the core beneath her panties. She stiffened as something marvelous took hold and held her there, making her exhale in little gasps that seemed in rhythm with her body.

It was over almost before it began, the tightness diminishing, then disappearing as quickly.

Nick was looking at her curiously. "Did you just climax?"

"I…I think so. A little." She could feel herself blush. She wasn't sure. "Can we turn out the light, please? I'm embarrassed."

"No need to be embarrassed. Nothing should embarrass a man and a woman when they make love."

"The light, Nick. Please."

"No, I want to see you. I *need* to see you, sweetheart. All of you." And with that he took the hem of her nightgown and lifted it over her head.

Lamplight shone through the room, showing her naked body to him for the first time. "Beautiful," he murmured, reaching out and resting the palm of his hand on her stomach, leaving it there as if soaking up the touch of her skin. Her pulse shimmied through her veins, building anticipation. She wanted him to touch her more.

So much more.

Instead he leaned down and placed his lips against her *there* and just as she recovered from the shock of it, he gave a deep groan and pushed himself off the bed.

Her gasp was not because he'd left her, but because he was shrugging out of his bathrobe. In the blink of an eye her focus was on him, her sensibilities shocked at seeing a man in his full glory for the first time. Transfixed, she reached out to touch him. She could see her hand shaking but once she slid around him, he was her rock.

The air grew thick.

"Sasha," he said in a guttural voice.

She thrilled to the sound of him, to the sight of him, and now if she could just keep on…

"I need to touch you, Nick."

He made a low sound deep in his throat and that

was all the encouragement she needed. Tentatively she ran the tip of her finger over the head of his erection. She wanted to see what power she had over him.

He jerked. "No more," he growled and took her hand off him, twisting away to take a condom out of the bedside drawer and roll it on himself, entrancing her by his very masculine action. She'd read about all this in magazines, but the reality was overwhelmingly intimate.

"Slide over," he ordered, and he joined her on the bed, where he grasped her waist and rolled her on top of him.

She felt a rush of heat at the full length of his body against her own for the first time, and the feel of his hands cupping her bottom.

Their eyes met.

She wanted to look away but couldn't. Not when she could feel that curl starting in her toes again, making her want to tighten her legs and grind herself against him.

Suddenly he rolled her over and slid on top of her like he was meant to be there. And then he nudged her legs apart and pushed inside her a little.

She winced at the slight pain.

He stilled, his eyes widening in shock. "You're a *virgin?*"

She wanted to deny it. Wanted to say that she was

experienced so he would keep making her feel this way. Only she couldn't lie.

"Yes."

He swore but amazingly didn't pull out. He took a deep breath and then began to move slowly, his eyes never leaving her face. Carefully he filled her, and when he was fully inside her he stopped.

"Okay?" he asked hoarsely.

She nodded, too emotional to be able to speak. Nick had made her a woman.

His woman.

He began to move, and the world faded away. No one else existed, and nothing mattered. It was just the two of them, and when she climaxed Nick followed, and they came together in their own private world.

After Nick returned from the bathroom he sat on the bed and took her hands in his. "Why?"

Sasha swallowed. "Why didn't I tell you? You said it would make a difference and I…well…I wanted you to make love to me."

His mouth softened with tenderness. "You silly goose. The difference would have been in the way I made love to you, not in whether I made love to you at all."

"Oh."

"Your first time needs to be handled gently." A moment later he grimaced.

She saw the hint of regret in his eyes. "Nick, you were very gentle with me. Thank you."

He kissed her briefly. "Thank you for saying that." Then he leaned back with a penetrating look in his eyes that made her uneasy. "I seem to remember you telling me that you'd slept with Randall Tremaine."

She'd been prepared for this.

"Yes, I did say that. But I was eighteen, and I didn't want you thinking our kiss meant anything to me so…" she lifted one shoulder in a shrug, "I made it up."

"You were saving face?"

"Yes."

He considered her. "Why haven't you ever slept with anyone?"

"Perhaps I wanted to save myself for my husband."

A tic beat in his jaw. "And I've taken that away from you."

"No!" She swallowed, feeling bad for him. "Nick, look, we've both lost a lot of things from this marriage but we've gained some things, too. I'm glad you were my first, okay?"

His gaze took on a piercing look that held hers for long moments. Then just as quickly it changed to a sensual warmth that made her heartbeat stutter.

He got off the bed and scooped her from the sheets. "Nick! Where are you taking me?"

"To the shower."

She didn't ask why. It became obvious when he stood her in the cubicle and began to wash her with tenderness and care, and with a gentleness that almost brought tears to her eyes. This rich, arrogant playboy had a capacity for caring she hadn't really expected.

Then his hand and fingers replaced the soap, creating a lather that had nothing to do with bathing and everything to do with making love.

Four

For a moment Nick was confused when he woke up the next morning. He could hear car doors shutting and voices talking, and usually he didn't hear those sorts of noises from his tenth-floor apartment in the city.

Then he remembered.

He was married now. And this wasn't his apartment. He was at the Valente estate and the sounds he heard were the caterers clearing up the last of the wedding reception.

Sasha!

He lifted his head to find himself weighted to the bed by the naked female sleeping against his chest.

He looked down at the top of her blonde hair, and heat surged through his veins.

God, she'd been a virgin.

Amazingly there was something totally satisfying about knowing *he* was the only man to ever touch her like he had. Knowing he was the first man to be inside her like he'd been. He'd never thought he'd be the sort of guy who indulged in that sort of thing. He wasn't usually some sort of he-man who beat his chest in triumph.

Yet this time he wanted to do exactly that.

A virgin, for Pete's sake!

And of course that meant she'd lied to him all those years ago when she'd told him she'd gone out and slept with Randall Tremaine. It had been a few weeks after the gazebo incident and at the time he'd put it down to the fickle ways of a woman not knowing her own mind.

It hadn't stopped him wanting to knock the other man out when he'd seen them talking together briefly at a party. He remembered thinking Randall had been playing it so cool. No wonder. The poor guy had been an innocent pawn in it all.

Totally innocent.

Just like Sasha.

Hell, was he blind or what? Everything had pointed to her being a virgin, only he hadn't been looking. He'd just thought her a little inexperienced.

He could see it all now. The shyness in her, her first climax, wanting the light turned off.

The thought of being inside her again made him groan softly, and he knew he could wake her up and take her again. And it would be good for both of them.

Damn good.

But this wasn't a woman he could make love to, then kiss goodbye. This was his *wife*.

That thought had him easing out of bed and heading for the shower. He'd already given up his freedom for this marriage. He wasn't giving up his work, too.

But tonight…yes, tonight…he was going to enjoy teaching Sasha more about making love with a man.

Sasha opened her eyes to find the sun streaming in through the windows and an empty bed next to her.

She was a woman in every sense of the word now. And her heart was still intact.

She'd been terrified last night. Deep-down terrified that somehow Nick's lovemaking would open up the floodgates on the love she'd had for him years ago. It had been a very real fear.

But she'd had nothing to worry about, thank heavens. Nick's expertise in bed had made it so very special for her, and while lingering memories of her teenage love may have played a part in her enjoyment, pure physical attraction had saved the day.

It was such a relief!

Yes, she could cope with a physical relationship, she mused, throwing back the sheets and taking a couple of steps, then felt herself blush at how pleasurably sore her body was in all the places he'd touched.

And kissed.

Her hot shower should have soothed her but she kept remembering Nick carrying her in here last night. The thought of it brought a lump to her throat. How gentle he'd been.

And caring.

By the time she was dressed she was ready to face the day. The main thing was that she didn't love Nick nor had he guessed she'd been in love with him years ago.

And that was something to celebrate, she decided, as she went down the staircase to the kitchen. Today was business as usual for her husband, and it would be for her, too. She had her own work to do.

She had plans.

Lots of them.

Her fingers itched while she ate breakfast on the terrace, her mind racing with excitement, eager now to get back to the designs she'd started a few weeks ago.

The house was an interior designer's dream. It had a grand salon with picture windows and French doors looking out over spectacular gardens and courtyards. There was also a formal dining room and family living areas with five bedrooms and bathrooms, a study upstairs and one downstairs, and a kitchen with modern conveniences in an old-fashioned style.

Before too long she'd spread herself out in the downstairs study, her ideas and thoughts spilling onto the paper, her enthusiasm for the project continuing to bubble as she worked past lunch.

"Have you been here all day?" Nick said from the doorway.

Startled, she looked up and her heart skipped a beat at the sight of him. He was so handsome, and she'd been intimate with him last night. The thought made her feel warm all over.

She quickly dragged her gaze away to her watch. "Is it six o'clock already?"

He started to scowl as he stepped into the room and came toward her. "You're working on plans for the redecorating?" A muscle ticked in his cheek. "So you're still going ahead with it?" he asked, stopping in front of the desk.

That warm feeling disappeared at his tone. She

leveled him a look. They hadn't discussed it further, but she'd assumed he would still let her redecorate. "I guess that's up to you. You're the boss."

His eyes narrowed. "This is your home, too, now, you know."

"I guess it is."

Not for a moment did she think she owned this house. How could she? It was Nick's. It would always be Nick's even if she stayed married to him for fifty years.

Her breath stopped at the thought.

He leaned over the paperwork and looked at her plans for the main dining room. A minute later he grudgingly admitted, "They're good."

Despite herself, she felt a thrill at his praise.

She shrugged. "They're just ideas. There's still a lot to be done."

He studied her. "This means a lot to you, doesn't it?"

"Yes."

There was a tiny pause. "Fine. Then you have carte blanche to do what you like."

"Really?" Excitement rushed through her, but she quickly reined it in and said more primly, "Thank you."

"But my old bedroom stays as is."

"Oh?" She didn't say she'd planned to turn his room and the one next to it into a larger suite. "If that's what you want."

"It is."

"Okay." She'd allow him that. After all, she had the rest of the house.

"I'm going to shower and change before dinner," he said, a possessive gleam in his eyes sweeping over her, making her panic.

She swallowed. Was he asking her to join him?

"Um…I want to finish something here first. I'll freshen up in a minute."

A knowing look in his eyes, he turned toward the door. "Don't be too long."

"I won't."

They both knew she wasn't about to follow him upstairs. As much as she suspected being in his arms was addictive, she had to keep her distance or risk becoming his sex slave.

She smiled to herself. Would that be so bad?

Reality returned. Perhaps she ought to remind herself that she hadn't even warranted an "I'm home, honey" kiss. Whether he wanted her in his bed or not, it was clear he wasn't going to treat her like a real wife outside the bedroom. Not when they were alone anyway.

Shades of her parents' marriage?

No, she wouldn't think that.

The thought was too painful to contemplate. Sasha looked down at her designs and started working on them again. Work had always helped her concentrate on the moment, holding unhappy thoughts of the past or the possibility of a lonely future at bay. Work had been her salvation.

Now, if only she could get the color just right for…

"Dinner's almost ready," Nick said, startling her again.

She looked up and saw he'd showered and changed and she wrinkled her nose at herself. "I totally forgot the time again, didn't I?"

"Obviously you're not falling over yourself to be with me?" he drawled, not looking in the least put out about that.

No doubt he'd have plenty of women who *would* fall over themselves to be with him, she mused. Well, she wasn't one of his women.

She held her head high. "No, I'm not."

He considered her. "You're not like other women, are you?"

Was that a compliment? She wasn't sure.

"I guess not."

His face closed up. "You've got ten minutes," he said gruffly before striding away.

For a moment she just stood there. What was all that about? Her virginity? Was he feeling guilty about it? There was no need.

After that she hurried to shower and re-apply a light coating of make-up, leaving her straight blonde hair to fall loose past her shoulders. Taking her cue from Nick's dark trousers and polo shirt, she didn't dress up too much for dinner, instead slipping on a summery dress made from soft material that fell just above her knees.

Fifteen minutes later she joined him in the dining room. The hint of pleasure in his eyes made her heart race as she walked to where he held the chair out for her.

They sat down at the table. Iris served dinner before mentioning that Cesare had called to remind him about the English launch of "Valente's Woman." Then the older woman left them to eat.

Sasha was curious. "When is the U.K. launch?"

"In a couple of weeks."

"It'll do well over there."

He nodded. "It'll do well everywhere."

She had to smile at that.

"What are you smiling at?" he asked.

"Your arrogance."

His mouth quirked at the corners. "It's the Valente way."

"I know."

Some lazy moments passed while they ate in silence. Sasha was still amazed she was now actually married to Nick Valente. Who would have thought it?

Not her.

Aware she needed to move away from such

thoughts, she made herself reflect on how much effort went into launching a new perfume. "You should go with Alex. He may need you with him."

"Alex can handle it. He and Olivia will make sure it goes off with a bang."

All at once she didn't want him staying home for her sake. "Just because we're newly married doesn't mean you have to stay home with me."

His lips twisted. "Are you trying to get rid of me so soon?"

"Of course not. I'm just thinking you have other commitments and being married shouldn't change that."

He held her gaze for a moment, then, "If I thought Alex needed me, I'd go. But he doesn't and frankly, I'd prefer to stay home."

She noted he didn't say "stay with *her*."

Strangely she was rather glad he wasn't going away and leaving her alone. She seemed to have had too much aloneness these past few years.

Had he?

She didn't think so.

They began to talk about the wedding—was it only yesterday?—and before too long Iris was serving dessert, and then not long after, they finished their dinner.

She wondered what was next....

Coffee?

Tea?

Bed?

"Would you like to watch television?"

She ignored the look in his eyes. He'd known what she was thinking. "That would be nice." She got to her feet, and Nick stood, too.

"You go ahead and I'll be with you shortly. I've got a couple of calls to make first."

She felt a smattering of disappointment, but she quickly pushed it aside. Time alone would let her pulse slow back to its normal beat.

An hour later she was still waiting for Nick to join her. Her favorite sitcom hadn't held her attention, and now a rather boring program was about to start. She could go get her designs and continue working, but she needed a break from them. What's more, she didn't want to interrupt Nick in the study. He could be on an important call.

She yawned.

She felt so tired.

Perhaps she'd just close her eyes for a moment or two.

The next thing she knew a pair of strong masculine arms were lifting her up and carrying her. She tried to clear her mind but she felt warm and protected and she just wanted to snuggle closer.

"Nick?"

"Yes."

It was so hard to open her eyes. "Put me down," she murmured. "I can walk."

"No."

She let out a small sigh. It was too much trouble to argue, especially with her cheek pressed against his chest, his heartbeat beneath it.

He was climbing the stairs now and he smelled so good, his clothes fresh but mixed with his own male scent, his breath retaining a hint of coffee. She'd never been carried by a man before. There was something to be said for all those movies that made it look so romantic being swept off her feet like this.

And then she realized something and she started to giggle. She couldn't help herself.

At the top he paused to look down at her. "What's so funny?"

"You're a little out of breath."

A gleam of amusement twinkled in his eyes. "Are you saying I'm too old to carry you up the stairs?"

"Would I dare?"

"Yes."

All at once she noticed his firm mouth curve up at the corners.

His eyes held a certain glitter. "I'm not too old…or out of breath…to make love to you, my sweet," he murmured, then carried her into their bedroom, kicked the door shut and stood her up against it.

His blue eyes smoldered for her in the lamplight

as he bent his head and kissed her. And he kept right on kissing her until it became a game between them that neither would give up. In the end she had to break away to catch her breath.

He gazed at her triumphantly and before too long he'd stripped the clothes from her body and kissed her again in much more intimate places.

And if he was out of breath by the end of it, he didn't show it. The only thing he showed was a passionate hunger for her that took her by surprise.

Sasha was in the pool when Nick returned early from work the following evening. She'd meant to be showered and changed by now but summer was almost over and she'd wanted to take advantage of the warm weather.

He sat down on the deck chair and loosened his tie, looking handsome but with dark shadows beneath his eyes. She felt guilty for keeping him awake last night, even if it *had* been mutually beneficial.

She trod water in the middle of the pool. "You look tired."

He seemed surprised she'd noticed. "Yeah, I guess I am."

She frowned. "All that driving into the city and back is taking a lot out of you." Commuting to the city took an hour and a half each way, not to mention putting in a full day's work.

He shrugged. "I'll get used to it."

"You shouldn't have to, Nick." She tilted her head at him. "Why don't you get yourself a driver? Your father's had one for many years."

His brow creased in consideration. "Hey, that's not a bad idea. I could hire a permanent driver and that way I can work while I'm in the car and not waste time." He gave her a smile. "Good thinking."

She gave a quick shiver as a late afternoon breeze skipped over her. "Thanks, but I'm sure you would have thought of it yourself."

His gaze dropped to the water lapping at the top of her breasts. "Probably," he said, his distracted tone giving the comment less arrogance.

Her nipples tightened beneath the pink bikini top at the sudden sensual look in his eyes.

He stood up and started undoing his shirt.

"Er…what are you doing?"

"Joining you." He discarded shoes and socks, then his hand went to his belt buckle. Soon he had stripped down to black boxer briefs that fitted him like a second skin, leaving nothing to her imagination.

Her heart thumped erratically. "It's getting a little cold in here."

He gave her a wicked grin. "Then I'll warm you up."

He dove into the pool and she watched him come toward her in the water like a torpedo. The urge to turn and swim for the other side was strong. The temptation to stay and have her defenses annihilated was more exciting.

In one whoosh he came up close to her body and rose to the surface, so close she felt him like a caress. He shook the water from his face and smiled, his wet hair plastered to his head, his sooty lashes spiked with moisture.

"Fancy meeting you here," he drawled, looking what he was: a drop-dead gorgeous male who'd caught the biggest fish in the pool.

Her.

Of course, she was the *only* fish in the pool.

"Yes, fancy that."

The late afternoon sun showed a mischievous gleam in his eye and all at once she knew he was up to something. "Nick," she warned, trying to escape, the water hindering rather than helping.

He laughed playfully and caught her by the waist, before lifting her in the air and tossing her backward. She took a breath just as she went under the water, her mind already on sweet revenge.

She'd get him back, she promised herself as she burst through to the surface. "Nick, you'd—" She gasped. "My bikini top's come off!"

"Really?"

She ignored the relish in his voice and started looking around. Then she saw a pink blob of material near the edge of the pool.

"There it is." She started to swim toward it, aware that Nick was swimming with her. She thought he was merely trying to help her, until they reached it at the same time and he snatched it up and threw it onto the concrete outside of the pool.

"Nick!" She glared at him as she covered her breasts with her hands.

"What?" His eyes danced with the devil.

"How am I going to get out of the pool now?"

"No one's around. Iris is in the kitchen and Leo's gone into Richmond for supplies."

"I'm not a prude but—"

"Yes, you are." He chuckled. "Look at you. I know your body intimately now and yet you're still covering yourself from me."

"You're still a stranger, Nick," she said without thinking.

His smile disappeared. "Am I?" His blue eyes deepened in color. "Then we'd better do something about that."

Without hesitation, he caught her by the waist and pressed her up against the side of the pool.

And then he kissed her.

At first his lips were cold from the water but they soon turned warm enough to have her melting against him. For long, languid moments she reveled in having his mouth take advantage of hers, but eventually he eased back from the kiss.

"Still think of me as a stranger?" he said, a very masculine expression of satisfaction on his face.

A minute ago she'd felt very feminine, but now his words brought her back to reality and she didn't feel in the least like being coquettish. "There's more than knowing a person physically, Nick."

His face closed up. "It'll do for now," he said and turned away. "Stay here. I'll get us some robes."

Sasha watched him heave himself out of the water and stride over to the cabana, all male muscle and sinew. She swallowed hard. What on earth had made her say something so deep like that? Maybe she really *was* a prude and saying that had been her only defense?

He came out wearing a thick white robe and carrying one for her. "I'll cover you as you get out."

Thankful he was still being conscious of her sensitivity, she began climbing up the ladder. It was probably silly to be overreacting but she'd never been one to flaunt her body outrageously and merely because she was no longer a virgin didn't change her way of thinking.

Just as she reached the top of the ladder she looked up in time to see Nick's eyes flicking over her naked breasts. Unable to stop herself, she flushed.

"Put your arms in here," he said huskily, and she did as she was told, feeling more secure once she had the robe cinched in at the waist.

Nick cleared his throat and stepped away from her. "It's still balmy. Would you like to have dinner out here?"

She'd half-expected him to make some excuse to retire to the study. After all, he'd frozen up when she'd started talking about feelings. Fool that she was! The last thing she needed to bring out in the open was any sort of feelings.

To hide her surprise, she pushed back her wet hair. "That would be lovely."

"Good. I'll tell Iris."

"And I'll go dress."

"Let's not bother."

"Er…okay."

He started toward the house, detoured slightly and stopped to pick up something, then came back and handed her the pink bikini top.

Their eyes met and she blushed. "Thanks."

"You're welcome." He turned and walked back toward the house.

She watched him for a moment with her heart thudding, unable to stop herself from admiring those firm legs beneath the bathrobe. She liked the dark hair that was just-so-manly and just-so-touchable and if she dared, when he came back she would love to run her palms up his legs, caressing them, caressing *him*.

All at once she realized she was squeezing her

bikini top. Giving it one last squeeze she dropped it in the pocket of her robe, then went to sit down at the table, her own legs kind of shaky.

And he'd called her a *prude?*

Not any longer.

A few minutes later Nick came back. "Iris will bring out dinner shortly. In the meantime…" He held out two glasses of wine and passed one to her, then went to sit in the chair opposite.

Made selfconscious by her thoughts, she looked away, pretending to concentrate on the guest cottage and glasshouse that could easily been seen from here. Mercifully, the gazebo where they'd shared their kiss was on the other side of the house.

The sound of clinking glass from behind told Sasha that Iris had come out on the patio area. She turned around and smiled as the other woman came toward them pushing a trolley. Before too long she'd left and Sasha and Nick were tucking into their steak and salad.

"How are the designs going?"

She glanced up and saw he'd noticed the paperwork on one of the small tables. She'd been working on them before deciding to take a swim.

"Really well." She hesitated. "Would you like to look over them after dinner?"

"Sure."

After that she turned the conversation to some of the problems she was having with one of the contractors, then they began to talk of the family and other general things.

Nick stood up as soon as they'd both finished eating, and walked over to her designs. Sasha followed him, her heart thumping, wondering if he'd like them. She'd gone to great lengths making sure everything suited the house just right.

"I'm very impressed with these. You've kept the charm of the place without taking too much away from it all."

A swell of relief filled her. "My intention was never to make major changes. I love this place as it is, too, Nick."

His eyes riveted on her face. "Yes, I can see that."

She flushed with pleasure, feeling her cheeks turn almost the same pink as the bikini she wore.

Or *didn't* wear, she mused, pulling the robe tighter over her breasts, seeing his gaze drop to where she pretended she wasn't naked underneath.

"You surprise me," he murmured, lazy seduction seeping into those blue eyes. "I'd have thought you'd put your bikini top back on."

All at once she felt a touch defiant. "Maybe I'm not quite the prude you think I am."

Taking her by surprise, he placed the tip of his finger at her chin. "Hmm, maybe not," he murmured, sending her heartbeat thudding into a mad gallop. Then his finger slithered down her throat to rest on her wildly beating pulse. "You look so damn sexy in that robe."

She moistened her lips. "Nick—"

"I could strip it off you here and now and you wouldn't stop me…would you?"

She was very much afraid he was right.

"And I could slide those tiny bikini bottoms off you and you wouldn't say a word…true?"

Heavens, yes! He could take her this very moment and she'd let him. He made her want to do things she normally didn't do.

How she wished she could lie. "Nick, you know you're right but—"

He dropped his hand away from her throat. "But?"

"Afterwards I would feel totally embarrassed if I thought Iris or Leo had seen us."

His eyes filled with satisfaction. "So you *are* a prude?"

She started to frown. "Are you pleased because I've admitted it? Or because you're right?"

"Both. I like to win."

And he would never give in until he did, she was sure.

Suddenly he said, "I can't help who I am, Sasha."

She looked at him and saw no apology, just a simple statement that made her succumb to her need for him. No, he couldn't help being who he was.

"Nick, please. Take me to bed."

Five

Every evening after that was like a mini-honeymoon for the rest of the week. The weather remained quite warm and Nick would come home and they'd swim in the pool, eat a lazy dinner until dark, then retire to the bedroom.

There Sasha learned she wasn't really a prude at all. She'd just needed to let go of her inhibitions, and with Nick's instructions she did.

And her heart was still intact.

Then one morning she ended up walking past Nick's old bedroom and for some reason she stopped and went in. The room had a large bed and furnishings befitting a teenager of wealth, done out in shades of light and dark brown. On the dresser there were school trophies for cricket, soccer and swimming.

She wasn't sure what she expected to find, but there was something more here, something that made her believe Nick was much deeper than she had previously believed.

She just didn't know what that was.

And perhaps it was best she didn't find out.

Let him be who he was, and leave it at that. She didn't want any more complications in her life.

And speaking of complications, Sasha got a sinking feeling in her stomach when her mother arrived a few hours later right at lunchtime, supposedly to see how things were going. There was nothing for it but to invite her mother to lunch. Not that she minded. It was just that today she seemed to have an agenda.

And Sasha had the feeling it was to do with her father.

"So, you've recovered from the wedding?" Sally asked as they sat down to a light lunch.

"Yes, I have." Until this moment Sasha hadn't let herself be upset that her mother hadn't called since the wedding. *Nick's* mother had managed to call several times.

"I'm sorry I didn't phone you, darling," Sally

said, as if reading her daughter's mind. "I just thought it best I leave you to…adapt."

Sasha gave a remote smile. "Thanks."

"Darling, it's always good to leave a newly married couple to their own devices."

"Is that what the wedding manuals say?" she muttered, then felt bad when she saw the crushed looked on her mother's face. "Mum, I'm sorry. All this has been a bit of a strain. I never expected to get married. Not for a long time anyway."

Sally nodded. "It's okay. I understand. But please remember that you've made your father and me so happy. I love that he's smiling again."

Ignoring the thought that her father probably had a new girlfriend, Sasha squeezed her mother's hand. "Then I'm glad."

Sally's grateful smile turned to a frown. "Darling, there *is* one thing…" she began, making Sasha tense. "There seems to be some sort of delay in closing the deal with Cesare. Your father can't wait much longer, I'm afraid."

"They're pretty busy with the launch in the U.K. and all, I'd imagine."

Come to think of it, she wasn't sure of the reason for the delay herself.

"I was sort of hoping you could ask Nick. Not straight out, mind you. Just see if there's a problem and what it is. I wouldn't ask if it wasn't so important."

Sasha swallowed. "Mum, this is an awkward position you and Dad are putting me in."

Again.

Her mother didn't seem to notice. "Nick's your husband. He'll tell you everything."

There were just so many things a mother could ask a daughter to do. "Nick and I are not in love, Mum. He keeps things to himself. I can't guarantee anything."

"If you could just try, darling."

Sasha sighed. "Okay, I'll see what I can do."

Her mother left straight after the meal, probably in case she said anything to change her daughter's mind. Sasha saw her off with a heavy heart. She loved her mother dearly but she'd never understand her love for a man, which totally submerged her own personality.

That would *never* happen to her.

Never.

And to prove it to herself, she would broach the dreaded subject with Nick at dinner this evening.

"My mother stopped by for lunch today."

Nick looked up from his meal and felt pleased for Sasha's sake. "Good. I don't think you've heard from her since the wedding, have you?"

"She's been busy."

"I'm sure." No doubt looking after Porter's every whim.

And at the expense of her daughter, Nick thought with a frown, surprised at the lack of attention Sally had actually given Sasha since their marriage. Wasn't a mother supposed to fuss over a newlywed daughter? Or was he just being a bit too old-fashioned?

Sasha moistened her mouth. "My mother does have a concern, though. She thought I might be able to help."

"And that is?"

"My father's waiting on a shipping deal to go through with the House of Valente, and apparently it's been delayed. He's not sure why."

Nick leaned back in his chair, and his lips twisted. "And he's sent *his* wife to ask *my* wife why?"

Sasha swallowed, looking uneasy. "He just needs to know, okay? Otherwise he might have to look at other avenues."

"Other avenues?" He almost snorted out loud. Porter was too lazy to go elsewhere when he had Cesare Valente on his side.

"This is business, Nick."

"Exactly."

Her chin angled. "What's that supposed to mean?"

"Stay out of the family business, Sasha."

She gasped. "I thought I *was* part of the family now."

His mouth tightened. "Not the business. That's got nothing to do with you."

"I see." Her green eyes turning cool, she placed her napkin on the table and stood up. "Then perhaps you should have made me sign a prenuptial. Then I won't be able to touch any of your precious family business if we ever divorce." On that note she walked out of the room.

Nick frowned as he watched her leave. They'd only just gotten married, so why the hell was she already mentioning divorce?

Or perhaps she really *had* married him for the money? No, he didn't think that any longer. Why, he couldn't say.

Besides, there was nothing to worry about. No way would she ever get any part of the House of Valente. The legal side of the business was wrapped up tighter than a ball of string.

Dammit, she should stay out of all this anyway. She had her job, and he had his. And what the hell was Porter playing at? The man had no scruples in hiding behind his wife and daughter's skirts. He never had.

It was just a pity the man was so good at detecting trouble. He was obviously suspicious about the delay in signing the contract. And with good reason.

Nick and his brothers couldn't quite put their finger on it, but there was something not quite right about the deal. None of them liked Porter, though this was more than not liking the man. It was a gut feeling that the wool was being pulled over their eyes. But with no real evidence, and unable to share their concerns with Cesare because of his health, they weren't going to be able to postpone the deal much longer.

Damn Porter Blake.

Suddenly Nick realized that Alex should be told the latest development. Yet he didn't want to say any of this on the telephone in case Sasha overheard him and reported back to her father. He grabbed his car keys and left the house.

After that he spent a couple of hours at Alex's place where they talked over the shipping deal once again, trying to find the reason it just didn't feel right. Nothing came to mind, and they reluctantly moved on to the upcoming launch in the U.K.

"Another cup of coffee, Nick?" Olivia asked, sticking her head around the study door.

He smiled at his sister-in-law. "Perhaps one more, Olivia, thanks."

Olivia's gaze slid to Alex. "What about you, honey?"

"No, nothing for me."

Olivia's gaze darted back to Nick, then Alex again, then she smiled oddly and left. Nick knew they were wondering why he wasn't eager to go home to his new wife.

"Problems with Sasha?" Alex said when they were alone again, a speculative look in his eyes.

Nick rubbed the back of his neck. "Just teething problems."

"I understand."

Nick thought about that. "Yes, you do, don't you?"

There was a moment's pause, then Alex said, "Sasha's turned out pretty good, considering what her father's like."

Nick shot him a twisted smile. "Whose side are you on?"

"I'm sure you'll work it out."

Nick suddenly had the urge to go home. So Sasha had only been trying to please her father. He shouldn't have snapped at her like that.

He stood up. "I think I'll give that coffee a miss."

Alex grinned. "I'll tell Olivia."

By the time Nick got home, Sasha was asleep. He showered and slid into bed beside her, careful not to wake her though he was tempted to pull her close. In the end he fell asleep. It had been a long day.

Sasha kept busy the next day going to various stores, but her mind was on Nick and his reaction last night. Stupid hurt had ripped through her at his response. She had hated to ask about the shipping contract but that's all she'd done. It wasn't a major crime. So why was he being so defensive about it?

Of course that threat of hers about a prenuptial had been a childish thing to say, but it served Nick right for drawing such a line in the sand. She already knew he didn't care for her. She hadn't needed to hear that she should stay in the background like a good little wife. It smacked too much of her father.

"You're late."

She almost missed her step as she came through the front door and looked up. Nick was waiting inside and demanding to know where *she'd* been? After he'd left her wondering last night if he'd gone to see an old girlfriend or two.

She placed her handbag on the hall table. "So we're keeping tabs on each other now?"

An odd sincerity flickered across his face. "I was getting worried, that's all."

Her anger cooled. "Okay, if you must know I've been out seeing some contractors. It took longer than I thought it would."

His eyes clouded and all at once he turned toward the living room, his movements somewhat jerky. "Well, I'm glad you're home."

Sasha frowned at his back. Was he embarrassed because he had worried? At the thought, a hint of tenderness trickled through her.

"You could have called me on my cell phone," she suggested quietly, following him into the room.

"I don't know the number."

Her little bubble burst.

"You only had to ask."

"I know."

It said a lot for their relationship.

"Anyway," he continued, "I phoned Iris earlier and told her not to cook dinner. I thought I'd take you out to a local restaurant."

Was this his way of apologizing?

"That would be lovely."

He looked pleased, then, "I'm sorry I snapped at you last night, Sasha. I wanted to apologize when I came home from Alex's, but you were asleep."

So, he'd been at Alex's place. Could she believe that now? Strangely, yes. She just wished she'd known that last night when she'd been upset and pretending to sleep.

"I'm sorry, too," she found herself saying. "I shouldn't have asked. I was worried for my parents' sake, that's all."

"I understand. I should have understood that, too. I—" His cell phone rang. "Damn. I have to take this call."

"Then you do that. I'll go get ready."

He was answering the call even before she'd finished speaking, but Sasha didn't mind. She climbed the stairs, excited now about going out to dinner with her husband.

Thank goodness the wedge between them seemed to have disappeared. She'd hated that her parents had come between them. Hated that Nick had stormed out and left her wondering. And hated it even more when he'd come home and hadn't taken her in his arms.

She was in the shower ten minutes later when the glass door opened and Nick, naked and somewhat aroused, stood there. "Move over, Mrs. Valente."

She didn't need to be told a second time. She willingly moved aside but only a little. Just enough to let him get up close and personal.

Later at the restaurant she and Nick were given a warm welcome by the owner, an Italian man called Angelo.

"I read in the papers that you marry, so tonight I'll cook you both something very special." He beamed at them, then hurried away.

"He seems like a nice man," Sasha said, making small talk as she looked around the restaurant. "You must come here often."

"I used to date his daughter."

"And he's still talking to you?" she joked.

His wry smile conceded the point. "It was very platonic. Angelo knew that."

"He must think highly of you," she said, then pondered the comment while the waiter poured their wine. Italian fathers weren't known for being liberal when it came to their daughters, especially when it came to playboys.

Yet this man had trusted Nick with his daughter? It didn't add up.

When they were alone again, Nick was the first to speak, "So, tell me about living in London. I know you said you lived with your aunt for a while, but you must have liked the place to stay so long."

She was surprised by his sudden interest.

"I loved it. It's such a vibrant city."

His brow arched. "You don't find Sydney vibrant?"

"Yes, but in a different way." She lifted one shoulder. "I guess I was ready to spread my wings and try new adventures."

"You evidently didn't try *too* many new things," he drawled, hinting at her virginity.

She shot him a smile. "I tried enough to keep me happy," she said, then laughed to herself when she saw him frown.

Let him wonder.

Then he said, "Your mother must have missed you."

She felt her smile dim. "I imagine my father did, too."

His eyes shuttered at the mention of her father. "I've been to London quite a few times. I should have stopped in to see you. We could have seen a show together."

"That would have been nice."

She pushed aside the hurt that he hadn't bothered, despite her knowing it was best this way. Having him drop by to see her would have been a painful reminder of the past.

Just then there was a commotion near the front door as people greeted each other with a lot of enthusiasm, giving Sasha the chance to concentrate on something other than the past. Italians really knew how to welcome each other. They were so warm and friendly and—

"Sasha?

She turned back to Nick. "Yes?"

"I said I have a surprise for you."

"A surprise?"

"You'll be happy to know that we'll be signing the contract for your father tomorrow. Now you can tell your mother not to worry."

Intense relief washed over her, then as quickly restrained itself. "Thanks, but I'll wait until it's signed."

His glance sharpened. "You don't trust me?"

"Of course I do."

"Then you don't trust your father."

She hardly dared to breathe. "What makes you say that?"

His eyes narrowed. "I've just realized something. This deal of his was why you changed your mind about marrying me, wasn't it? It wasn't only about merging our two families. Your father wanted to make sure the deal went through, so he forced you to marry me."

Her brain stumbled. Her father would kill her for admitting this, but she couldn't lie.

"He was worried, yes. He thought he might be undercut by a competitor."

"So he made sure he wasn't," Nick said cynically.

Sasha couldn't argue with that. Still, she had to stand up for her father. "I think it's understandable he'd be worried about losing the tender."

Nick's eyes riveted on her, and all at once a mask came down over his face. Perhaps he knew the conversation was leading them places neither of them wanted to go.

He inclined his head. "You're right."

Thankfully Angelo appeared with their meal, and Sasha smiled and praised the food but somehow the evening had been spoiled. Talking about their families always caused friction.

They ate in silence for a while.

"By the way," Nick said eventually. "I've invited a couple of people to dinner Friday night. If you could coordinate it all with Iris that would be great."

All at once she felt a chill. "That's only a couple of days away."

"I know, but they're visiting from Europe and only have Friday night free."

"So it's a business dinner?"

"Yes."

"And you want me to arrange it all and host it as well?"

"Of course."

Her heart sank at his assumption that she would drop everything for him. Not only did she have a late afternoon appointment with one of the contractors, but it reminded her of her parents, her father snapping his fingers and her mother jumping to it.

She'd sworn never to be like her mother.

"You're quiet," Nick said after a few minutes more of silence.

"Am I?"

He looked at her sharply. "What's the matter?"

Her disappointment in him was immense. She should have known not to let herself get close to him again. She would only get hurt a second time.

"You brought me out to dinner to sweeten me up, didn't you?"

His brows drew together. "What are you talking about?"

"Actually I'm surprised you even did that," she scoffed. "Did you think I would say no, Nick? Well, you're right. I *am* saying no."

His face hardened. "No to what?"

"To arranging your business dinner and playing your hostess."

"You're my wife."

She bristled. "Yes, not your slave to be told what to do and when to do it."

He sat back, his eyes assessing hers. "Where's all this coming from?"

"I'm sick of being expected to drop everything for everyone else. First my parents expect me to give up my freedom for them, and now you think I should just fall in with whatever plans you make."

And truth to tell, she was sick of being a nobody to Nick. Because that's what it all came down to. He hadn't been interested in her years ago. He still wasn't interested in her.

Not as a person.

A pulse began to beat in his cheekbone. "I didn't mean to treat you like your father does."

She gave a silent gasp. Clearly he thought of her as her father's lackey as well. "Thanks very much."

"You know what I mean."

Hurt gnawed at her. "Unfortunately, yes, I do."

His gaze rested on her face with a hint of regret. "Sasha, I'm sorry. I'll take them to a restaurant in the city. You don't need to come."

She sighed, suddenly feeling bad yet knowing she shouldn't. "Nick, if you were to *ask* me, then I don't mind hosting the dinner. I just don't like the expectation that I have to do it."

He considered her across the table. "Then would

you mind being my hostess on Friday, Sasha? I'd really appreciate it."

Her heart thudded at the sincerity in his tone. "Yes. I'm happy to help." She would reschedule her appointment with the contractor.

His shoulders relaxed a little, and there was an odd amusement in his eyes. "You're quite fiery when you're upset. I never noticed that when you were growing up. You were always quite shy."

Shy and in love.

Her stomach did a flip at the thought. "Perhaps I didn't want you to notice back then," she lied.

"And now?"

She took a moment to answer as past hurts rose in her throat. "I'm older. I want respect."

"You always had my respect, Sasha."

"No, Nick. I didn't."

He went still, his eyes probing hers. "Then I'm sorry if I made you feel that way. It wasn't intentional."

"I know." And therein lay the crux of the matter. It was another example of her meaning less than nothing to him.

Angelo reappeared to check that their meal was enjoyable and Sasha welcomed the interruption. She'd said more than enough. If Nick didn't think she mattered, then she wasn't going to force him to change his mind.

She had her pride after all.

Six

Nick phoned Sasha late the following morning to tell her the deal had been signed and that Alex was calling her father now to tell him the news.

Enormously relieved, Sasha thanked him for letting her know, then waited for her mother to call and share in the good news and perhaps say thanks.

Her mother didn't call.

"No doubt your parents were relieved," Nick said when he came home.

"No doubt they were."

He froze. "You mean they haven't called you?"

A lump lodged in her throat. "No, but they were probably busy."

"They weren't too busy to ask you to spy for them," he rasped.

She sucked in a sharp breath. "It wasn't like that."

A pulse beat in his cheekbone. "Not on your part, but they got what they wanted from you. They used you, Sasha."

He was right, and on one level she was warmed by his concern for her, but loyalty to her mother kept her quiet. "Let's forget that for now."

"Can you?"

"No." If she thought about it the pain would overwhelm her. She'd always known she came second with her mother, but until recently she hadn't realized just how low down on the scale she was compared with her father.

She pretended to dismiss it all. "Come on. I want you to pick a color scheme for the study. I can't decide by myself."

He made a dismissive gesture. "Any color will do."

"No, Nick. You'll be using it a lot, so it's important I get your input."

"You'll be using it, too."

"Exactly. It's something we need to choose together."

He suddenly broke into a sexy half smile. "You're very good at getting your own way. Subtle but very effective."

She found herself smiling back. "That's always been my policy."

The rest of the week went quickly and before she knew it, it was Friday. She was nervous about hosting their first dinner, and of course she helped Iris arrange it all, but there was a difference in doing it because she wanted to and not because it was expected of her.

"You look beautiful," Nick said when she'd finished dressing in a blue dress that hugged her body in all the right places, her blonde hair up in a chignon, delicate diamond earrings at her ears.

Silly delight rippled through her. "Thanks." Her eyes slid over his dark suit and white shirt that did him full-on justice. "You're looking quite spiffy yourself."

He smiled. "Spiffy, eh?"

She smiled back then saw him fiddling with his tie. "Here, let me do that for you."

"You don't mind?"

"No, I like doing up men's ties," she quipped as she stepped close to him and began working on the tie.

His smile vanished. "Just how many men's ties have you done up?"

"The odd one or two."

He stared down at her, then must have seen her lips twitching because he broke into a grin. "I think you're making that up."

"Am I?"

"You'd better be," he pretended to growl, sending a thought flashing through her mind. He *liked* being the only man to make love to her.

Well, well, she mused. Who'd have thought he'd be so old-fashioned?

"You're not nervous about tonight?" he asked, dragging her from her thoughts.

"Yes, I am."

"You don't show it."

"Neither do you."

One brow rose. "Who said I was nervous?"

"You usually don't have trouble doing up your tie."

"Thanks for noticing," he said wryly.

She finished her task and patted the tie. "There. That's better."

He turned away to look in the mirror. "Perfect."

Yes.

He was.

She cleared her throat. "So this dinner is important, is it?"

He reached for his jacket. "Yes and no. Alex has already made the deals to launch 'Valente's Woman' in France and Germany. I just need to keep relations agreeable between us until the launch."

Sasha realized that this must be all quite new to Nick. Previously Cesare and Isabel would have hosted any clients, and then Alex and Olivia, but this time it fell to him. No doubt he would be an accomplished host as a playboy bachelor, but this was the first time he'd be hosting a dinner in his own home as a married man.

She felt bad now for refusing before. "You'll do fine," she said, prompting an arrogant smile from him.

"I know."

And he did.

Extra fine, Sasha thought sourly an hour later as she watched Claudine, the beautiful wife of the French businessman, flirt with Nick from the moment she set foot in the house.

In the meantime the German couple just sat back and smiled, along with Jacque, who didn't appear concerned by his wife's behavior.

It concerned Sasha, especially when Nick looked thoroughly smitten by the gorgeous brunette leaning close to him and talking French in a low, husky voice.

"Ooh, Nicolah, you are teasing me," she said in her accented English, laughing sexily as she squirmed in her seat.

"No, really," he teased. "If you're going to the fashion show tomorrow make sure they don't mistake you for one of their models."

Claudine preened. "Perhaps I will need you to

come with me and protect me." She looked at Sasha. "Would you mind if I borrowed your husband tomorrow, Sasha?"

Her blatant approach took Sasha's breath away. And Nick, the rat, was sitting there smiling and thoroughly enjoying himself and probably expected she would say yes.

She'd be damned if she'd be humiliated like this.

"I'm sorry, Claudine, but I need him tomorrow," she said sweetly, smiling at Nick like her very existence depended on him.

"Ooh," Claudine pouted at Nick. "Another time perhaps, Nicolah?"

"It's a date."

Sasha could feel the humiliation rise up in her throat but she refused to look at the others at the table. A date with a married woman? Wasn't he forgetting something? Like he was now a married man himself? This was going beyond being more than a good host.

Or perhaps he just didn't care. Perhaps he was too focused on making a conquest to worry about what this meeting was all about. Worse, perhaps this was how he did business as a playboy.

A reputation well earned?

Thankfully the German woman, Freda, asked Sasha about her plans to redecorate and the conversation turned to interior design. She was busy answering questions when she heard Claudine ask Nick if he could show her where she could freshen up.

"That's okay, Claudine," she said instantly. "I can show you."

"Oh but…you are talking to Freda."

"No, that's fine. I want to freshen up, too."

The woman pouted again, but Sasha ignored it, just as she ignored Nick as she passed him on her way out the door. If he dared to chastise her later, then he was in for a rude shock.

"Your name is French?" Claudine asked as they walked down the hallway. It was the first personal thing she'd said to her all night.

"No. It's spelled S-A-S-H-A, not S-A-C-H-A."

"You are not French then?"

"No."

Claudine gave a grunt, evidently not impressed by a non-French person using a French-sounding name.

Then the woman sent her a sideways glance. "Nicolah is so handsome."

Aah, now they were getting to the main thing.

Sasha just smiled. "Very."

And he's mine, she wanted to say.

"Jacques does not like the fashion shows." She sighed deeply. "It's a pity Nicolah cannot come with me. I'm sure he would like that."

Sasha opened the bathroom door. "Family always comes first with Nick."

And as she shut the door behind the woman, Sasha realized that was the truth. His family did always come first.

Just not his wife.

Nick was glad to see the back of their guests. Now all he wanted to do was go to bed—with Sasha.

"That went well," he said, coming into the bedroom after he'd turned off most of the downstairs lights. Sasha was sitting in front of the dressing table, taking off her jewelry. She looked so right, so very feminine, and for the first time he felt thoroughly married.

It wasn't a bad feeling.

"For some," she said coolly.

Her unfriendly tone dragged him from his pleasant thoughts. "What do you mean?"

She spun around on the stool, and suddenly sparks were flying from her green eyes. "I'm sorry if I spoiled your plans for tomorrow, Nick, but I didn't think it right you go out on a *date* with another woman when you're already married to me."

He stared in amazement, then snorted. "You didn't think that was for real, did you? Claudine was just flirting."

And mild flirting at best. He'd known women who came on a lot stronger than that.

"Is that why she was practically begging me to let you go to the fashion show with her?"

"When?"

"When I escorted her to the bathroom."

He shrugged. "She's French. She does things over the top."

"Not with *my* husband she doesn't."

A crazy thought blew him away. "You're jealous!"

Her slim shoulders tensed. "Don't be ridiculous. You promised to be faithful, and I expect you to keep that promise, that's all."

Okay, so she wasn't jealous.

And now he was getting annoyed. His word was good enough for the rest of the world. It should be good enough for his wife.

"Look, I told you I take my marriage vows seriously, and I do. There's no way I'll be unfaithful to you."

"I'm trying to believe that."

He considered her tight mouth. "You've really got a thing about this, haven't you?"

She hesitated, then, "Yes, I do. I've spent a lifetime watching my father having affair after affair and my poor mother putting up with it. Not me. I won't put up with it. I won't allow myself to be humiliated in such a way."

The words were heartfelt, and something kicked inside him. "So you know about your father's affairs?"

"Doesn't everyone?" she said with a catch in her voice.

"Does your mother know?"

"We've never mentioned it, but I'm sure she does." She straightened her shoulders. "And I won't ever let myself be put in that position."

"I'm not asking you to."

Her expression clouded. "It's all about respect, isn't it?" she said, as if talking to herself. "Respect for another person."

"You've got my respect."

She focused back on him. "But I didn't always have it, did I?"

The muscles at the back of his neck tightened. She'd mentioned respect the other day, too, and he'd let the comment pass. Not this time.

"Why do you say that? I've always treated you with respect."

"If you'd respected me years ago you wouldn't have gone off with that girl after our kiss."

The comment staggered him. "What are you saying? That our kiss *mattered* to you back then?"

She held his gaze for a moment, and her delicate chin rose higher. "You gave me my first kiss, Nick. And yes, it mattered."

He expelled a breath.

"But you didn't care, Nick."

She was wrong about that.

"You've got no idea how hard it was for me to walk away from you, Sasha. But dammit, you were only eighteen. You had your whole life ahead of you."

"So did you."

"I don't deny that. I was only twenty-five. I didn't want a serious relationship. It wouldn't have been fair to you—to either of us—if I'd taken what you'd offered."

"I felt humiliated," she said quietly. "More so when you left with another girl."

He swore low in his throat. "I'm sorry. That hadn't been my intention."

He'd gotten the hell out of there with the other girl—he couldn't even remember her name now—not to humiliate but because Sasha was a siren…a little witch…who'd suddenly developed a body and a face to die for.

Knowing himself, he would have taken what was offered and moved on.

Knowing Sasha, he couldn't have done that to her.

She gave a shaky sigh. "That was the worst part. You had no idea how devastated I was."

His heart jolted inside his chest. Had this been more than Sasha testing out her newfound womanly ways?

"Sasha, did you have a crush on me?"

For a moment their eyes locked.

"Yes, Nick. I did. I was a young girl in love with the man of her dreams."

Oh hell.

Dare he ask....

"Are you still in love with me, Sasha?"

Her eyelids flickered. "I'm fond of you, Nick, but that's all." As if the thought didn't deserve any further comment, she spun on her stool to face the mirror again and began brushing her hair.

It was odd but his stomach felt like it had just been hollowed out. She hadn't missed a beat in her answer. Love definitely wasn't in her agenda.

Not that he would have known what to do if she *had* said she loved him. He hadn't figured on *that* in their plans. He'd be happy with fondness between them.

And desire.

That was enough.

He walked up behind her and put his hands on her shoulders, looking at her through her reflection. "Amazing as it may seem to you, you're the only woman I want in my life right now."

And that was the truth.

The brush stilled in her hand. "I...I am?"

Her stutter was charming and made his heart pound against his ribs. She may not be in love with him, but she was so very beautiful.

"Yes," he murmured, sliding the neckline of her dress aside and kissing her bare shoulder. "Let me show you."

* * *

At breakfast, Sasha was still recovering from Nick's questions last night.

Are you still in love with me, Sasha?

No, she wasn't, but the question had made her uncomfortable. Love wasn't an easy subject to discuss at any time, but talking about it made it seem more real, even possible.

It was a possibility she didn't want.

Just then, Iris opened the door to the breakfast room and Cesare and Isabel came walking in.

Nick put down his napkin in surprise. "Dad, what are you doing here?"

Cesare's step seemed to hesitate. "Son, I have something to tell you."

Sasha saw Nick stiffen.

"What's happened, Dad?"

Cesare sat down on one of the chairs, his face paler than usual. At the same time, Isabel hugged Nick, then straightened but kept her hand on his shoulder in a comforting gesture. Sasha swallowed hard. This was definitely bad news.

"It's your mother, *figlio mio*." The older man paused. "She fell asleep at the wheel of her car last night and crashed into a parked truck."

Sasha gasped.

Nick sat like stone. "And?"

"She's dead, Nick. She died instantly."

Pain for Nick squeezed Sasha's heart as Isabel squeezed his shoulder.

Nick didn't move. "Had she been drinking?"

"We don't know. Perhaps."

Nick's lips twisted. "More than likely she was coming home from a party."

Cesare inclined his head. "She lived life on her terms, Nick."

"You don't have to tell me that, Dad," Nick said, jumping to his feet and going over to the patio door. He stood looking out over the sunny courtyard.

"At least she didn't suffer, honey," Isabel murmured. "None of us would want that."

Nick let out a deep sigh but didn't turn around. "No, I wouldn't have wanted that."

Seconds passed without anyone speaking as if in deference to the dead.

"They're arranging the funeral for Tuesday in Melbourne," Cesare finally said.

"I won't be going."

Cesare's mouth clamped in a thin line. "She was your mother, son."

"Really?" Nick turned around to face them, the lines of his face rigid.

"I know how you feel, but the world is made up of different people. We have to accept that."

"*You* accept it." Nick tilted his head. "Actually, you accepted that years ago, didn't you?"

Cesare stiffened. "Your mother wasn't the woman I thought she was when I married her, I know. But I did learn to accept that's how she was."

"I'm sorry, but I can't be so generous."

Cesare's gaze held his son's. "The best thing that came out of our marriage was *you*, Nick."

Sasha's throat thickened.

A muscle ticked in Nick's cheek. "Emotional blackmail won't work this time, Dad. I won't go to the funeral. I don't owe her anything."

Cesare was having none of that. He straightened his shoulders. "Julieann was a Valente, if even for a short while. She should have someone from the Valente family go to the funeral."

"You go then."

Cesare glanced at Isabel then back. "I can't. I would if I could, but—"

"His doctor won't let him go," Isabel said. "He's worried it will be too much for your father."

Cesare made a dismissive gesture. "The doctor's just being too cautious. He thinks you'll sue him if I die."

Isabel tutted. "Now, you know that's not true, Cesare." She looked at Nick. "For what it's worth I don't think you should be forced to go either."

"Thanks for your support, Izzie," Cesare muttered.

She looked at her husband. "I don't care what you

say. I don't think anyone should have to go if they don't want to, Cesare."

For some reason, Sasha thought of her own father and how she'd feel if he'd walked out on them years ago. Would she have been forgiving of him?

Probably not.

Of course, it may have turned out better if her father *had* left them. Her mother may have had a chance at a decent life.

"I'm not going, Dad."

Cesare got to his feet, his mouth firming with purpose. "Then it's up to me." He shot Isabel a look. "And no more about it from you, my darling wife. I—" Suddenly he turned pale.

"Dad?" Nick raced over while Isabel gasped, then took some tablets out of Cesare's jacket pocket.

"Here, darling. Put this under your tongue."

A short while later Cesare started to get his color back and everyone breathed a sigh of relief. If the older man had been hoping for effect, he couldn't have chosen a better moment.

Nick stood looking down at his father, his eyes unreadable. "Okay, Dad. You get your wish. I'll go to the funeral."

Cesare looked relieved. "Thank you, *figlio mio*. This means a lot to me."

"I'll go with him," Sasha said, wanting them to know she'd be there for Nick.

Nick spun toward her. "No."

"But—"

"No." Without another word, he turned and walked out of the room.

Sasha's heart sank, but she wasn't about to give up.

"Go with him, honey," Isabel said. "He needs you."

Sasha nodded. He needed someone, but she wasn't sure it was her. "I intend to, Isabel. Don't worry."

After that, the older couple left and Sasha saw them off. For all that she understood why Cesare wanted a Valente at the funeral, like Isabel, she did think it unfair to ask Nick to go. Did they really need someone to represent the family? Wasn't Cesare showing the woman more compassion than she'd shown him and their son?

But it wasn't her place to say anything.

She knocked on the study door and went in. "Nick—"

"No, Sasha."

"But—"

"I'm going alone."

She stopped in the middle of the room and glared at him across the desk. "Would you let me finish a sentence or are you taking a page from my father's book now?"

He flinched.

"Nick, look. I know we were forced to get married, and I know we didn't marry for love, but I…care about you. I'm your wife, and I should go with you at a time like this."

A nerve pulsed near Nick's temple. "It's a funeral for a woman you didn't even know, Sasha. There's no reason for you to attend."

"I may not have known the woman, but I know her son very well. *He's* reason enough for me to go."

His eyes darkened as silence hung in the air. She meant every word. She wouldn't back down over this.

Something shifted in his expression as he looked at her. Finally he said, "As you wish."

Her heart thudded with relief. "Thank you."

He picked up the phone. "Now, if you don't mind, I have some arrangements to make." Clearly he wanted to push her out, both of the room and emotionally.

Still, she hung on. "Would you like me to do all that?"

"Thanks, but my PA knows my requirements."

She inclined her head and went to leave the room. It was obvious he'd given all he had to give right now.

"Sasha?"

She stopped and turned. "Yes?"

"Thank you," he said brusquely.

She nodded and shut the door behind her, not

sure what he was thanking her for—wanting to go to the funeral with him, or offering to help. Her heart swelled inside her chest. Nick really did appreciate her efforts.

He had finally noticed.

Seven

With Alex using the family jet in England, making it unavailable to take to Melbourne, Nick was glad he'd hired another plane. At least this way he wouldn't leave the tainted memories of the funeral in the family jet and could put it all behind him once it was over.

He only wished Sasha had stayed at home, he thought, watching her in the leather chair opposite as she stared out the aircraft window. She was dressed appropriately in black and looked elegantly sedate, but he still didn't think this funeral was the place for her. He appreciated her concern, but it wasn't warranted. He could handle this by himself.

Dammit, his mother didn't deserve to have Valente representation at her funeral. Okay, so his father had wanted to do the right thing, but then, his father had always wanted to do the right thing. The older man just hadn't known there had been a price to pay.

And that *he'd* been the one to pay it.

An hour later they pulled up outside the church and a knot tightened in Nick's gut. Just as he squared his shoulders he heard Sasha gasp.

"It's beautiful," she murmured, looking up at the church through the limousine window.

He took a glance but he wasn't really interested in a building right now.

She sat back on the seat and winced. "Oh, Nick, I'm sorry. This isn't the right time to say that."

"It's fine."

She shook her head. "No, I was being insensitive. It's just that this is the type of church I always dreamed I'd be married in."

That caught his attention. "You did?"

She flushed, then gave a shrug. "Sorry. It took me by surprise when I saw it."

Just like she was taking him by surprise.

"No need to apologize," he said, as the driver opened the car door.

Nick had the strangest feeling when he saw his mother's casket near the altar. He stopped inside the door, his legs unable to move. This was his *mother,* something inside him screamed.

And then he felt Sasha touch his arm and at that moment he was truly grateful to have her with him.

The service was brief with only about twenty people who'd bothered to come. Two of the men he remembered as her husbands from years ago. Not much for a life spent with five husbands and various lovers.

A life spent on the edge.

Outside the church a man in his early sixties came up to him and shook his hand. "Nick, she would have been so happy you came."

Nick's brows flattened. "And you are?"

"I was Julieann's husband."

"Husband?" Nick bit back from asking which one.

"Her last one," the man said, reading his mind. "My name's Ted, by the way."

Ted's eyes darted to Sasha. "And this must be your new wife," he said, startling Nick, then explained, "Julieann read about your marriage in the papers."

Nick grimaced inwardly. He wondered how long before his mother would have found a way to make use of that knowledge.

"How long were you married, Ted?"

"Five years." The older man's eyes didn't waver. "She'd changed, Nick."

"Really? So she wasn't drunk behind the wheel of her car when she died?"

"No, she wasn't," Ted said firmly. "She'd been working the nightshift at an old people's home. She fell asleep because she was tired."

"My mother would never have been working. Period. And certainly not working to help anyone else."

Ted began to look upset. "I told you, she'd changed. Believe me, she had."

Nick held himself in check. Nothing would convince him of that statement. "It doesn't matter if I believe you or not. It's over."

The older man blinked rapidly, then reached into his pocket and pulled out an envelope. "I think you should have this."

Nick didn't take it. "What is it?"

"It's a letter. To you. She was planning on sending it, but kept putting it off until she felt you were ready."

Nick still didn't take it. "I don't want it. It's too late."

Ted continued to hold out the envelope but his hand shook a little now. "Then it won't do any harm for you to read it."

Nick stared hard at him. "Were you good to my mother, Ted?"

Moisture refilled Ted's eyes as he straightened. "Yes, I was."

"Then I'll take it for your sake." Nick took the envelope, aware of the other man's relief. He couldn't promise to ever read it. "I'm sorry for your loss, Ted."

"I'm sorry for yours, too, son."

Swallowing a lump in his throat, Nick cupped Sasha's elbow and walked her to the limousine. Ted had no need to offer condolences for losing his mother.

You couldn't lose something you had never had.

After dinner that evening, Sasha wasn't surprised when Nick said he was going to do some work in the upstairs study. He'd already spoken to his father about the funeral, and then Alex had called from London with concern in his voice.

She knew Nick was upset and he needed to be alone to think about the day's events. She understood he was having trouble assimilating what Ted had told him about his mother, how to fit that image into the person Nick knew her to be. She could only imagine the thoughts going through his head right now.

Of course, he hadn't needed to hear her exclaim over the church like they were attending a joyous wedding instead of a solemn funeral. Yet she hadn't been able to stop herself. The moment she'd seen it, she'd fallen in love with its picture-book setting. The perfect picture for the perfect wedding she had dreamed about.

She sighed and pushed aside her wistful thoughts as she settled down to do some work of her own. For once, time dragged. She wanted to go and see how Nick was doing.

For a few hours she held back, but at nine o'clock she couldn't wait any longer. She went upstairs and knocked on the study door, only to find him nowhere to be seen.

And then she saw the letter from his mother lying open on the desk. Her heart started to thud.

Hurrying to the window she saw his car was still parked outside in the driveway. Then she checked their bedroom but he wasn't there either. She was about to go downstairs and check the kitchen when she noticed a door open at the far end of the landing.

Nick's old bedroom.

She found him sitting on the side of the bed in the dark, the light from the hallway spilling across the center of the room, showing him with his elbows on his knees, staring down at the floor.

"Nick?" she murmured with concern, wanting to rush to him but not wanting to intrude in a private moment.

He lifted his head. "Sasha."

"Are you okay?"

A moment's silence, then he straightened. "Yeah, I am."

She took a few steps into the room. "I went to look

for you in the study." She hesitated. "Um…I saw your mother's letter was open and I was concerned for you."

"Did you read it?"

"No! I would never do that."

He grimaced. "I wasn't accusing. I thought you might have read it to see if it had upset me, that's all."

"And has it? Upset you, that is."

"Yes and no." He took a ragged breath. "No, because my mother truly was genuinely sorry for all she'd done. Yes, because it's too late to tell her I forgive her."

Stunned surprise rippled through her and she sat down on one of the brocade chairs. "You forgive her?"

He nodded. "My mother was never the type of person to ask for forgiveness. You see, she never actually realized she needed forgiving in the first place." He gave a half smile at that. "And I would've said a leopard never changed its spots, but some things happened to Julieann that had a profound effect on her."

"What was that?"

"She fell in love for the first time ever. With Ted." He gave a tiny pause. "And she got cancer."

Sasha's heart saddened for the woman. "Cancer?"

"Yes, and she recovered but it made her look back on her life and see all the hurt she'd caused. Believe me, I know the woman my mother was in her younger years, and she would never have written that letter. Never."

Sasha knew he would never let himself be fooled by anything insincere. "I'm glad she changed for the better."

"Me, too." Then his brows pulled together. "I guess for once my father was right and I was wrong. If Dad hadn't convinced me to go, I'd probably have received the letter in the mail and not read it at all. I know for sure I wouldn't have been so quick to forgive, but meeting Ted today convinced me he was genuine. And that the letter was, too."

"I liked Ted."

"Me, too. He's much better than her previous husbands. There were five," he said before she could ask. "And apart from Ted, they were all after my mother for the money she could get out of my father."

Sasha's forehead creased. "Did your father just hand over money whenever she asked for it?"

He shook his head. "No, it wasn't quite like that. From the time I was seven she'd turn up here every couple of years until I was twelve, and insist on my staying with her and her current husband for a few days while they were in town." His lips twisted. "Naturally she'd insist on being paid 'expenses' and then blow it all at the races."

Sasha listened with rising dismay. She was beginning to see why Nick had disliked his mother so much.

"My dad didn't want to stop me from seeing her, but he would always ask me if I wanted to go. I thought he wanted me to, so I did." He shrugged. "I've never told him the truth."

Her eyebrows rose. "Your father didn't realize this? He just handed you over to a woman who had no respect for anyone or took no responsibility for anything?"

"He thought he was doing the right thing. Besides, he told me years later he had someone keep an eye on me while I was away, and he thought I was having an okay time. She'd dump me on her parents, you see, while they went off to the races, so he thought I was getting to know my grandparents. They couldn't have been less interested in me if they'd tried."

Oh, poor Nick. "What did you do when you were with them?"

"Sit and watch television. I was miserable and couldn't wait to get back home." He took a shuddering breath. "It was only a few days, but it felt like a lifetime."

"And there would've always been the fear that you would never come back home again," she said half to herself.

A muscle began to throb in his cheek.

She stared aghast. "Oh my God. That's why you won't let me redecorate this bedroom. This was your sanctuary whenever you returned home, wasn't it?"

He nodded with a taut jerk of his head. "Yes. I felt safe here. I still do. I used to imagine they would never get to me here."

Her heart constricted. "Oh, Nick. I'm sorry you had to go through all that."

"Hey, it wasn't so bad," he said, making light of it now.

"Yes, it was."

A look of discomfort crossed his face. "Okay, so those times were bad, but I always made it back home and that's the important thing."

She looked at Nick and something tumbled around in her chest. She could imagine him a little boy or a young teenager putting on a brave face, terrified of going with his mother and her latest new husband, not knowing if he would ever come back to those who loved him.

The urge to hold him was strong and she stood up and went to stand between his legs, pulling his head against her breast in a comforting fashion. He didn't resist, and they remained like that for a while.

Only, suddenly, she wanted more tonight. She wanted to show him that this was their home and she was his wife and he had no need to fear being abandoned ever again.

She turned his head up to her. "Let me make love to you, Nick."

His eyes flared with desire. "Yes, Sasha," he said in a low, raspy voice. "I need you to love me tonight."

His words cut the air from her lungs.

Love him?

Oh God, she thought as she bent her head and began placing soft kisses down his cheek until she came to his mouth.

She already did.

Eight

The next morning Sasha felt Nick's lips on hers in a brief goodbye kiss, but she kept her eyes shut until she heard him leave the room. Then and only then did she carefully open them to a new morning and a new beginning, one where she knew she would have to be strong.

She loved him.

If it hadn't been for all the smoke and mirrors caused by their forced marriage she'd probably have seen it coming. As it was, it had taken a private man like Nick to share his painful past with her to make her see what was truly in her heart.

She'd never stopped loving him.

She'd merely been convincing herself otherwise because it hurt too much to admit she loved a man who would never love her back. He couldn't. He wasn't the type of man to give up part of himself for love of a woman. Even now, she knew he didn't love her. He liked her, and she was sure he liked her even more with each passing day, but there was no way she could tell him she loved him.

He wouldn't want to know.

And his rejection of her would be far worse this time. They were adults now and their feelings ran deeper and more lasting, and to bring it out in the open would ruin any chance of a happy marriage between them.

A marriage now based on friendship.

Not love.

No, she'd have to be happy with what she had. The alternative of a divorce, or of Nick feeling uncomfortable around her was too much to bear.

Better to keep it a secret.

Of course, for all her self-talk, when he returned home that night and kissed her hello, then took the stairs two at a time to go shower and change, Sasha's heart skipped a beat as she realized something. This morning's kiss before leaving for work had been the first time he'd kissed her goodbye.

And now this?

Things had definitely changed for the better between them. Perhaps one day...

No, she dared not think it.

"By the way," he said over dinner later. "I'm happy for you to redecorate my old bedroom now."

She blinked. "You are?"

"Yes. Give it a whole new look and turn it into a spare bedroom. Do whatever you want. You're the expert. I don't need it anymore."

Her insides turned soft. "No, you don't, do you?"

He seemed much more relaxed. "Sasha, I think it's time we had some fun. Would you like to go to a party on Saturday night? Friends of mine are celebrating their fifth wedding anniversary."

She liked that he was asking her and not merely expecting her to go. More importantly it was as if he actually *wanted* to be with her.

"I'd love to go to the party with you."

He flashed her a smile. "Good."

That smile made her senses spin and took her right through the week, especially when he continued to kiss her goodbye and hello every day. It was as if he truly considered her his real wife now.

There were about fifty people at the party held at a gorgeous mansion overlooking the Parramatta River. Nick's friends, Fiona and Boyd, were warm and friendly.

"We're so sorry we missed your wedding," Fiona said. "We were overseas at the time but it was a nice surprise when we came back."

"Surprise?" Boyd laughingly choked. "I was totally shocked when Nick told me he was married. Who'd have thought the playboy would ever get married, let alone so quickly?" He got an elbow in the ribs by his wife. "I mean…well, you know what I mean."

"Yeah, Boyd, we know what you mean," Nick teased and left it at that.

Sasha was grateful Nick didn't tell them the truth. She hadn't cared at the wedding if everyone had known, but now it was a matter of pride.

And a matter of love.

Over the next hour Nick kept her by his side, not leaving her for a minute while they mixed with a small group of friends. They were laughing at something one of the wives said when suddenly a blonde beauty pushed through the group.

"Darling!" she squealed, throwing her arms around Nick's neck and hugging him. She leaned back and kissed him full on the mouth before saying, "Darling, I'm back. Aren't you glad to see me?"

There was dead silence in the group.

Sasha swallowed hard as she looked at the beautiful blonde, then Nick, seeing the shock before a mask came down over his face.

Effortlessly he extricated himself from the

woman's arms and slid his arm around Sasha's waist and said, "Brenda, I'd like you to meet my wife."

The other woman gasped, her eyes darting in disbelief to Sasha and back. "Your *wife?*"

"That's what I said."

The blonde's face began to crumble. "Oh, Nick, how could you!" she choked, spinning on her heels and racing out to the patio.

The silence continued.

Nick's mouth tightened as he turned to Sasha. "I'd better go sort this out."

Sasha nodded. It was the right thing to do, the only decent thing to do, so why was she feeling uneasy about it all? He strode away, leaving an uncomfortable quiet.

Then Fiona took matters into hand. "These things happen," she said sympathetically, giving Sasha's arm a pat.

Sasha cleared her throat. "Yes, they do."

Then one of the men started talking about something else and the conversation started up again somewhat awkwardly, everyone no doubt wondering what was going on out there on the patio and none more than herself.

She held her head high and determined to keep on doing so, but inside she was feeling less than certain. Who was Brenda, and how much had she and Nick meant to each other?

It seemed forever before he returned. His jaw was clenched as he came up and slipped his arm around her waist again, pulling her close. "Right, I'm back where I belong now."

She knew he meant to comfort her but their relationship was such that she didn't know which way the wind would blow. All this could be for show.

She winced. What was the matter with her? It *was* all for show.

All at once Brenda appeared at the open doorway, tears streaming down her beautiful face as she gave a loud sob and ran through the room to the front door. Every pair of eyes watched her, then all those eyes seemed to turn and look at her and Nick.

Sasha wanted to sink through the floor.

"Let's dance," he rasped, taking her drink and handing it to Boyd. Then he led her toward an area set aside for dancing.

He pulled her into his arms. "Don't ask."

"Nick, I—"

"Later. Right now I want to dance with my wife."

She kept quiet but as she looked into his angry blue eyes she had to wonder if there was a reason he had called her his wife.

Was it to remind her that he was married to her?

Or was it a reminder to himself?

Thankfully by the time they'd finished their

dance, the commotion Brenda had caused had receded into the background. Everyone had gone back to enjoying themselves and she was touched that some of the ladies seemed to be going out of their way to be nice to her.

She just hoped it wasn't from pity. She couldn't bear that. Not when she'd seen so many others pity her mother over the years.

They stayed at the party for an hour after that, more out of pride than not, Sasha knew. Once in the car, she couldn't hold back any longer. She had to know.

"Do you love her?"

Nick's hand stilled on the ignition key. "Of course not."

"She loves you."

His mouth tightened as he lowered his hand. "She thinks she does. She'll get over it."

Just like *she* had got over him years ago?

Just like *she* would have to get over her love for him now?

"That's so hard-hearted, Nick."

"What do you want me to say, Sasha? I'm married now. I can't help her."

Pain wrapped around her heart. "Would you help her if you *weren't* married?"

He shot her a hard glance. "No."

Is that all he had to say?

"Look, she went overseas and married someone else, and now she's walked out on that marriage after six months and is pretending she still wants me? No way."

She swallowed hard. Couldn't he see what was right in front of him?

"Maybe she really does love you."

He made a harsh sound. "Sure. Brenda came back through that room knowing everyone would feel sorry for her. Don't you think a truly broken-hearted person would leave by the back door and away from prying eyes? Does all that sound like love to you?"

Her heart began to fill with relief. "No, I guess it doesn't."

"I was the one who broke it off. Brenda was a fling, that's all. I would never have married her."

"Never?"

"Never." He reached out and put his hand over hers. "I'm glad I'm married to you."

She ignored the warmth of his skin against her own. "Why?"

He blinked. "Why?"

"That's what I said."

Withdrawal came over his face before he turned back to put the key in the ignition. "There's a whole heap of reasons."

Yes, and none of them were love.

He glanced back at her. "Sasha, don't let her get to you. She's someone from my past and I can't change that. But don't let her into our future, okay?"

He was right.

"Okay."

He waited a moment more, his eyes reading hers as if to be convinced, then he started up the engine and headed for home.

"Are you sure you don't want to come with me to my parents' place?"

Sasha placed her hairbrush down on the dresser and looked at Nick. "No, I'd only be in the way."

The Valente men were getting together at Cesare's apartment now that Alex was back from London. And Isabel was having Sunday brunch with a friend, so it was no use going with Nick just to sit and listen to the men talk business.

"You wouldn't be in the way," he said, a touch of gruffness to his voice.

Tenderness filled her but she tried not to show it. She'd accepted what he'd said about Brenda and it was forgotten. Now she just wanted to get on with her life.

With Nick.

"No, I've got lots of things to do here."

He went to kiss her then stopped to hover just above her lips. "So you're okay about Brenda?"

"Yes, I am."

And she was.

He kissed her then, a long lingering kiss that was meant to reassure her.

And it did.

Until she answered the phone an hour later and a woman asked to speak to Nick.

"He's not here at the moment," Sasha said, her fingers tensing around the handset. "Do you want to leave a message?"

"Tell him it's Brenda." The woman's pause was definitely for effect. "I'm returning his call."

Sasha held on to her composure. "His call?"

"Nick called me a little while ago and said to call him back. I thought it was from this number. This is his parents' old number, right?"

Her words implied that she knew his parents' number very well.

Sasha drew herself up straighter. "Yes, this was Cesare and Isabel's house. It's mine and Nick's now. I'll pass on the message that you called."

Her hands were shaking as she hung up the phone and for a moment she felt a silly sense of triumph. Then it hit her.

Nick had called Brenda.

To meet with her?

Or to tell her to leave him alone?

All at once Sasha's doubts rose again like weeds

in a garden. She tried to mentally cut them off at the roots but they went too deep.

Was Nick lying?

She'd believed him about not being in love with Brenda, but was she being a fool to be so accepting? Had she *wanted* to believe him because of her love for him? Had it blinded her to his faults? Made her weak to his lies?

No, she didn't want to believe any of that, but the scenario was all too familiar. Memories of her parents' marriage were always at the back of her mind, her father always so glib at assuring her mother he was working when he was out with his latest girlfriend. Her mother always accepting his assurances. Sasha was certain her mother hadn't always believed him, but she'd forgiven him anyway.

Was this the same situation between her and Nick?

Was she like her mother?

And was Nick more like her father than she wanted to admit?

All at once she had the urge to go see her parents. Perhaps by merely being around them she'd find she was just being silly.

An hour later her mother's eyes lit up with surprise when she opened the door. "Darling, what are you doing here?" she said, giving her daughter a kiss. "And where's Nick?"

"He had to go see Cesare about work," Sasha said, stepping inside.

"Men! Your father's not here either. He went into the office to fix something or other. On a Sunday, too!"

Sasha turned to hide her face so that her mother couldn't read the suspicion in her eyes. Was that just an excuse? Was her father out with his latest mistress?

"Anyway," Sally said. "It's just us girls today. We can catch up over coffee."

"That would be nice, Mum," Sasha said, regretting having come now. Instead of doubting her suspicions about Nick, this visit was only reinforcing that she could never be like her mother and so accepting of her husband's lies.

And if she couldn't trust Nick, then how could she stay married to him?

They chatted over coffee on the patio until Sasha's cell phone rang. It was one of the contractors handling the renovations. "Let me just get a pen and paper," she said, looking around for her handbag, remembering she'd left it on the kitchen table.

Sally waved her toward the study.

Sasha nodded and entered by the French doors, hurrying over to her father's desk. By the time she ended the call, she had the feeling this particular contractor was going to be more trouble than he was worth.

She sighed as she turned to leave and knocked

into the bookcase, causing a large vase to fall on the carpet and break.

"Oh no," she muttered, crouching down to pick up the pieces. She hoped it wasn't irreplaceable.

Suddenly she realized there was some rolled up paper in the vase that had now spilled out. She picked it up. Her father wouldn't be pleased to have his things all over the place, though why he would tuck them in a vase like this—

A shiver of apprehension slid down her spine as the paper unraveled and the name "Valente" caught her eye. She didn't mean to pry but the words "correct figures" had been written in pencil at the top of the paper.

Then she noticed another sheet of paper underneath it, looking like a duplicate of the top sheet except that the numbers were different.

She blinked, then reread them. Was she seeing what she thought she was seeing?

She swallowed hard. Oh God. It hadn't been enough for her father that she had married Nick. Porter had falsified the numbers to win the contract by undercutting the other tenders by one hundred thousand dollars. No wonder these papers were hidden away.

God, did Nick know? Was that why they'd delayed signing the contract a few weeks ago? She shook her head. No, if Nick knew he'd have done something about it.

Definitely.

"What are you doing with those?" her mother suddenly said in an accusing tone.

Sasha's head shot up, trepidation filling her. "You know, don't you?"

Sally rushed toward her and snatched the papers to her breast. "Know what?"

"That Dad falsified the numbers to win that latest contract."

"Don't be silly."

"Mum, I saw the paperwork. It's there in black and white."

Her mother flushed, then paled. "Darling, you can't say anything. Promise me you won't."

Sasha gasped. "I can't make a promise like that. What Dad did isn't only morally wrong, it's illegal."

Sally's face screwed up. "Yes, and he could go to jail. Oh dear God."

"Maybe he should have thought of that."

She grabbed Sasha's arm in desperation. "Darling, you can't do this to your father. He can't go to jail." She began to sob. "Besides, the deal's already—" another sob "—signed and delivered and—" sniff "—no one's ever going to know. Not unless you tell them."

"I can't *not* say anything, Mum."

"He's your father."

"Yes, and I'm married to a Valente."

"The Valentes have plenty of money. They won't miss this."

Sasha couldn't believe she was hearing this. "Mum, I can't—"

"Darling, look, don't do anything yet. Think about it all first. I'm sure you'll see that remaining quiet is the best thing."

"Mum—"

"Promise me, darling," her mother said, her voice getting shrill. "At least promise me you won't do anything just yet. Give me a chance to speak to him. I'll get him to pay back the money somehow."

Sasha was torn and confused and she just wanted to be alone for a while to think things through. "I don't know."

"Getting the contract freed up other monies and your father has the money to pay the Valentes back now. He'll have to find a way to do that without raising suspicion, but I promise he'll rectify the situation."

Could she believe that?

Did she even have a choice?

She sighed. "Okay, I won't do anything yet."

Her mother hugged her. "Thank you, darling, thank you. We'll sort things out, you'll see."

Sasha made a hasty exit after that. It was hard to believe her father had done such a thing.

It was even harder to believe her mother was sticking up for him.

Nine

"Something wrong?" Nick asked, watching as Sasha jumped slightly, her green eyes looking nervous all of a sudden.

"Wrong? Why do you say that?"

He'd been watching her over the top of his newspaper. "You were quiet during dinner and didn't eat much, and now you've been staring at the television like it has you under its spell."

A hint of pink stained her cheeks. "I find this show fascinating."

He looked at the television screen and saw they had gone to a commercial. "You were watching the news, Sasha, and I wouldn't exactly call the news fascinating. Interesting, but not fascinating."

"That's your opinion."

"Let's not quibble about words. Something's the matter." He hesitated to bring this up but "If it's about the party and Brenda—"

"It isn't," she dismissed without hesitation. "And I'm not giving that a second thought, okay?"

"Okay."

There was something definitely bothering her. She was too pale and not herself.

"I guess it's the renovations," she suddenly said. "There was a lot of work to be done in the initial stages."

Why did he have the feeling she was just saying that to stop him prying further?

"Is it too much for you?"

She looked horrified. "No! That wasn't what I meant. I love it. I really do. But with coming back from England, then the wedding, then working on the redesigning, I suppose I'm just a little tired tonight."

It made sense yet....

The news returned and she pasted on a smile that surpassed the false one on the newsreader's face. "The news is back on."

"Then don't let me stop you from being *fascinated,*" he drawled.

Her smile couldn't hide her wariness as she

returned to look at the screen. He still wasn't convinced there wasn't something troubling her.

He was even more convinced ten minutes later when he heard the telephone ringing out in the hallway and Sasha didn't move. She didn't even appear to hear it. Normally she would get up to answer it straightaway.

He was just about to do it himself when he heard Iris pick up the phone. Then the housekeeper popped her head around the door. "There's a telephone call for Mrs. Valente. It's her mother."

Apprehension crossed Sasha's face, then vanished. "Iris, please tell my mother I'll call her back later."

"Yes, Mrs. Valente."

Nick scowled as the other woman left. "You don't want to speak to your mother?"

She darted a look at him, then away. "I only saw her today. It can wait." She turned back to the television but there was a flush to her cheeks that gave her away.

Something was definitely wrong.

And it had something to do with Sally Blake.

Half an hour later he walked into the kitchen and found Sasha talking on the telephone.

"I said I wouldn't say anything," she was whispering, "and I won't. But—" Suddenly she saw him standing in the doorway and went pale. "Mum, er… I've got to go. Nick's just walked in." She hung up.

Nick leaned against the doorjamb and crossed his

arms. Her words had been a warning to her mother, not a comment.

"Is the hot chocolate almost ready?" he asked, reminding her why she'd come here in the first place.

"Wh-what? Oh yes. I was just about to make it." She hurried over to the refrigerator and took out the milk.

"Your mother has a problem?"

She darted him a look. "You heard?" Without waiting for an answer she turned and took some mugs out of the cupboard. "It's um…women's problems," she said, not looking at him now. "Nothing you want to know about."

So, she was using that age-old excuse, was she? How could he refute it?

"Nick, why don't you go back in the living room. I'll bring in the drinks shortly."

He nodded, then turned and let her be, but if she thought she'd convinced him that nothing was wrong then she was in for a shock. He fully intended to keep an eye on things. Sally Blake had a secret and Sasha knew what it was. And that was fine as long as it didn't impact Sasha too much.

But by her reactions, it did.

Sasha had a restless night until Nick growled and pulled her into his arms, where she promptly fell asleep.

But her thoughts returned as soon as she opened her eyes the next morning. Dear Lord, how could her father cheat Cesare that way? Not to mention the whole Valente family? How could he cheat his *own* family like that? It put her in a terrible position.

"How about meeting me for lunch today?" Nick suddenly said, doing up his tie. "You're coming into the city anyway to talk to your suppliers."

His words brought her back to the moment and Sasha rolled on her side and watched Nick finish dressing for work. He was so handsome. So virile. She loved him so much.

And she might have to give him up.

Oh God, this might be her last chance to spend time with her husband. Her world would fall apart soon enough.

She leaned up on one elbow. "I'd love to have lunch with you, Nick."

He looked pleased. "Good. Leo will come back and pick you up in a couple of hours. He can drive you around while you do your business."

"I can drive my own car."

"Leo's not doing anything until he takes me home again. You may as well make use of him."

Her lips curved upward. "Make use of his services? Yes, I think I can do that."

"Hussy," he murmured, kissing her before he left.

She lay there in bed, just letting her love for Nick

be a part of her. *He* was a part of her, and she would never doubt that again.

She had her mother to thank for realizing that. Going to her parents' place yesterday had shown her Nick was *not* like her father.

Nor was her parents' marriage the same as her own marriage. At first she'd been scared and had projected her fears onto Nick. Nick Valente would not do what her father had done. Nick was good and honest. He'd been open and aboveboard about everything. And despite Brenda's phone call, Sasha was convinced the other woman had just been trying to make trouble. If Nick had called Brenda then it had been for an honest reason. She'd bet her life on it now. Nick was to be trusted.

Her father was not.

She kept those good thoughts of Nick close to her heart for the rest of the morning. Hopefully having only good thoughts would keep the bad thoughts at bay.

"You seem to be enjoying the view," he said over lunch at the harborside restaurant.

Sasha turned to look at him with a smile. "Their menu boasts they have the most glorious view in the world. I was merely checking it out."

"And?"

She surveyed the Harbour Bridge and Opera House through the large glass windows. "I'd say their claim is well-supported."

He smiled, then, "So, what's on the agenda for the rest of the day?"

"I've got a couple more places to visit before I finish up."

He took a sip of wine. "By the way, how's your mother today?"

She dropped her gaze to her plate so he wouldn't see the panic in her eyes. She was sure he hadn't believed her last night about her mother's medical problems. If the positions had been reversed she wouldn't have believed him.

Taking a breath, she looked up. "I only spoke to her last night, so I don't think anything's changed since then."

His eyes had a speculative look. "Aren't you concerned for her health?"

"Of course, but it's nothing urgent. My mother will be fine." Time to change the subject. "By the way, you didn't tell me about the U.K. launch. Did it go well?" She'd been understandably preoccupied last night and had forgotten to ask him about it.

His gaze held hers for a second too long, as if he was considering why she had changed the subject. "It went very well by all accounts. We're launching it on the Continent next."

She was grateful he didn't mention Claudine and any upcoming launch in France.

"It's a gorgeous perfume, Nick."

"I notice you wear it a lot."

"It's my favorite."

"It's every woman's favorite."

She smiled at the usual show of Valente arrogance, and all at once he smiled back with the full power of a Valente smile. The breath hitched in her throat.

The waiter returned to refill their glasses, allowing her to mentally break free of Nick.

When they were alone again Nick said, "How would you like to go on a harbor cruise on Wednesday? We have some prospective customers visiting from the States and I need to take them out to lunch and show them the sights. They're only here for a couple of days."

For a second, sharp anxiety twisted inside her. Would her father have paid back the money by then? Or would she have to gather her strength for Friday's deadline? How *did* a person knowingly send their father to jail?

"The women aren't anything like Claudine," Nick reassured her, thankfully reading her hesitation wrong.

"It sounds like fun."

They ate in silence for a while, until Sasha's cell phone rang. She left it in her handbag, ignoring it and wishing she'd thought to put it on silent.

"Aren't you going to answer it?"

"No."

"It could be important."

Nothing was as important as lunching with Nick. Every second with him counted.

She gave an unconcerned shrug. "It's only about the renovations. I'll get to it later."

Her phone stopped ringing.

"Would you like dessert, madam?" the waiter asked, suddenly appearing at her side.

"Um…" Her cell started to ring again. She opened her handbag and went to turn it off, but not before she caught the number displayed. It was her mother.

"No, just coffee," she said, trying to appear unconcerned as she switched the phone off.

Nick asked for coffee, too, then glanced to Sasha, "Was it a contractor?"

Flustered, she said the first thing that came to mind. "What? Oh, no, it was just my mother. I'll call her back later."

Nick's eyes were full of questions. "I'd have thought you'd want to talk to her."

Oh hell. Was she giving too much away?

"It's not exactly a subject to be discussed over lunch," she pointed out.

Nick grimaced. "True."

Just then Nick's cell phone began to ring.

He glanced at it. "I don't know that number."

"Let me see." Her heart sank. "It's my mother."

He frowned. "Then it must be important if she's calling me," he said, handing it straight to her.

There was nothing for it except to answer the phone, but Sasha got a shock as she listened to her mother's tearful voice. Oh God, she shouldn't have ignored her previous calls.

"My father's had a heart attack," she whispered to Nick in an aside, then spoke to her mother again. "I'll be there as soon as I can, Mum." She finished the call.

"*We'll* be there soon," Nick said, gesturing to the waiter, and a few minutes later hurried her out to the waiting car. "What's his condition?"

"I don't know."

Could *she* have been the cause of this? Her mother would have had to tell him she knew. And having his daughter threaten him with exposure and probable jail would certainly cause him stress enough to have a heart attack.

Yet how could she *not* do something about what she knew, she wondered, feeling like she was shriveling up with stress herself as they headed to the hospital.

Nick squeezed her hand. "You know, my dad's heart attack looked bad at first but it ended up only being a mild one."

She'd forgotten about Cesare's heart attack. Suddenly she felt guilty. "Nick, you shouldn't have come with me. I appreciate it, but I don't want you to go through it all again with my father."

"Don't be silly, Sash," he said gruffly. "I'm your husband."

Warmth rose up inside her and she had to blink back tears. He'd called her "Sash"—the name he'd called her years ago. It was something she'd forgotten until this moment.

"He'll be fine." He pulled her close and she leaned into him, grateful for his presence, comforted by his arms around her, and the now familiar scent of him.

It was only as they were walking toward her mother in the waiting room that Sasha had a tense moment of apprehension. Would her mother inadvertently say something in front of Nick about how Porter had taken the news? Would she blame Sasha's ultimatum for all this? Nick would have to ask why.

"Mum?"

"Oh, Sasha," Sally cried and hugged her.

Sasha returned the hug, relief easing through her. It didn't look like her mother was about to barrage her with blame. "How is he?"

Sally moved back. "I don't know. They told me to wait here." She sniffed. "But it's been ages now and no one will tell me what's happening."

"I'll find out," Nick said ominously, spinning on his heels. "Stay here." He strode out the door toward the nurses' station.

Sasha led her mother back over to her seat. "Mum, what happened?"

Sally gave a shuddering sigh. "When your father got up this morning he said he had indigestion so he took some antacid and went off to work. The next thing I know…" her voice shook "…they called me to stay he'd been brought here in an ambulance."

"So you haven't seen him yet?"

"No."

"Mum, did you—"

Nick strode back through the sliding glass doors. "The doctor's coming out shortly to talk to us."

"Oh God," Sally said and started to sob.

They didn't have to wait long for the doctor, and Sasha put her arm around her mother's shoulders as he told them the news that it didn't look like it been a heart attack at all.

"We're running more tests, but it appears it wasn't."

"Thank God," Sally said.

"What could it have been, Doctor?" Sasha asked.

"I'm not sure. We'll be keeping him here overnight. He's in a private room and Mrs. Blake can stay with him, if you like?"

"Oh, yes," her mother said. "Can I see him, Doctor?"

"He's resting, but I don't see why not." He paused. "But only Mrs. Blake for now."

Sasha watched her mother and the doctor leave

the room. It was wonderful that her father was going to be okay, but he still had to face tomorrow.

And so did she.

"Nick, why don't you go back to work? I'll stay here with Mum until we know more."

His jaw set stubbornly. "No. You need me. I'll stay."

"Seriously, I'll be okay. Besides, it'll probably be hours." She leaned forward and kissed his cheek. "Thank you, but it's no use just sitting around here doing nothing. I'm fine."

His gaze rested on her. "If you're sure?"

"Yes. Now go." It would give her the chance to talk to her mother in private. Sasha couldn't imagine she *wouldn't* have told her husband about yesterday, but she needed to know for sure.

Hours later her father had been given a cautious all clear and Sasha was allowed in to see him, but in the end she didn't get to ask her mother anything. Sally wouldn't leave her husband's side.

And as Sasha looked at her father sleeping peacefully on the bed, she wished so much that it could have been different. If only her father was a different man…a different person.

If only he was a better husband and father.

If only she could love him more.

Sasha finally arrived home around nine and found Nick asleep on the sofa in front of the television.

She'd expected to be home much sooner, so that when he'd phoned her she had even insisted he go straight home and not come to the hospital.

Now, standing in the doorway her heart softened as she looked at Nick. He was such a part of her. He'd always been a part of her. It would be like losing a limb to do without him.

For a moment her vision blurred. She blinked back the tears and turned away to hurry to the kitchen. She wasn't hungry but Iris had put a portion of lasagna in the oven for her, so she'd have to make the effort to eat it.

But first she showered and changed into her silk nightgown and robe, then put the lasagna on a tray and took it into the living room.

Hungrier now than she'd realized, she turned the television down low while she ate her food and watched Nick sleep. She thought the smell of the food might wake him, but it didn't, and she was sipping at her decaffeinated coffee and deciding to cover him with a blanket when his eyelids lifted.

For a moment he looked disorientated. Then he sat up and ran his fingers through his hair. "Damn, I fell asleep, didn't I?"

She gave an understanding smile. "You were tired."

"What time is it?"

"Almost ten."

His eyes grew alert. "You must be exhausted yourself."

"I'm better now that I'm home." And she was.

He scrutinized her more. "How's Porter?"

"They'll keep an eye on him overnight, but they're confident it wasn't a heart attack."

His face relaxed. "See, I told you there was nothing to worry about."

"I know."

All at once his gaze noted her night attire, and the air stilled. His eyes burned into her, making her heart skip a beat. She waited for him to get to his feet and pull her into his arms.

Only, he seemed to withdraw. "I think I'll use a spare room tonight. You need your sleep."

Disappointment filled her. "I won't be able to sleep without you," she said, putting herself on the line…putting her heart on the line and hoping he didn't notice.

The light of passion flared in his eyes again but was banked as he stood up and held out his hand. "Fine. We *sleep,* and that's all."

Her heart expanded at his thoughtfulness. He wanted her yet was prepared to put her needs first. Or what he *thought* she needed.

Happy to just be able to share his bed, she put her hand in his and together they went up the stairs. He made no attempt to make love to her, but he held her in his arms until she fell asleep. And she found that was just as welcome as making love.

She was home.

And she was where she wanted to be.

Ten

Cesare phoned the next morning to see how Porter was doing and Nick put the phone on loudspeaker so both he and Sasha could talk while they were getting dressed.

"Dad, it wasn't a heart attack." Nick went on to explain.

"Grazie a Dio!" Cesare said with relief.

"We've just called the hospital and he's already been released," Nick continued. "Sally will look after him. I'm sure she'll make him take things easy."

"Yes, she's a good woman." Cesare paused. "Sasha, your father's a good man. He gives so much of himself to everyone. It would be a great loss if anything had happened to him. He's the consummate businessman."

Sasha wanted to choke. If only Cesare knew….

"Thank you, Cesare," she managed. "That's kind of you to say."

Cesare ended the call after that and Nick kissed her good-bye, but as he drew back he hesitated. "Are you sure you don't want me to get out of the harbor cruise tomorrow? Alex or Matt can step in."

Tomorrow was Wednesday.

Only two more days until Friday.

The thought of having to force her father's hand pressed down on her. She felt sick at heart over him cheating the Valentes out of money.

She schooled her features. "No. I'll be fine."

Nick held her gaze a moment more. "Okay. See you tonight."

"Yes," she said, putting on a brave face.

As soon as he left, she finished dressing. She would go see her parents. Now that she knew her father hadn't had a heart attack, he had to rectify the situation soon. She couldn't go on like this.

No one answered the front door when she rang the bell, despite her father's favorite music coming from inside the house. Then she realized it was coming from the back patio, so she went around the side and opened the gate.

To her shock, she found her father sitting on the lounger in the back garden, smoking a cigar and drinking whiskey. He looked like a man who was celebrating life.

Or something else?

Suddenly it hit her.

"Oh my God," she accused, seeing him jump with fright as she strode toward him. "You didn't have a suspected heart attack at all. You made it up."

The blood siphoned from his face, then he turned red. "Don't be stupid, child. Of course I didn't make it up."

"I don't believe you."

He stabbed out his cigar. "You think I'd put myself through all those medical procedures, not to mention worrying you and your mother, for the fun of it?"

"Yes! You were desperate. And you didn't give a damn about me or Mum." Sasha swung around when she heard her mother come out on the patio behind her. "Mum, I can't believe you were a part of this."

Sally's eyes widened in alarm. "Wh-what?"

"Leave your mother out of this. She didn't know."

Sasha gasped. "So it's true."

"Know what?" Sally said, looking from one to the other.

"That Dad faked his heart attack so I wouldn't tell the Valentes about his falsifying records."

"No!"

"He thought I'd feel guilty enough to overlook the fact that it wasn't actually a heart attack. No doubt he planned on milking it for all it was worth."

"Porter?" Sally whispered.

"Sally, don't look at me like that. I was only thinking of you. What will happen to you if I go to jail?"

"How magnanimous of you, Dad," Sasha snapped.

"Mind your own business, Sasha," he growled.

She stared hard at him. "You don't regret what you did at all."

"Of course I do."

She knew he didn't. He only regretted getting caught.

"Dad, unless you tell me here and now that you're going to make things right and pay back the money, I'm going to tell Nick what you've done."

He turned white. "You don't mean that."

"I do."

"But I'm your father."

"Emotional blackmail doesn't work on me anymore." She pulled back her shoulders. "Now tell me that you'll make things right, or I go tell Nick right this minute what you've done."

He blanched. "Okay, okay. I'll pay it back, but it might take me a couple of days."

"You've got until Friday." She turned and walked away, her heart so heavy she was surprised she could walk at all. She'd never had much love or respect for her father but she had even less now.

Of course, she wasn't fool enough to trust him. And how the heck was she going to believe him on Friday anyway?

Yet there was a bigger picture here.

How was she going to look Nick in the eyes for the rest of her life and pretend this wasn't between them?

Sasha could feel Nick looking at her throughout dinner but she couldn't seem to lift her spirits. A black cloud hung over her head. It was only a matter of time before it all poured down on her.

After they'd eaten and moved into the living room, she still couldn't relax. She couldn't get interested in the unfolding legal drama on television. She had enough legal drama of her own right now.

And she was terrified her mother would call and put pressure on her to give her father more time, or to beg her to change her mind. She didn't want the stress of even talking to her mother right now and certainly not in front of Nick.

An idea occurred to her.

"I think I've got cabin fever, Nick. Let's go out for a drink somewhere."

He blinked in mild surprise and put aside some paperwork. "Will one of the local pubs do?"

"Yes, there's some lovely pubs around here. And

can we turn our cell phones off, please? Let's not have any interruptions."

He shot her an odd look. "If that's what you want."

Half an hour later they were sitting in the corner at a local pub, sipping their drinks. The hotel was on the heritage listing as were many buildings in the Hawkesbury district.

"Any special reason for the cabin fever?" he asked, leaning back in his chair, his eyes watchful.

It sounded a ridiculous thing for her to say now. They'd been out of the house a lot lately and cabin fever was the last thing she'd have.

She wrinkled her nose. "I guess it's more that we haven't had much time to ourselves."

He nodded. "And all that with your father didn't help either, does it?"

She gave a silent gasp. "Wh-what?"

"With Porter being in hospital."

"Oh." She swallowed. "Yes."

His look sharpened. "You've been tense all night. Are you sure you're telling me everything? He's not taken a turn for the worse, has he?"

"No, he's fine." Panic bounced inside her. She had to get thoughts of her father out of Nick's mind and onto something else. Otherwise she might give herself way. "Brenda called me, you know."

He straightened in his chair. "What? When?"

"Sunday morning after you went to your father's place. She said she was returning your call."

The look in his eyes turned hard and dangerous. He would be a formidable enemy. "She did, did she?"

"So you didn't call her?"

"No." His gaze focused back on her. "Did you think I had? Is that why you didn't tell me before now? You've been worrying yourself sick about it."

"No, that's not it at all. I figured you just wanted to tell her to stay away from you."

"I'd already told her. And she knows the score. She was just trying to cause trouble." He stared at her. "And succeeded."

"No, she didn't." Brenda had tried to make her doubt Nick, but in the end she hadn't succeeded.

Nick's eyes were razor-sharp. "You've been upset all evening. In fact, you haven't been yourself since Sunday at the party."

Somehow she held it together. Sunday was when she'd learned what her father had done.

"I told you it's because of everything else." She swallowed past her dry throat. "I believe you, Nick. I swear I believe you."

He studied her face, taking his time to measure her words. Finally a gentle look came into his eyes. "Thank you," he murmured.

Her heart tilted inside her chest.

In the end they stayed for over two hours, talking

about nothing much in particular and listening to a folk singer. Sasha could feel the tension easing out of her as the wine took hold.

"I think that did us both good," Nick said on the drive home.

She leaned her head back against the leather seat and smiled sideways at him. "We should do it more often."

He chuckled. "I believe you're slightly drunk, Mrs. Valente."

"Enough to take the edge off my pain," she said without thinking.

His scowl was instant. "You're in pain?"

She bit her lip and thanked heaven he had to concentrate on the road. "I had a headache before," she lied. "I thought it was going to turn into a migraine."

He darted a look at her. "Do you often get migraines?"

"No." But she had the feeling she may well start after all this.

Without warning, he gave a crooked grin. "Don't worry. I'll kiss you better if it returns."

"Then it'll be worth it."

"Don't say things like that when I'm driving," he pretended to growl.

She just smiled.

They arrived home and he parked the car in the sweeping driveway, but something happened inside her as she watched him come round to open the passenger door. A sense of impending doom centered in her chest. Suddenly she had the feeling this was all coming to an end.

"Come on, milady," he drawled, holding his hand out.

She vaguely heard him. This moment was far more important than joking or teasing or anything else in this world. God, she loved this man. How could she ever tell him the truth?

She stood up and cupped his face with her hands. "Make love to me, Nick. Make me forget all my headaches."

He looked down at her, his brows drawing together. "What's all this about?"

"Nick, don't talk. I need you tonight. Make me yours."

He opened his mouth to speak, then must have thought better of it. He released his breath and lowered his head.

After that it seemed like they kissed all the way to the bedroom. And in the bedroom…dear God, in the bedroom…their lovemaking took on a poignancy she was sure Nick felt, too. There was a deeper focus in his eyes as he looked at her. A longer than usual pause as he entered her.

And when he made her *his*—perhaps for the last time—her heart hurt.

Eleven

Sasha's pace quickened as she stepped from the elevator and walked toward Nick's office in the House of Valente building just before noon. Her sense of impending doom from last night had alleviated by the time she woke this morning, making her realize it had mostly been the wine.

But not all.

There was still a heavy feeling inside her that she'd been trying to push aside all morning, and it hadn't helped that the hours had dragged until it was time to come into the city for the harbor cruise. She'd needed to keep busy.

And she'd needed to see Nick again. Hopefully being with the man she loved would help push away those demons and doubts riding on her shoulder.

"He's in the conference room," Nick's personal assistant said. "I'll just let him know you're here." She went to press the intercom.

"That's okay, Joyce. I can wait in his office."

"No, he said to tell him when you arrived. It's only the family in there anyway."

Knowing he was waiting for her filled Sasha with pleasure, more so when Joyce said to go straight into the conference room.

"Thank you." Sasha's steps were lighter as she continued along to the end of the corridor. The view of the harbor through the panel of windows called out to her and she was really beginning to look forward to the cruise today. The harbor breeze could be just what she needed right now, especially if she was sharing it with Nick.

"Come in," Cesare called out in response to her knock.

Sasha opened the door with a smile. She had to admit she really liked being a part of the Valente family. Growing up, she'd often been a little wary of Cesare but he was a good man and so were the others.

"Well, well," the older man in question said as she came toward three of the Valente men sitting at the conference table. Nick was standing at the window looking out, his back to her. "You're just in time."

Sasha's steps faltered at his tone. "I…am?"

Why hadn't Nick turned to face her?

"In time for what, Cesare?"

"For me to have your father arrested for fraud."

Sasha's heart dropped to her toes.

"We've found out what he's been up to. Did you think we wouldn't?"

Sasha couldn't find her voice.

"I can't believe Porter thought he could get away with it," Cesare continued. "Does he think the Valentes are stupid? And you were in on it, too, weren't you, girl?"

She gasped at the accusation, aware of three sets of eyes upon her, but the eyes that mattered—Nick's eyes—were still turned away from her.

"And I, fool that I am, wanted Nick to marry you. I thought you were perfect for my son." He gave a harsh laugh. "No wonder Porter wanted you to marry Nick, and no wonder you agreed to the marriage. If it was all in the family he'd get that contract, no questions asked. Of course you had to say no first, didn't you? That way you could dangle yourself as bait in front of Nick and—"

"Enough!" Nick spun around, his face taut as he glared at his father. "You're accusing Sasha without any evidence. You don't know she was involved in any of this."

"Then ask her, *figlio mio*," Cesare said. "Ask her, and then we will know."

She watched Nick hesitate, and felt like she'd been slapped in the face.

He doubted her.

Then he straightened his shoulders and walked toward her. "Sasha," he said, his voice quiet but firm, his eyes with a hint of pleading in them. "Please tell me you didn't know about any of this."

A moment crept by. The others receded into the background. There was her and Nick.

Only her and Nick.

And soon....

She trembled. "I...I...can't."

He sucked in a sharp breath.

"Nick, I—"

His glare silenced her. "No excuses."

"But—"

"This was your sick way of getting revenge, wasn't it?" Disgust filled his eyes now. "Very clever, Sasha."

"Revenge? I don't know what you mean."

"Remember that kiss in the gazebo? Remember how you thought I'd rejected you? You wanted to pay me back for that, didn't you? You wanted your revenge."

"No!" she whispered, her voice threadbare.

"Yes."

At that moment, she knew it was over. He wasn't prepared to let her explain any of this. He wasn't even prepared to ask if there were extenuating circumstances, nor give her the benefit of the doubt.

And could she really blame him?

Giving a small cry, she spun away and ran from the room. It was over.

"I'm sorry, *figlio mio,*" Cesare said, coming up behind Nick and putting his hand on his shoulder.

"Not as sorry as I am, Dad." Nick's gut was one big knot of pain. He'd trusted Sasha. Trusted her like he'd trusted no other woman.

He should have known she'd let him down.

Cesare's mouth tightened. "*Santo cielo,* I'm going to see Porter myself!"

Alex jumped to his feet. "No, Dad. We can handle this."

Cesare clenched and unclenched his hands. "I want to see his face. He was my friend, and now he's a traitor."

"You're getting upset, and that's not good for you. Matt and I will go see Porter. Let Nick take you home."

"No," Nick growled. "I'm going to see Porter." He had more than a vested interest in all this.

Alex nodded. "Then Matt can take Dad home."

Cesare complained but he was shaken and obviously realized it was best he not be there to confront his now ex-friend. He left with Matt, and Nick and Alex took off for the Blakes' house.

Sally turned white when she opened the door to them. It was evident she knew why they were here.

Porter was eating dinner, and he went white, too, as Nick and Alex strode into the dining room.

Alex spoke first. "Porter, I've come to tell you that we're filing charges for fraud against you."

Sally gave a wailing cry behind them, but they ignored her.

The older man's face screwed up. "So Sasha told, did she? I should have known not to trust that daughter of mine. She finds out a couple of days ago and threatens to blow the whistle unless I—"

Nick stiffened. "*What* did you say?"

Porter made a harsh sound. "I said my daughter was going to blow the whistle on her old man. Can you believe it?"

Nick looked at Porter. "Yes, I can." Then he looked at Alex, who nodded in understanding.

"Take my car," his brother said, tossing the keys at him. "I've got a lot more to say to Mr. Blake."

Somehow Sasha managed to find some semblance of control by the time Leo dropped her off at home. She'd never been more grateful for the dark glass panel between them as she huddled in the corner of the back seat, unable to stop the tears from flowing.

Iris took one look at her face and was full of concern. "Mrs. Valente, is there something wrong?"

Sasha almost laughed out loud. Everything was wrong. And nothing could make it right.

Not ever.

"Are you ill? Would you like me to call a doctor?"

Sasha headed for the stairs. "I'd just like to be alone, Iris."

The housekeeper was clearly reluctant to accept that, but inclined her head. "If you wish, Mrs. Valente."

"I do."

Sasha made her way to the bedroom, sick with anguish. She threw some water on her face, hoping the coldness would take away her inner pain, but knowing it was a losing battle. She was burning up inside, her despair like a flame inside her, growing higher and more intense. An iceberg could not put it out.

She knew what she had to do. Nick would no longer want her in his house or in his life and she wouldn't wait around for him to kick her out. He would be glad to see her gone. No doubt he would even get someone else in to oversee the redecorating.

Her throat tightening, she began to throw some of her things in a suitcase. She would get the rest later.

Or better still, leave them for charity. She wouldn't want any reminders of her marriage.

Just then there was a tap at the door and she swallowed a moan. "Come in."

The housekeeper's eyes widened when she saw the suitcase on the bed. "Um…your mother's on the phone, Mrs. Valente."

Sasha's nerves tensed. "I don't want to talk to anyone right now, Iris."

"She says it's urgent."

Sasha winced, then realized it was best to take the call. She felt too raw to give her mother the support she needed right now, but once she pulled herself together, she'd manage it in the future.

Somehow.

She picked up the phone. "Mum, I—"

"Sasha, how could you! You said you would give your father until Friday and now you've gone and told the Valentes. You've betrayed your own family."

She then went into a tirade about Porter going to jail and that her daughter had sent him there, and at that moment Sasha finally understood something. No matter what her father did, her mother would always make excuses for him.

And her daughter would come a poor second.

Sasha quietly hung up. Her mother was welcome to do what she wanted with her life, but *she* wasn't about to help her do that any longer.

It was over.

Just like her marriage to Nick.

There was only one place where she'd found a measure of peace before. She would go back to London. There was nothing for her here.

Nick drove home as fast as he dared. Last night when Sasha had begged him to make love to her, she must have known something was about to happen. She should have told him the truth. She should have said something.

Anything.

Then he remembered how she'd tried to tell him the truth back in the conference room, only he hadn't wanted to listen. He'd accused her of revenge.

Dammit all to hell.

He took the stairs two at a time, not believing Iris's words that Sasha had packed her things and gone. Then he saw some of her clothes missing from the wardrobe and the dresser now empty of her possessions.

And he felt empty deep inside.

So empty he wasn't sure if he could live without her. *Not when she'd taken his heart with her.*

He sucked in a lungful of air. He hadn't seen it coming, but he loved her. It hit him fair and square between the eyes. He could not deny it.

And now he couldn't even tell her. He had no idea where she'd gone, except that he knew she wouldn't go home. After what he'd seen, her parents wouldn't want her.

Well, he *did*.

He strode to the telephone beside the bed and called Joyce. He'd turn this city over until he found the woman he loved.

Twelve

Sasha tightened the belt of her bathrobe, then began toweling her hair dry as she walked into the bedroom. She probably should order something to eat except that she didn't have an appetite. It was going to be a long time before—

"Sasha."

Her head shot up, her heart slamming against her ribs at the sight of her husband standing in her hotel room. "Nick!"

Their eyes locked, but she could tell nothing from his expression.

"Yes, Sasha. It's me."

Her mind tried to take it in. He was here. Oh God, Nick was really here. But how? Why? She dare not hope. No, not even the tiniest bit.

Placing the towel on the table, she pushed back her wet hair and faced him. "How did you find me?"

"You used your credit card to book the hotel, and then again for your flight to London tomorrow."

She hadn't thought he'd be looking so she hadn't given it a second thought. Then she realized why he'd come looking for her. The disappointment was immense.

She thrust back her shoulders. "Look, if you want more details about my father, you've had a wasted journey."

"I already know the details."

Her forehead creased. Was he playing some sort of game with her? "Then there's nothing to say."

"There's plenty to say." He paused and suddenly regret seemed to cut through him. "I'm sorry, Sasha."

"S-sorry?"

"For not trusting you."

She swallowed hard. "I don't understand."

"I shouldn't have been so quick to believe you'd have anything to do with what your father did."

She searched his eyes. "You believe me?"

"*Now* I do. But it wasn't until Porter inadvertently told us your involvement that I realized I'd misjudged you." He took in a lungful of air. "I'm sorry, Sasha. I'll say I'm sorry every day for the rest of our lives if that's what it takes."

Her heart began to wobble. "You want me to come back to you?"

His expression opened up fully for the first time ever. "How can I live in that great big house without the woman I love to share it with me?"

"Nick, are you—" She moistened her mouth. Dare she say the words? "Are you saying you *love* me?"

"Yes."

Her heart jumped with joy but still she held back. She was too scared to believe it. There had to be another reason.

"Is this your revenge, Nick? Are you going to get me to admit I love you and then walk away?"

There was a flash of pain in his eyes. "No. The only direction I'm walking in is *to* you." His steps did exactly that. And then he stood in front of her, his gaze achingly intense. "Do you love me, Sasha?"

She looked up at him and could fight it no longer. "Yes, Nick, I do. I've always loved you. I always will."

He pulled her close. "Oh God, I love you, Sash," he said thickly, his deep voice caressing her ears.

"Nick," she murmured, love swelling within her.

He drew her close and kissed her. She inhaled him in like he was the very air, his heartbeat merging with hers, his touch purring along her skin, his scent mingling with her own. She'd never felt more alive.

Or complete.

He moved back but held her within the circle of his arms. "Last night I knew there was something going on with you, but I didn't know what. And today, I didn't know if you could forgive me." His lips brushed hers. "I just have to say it again. I love you."

"I'll never get sick of hearing you say it," she whispered, the love in his eyes stealing her breath. "I love you so very much, Nick."

He hugged her tight for a short while, then eased back. "I had some bad moments on the way over here, let me tell you."

"Perhaps I gave in too easily then?" she teased.

His lips twitched. "If you hadn't, I'd be a nervous wreck by now."

"You a nervous wreck? Never!"

"You're right," he said, making her smile at his Valente arrogance. "I'd never be a wreck because I wouldn't have let you go in the first place."

"I can't fault that reasoning."

His hands tightened on her waist. "Speaking of giving, you give so much of yourself, trying to balance it all so that no one will get hurt. Your parents don't deserve you. *I* almost didn't."

"Nick, I should have told you as soon as I could,

but I was torn. How could I be responsible for sending my father to jail?"

"You weren't responsible for anything."

"I was responsible to you as your wife. I should have made him tell you in the first place."

His mouth tightened. "Your father is the one who should have been responsible."

She winced, then, "You know, I'm glad it's over now. It would have always been between us because *I* would have known."

"I can guarantee it won't be between us now."

Her heart rolled over as she looked up at him. "Oh, Nick."

"Call me darling."

"Darling," she murmured. Then she remembered something else. "What about your family?"

"They'll know the truth by now. They won't hold anything against you."

"But Cesare—"

"Loves you like a daughter. It's the reason he was so hurt. He will apologize and no more will be said about it."

His words gave her joy. "I love your family, Nick."

"As long as you love me more."

"Oh, yes! Far, far more."

He glanced at the bed. "Seeing that you've already paid for the room…"

She arched one of her eyebrows. "Are you suggesting I go to bed with you, Nick Valente?"

"Do you have a better suggestion, my darling?"

"Not a one."

With their hearts finally open to each other, he drew her down on the bed beside him and at that moment she finally acknowledged something to herself. Loving Nick was no longer the worst thing that could happen in her life.

Loving Nick was the *strongest* part of her life.

Epilogue

Nick watched his very beautiful wife come toward him in the church and his heart swelled with love. He'd ruined Sasha's dreams seven years ago, and then almost ruined them again more recently. This time he was going to make sure her dream came true.

A lump formed in his throat when he saw her blinking back tears during the service. He never knew life could bring such happiness as he'd had the last few weeks with Sasha.

"Darling, thank you," she murmured after they walked back down the aisle past the Valente family, who were their only guests. "The church is so beautiful."

He'd searched high and low to find the perfect church for her and finally found it up in the mountains. The historic church had stained glass windows that looked out over the valley to the ocean where the heart of Sydney could be seen many, many miles away.

Outside the church his family…no, make that *their* family…gathered round to congratulate them and have their picture taken for posterity.

"There's one more thing I want to do," he whispered in her ear.

"What's that?"

"I'll show you later, my love."

And he did.

That night the moonlight shone over the silhouette of a couple kissing in the gazebo. And this time when Nick left to go back to the house, he wasn't alone.

He had Sasha by his side.

As it always would be.

* * * * *

INHERITED:
ONE CHILD

DAY
LECLAIRE

To the four-legged wonders who share our lives and
give us such unstinting love and devotion. To those
who have come and gone…Yoson and Brutus,
Little John and Thursday, and Annie.
And those who give us daily joy…
Yoda and Ruggy, Athena and Guinness.

Prologue

"You have no choice, Jack. If you want to keep custody of Isabella, you're going to have to marry."

Jack Mason glared at his lawyer. "You know I swore I never would."

Derek dismissed that with a wave of his hand. "So you've said. Ad nauseam, I might add."

"Then let's move on, shall we? What's my next option?"

"Jack, I'm telling you flat out. There is no other choice." Derek leaned a hip against his desk while Jack prowled the length of the office. "Look, we've been friends since our college days. You may not have told me all that went on between your parents, but having met your father, I can guess. That doesn't change the facts. CPS is very concerned about your niece, thanks to that psychologist's report."

"I wish I could call the man a liar." Jack thrust a hand through his hair and blew out his breath in a long sigh. "But he was simply stating the facts. It's been three months since the plane crash and Isabella isn't adjusting at all. Her tantrums have escalated. And she's still not speaking."

Sympathy lined Derek's dark face. "Providing your niece with a stable home life and continuing with therapy will go a long way toward changing that."

"I've hired nannies for her." Jack could hear the defensive edge in his voice and fought to eradicate it. Getting ticked off at the one person squarely on his side wasn't his best strategy. "I have a business empire to run, Derek. Isabella is only five. I can't be her caretaker 24/7."

"Child Protective Services is well aware that you've had an endless stream of nannies since March. According to the letter I've received, they're not happy about it. And frankly, Jack, it's not helping with Isabella's recovery." Derek hesitated. "There is another alternative."

Jack lifted an eyebrow. "Go on."

"Let her go. You can afford to find a good home for her. The best possible home. A home with two parents. Someone who has the time to commit to Isabella's well-being."

"I can't do that." The words were ripped from him, low and guttural. "I won't."

Derek didn't bother to pull his punches. "That's your guilt talking. Isabella survived the plane crash and your sister and brother-in-law didn't. You also believe you should have been on that plane with them."

Jack couldn't deny it, not when it was the truth. "I was supposed to be. If I had been… If I hadn't let work delay me…"

"You'd most likely be dead, too, and Isabella would be in the exact same position she is now," Derek stated with brutal logic. "In need of two stable parents who can give their full attention to her needs—something you aren't in a position to do."

"I won't desert her." Jack continued to pace the width of his office while frustration ate at him. "I just need to find the right person. It's taking a bit longer than expected."

"You need a wife. The caseworker is old-school, Jack. And she's from the north. She doesn't care how much money you have or what your name is, or whether your ancestors were among the first residents of Charleston. Her only concern is Isabella."

Jack shot his friend a black look. "And mine isn't?"

Derek's expression softened. "I know you care about your niece. But you've seen her exactly twice since Joanne adopted her, both times when she was little more than a baby. You have no blood ties. You're a stranger to her. And ever since the psychologist released his evaluation, Mrs. Locke has made it clear that she doesn't consider you a suitable guardian. She's actually mentioned placing Isabella in a treatment facility."

Stark fury gripped him. "Over my dead body."

"You won't have any choice in the matter. They'll simply come and take Isabella from you—by force, if necessary." Derek took a seat behind his desk and released a sigh. "What happened, Jack? You were supposed to talk to Mrs. Locke. *Sweet*-talk her, to be precise."

Jack grimaced. "There isn't sufficient sugar on earth to sweeten up that woman."

"You should have made more of an effort, instead of throwing her out of your office. Her opinion will carry a lot of weight in court, as will the psychologist's findings."

"Are you saying that ticking her off wasn't my best business decision?" Jack asked drily. When his friend maintained a diplomatic silence, he allowed the moment to stretch while he considered his options. Not that there were many. "What if I do what you suggest and marry?" The words grated like ground glass in his mouth.

"Then you have a real shot at retaining custody, assuming the Locke woman believes the marriage is genuine. I strongly recommend you choose a bride who has experience dealing with special-needs children. A teacher or a social worker. A do-gooder type who will devote all her time to Isabella's welfare."

"Just like that? Find a do-gooder and marry her." Jack folded his arms across his chest. "And how do you propose I accomplish such an amazing feat?"

"I recommend you find her the same way you found your nannies. You advertise."

Jack stared in disbelief. "You want me to advertise for a wife?"

"No, I want you to advertise for a nanny and then marry her. You find a woman you can live with until CPS signs off on the case, and I'll draw up an ironclad prenup."

Jack had never considered himself slow on the uptake. But this left him totally at sea. "How the blue blazes am I supposed to convince the woman to marry me? Lie to her? Trick her? Pretend I'm madly in love with her?"

Derek shrugged. "If you want. Personally, I'd recommend a far simpler method."

"Which is?"

"Hell, Jack. How many billions do you have moldering away in various financial institutions? Even I've lost track. Take a healthy chunk of it and buy the damn woman."

One

Jack Mason knew he was in trouble the minute he saw her.

He didn't know why she snagged his attention, considering she sat in a room crowded with nanny applicants of all shapes, colors and ages, none of whom possessed a clue about his true intentions—choosing one of them for his wife. This woman dressed in a somber black pantsuit that wasn't the least eye-catching, so perhaps his reaction had something to do with the way she sat reading a paperback novel…perfectly composed and preternaturally still, an expression of absolute patience on a face more striking than beautiful.

Jack examined her with greater care. Interesting. Everything about her appeared quiet and understated. She'd pulled her hair into ruthless obedience, anchoring the ebony mass into a tight knot at her nape. In addition, she'd used a restrained hand with her makeup, just a hint of color on her cheeks and lips. A light brush of taupe across her eyelids drew attention to a startling pair of deep-set eyes that wavered somewhere between honey and gold and were framed by lush black lashes. She looked impossibly young, and yet one glimpse of those eyes warned of someone who'd been through the pits of hell and back again. They overflowed with ancient wisdom and intense vulnerability.

Was that why he'd keyed in on her from all those crowding the room? And what, in particular, about her appearance aroused such intense interest? It was something subtle. Something that stirred instincts he'd honed during his years surviving in the shark-infested waters of the business world. Those instincts warned that this woman, while appearing so calm and controlled on the outside, seethed with secret passion. It was almost as though he sensed the ebb and flow of those restless seas and reacted on a visceral level to a call only he could hear.

If they'd met anywhere else, he'd have moved in on her and cut her from the crowd. He'd have found a way to break through that carefully cultivated self-control and release the inner passion. It had always been that way with him. He'd always responded to the essence of the woman swirling beneath the surface and felt the burning need to strip her down, layer by layer, to that passionate inner core.

This woman would have many layers, fascinating layers. Layers he could explore intellectually and physically. And he wanted to develop—wanted with an intensity he hadn't experienced in years.

One of his prospective "wives" coughed, snapping Jack's concentration. Awareness of time and place returned, along with an irritation that he'd allowed such pointless speculation to distract him. He forced his attention back to the business at hand—securing a woman who could act the part of both nanny and wife. On the verge of calling the next name on the list, the door to the outer office flew open and his niece burst in.

Her short, curly hair stood out from her head in matted golden-brown spikes that had yet to see a brush that morning, and he could tell what she'd eaten for breakfast with a single look at her shirt. She'd worked a hole into each knee of her new jeans—with a pair of scissors, by the look of it. And she'd used her watercolor paints to turn her face into a startling mask of red and black swirls.

Isabella scanned the room in frantic anger, her olive green eyes narrowed to slits. Taking a stance dead center in the room, she balled her hands into fists and then opened her mouth, letting out a scream loud and shrill enough to cause the windowpanes in his office to shiver in protest. For a split second, everyone in the outer room froze. Jack considered taking control of the situation, but then decided to wait and see how his nanny applicants reacted.

Some of the women took decisive action. They bolted for the door. Jack sighed. Three down. Several of the others exchanged uneasy glances, clearly uncertain how to respond to the crazed child who'd erupted into their midst. One large-set, no-nonsense woman rose and approached Isabella.

"You stop that this instant," she demanded.

Isabella responded by kicking the woman in the shin and increasing the volume and shrillness of her scream-

ing, something Jack would have thought an impossibility.
But somehow, his darling niece managed it. The woman
exited, muttering furiously beneath her breath—four
down—and Jack thanked his lucky stars. He didn't think
he could handle a wife with a moustache. Nor did he think
Mrs. Locke would believe theirs was a real marriage.

Successfully having rid herself of four of the applicants, Isabella took control of the room. She darted from
person to person, giving them an exclusive, one-on-one
performance. Each reacted differently. Some attempted
to cajole. Others took the first woman's approach and
made demands. One actually threatened Isabella with a
spanking. Several made shushing noises. Only the woman
in black didn't react. She continued to sit quietly, reading
her book as though she neither saw nor heard the chaos
exploding around her. Isabella took note and her jaw
assumed a determined slant.

Jack winced. Hell.

Rushing over to stand in front of the woman, Isabella
gave full throttle to her displeasure. It didn't make a bit of
difference. The only response was a leisurely turn of the
page. Finally, Isabella's voice gave out and she croaked
into silence. Only then did the woman look up. For an
instant the two stared at each other, a silent contest of
wills.

An odd expression burned in the woman's eyes, something that might have been fear combined with an intense
vulnerability, which didn't bode well for her ability to
control a child of Isabella's willful nature. In the next
moment, the look vanished, replaced by a gentle relentless-
ness, a searing look of hope combined with determination.

The expression took his breath away. She'd only been in Isabella's presence for mere moments, and yet he could practically see her weaving an emotional connection with his niece.

She said something to Isabella in a voice so soft it didn't carry any farther than his niece's ears. Then she stood and walked to the door. Opening it, she scanned the area. "Who's in charge of this child?" Jack heard her ask.

The temporary babysitter he'd hired, who'd no doubt been cowering in the hallway, reluctantly stepped forward. "I am."

Without another word, the woman ushered Isabella through the door and, before the child could react, closed it decisively in her face. Then she returned to her seat, picked up her book and resumed reading. A scattering of applause broke out around her, not that she took any notice. Even so, Jack could tell the incident had affected her. A telltale pulse throbbed at the base of her throat, betraying her agitation. It impressed the hell out of him that she could hide her reaction so well. He checked his watch and grimaced. Time to move this show along.

He called the next name on the list. "Annalise Stefano."

He wasn't the least surprised when the woman he'd been studying tucked away her book, shouldered her purse and stood. Somehow, the name fit. She walked toward him with a long, easy stride that suited her lean, coltish build. A tiny curl sprang loose from the tight control she'd attempted to impose on it and bounced against her temple in joyful exuberance. He almost smiled. Her hair was one of the layers he'd love to peel away. How would she look with all those curls tumbling down her back in total abandon?

"I'm Annalise," she said, and offered her hand. "It's a pleasure to meet you, Mr. Mason."

He took her hand in his and felt the odd dichotomy of fine bones in opposition to a tensile strength. Did it reflect the woman? He suspected it did. He forced himself to release her, when in truth he experienced a sharp desire to tug her closer, if only to see how she'd react, to see how deep that self-control ran. Not good. Whomever he chose for this job would be his temporary wife, a woman he'd want out of his life as soon as feasible. That meant their relationship could be boiled down to two words.

Hands. Off.

"Ms. Stefano," he said. "Come with me." He started to close the door to his office and caught a glimpse of another of the applicants scurrying toward the exit. Hell. Five down, though at least it was the one who'd advocated spanking. He closed the door and waved a hand toward one of the two chairs in front of his desk. "Have a seat while I review your résumé."

He scanned it quickly to refresh his memory. Right, right. He remembered this one. He'd almost rejected her out of hand because she had so little practical experience. What had tipped the scales in her favor was the fact that she'd received her teaching certificate in early childhood and elementary education, as well as in special ed, and that she'd possessed glowing recommendations. They were right in line with the qualifications Derek recommended in his future bride.

"I assume my assistant explained why I'm in need of a nanny?"

"Yes, she did. I also read about the tragedy in the newspapers, Mr. Mason. I'm very sorry for your loss."

He inclined his head, relieved that he didn't have to go into lengthy explanations. The papers had been quite thorough in that regard. "I'm afraid you had the pleasure of meeting my niece, Isabella, a few minutes ago."

Annalise offered a quick smile, one that transformed her face, lifting it from striking to luminescent. "So I gathered."

"As you can see, she's having a difficult time making the transition." He held out his hands. "And who can blame her? Not only did she lose her parents three months ago, but she's been uprooted from her home in Colorado."

Sympathy radiated off Annalise and her eyes glittered with a wealth of emotion. "That explains a lot about her current behavior."

Jack inclined his head. "When she first came to live with me, I contacted an agency to hire a qualified daytime caregiver. I went through their entire portfolio the first month. The longest stayed a week. The shortest clocked in at just under an hour. Since then, I've decided to take matters into my own hands and hire someone myself. Which brings me to your application, Ms. Stefano."

"Please call me Annalise."

"Fine. Annalise it is." He paused on the first page of her application. "You're qualified to teach elementary school. Why have you applied for a position as a nanny?"

She didn't hesitate, clearly anticipating the question. "I'm interested in attaining my master's before taking on a teaching job. This position will provide me with more flexibility than teaching and fewer hours of preparation while I pursue that goal."

He tilted his head to one side. That would fit in with his

own plans. She could pursue her master's program—a program he'd be only too happy to pay for—while playing the role of devoted wife and mother. "Would you be willing to commit to an employment contract of two full years? And would you be willing to homeschool Isabella, if needed?"

She folded her hands in her lap and met his gaze dead-on. "It will take me two years to complete my master's program, so that aspect isn't a problem. Since it's the end of the school year right now, your niece and I will have the summer to work out a comfortable routine before fall classes begin. If you want to initiate a schooling program for her at that point, I'll have the next few months to put together a curriculum that meets with your approval. Then I can implement Isabella's lessons while I begin evening classes toward my master's."

Despite her outer calm, he sensed a certain level of ner-vousness—almost anxiety—and couldn't help but wonder what caused it. He allowed the silence to drag while he considered the various reasons for her turmoil. She could be nervous because she was lying to him about some-thing, in which case he'd find a way to get to the truth. The irony of that fact didn't escape him, considering this entire interview was a huge fraud. Even so, he needed to trust his future wife, which meant all the cards on the table. Of course, she could be nervous because she didn't handle interviews well. One other possibility occurred to him, one that caused his gut to tighten and an unwanted hunger to gnaw at him.

Maybe *he* made her uneasy. Maybe she'd experienced the same odd awareness that he had. She didn't break the lengthy silence with a rush of nervous explanations the way many would have. That fact alone impressed the hell out of him.

"Let me be frank, Annalise. I'm concerned that you may change your mind midsummer and take a teaching position, leaving me to go through this process all over again. Isabella's had enough trauma and loss in her life without experiencing another so soon."

"That won't happen."

Instinct told him that she spoke with absolute sincerity. Even so, he sensed an intense emotional current that continued to ripple just beneath the surface, though he still couldn't quite pinpoint the reason for it. Perhaps it was a simple case of interview jitters. He glanced down at her file.

"I see you've also had some training with special-needs."

She stilled in the act of brushing another loosened curl away from her eyes. Her expression grew troubled. "Has Isabella always been a special-needs child? Or is today's incident related to the plane crash?"

He hesitated, choosing his words with care. "It started after she came to live with me. I want to make sure I hire someone who can help her adjust. Frankly, I don't think you have the necessary experience."

"Is she seeing a counselor?"

"I don't have much choice in the matter. CPS has insisted."

She raised an eyebrow at his dry tone. "With good reason. Children of that age can be manipulative. If she feels like you're cutting her some slack because of her loss, she'll use that for as long as it works. You should also consider talking to one yourself in order to learn how to best provide for her needs."

He leaned back in his chair and lifted an eyebrow. "Do I look like the sort of man who can be easily manipulated? Or is it just that you don't think I can provide for her needs?"

"Look, I'm not saying you can't or shouldn't give her love and stability and reassurance. I'm just suggesting you don't allow pity to make you too indulgent." Then she grinned, the vibrant flash of it arrowing straight through to his gut. "And now I've moved from dispensing unwanted advice to lecturing. It's well-intentioned, honestly."

He knew it, just as he knew it was advice identical to that of the psychologists he'd consulted. "How would you deal with her temper tantrums? If I hire you, you won't be able to do what you did a few moments ago and hand Isabella off to someone else. Next time you'll be the one in charge."

"I'll try a variation on what I did today. Ignore her screaming when practical, making sure she can't injure herself. Remove her from the situation when necessary, particularly if we're in public. Afterward, talk to her in a calm fashion and make it clear that her behavior is unacceptable. In time, when she doesn't get the response she's hoping for, she should stop." She offered a wry smile. "Of course, then she'll try something else."

Curiosity filled him. "What did you say to her before you put her out?"

"I told her that screaming is unacceptable behavior, and that there are consequences when she chooses to resort to a tantrum."

"What sort of consequences?" His eyes narrowed. "Do you believe in spanking?"

"No, I don't," she retorted crisply. "Do you?"

A smile loosened his mouth before he could prevent it. "No."

"That's a relief."

"So, if you don't utilize corporal punishment, then how do you plan to change her behavior?"

He was genuinely curious, since none of the methods he'd attempted had worked. Of course, he had not been consistent, nor had he been Isabella's main caregiver except for those first weeks immediately after the plane crash. Right on the heels of her release from the hospital, his work obligations had taken up most of his time, limiting the hours he spent with her. Plus, he doubted the interim sitters he'd employed had helped the situation. There hadn't been any consistency in his parenting and it showed.

"Is she intelligent?"

"Highly."

Annalise nodded. "She needs to be challenged intellectually, as well as physically, in order to help her stress level. In other words, she needs to engage in activities that will allow her to cope with her grief and confusion and work through them at her own pace. It would help to have a daily schedule that doesn't vary, so she knows that every day she gets up at the same time, eats at the same time, goes to bed at the same time, all of which gives her a feeling of security."

"She doesn't have that right now."

Annalise lifted a shoulder in an expressive shrug. "Because she's so young she may not be able to verbalize her fears and concerns. It would help to find creative outlets that allow for that expression. Painting or coloring, games that require organization, regular exercise, other children she can socialize with so she can just be a quote-unquote child for a while." She paused. "Does she have nightmares?"

"Yes."

Annalise nodded, as though not surprised. "She may also revert to behaviors she exhibited at a far younger age, such as thumb-sucking or bed-wetting."

"I haven't noticed any of that, so far." Well, except for one not-so-minor detail that he'd neglected to mention— her refusal to speak.

Annalise leaned forward. "As I said, continuing with a counselor is vital. He can help you and Isabella's main caregiver develop some strategies to assist in her recovery."

Annalise was right and he knew it. He glanced down at his list of questions and moved on to less complicated issues. "I'm sure my assistant mentioned that this job is five days a week, daytime shift."

"Will you be hiring a nighttime caregiver?"

"I did that right after I brought Isabella home from the hospital. Mrs. Walters will arrive at the end of your shift and cover until I get home. She also stays overnight when I'm out of town on business. If I needed you on an occasional night, would that be a problem?"

"Not at all."

So far, so good. He tapped a finger on the list of questions and moved on to the next issue. "Do you have a first-aid certificate?"

"Yes, as well as a criminal-convictions certificate."

He flipped through the file until he found them. The first-aid certificate was recent and, as expected, she didn't have a criminal record. "Do you have any problem with my running a background check?" The slightest hesitation combined with a hint of worry passed over her features. His gaze narrowed. "Problem?" he asked coldly.

She shook her head. "No, I can see where you'd need to do that. I'd just appreciate some time so I can warn my friends and relatives."

"Warn?"

She sighed. "Alert. Is that a better word for it? I'd like to call them first and ask for their cooperation, so they're not taken by surprise."

"Fair enough." If she really was hiding anything, his private investigator would find it. He moved on. "Do you smoke?"

"No."

"Are you involved in an intimate relationship?"

Again, she hesitated. "How is that germane?"

He studied her curiously, wondering if he'd hit on something. "I need to know if you have any obligations that may interfere with your ability to give Isabella your full attention." Or prevent her from becoming his temporary wife. "I also need to know about anyone who may come into regular contact with my niece so that I can have them checked out."

"Of course." She inclined her head and another curl escaped, this one just behind her left ear. The shiny black ringlet bounced against the long line of her neck, providing an irritating distraction. "No, to answer your question, I'm not in an intimate relationship."

He lifted an eyebrow. "What about a casual relationship?"

A hint of color marched along the sculpted curve of her cheekbones. "I'm not in any sort of relationship at all."

He fought the satisfaction her response elicited. "How do you get along with your family?"

He'd caught her by surprise again. "There's just my father, and we get along fine."

"How often do you see him?"

Her brow puckered in bewilderment. "Once a week. Sometimes more often, now that I'm back in South Carolina."

"Does he live in Charleston?"

"Jim Isle, born and bred."

"How much contact do you anticipate he'll have with Isabella?"

To his surprise, a flash of alarm flickered through her eyes, darkening the honey gold to a deep amber. "I…I don't anticipate there being any contact between them."

He digested that for a moment. "Why not?" he finally asked.

She floundered for an instant. It was the first time he'd seen a serious crack in her composure and it filled him with curiosity. "Because my time with Isabella is business related and the time I spend with my father is personal. I really don't see the two crossing paths."

Interesting. "You believe in keeping your work and home life separate?"

"Don't you?" When he didn't respond to the question, she brushed it aside with a fleeting wave of her hand. "Yes, I prefer to keep the two parts of my life separate."

"Is there some reason you don't want your father to come into contact with Isabella? Does he have a criminal record? Would he be a bad influence on a child?"

"No," she instantly denied. "Not at all. My father is a

good man. I just prefer to keep my family life private. Is that a problem for you?"

"I have no objection either way."

Surprise swept across her face, followed by relief, before she masked her emotions behind a facade of calm serenity. It was an interesting transformation to watch. He suspected her exquisite self-control was an innate part of her personality, and he couldn't help wondering what circumstances had occurred in her life that had required her to develop this ability. Had she also experienced trauma? Was that why she shrouded herself in unruffled composure, as a way to combat the whirlwind of strife and turmoil?

He took a quick stab in the dark. "You mention your father, but not your mother."

She took a quick breath. "My mother died when I was twelve."

"A difficult age to lose a mother."

A dry smile kicked up the corner of her mouth. "Is there a good age?"

"No. Even so... You must have learned coping mechanisms."

"Eventually."

"Would any of them help Isabella?"

"Some." She considered briefly. "In theory."

"Why in theory?"

"Because Isabella isn't me," she explained. "What worked for one person might not work for another. It's not a one-size-fits-all."

He leaned back in his chair and studied her for a long moment. He was tempted to hire her. So very, very tempted.

Again, he sensed a ripple of tension just beneath her calm expression. "You've met Isabella. You see how much work it's going to take to get through to her. Why do you want this job so badly?"

Annalise moistened her lips and answered with care. "Isabella needs help. Maybe I can give her that help. At the very least I'll find out whether I'm capable of handling special-needs children."

"I'm not sure I want to hire someone who regards this as an experiment or a test of their capabilities." She didn't respond to the observation, though he could tell his comment worried her. "There's one other detail you should know about Isabella."

"Which is?"

He decided to lay it out for her. If it scared her off, he'd know she was wrong for the job. "After we explained what happened to her parents, my niece stopped speaking."

Annalise inhaled sharply. "She doesn't talk? Not at all?"

"She screams. That's her communication of choice. So you can see why I'd like the most experienced person possible for this job."

"Yes, I can understand that," she conceded. "But I'd still like a shot at the position."

Jack released his breath in a slow sigh. There were two reasons he didn't plan to hire Annalise Stefano, despite the urge to do just that. The first and most important was that she didn't have the necessary experience. Good instincts, but little hands-on practice. What if Mrs. Locke decided Annalise wasn't knowledgeable enough? He'd have precisely one shot at this. If the caseworker gave the thumbs-down, he couldn't run out and find a replacement bride. No, whoever he chose would have to be as close to perfect as possible.

The second reason he hesitated was the attraction he felt toward Annalise. It didn't bode well for a successful working relationship and threatened unending complications down the road. Plus, it didn't make sense to keep such blatant temptation in his home. Too risky.

He flipped the file closed. "I appreciate you coming in for this interview."

She fought to maintain her composure. "You've already made up your mind, haven't you?" A dark, husky note slipped into her voice and he gained the impression that she'd pinned a lot of hopes on this job. "You're not going to hire me." It wasn't a question.

"I'm sorry, Ms. Stefano." He let her down as gently as possible. "You've only just completed your studies. You haven't had any practical experience. I need someone who's actually worked with children like Isabella."

She didn't argue, although he suspected she wanted to. "If you change your mind, you have my number." She stood and approached his desk, holding out her hand. "Thank you for considering me, Mr. Mason."

He took her hand again, experiencing that same oddly appealing dichotomy of strength overlaying fragility. Of vulnerability warring with quiet determination. He didn't doubt she'd have thrown her heart and soul into helping Isabella, and he couldn't help but wonder if he was making a horrible mistake in not choosing her. He deliberately quashed any doubts. Doubts equaled weakness, and he learned at his father's knee never to allow weakness to influence a business decision.

Releasing Annalise's hand, he picked up the list of applicants and escorted her to the door. He opened it and froze. The outer office was deserted. Not a single person remained.

"Well, hell."

Annalise planted her hands on her hips and surveyed the empty chairs. "I don't suppose you'd care to reconsider that job offer?"

What choice did he have? Time was of the essence and Annalise had come close—very, very close—to fitting the profile he needed for both a nanny and a wife. "As a matter of fact, I would like to reconsider."

She nodded. "I thought you might." Her brilliant smile transformed her appearance once again. "When would you like me to start?"

In the distance, a shriek of anger penetrated the walls. Jack released an exhausted sigh. "Is now too soon?"

"That depends."

He regarded her warily. "On what?"

"Before I give you my answer, I'd like to get the opinion of one of the top businessmen in the country." She slanted him a teasing glance. "Would this be a good time to ask for a raise?"

Nothing about the events of today were funny, and yet he found himself grinning, anyway. "I'm sorry to say that now would be an excellent time." He waved her back toward the chair in front of his desk. "Why don't you make yourself comfortable while we discuss an early-start bonus."

Two

Mary opened the door to Jack's office and regarded him with sympathetic eyes. "Ms. Stefano has asked to see you," his assistant informed him. "Sorry, boss."

He checked his watch. His brand-new nanny-slash-prospective-wife-to-be had lasted all of thirty minutes. He'd hoped for longer, but he was a realistic man. Isabella had driven away the best of the best. What chance did someone with Annalise's lack of experience stand?

"Does she have Isabella with her?"

"No. She requested that the babysitter stay. He's keeping an eye on your niece for the moment."

Jack sighed. "Send her in."

Annalise appeared a moment later, entering with that loose, hip-swing stride he found so attractive. More curls had escaped the tidy knot, bubbling down her back and around her face in gay abandon. Her startling eyes, now a darker shade of honey-gold, were tarnished with concern.

"Mr. Mason—"

"Might as well make it Jack."

She nodded impatiently. "This isn't working, Jack."

"I have to admit. You disappoint me." He leaned back in his chair and drummed his fingers against the leather armrest. "You also win the prize for shortest nanny on record."

She froze, blinking her long sooty lashes at him. "Shortest—" Her breath exploded in a short laugh. "No, you don't understand. I'm not quitting. I'd like to get Isabella out of here. We need to work together one-on-one away from your office. If we're going to establish a routine, we should do that right from the start." She lifted an eyebrow. "Unless you intend for us to come in and disrupt your work every day?"

"Of course not." He checked his watch and frowned. "I was planning to take you home at lunchtime."

Annalise shook her head. "That won't work. There's too much going on here, too much excitement. It's getting Isabella riled up. We should leave now, and then I need you to sit quietly with her for a time and explain who and what I am. It would help with the transition."

Jack frowned. "You haven't already done that?"

He caught her unexpected flash of temper before she reined it in. "You're her uncle, which makes you the authority figure," she explained. "Isabella needs you to organize her world and then set the boundaries for that world. At school—even at day care—children learn very quickly that the teacher is in charge of them and the classroom, but that the principal oversees the entire school and is the ultimate authority figure. If you're putting me in charge—as the teacher—you, as the principal, have to be the one to explain the rules so she knows that you back me up and that she'll be sent to the principal's office if she doesn't behave appropriately toward the teacher."

"Fine. I can take care of that right now."

Annalise shook her head. "There are too many distractions here. It's better to do it in the setting where we're going to spend most of our time."

"I have a full schedule today."

Her mouth took on a stubborn slant. "No, right now you have a family obligation that takes precedence over your full schedule."

"Damn it." He allowed himself an entire ten seconds to stew. "You're right, of course. I don't like that you're right. But, Isabella comes first."

She didn't attempt to disguise her relief. "You have no idea how happy I am to hear you say that."

"Go pack her up. Tell the sitter he can leave. I'm sure he'll be only too happy to run for the nearest exit." He lifted an eyebrow. "You sure you don't want to join him?"

Stark emotion shifted through her gaze, rousing his curiosity. For some reason his niece had made quite an impact on Annalise. He'd seen that look in others when they'd seized on a project or an idea that touched them in some way. In just the short time since he'd hired his new nanny, she'd bonded with Isabella and would do whatever necessary to make certain the relationship worked.

"I'm staying," she said quietly, confirming his conjecture.

For the first time Jack felt a stab of genuine hope. So far, so good. "Thank you, Annalise."

Once his PI had gone over her background and given the all clear, Jack would move his marriage project to the next stage. In the meantime, if Annalise became emotionally connected to Isabella, so much the better. It might make her more amenable to his proposal. All he had to do was find the right buttons to push to convince her to cooperate, something he hoped the investigation might assist in uncovering.

The ride to his home was accomplished in blissful silence. Isabella went into her booster seat without a word—or rather, sound—of complaint. He wished it signaled an improvement, but he suspected she was merely resting up for the next round.

Heading into the South of Broad neighborhood of Charleston, Jack turned onto Battery and hit the remote control for the electric gates. Beside him, Annalise reacted to her first glimpse of Lover's Folly with a soft gasp. "Home sweet home," he murmured. "Hope you like it."

Whatever facade she'd managed to don over the past few hours crumbled. "You live here? This is your home?"

Even he had to admit the four-story, nearly eleven-thousand-foot residence created quite an impact. Meticulously renovated over the past several decades, it boasted views of Charleston Harbor and James Island, and was listed as an exceptional example of historic architecture.

"It's called Lover's Folly, and I inherited it from my paternal grandmother, much to my father's annoyance. He assumed he was next in line to own the place. It's been in the family since the mid-nineteenth century, a decade or so before the War Between the States. My ancestors bought it from the original owner."

"Why is it called Lover's Folly?"

He pulled his Jaguar into the two-story brick carriage house, the structure large enough to house a half dozen vehicles, if he were given to that sort of excess. His housekeeper, Sara, shared the two bedroom apartment above the garage with her husband, Brett, who was employed as the gardener and general handyman.

"It was constructed as an apology to the man's wife—" He spared a quick glance toward the backseat. To his relief, Isabella was sound asleep, no doubt worn out from her morning exertions. He lowered his voice. "When his wife found out he'd been keeping a mistress in high style, she demanded recompense. He had this house built to make up for his folly."

A smile trembled on Annalise's mouth. "For his folly for taking a mistress or for getting caught?"

Jack grinned. "No one's quite certain, though there's been endless speculation about that." He exited the car and gently extracted Isabella from the backseat. She murmured groggily before burrowing against him and nodding off again. It was rare moments like this that convinced him he'd done the right thing, that this poor little mite needed him. "She's exhausted, which means she'll nap for a while. Enjoy it while it lasts."

"I gather it doesn't last long?"

"No."

That single, terse word said it all. He led the way into the kitchen and introduced Annalise to Sara. The housekeeper offered a warm smile before turning a wary eye on Isabella. "Little Madam is worn out, I see. But it must have gone well, considering you managed to hire another nanny."

Jack slanted Annalise a quick, encouraging look. "One who plans to stay, I hope." He inclined his head toward the steps at the far end of the kitchen. "I'll be up in the nursery if you need me."

He ascended the back staircase, climbing to the second floor. The nursery wing occupied the right-hand side of the U-shaped mansion. It had been designed in the days of large families and live-in servants, and consisted of four bedrooms, plus the nanny's quarters, and a huge playroom. He carried Isabella into the room she'd chosen for herself. It overlooked a large patio and yard, and was enclosed by a towering stone wall. After settling his niece in her bed, he picked up the baby monitor and hooked it to his belt. Then he motioned to Annalise and escorted her to the playroom, where they could talk without disturbing Isabella.

The instant they entered the room, Annalise spun around to face him. She did her best to hide it, but she was seriously rattled. A deep flush sculpted her sweeping cheekbones, while her eyes rivaled the sun in their intensity. Though she stood without moving, the ringlets which had escaped her control trembled in agitation.

She took a deep breath, drawing his attention downward to where the vee of her jacket clung to the attractive swell of her breasts and traced the outline of her narrow waist and the womanly flare of her hips. For some reason the nondescript black suit didn't seem so nondescript anymore. Not when he examined all it concealed.

His nanny was a knockout.

"Color me officially overwhelmed," she announced.

"I have every confidence that you'll acclimate," he replied.

Worry dug a small line between her brows. "I'm not so sure. I've only seen the smallest fraction of this place and I'm already blown away."

"Relax, Ms. Stefano. One of the reasons I hired you was your impressive self-control."

"No, the reason you hired me was because all the other rats had deserted the sinking ship." She paced off a small measure of her agitation, giving him an excellent view of her endless legs and gloriously rounded backside. She spun around to face him. "Is this the sort of home Isabella came from?" she asked. "Was she accustomed to this sort of grandeur? To living among so many antiques?"

Jack forced himself to ignore the tantalizing view and focus on the business at hand. "No, Joanne and her husband, Paul, lived a far more simple life."

Annalise's expression grew troubled. "So many changes, poor baby," she murmured. "It must be even more overwhelming for her than it is for me."

"This is where and how I live. In time, my niece will become accustomed to it. She won't have any choice." He lifted an eyebrow. "Unless you expect me to sell a home that's been in my family for over a hundred and fifty years?"

She waved that aside. "No, of course not." She regarded him in momentary silence and he could see her marshaling and organizing her thoughts and impressions. "May I ask a personal question?"

Not a road he wanted to head down. Nonetheless, he inclined his head. "Feel free."

"How did you gain custody of Isabella? Did your sister request you as guardian in her will?"

"It would have simplified matters if she had. Unfortunately, she didn't."

"So, you simply took your niece in? There was no one else?"

Anger flashed through him. He planted his fists on his hips and faced her down. "You say that as though you don't consider me an appropriate guardian."

She hesitated. "That's not the word I'd use. You have a…a magnificent home. You're a successful businessman. You're well-intentioned—"

"But?"

She frowned. "Weren't there any other family members willing to take her? Someone who has more time to devote to her care?"

"No. Paul has a sister. She flat out refused."

"Flat out? But, why?"

"Because Isabella isn't blood kin. Joanne and Paul adopted Isabella when she was only a few days old. For some reason, that let Paul's sister off the hook."

"And put you on it?" Annalise had adopted an expressionless mask again. But he'd begun to realize that the less emotion she showed, the more she felt. "Is that why you took her in? Because no one else stepped up?"

He gave her the look that would have most men in his rarified world trembling in their Berluti loafers. "Ms. Stefano, I hired you as Isabella's nanny, not as my personal pop psychologist. My reasons for assuming guardianship of Isabella have nothing to do with you or the job you are to perform. A job for which I'm paying you quite a lot of money."

To his amazement, she didn't back down. In fact, she took a step closer. "Have I hit a hot button, Mr. Mason?

Did you feel obligated to take her in? Are you protecting your image? Concerned with media scrutiny? Is that why Isabella's here, so your personal and business image don't take a hit?"

Fury vied with a primal awareness, one with a raw, sexual edge. Or perhaps the fury exacerbated the awareness he'd experienced the first moment he'd set eyes on her. "You are walking a very thin line, Ms. Stefano. If I had anyone who could take your place, I'd fire you on the spot."

"For asking tough questions? Or do my questions hit a little too close to home?"

Her questions were identical to those Mrs. Locke had asked. That alone gave him pause. He was a private man who kept his personal life as far from the high beams of the media headlights as possible. He also kept his emotions under tight control, even tighter than Annalise did. Another lesson he'd learned at his father's knee. As much as he hated the idea, he needed this woman. Isabella needed her. She might be the only person capable of keeping his tiny family intact.

He forced himself to answer her. "Other than Paul, Isabella was the most important person in my sister's life." He swallowed past the tightness constricting his words. "At one point, Joanne was the most important person in mine. Isabella is part of my sister, all that's left of her. My niece is hurting and I have no idea how to help her."

The anger drained out of Annalise. "You hired me to take care of Isabella. And that's what I intend to do." She gestured in the general direction of his niece's bedroom. "Tell me something, do you think that overstuffed toy factory you call a bedroom is in her best interest?"

What the hell was she talking about now? "It's the smallest of the bedrooms. She chose it herself."

Annalise's breath escaped in a quiet sigh. "The issue isn't the square footage of her room. I couldn't even say what size it is because it's stuffed to the rafters with toys and games."

"I'm just trying to create a home for her."

"By buying her *things*. That's not how you create a home. Isabella doesn't need *things*. She needs love and attention."

"I'm doing the best I can." He hated the gritty quality that climbed into his voice.

Annalise took note and a softness slipped into her voice. "Your niece doesn't need more stimulation, Jack. She needs less."

For some reason, her use of his first name had a devastating effect. He forced himself to listen to Annalise's words, when what he really wanted to do was yank her closer and see if all that passion would spill over into their embrace. Would spill onto him. She gave so generously of herself to a little girl she didn't even know. How would it feel to have some of that emotion directed at him?

The instant the thought blazed through his mind, he rejected it. Damn it to hell! Had he lost every ounce of common sense? This wasn't part of the plan.

He deliberately turned his back on Annalise and walked to the window, giving himself some much needed breathing room. Resting his arm on the sash, he gazed out at the backyard. It had been designed as a peaceful haven, secluded from the bustle and noise of the city traffic. He retreated there whenever he had a tough business decision to make—or a tough personal one. It was there that he'd made the final determination to accept responsibility for Isabella. It was there he'd come to the conclusion that he'd have to marry in order to retain custody of his niece. Would it be Annalise who ultimately became his wife?

He turned around, surprising a look of compassion on her face. "CPS wants to take Isabella away from me," he found himself admitting.

Annalise couldn't quite control her flicker of alarm. "Why? What did you—" She broke off abruptly. "What concerns them?"

"That's not what you were about to say." It was his turn to close the distance between them. "You were wondering what I'd done wrong that caused CPS to step in."

Her breathing quickened as she finally seemed to sense she'd pushed him too far. "Why are they involved?"

"I already told you. Paul and Joanne didn't designate a guardian. CPS needs to make sure I'll do an adequate job." His mouth twisted. "So far they're less than impressed."

"But you mean to change that."

He fixed her with a fierce look. "Allow me to make myself clear." He paused to give his words more impact. "I'll do whatever I must in order to keep Isabella. Any. Damn. Thing. Is that clear enough, Ms. Stefano?"

"Annalise."

Why didn't she back down? Did she know nothing about his reputation? Or did she simply not care? "You're not the least intimidated by me, are you?"

She lifted an eyebrow. "Should I be?"

"Yes," he stated baldly. "But you're like a damned dog with a bone. You just don't let go."

She stunned him by leaning in and offering a teasing smile. "Isn't that precisely the sort of person you want on Isabella's side? I'm a fighter. And you're right. I don't give up."

He paused to consider. He did need someone like her, someone who'd help him take on Mrs. Locke. Maybe it was time to listen to her. "What do you suggest?"

She didn't hesitate. "Two things. First, simplify Isabella's environment so she isn't so visually stimulated and overwhelmed. Second, I suggest you take a few weeks off work and spend time with her in a—" she spared a brief glance around "—shall we say, in a more basic setting."

"I can't afford to take a few days off right now, let alone a few weeks."

Annalise tilted her head to one side, and more curls escaped from the knot at her nape, tumbling down her shoulders and back in glorious abandon. No wonder she attempted to maintain such tight control over her hair. It was every bit as willful as the rest of her. Her eyes darkened as she regarded him.

"I thought you were willing to do whatever it took to keep custody of Isabella," she said. "Any. Damn. Thing. Remember?"

"I have a business empire to run."

"Then let her go."

The softly spoken recommendation—identical to the one his lawyer, Derek, had made—hung in the air between them, vanquished only when he released a single, harsh expletive. "I must have been insane when I hired you."

"Would it help if I promise I'll always put Isabella's best interests first?"

"I don't doubt that for a minute." He forked his fingers through his hair. Every instinct told him she was right. He'd just been looking for an easier solution. He should have known he wouldn't find one. Building his import/export business had been no different. It had required total dedication and had demanded his attention every hour of every day, and then some. "Fine. We'll try it your way for now."

Her grin blew him away. "Thank you."

He snagged the collar of her suit jacket and tugged her close. Close enough that he could feel the explosion of her breath against his jawline. "We'll try it your way for now. But one stumble and that changes. Are we clear, Ms. Stefano?"

"Are you a perfectionist, Mr. Mason? Are your employees expected to be just as perfect?"

She'd reverted to a more formal manner of addressing him and he could guess why. Since she couldn't pull free of his hold without losing their small battle of wills, this was her subtle way of putting some distance between them. "Jack," he reminded her. "And yes, I am a perfectionist. I can afford to be—just as I can afford to hire the very best and expect them to give me precisely what I want."

She didn't cave, not one inch. Instead, she continued to gaze at him with those ancient, deep-set eyes, eyes that seemed to alter color with her every mood change. Right now, they reminded him of tarnished gold. "In that case I'll have to see that you get your money's worth."

His gaze dropped to her mouth, a mouth full and lush and red, and more enticing than the legendary apple Eve had offered Adam. "I'll hold you to that," he warned.

Temptation beckoned, urging him to take a bite of sin. He didn't bother resisting. Something about this woman made him want to stake his claim, to gather up all that passion and energy she tried so hard to hide and allow it to storm through him. He'd been so cold for so long. He needed her heat, needed to feel the flames of desire. To—just this once—release the rigid control which governed every aspect of his life. What harm would this one time make?

Was she as curious as he to see where their embrace took them? He could spare her the suspense. He'd accomplished step one of his marriage project. He'd hired a nanny who would put his niece's best interests first and stick around long enough to satisfy CPS. Now for step two. To engage her emotions just enough that she'd cave to the insanity of marrying him.

He lowered his head and captured her mouth with his. He half expected Annalise to yank free of the embrace, but to his relief, she didn't resist. Nor did she burn with the same fire sweeping through him. Instead, she responded with a heady delicacy. Her mouth turned soft and responsive, yielding for those first seconds. Then her lips parted ever so cautiously, and she deepened the kiss.

Rational thought disintegrated. All he could think about was the woman in his arms and how quickly he could strip away the layers of clothing until burning flesh collided with burning flesh. He skated his hands down her back and cupped her lush backside, pulling her more fully against him. His groan slid from his mouth to hers.

A soft moan hummed in her throat and she slid her hands across his chest to his shoulders. "Jack…"

The sound of his name, overflowing with feminine

desire, swept away the final remnants of his self-control. He urged her backward across the room toward the padded window seat overlooking his cloistered garden. The back of her legs bumped against the half-wall and she teetered on the edge of tumbling. He grinned against her mouth, preparing to follow her down onto the thick cushions, when an unmistakable noise distracted him. The sound of weeping crackled through the baby monitor clipped to his belt.

He released Annalise, and for an endless second their gazes locked and held. Shock and disbelief glittered in her eyes, though whether directed at his actions or her own, he couldn't quite tell.

The breath exploded from her lungs and she shook her head. "Oh, no. *Hell,* no. This is not going to happen ever again, Mr. Mason. Are we clear on that point?"

"Crystal. And just so you know?" He traced a finger along the curve of her cheek and watched as her eyes overflowed with helpless desire. She fought it, but it was there for him to see. "It will happen again, for one reason and one reason only."

Her chin shot up. "And what's that?"

"I doubt either of us will be able to keep our hands off each other."

With that, he turned and left the room, unwilling to admit even to himself how difficult he found the choice.

Three

Isabella crouched in the middle of the large bed, lost amid the piles of pillows, dolls and stuffed animals. He crossed to sit on the edge of the bed. Annalise appeared in the doorway behind him and stepped hesitantly into the room.

"Hey, Baby Belle," he murmured. It had been his sister's nickname for her daughter and using it often helped soothe Isabella. "All done with your nap?"

She stared up at him, her green eyes dewy wet and far too resigned for a child of five. She nodded in response to his question before turning her attention to Annalise. To Jack's surprise his niece didn't scream as she often did with the other nannies he'd hired. Nor did she appear the least interested. Instead, she stared with apathetic acceptance. He sighed. Too many changes in too short a period of time.

"Isabella, this is Annalise. She's your new nanny. The three of us are going to spend the day together getting to know each other."

Recalling Annalise's concern about the room, Jack swept a swift assessing glance around. Now that he looked—really looked—the place resembled nothing more than a toy store that had exploded in messy exuberance. She was right. The kaleidoscope of colors created an agitated blur that didn't allow the eye to settle. Why the hell hadn't he noticed it before?

"You know—" he offered tentatively "—it's pretty crowded in here, isn't it? There's hardly any room for you, let alone all these toys. I wonder if your new nanny can fix that problem."

No response from his niece, but Annalise caught the ball he lobbed in her direction and put it in play. "You're right, Jack. It is too crowded in here." She took a seat on the floor, folding her lanky frame so her height wouldn't seem as intimidating. "I'll bet your toys would like to have their own room so they're not so uncomfortable crammed in here. What do you think, Isabella? Shall we pick out a special room where your dolls can stay when you're not playing with them?"

A debate raged in vivid detail across Isabella's face. She shot Jack a questioning glance. At his smile of encouragement, she nodded in agreement.

"Why don't you pick out your favorite dolls and put them on the bed," Annalise suggested, pitching her voice so it remained calm and nonthreatening. "They'll stay here with you. Then we'll pick out a special room for the others."

Isabella hopped off the mattress and made a beeline across the room. She seized a porcelain doll that had seen better days and placed it with great care on the bed. To Jack's amazement, she turned and faced Annalise, waiting for the next instructions.

"That's the only one?" he prompted. He couldn't explain why he was so horrified when she nodded. "If you want another—"

Annalise shook her head in silent warning. "What about the stuffed animals?" she asked. "Are there any who should stay with your doll?"

This time Isabella gathered up three: a threadbare puppy, a cashmere-soft kitten and a ferocious lion. Over the next half hour, Annalise worked her way through each type of toy until the favorites had been whittled down to a select couple dozen.

When she'd finished, Jack found he had to swallow hard before speaking. "They're all the toys she brought from home," he commented in a rough undertone. "She's spent three full months here with hundreds of brand-new toys and all she wants—"

To his horror, he couldn't finish his comment. Fresh grief welled up inside, ripping through him. What was money in comparison to Joanne and Paul? What were all these toys he'd drenched his niece in, compared to the lives of her mother and father? He'd trade every penny of his billions to have his sister and her husband alive and well. But that wasn't possible. And so Isabella clung to the tattered remains of that old life while he clung to Isabella.

Beside him, Annalise gathered his hand in hers and

squeezed gently. She waited until he'd regained his self-control before continuing. "Anything you've forgotten about?" she asked Isabella.

There was a momentary hesitation and then she darted to the small bedside table and snatched up a picture frame, hugging it close. It was too much. Jack was at Isabella's side in an instant, lifting her into his arms. He took a seat on her bed and cradling her close. "Don't worry about your pictures," he murmured. "They all stay in here. Every last one of them."

Gently he pried the frame from her grasp so they could both study the photo. Joanne and Paul beamed out at them, a slightly younger version of Isabella tucked protectively between the two. He ran his index finger over his sister's image. Memories crashed over him like waves advancing before a storm front.

"Your mom and I looked alike, didn't we?" he managed to ask his niece. Not that he expected a response. To his surprise, she leaned her slight weight against him and nodded.

His sister's rich, brown hair was a couple shades lighter than his, the highlights more red than the gold that streaked his own hair. But they shared the same facial features—straight, bold noses, full mouths, squared jawlines. Even the direct intensity of Jo's black eyes was identical to what he saw reflected in his mirror each day. These were characteristics they'd inherited from their mother, something that connected the three of them.

"God, I miss her," he said. Isabella curled tighter into his embrace and he could feel her shoulders tremble, feel the dampness of tears soaking into his shirt. He wrapped her up close and planted a kiss in her matted curls. "We'll get through this, Baby Belle. I swear we will. You and I are going to be a family. It won't be the same as it was. But we'll figure it out. Somehow we'll manage."

He didn't know how long they clung to each other. Throughout it all, Annalise remained quiet and motionless, giving them the time they needed to weather the storm. When the last hiccupped sob had long faded, Jack drew Isabella to her feet. His hand swallowed hers as he led her to the bedside table. Carefully, he returned the photo to its place of honor.

He crouched beside her. "They'll always be watching out for you, Isabella. Just like I will. Okay?"

Isabella nodded solemnly. Then Annalise crossed to join them. "Why don't we go find that special room for the rest of your toys?" The gentle suggestion came at the perfect moment, helping to distract them from their sorrow. "Anytime you want one of the toys from that room, you can trade them. That means you pick one of the toys from in here and put it in the special room and take the toy you'd like to play with instead and bring it in here to live with you. Is that all right?"

Isabella sought Jack's reassurance before nodding. Over the next hour, they made a production of choosing the perfect "special room" and transferring toys. When they were done, his niece's room had been transformed from a toy store into a peaceful, uncluttered bedroom. Her favorite toys decorated the shelves lining her room, each assigned a place of honor. He noticed that all the books remained, as well as a small play station that contained puzzles, coloring books and other educational toys.

"Makes quite a difference, doesn't it?" Annalise murmured. "This gives her a safe haven that should help her relax."

"Instead of a place guaranteed to agitate."

He glanced at her, driven to mention what had happened in the playroom. Before he could, she spoke again. "Did the caseworker see Isabella's room with all the toys?"

He grimaced. "Yes."

To his surprise she rested a hand on his arm and gave a reassuring squeeze. "Don't worry. I'm sure it will help once she sees the changes you've made."

It was the second time they'd touched since their embrace in the playroom. Not that she seemed aware of that fact. He wound one of her curls around his finger and tugged. "The changes *you're* making, don't you mean?"

She stilled and her pulse fluttered at the base of her neck. Standing this close he could see the smooth, rich texture of her skin, the color a gorgeous creamy shade accentuated by her dark hair. The attraction he felt drew him, even as he fought to hold himself at a distance. He shouldn't be experiencing these emotions. They weren't part of the plan. And yet, they were undeniable. What the hell would happen once they eventually married?

If they married, he hastened to correct himself. He had a long path to walk from here to the altar. Considering Annalise's willful nature, it wouldn't be an easy one.

As though underscoring that point, she eased free of his touch and focused her attention where it belonged…on Isabella. "I couldn't have made any changes if you weren't here to reassure your niece and lend support." She shot him a warning look. "Nor will I be able to make any more if we're not in agreement on how our…relationship should progress from here."

He had to give the woman credit. Subtle, yet direct. Too bad she hadn't chosen to enter the business world. She'd have been a natural. "So, what's next on the agenda?" he asked with a calm he didn't come close to experiencing.

"Lunch, I hope." A swift smile flashed. "Dare I suggest something casual, either al fresco or in the kitchen?"

"We'll eat on the patio. Sara's not too keen on having her kitchen invaded," he explained.

The choice proved a rousing success. The serene location had a beneficial effect on Isabella. After they arranged for a place setting for her doll, she ate without protest or tears, and afterward played beneath a nearby tree, rocking her "baby" while humming tuneless reassurances.

"It won't last," Annalise offered. She dipped a hand in a glass bowl containing a selection of olives and popped one in her mouth. "I just want to warn you so you don't get your hopes up."

"And here I was assuming you had waved your magical wand and fixed all our problems."

She cocked an eyebrow. "Sorry. The fairy godmother association hasn't issued me my official wand yet. Until they do, we'll have to handle this the old-fashioned way."

"Hard work and luck?" he guessed.

"Mmm. We *were* lucky today. Tomorrow…?" She shrugged. "Who knows? I do have another suggestion, however."

"Go on."

"If there's any way you can arrange it, we should insti-
tute step two as soon as possible. Can you take a couple
weeks off sometime in the near future?"

"And go where?" A hint of cynicism crept into his
voice. "The Caribbean? Hawaii? Europe?"

"Is that what you think I'm after? A free vacation?"
Laughter brightened her eyes. "No way, ace. I'm talking
low-key. A little bungalow on one of the islands around
here. Someplace modest where the three of us are tripping
all over each other so we're forced to bond."

"Dangerous, all that bonding."

Color dotted her cheeks and he could see the reflection
of those moments in the playroom mirrored in her eyes.
"Focus, Mason. I'm talking about bonding with Isabella,"
she stated tartly. "Once we've spent some quality time
together, we can come back here. It would help if you
could transition to working part-time and hang around
here with your niece the rest of the day."

"Hell, honey. If I do all that, what am I paying you for?"

Annalise didn't take offense, though her chin jerked
upward an inch in open challenge. "You're paying me to
help Isabella adjust to a brand-new life, a life she didn't
expect or want or ask for. You're paying me to get CPS off
your back, although you neglected to mention that small
detail during our interview."

"Sorry." He scrubbed his hands across his face.
"You're right, of course. I'm not handling this well.
Blame it on exhaustion."

It took her a minute to work out the reason. "Isabella's
nightmares?"

He nodded. "It's hard to get her settled afterward. I'm

down to about five hours a night. She can sleep during the day to make up for it, but I can't."

"That explains a lot. Isn't there someone who can cover for you at night? What about the woman you mentioned during the interview?" She fumbled for a name. "Mrs. Walters?"

"She's here five to ten but refuses to live in. And I've had enough trouble finding someone for the day shift without running the risk of losing Walters. I need her for those occasions I work late or have a meeting out of town. Besides, the nights I'm with Isabella…" His mouth compressed. "You've talked about my bonding with my niece. Well, the nights when I sit with her, comforting her while she drifts back off to sleep, those are the times we come closest to bonding."

Annalise nodded in perfect understanding. "And you don't want to give them up."

"No." His response caused a hint of relief to flicker across her face. His back teeth clenched. "My guardianship of Isabella isn't just about duty, Ms. Stefano, despite what you clearly believe."

A smile quivered at the corners of her mouth. "Do you realize that whenever you're annoyed with me, you revert to formality?"

"Take it as a warning."

Annalise's smile grew and Jack stared in disbelief. Why didn't she react the way every other intelligent person within his sphere of influence did when confronted with the predatory side of his nature? She should be quaking in her sensible flats. She should be utterly intimidated by the slightest frown. Hell, she should be doing precisely what he said without a single word of argument. Instead, she helped herself to another olive and popped it in her mouth as though lounging across from a man capable of destroying her world was an everyday occurrence.

"Do you have no sense of self-preservation?" he demanded.

She blinked, mildly startled. "Excuse me?"

"You are familiar with my name, I assume? With my reputation?"

She frowned. "Sure. Who isn't?"

"What, may I ask, do you know about me?"

She shrugged. "You're thirty. You're rich. Powerful. You were supposed to go into the family business with your father. Instead you walked away. When you were cut off from the Mason purse strings, you built an import/-export empire from scratch that succeeded in eclipsing your father's in the business world. You've been linked, romantically, with some of the most beautiful women in the world." She blinked at him in open bewilderment. "Is it important that I know your history? Will it help somehow with Isabella?"

He gritted his teeth. "No, but it should help in *our* dealings."

Her eyes narrowed, then widened. Her mouth gave another betraying quiver before she bit down on her lip to suppress it. "I'm so sorry, Mr. Mason. Have I neglected to treat you appropriately?"

"Instant obedience to my every whim would be appreciated," he responded dryly.

A gurgle of laughter escaped. She leaned forward and pitched her voice to an ingratiating purr. "Very well, sir.

Your every wish is my command, no matter how boring and tedious all that instant gratification may become."

He fought for a control that should have come without thought or effort. But ever since Annalise had entered his life with her distinctive hip-swinging stride, that control had eluded him. He couldn't help himself. He released a barking laugh, unable to recall the last time he'd felt such genuine amusement. Isabella's head jerked up and she stared at him in open disbelief, as though the sound was not only unheard of, but downright impossible. Sorrow caused his humor to fade. Was his laughter really such a rare occurrence?

Annalise followed the progression of his thoughts with uncomfortable accuracy. "Okay, I get it. You're a ruthless businessman. But who are you to Isabella? How do you want her to respond to you, Jack? Should she fear you, or should she look on you as her kind and loving uncle?"

He shook his head. "It's not like I have a choice. I am what I am."

"Are you saying you're incapable of kindness? Of love?"

He turned his gaze on her, one he didn't doubt reflected the wintry coldness that seized hold. "Those qualities were eradicated long ago. What I can give my niece is a home, financial security and as much attention as I can spare."

"Got it. That sounds a lot like duty and obligation to me. And yet, not two minutes ago you claimed that wasn't why you took Isabella in. You might want to consider which is most accurate." She fixed him with an unwavering stare. "And I suggest you choose one that CPS will buy."

"You want me to lie?"

"Right now, I'm not sure even you know what's truth and what's lie."

He swore beneath his breath and surged to his feet. He'd had enough of this touchy-feely stuff. Time to take control, and this time he wouldn't let Annalise wrest it away again. "I think we need to discuss what happened earlier in the playroom."

His comment struck a nerve. She deliberately turned her head in Isabella's direction. His niece remained fully engaged with her doll. "I believe I already addressed that issue. It won't happen again."

"Time will tell."

She followed his example and thrust back her chair. He couldn't begin to imagine the amount of inner fortitude it took for her to stand and face him. But somehow she did it. "I have no excuse for what took place earlier. I will tell you I'm no stereotype, despite that unfortunate incident. You're paying me to take care of your niece, not be your mistress. Decide now, Mr. Mason. Which do you want? A nanny or a mistress?"

"And if both roads end up in the same place?"

"I'll quit before I become your mistress. Is that clear enough?"

"Quite." He leaned his shoulder against one of the beams supporting the wooden canopy that shaded the patio and folded his arms across his chest. "There's only one small problem."

"Which is?"

Her poise wasn't as secure as she'd like to pretend. He'd always been excellent at reading people and Annalise proved no exception. He caught the slightest quaver of her voice and the helpless balling of her hands. Even more telling, the pulse in her throat fluttered like a moth struggling to throw itself into the flames. And like that moth, she was irresistibly drawn to something guaranteed to deliver her into the arms of certain disaster.

His arms.

"I have a strict policy forbidding interoffice fraternization."

"I don't work in your office." The instant the words escaped, she inhaled sharply, aware of how much she'd given away with that single thoughtless comment. "I mean—"

He cut her off without compunction. "That policy extends to all my employees. I've never treated anyone who works for me with anything other than complete and utter professionalism." He paused deliberately. "Until today. Until you. Why is that, do you suppose?"

Her eyes darkened and she shook her head in open denial. "I have no idea."

"Yes, you do." He hadn't budged an inch, and yet for the first time since they'd met, she took a step backward. "Something unexpected happened between us. Something that caused me to ignore one of my cardinal rules. Do you have any idea how unusual that is?"

"If CPS suspected we were involved, it would cause untold problems," she was quick to say. "You can't afford to risk that, not if you're sincere about keeping custody of your niece."

"I'm dead serious."

"Then her needs must come first."

"I agree. But that doesn't change what happened today."

He straightened and took a step in her direction. "Nor does it change what's occurring between us right now. If our reaction to one another is this bad after one day, what will it be like after a week…a month…a year?"

"Stop it, Jack." He could see she wanted to continue her retreat, wanted it with an intensity that flowed off her in hot, desperate waves. A painful vulnerability settled over her, one that affected him more profoundly than he thought possible. She held up her hand to halt his forward progress. "Are you trying to convince me to quit? If that's your goal, you're succeeding."

He shook his head. "I don't want you to quit. But I'm not going to pretend that the attraction between us doesn't exist. In order to make our relationship work, we have to deal with what we're experiencing and decide how to handle it."

"Fine. That's easy enough." She sucked in a quick breath while scrambling to take charge of the situation. Not that he'd let her. "We ignore it. We are careful to never be alone together. And we absolutely, positively keep our hands off each other."

"My hands were only a small portion of the problem."

Her gaze flashed to his mouth. "Hands. Arms. Lips. And every other part of your body."

He continued toward her, booting her chair out of his path. It skittered across the flagstones with a squeak of surrender. "That's one option, I suppose."

"Oh, God," she whispered. "Please, Jack. It's the only option. If we can't control ourselves, I'll quit. I won't have any other choice. I can't lose control. I can't. Not ever again." She ground into silence as he halted a mere foot away.

Curiosity consumed him. "What happens when you lose control?" he asked softly.

To his concern, her chin quivered. "Nothing good."

"A lesson hard learned?"

"Exactly."

"Then I won't touch you first."

Jack hated making the promise. He was a ruthless man. A man who let nothing stand between himself and his goals. A man who'd learned the hard way to give no quarter. But a single anguished look from a pair of tumultuous golden eyes had him relenting. Softening. Clearly, he'd lost his mind.

Annalise's relief was palpable. "Thank you, Mr. Mason," she said formally.

He turned from her, furious with himself for not taking advantage of what he'd been able to accomplish so far. Time was still of the essence. He needed to move her from the role of nanny to the role of wife as soon as possible. Even so, he couldn't bring himself to hurt her in the process.

"No problem." He glanced over his shoulder, forcing out a teasing smile. "If you change your mind, feel free to say something."

Her mouth relaxed into a shadow of her old grin. "You'll be the first to know, I promise."

His cell phone vibrated and he checked the caller ID. "It's my lawyer," he explained to Annalise before distancing himself from her and taking the call. "What's gone wrong now?"

"Aren't we in a glass-half-empty mood."

"Do I have reason to be?"

"Only if you haven't found someone," Derek admitted.

"I found someone." He spared Annalise a brief glance.

She'd joined Isabella beneath the tree, sitting close enough to participate in his niece's play, without invading the little girl's territory. "The trick will be keeping her. I may have pushed too hard, too soon."

"That's not like you."

"There's a reason for that," Jack responded wryly. Like having difficulty keeping his hands off her. "What's wrong now?"

"Actually, it's mixed news. I managed to postpone Mrs. Locke's next visit. Told her you and the new nanny and Isabella were all going off on a little trip together so you could bond."

Bond. The word continued to haunt him and had him clamping his back teeth together. "I thought you said the news was mixed. That sounds like good news to me."

"It would be if Locke hadn't also informed me that she plans to make a final report after her next visit."

"What?"

"Calm down, Jack. I'm going to fight it and I'm pretty certain I'll be able to delay things again. But it would help if you had a loving wife cum nanny in tow the next time the Locke woman comes calling."

"I'm working on it."

"Work harder. Does this one have the qualifications I suggested?"

"Yes. Not a lot of experience, but she does have the appropriate educational background."

There was a delicate pause, then Derek asked, "What's she like?"

Jack's focus strayed in Annalise's direction again. "Different," he stated succinctly.

"Good different?"

"Let's just say that our marriage won't be dull." A sudden thought occurred to him. "Before I forget, I need you to contact our private investigator and have her thoroughly checked out. I know he did a preliminary run on all the applicants. Tell him to dig deeper on Annalise Stefano. I don't want any surprises that might come back to bite us."

"I'm on it. So, where are you going for your vacation?"

The question caught Jack off guard. "Come again?"

"I told Locke you were going away. That wasn't just hot air. You're going to have to actually do it."

"I can't afford the time right now." He felt like a broken record.

"Find a way." Before Jack could argue, Derek added, "What the hell do you think will happen if Locke discovers you've been going into work? She won't be happy."

"Damn it, Derek."

"It's either that or you take my earlier suggestion. Let Isabella go. You can find a good home for her. Then you can give your business all of your attention. You don't have to marry. You don't have to deal with CPS. No more headaches. No more stress."

No more Isabella.

Jack closed his eyes. "Enough. I'll do it."

"Have a nice vacation."

Jack snarled a final comment before flipping his phone closed and crossing the yard in long, ground-eating strides. Annalise and Isabella peered up at him with identical looks of curiosity.

"Good news," he announced. "Pack your bags. The three of us are going on vacation."

Four

Bright and early the next morning, Jack had all the luggage loaded and Isabella and Annalise installed in the car. She turned to him as they pulled down the driveway and smiled brightly.

"So, where are we going?" she asked.

He eased into the boulevard traffic before sparing her a brief glance. "You'll be pleased to know that I took your advice. I've arranged for us to stay at a small bungalow on the beach."

He was careful not to use the word *vacation*. When he'd said it the previous day, Isabella had reacted with something approaching hysteria. It wasn't until Annalise made the connection between the word and the accident that had claimed the lives of Joanne and Paul that she'd been able to figure out a way to comfort his niece.

Annalise grinned. "A bungalow on the beach, huh? Sounds fantastic."

"It's not quite as modest as you requested," Jack warned. "But I think it'll do."

"I'm sure it'll be perfect."

Her quiet confidence in his abilities affected him more than he cared to admit. He was thirty years old with a first-class education. He came from one of the oldest families in all of Charleston. He owned and operated a billion-dollar international company with countless employees at his beck and call, most of whom were confident in his overall abilities. But for some reason, he responded to Annalise's admiration like a cat being presented a bowl of cream. If he wasn't careful, he'd start purring.

"Part of the problem is that I need someplace that will allow me Internet access so I can stay in touch with the office."

"Of course," she agreed. "Perfectly understandable."

"And a location that protects our privacy."

"An unfortunate aspect of your position in life."

"Luckily, I have a friend who owns an estate with a guesthouse right on the water. He's in Europe for the summer, so we're welcome to stay for as long as we want. It's only two bedrooms, but it has a kitchen." A sudden thought struck. "Do you cook?"

"Yes."

"Okay, now for the important question. Are you willing to? I realize it's not part of your duties, but I'd be happy to compensate you for the additional work."

"That's not necessary." Annalise turned her head to stare out the window. "I'm happy to help out."

"And yet, you sound annoyed." A sudden thought struck, one he could scarcely credit. "Have I offended you by offering to pay you extra?" he asked.

Annalise released a sigh and shifted in her seat to face him again. "Yes. The ridiculous part is, I can't figure out why."

Maybe not, but he could. "It's because of what happened yesterday. In the playroom," he clarified.

She stiffened. "You mean when we—" She broke off and spared Isabella a quick look. "You know."

"Yes, I mean when we *you know*. The 'you knowing' blended business with personal."

"Then I suggest we unblend them since there won't be any more of either 'you,' let alone 'know,' ever again."

He shrugged. "We can try, though I doubt we'll succeed. How do you take the color green and turn it back into blue and yellow? We can say we're going to keep all the colors separate, that we'll resist the temptation to…er…blend. But I can't even offer to compensate you for the extra duties you'll be taking on these next couple weeks without it offending you."

"I'll get over it, just as I'll get over the urge to do anymore blending."

"Be sure to tell me how that works for you. I'm afraid I'm still a vivid shade of green."

An attractive blush tinted her cheeks. She deliberately twisted around and engaged in a one-sided conversation with Isabella. He didn't push. There'd be plenty of time over the next couple of weeks to tempt her with more blending. Even if he couldn't engage her on a personal level, he hoped she'd become so attached to Isabella that she'd be willing to accept his proposal for his niece's sake. He just needed to find the right lever that would tip the scales in his favor.

He ignored the small prick of conscience that prodded him for his cold-blooded plan. He couldn't afford a conscience, not if he wanted to keep custody of Isabella. If his father had taught him nothing else in life, Jonathan Mason had proved himself an expert instructor on how to pursue one's goals with ruthless disregard. Nothing mattered but the end results. Not compassion. Not kindness. Not any of the gentler emotions.

Jack had been brought up with a single motto: *No matter what it takes*. And that was how he would respond to his custody battle. When it came to Isabella, he would do whatever he had to, no matter what it took.

He pulled into a broad drive, guarded by a ten-foot-high stone wall and a high-tech electronic security gate. He keyed in the code Taye had given him and, once the wrought-iron doors swung open, drove toward a mansion even more elaborate than his own. Beside him, Annalise's jaw dropped. He turned down a narrow, graveled pathway, just wide enough for his Jag, and followed it for several hundred yards to a bungalow snuggled between beach and marsh.

Beside him, Annalise relaxed, possibly because the bungalow was an exercise in simplicity in comparison to the main house. "It's lovely," she said with all sincerity.

He smiled in satisfaction. "I hoped you'd approve." He thrust his door open. "Come on. Let's check it out."

Even Isabella lost her more typical apathetic mien and showed some enthusiasm. She darted into the bungalow behind him, one arm wrapped around her doll, the other around her stuffed lion. Jack couldn't help but wonder if the lion was meant as a protector—not that he'd blame her if that were the case. If it added to her sense of security, he'd surround her with a dozen lions.

The front door opened onto a small foyer, which accessed the main living area and a small dining room that he could use as a temporary office. On the far side of the dining room was a snug kitchen. A hallway branched off the living room and he led the parade in that direction, fairly certain they'd find the bedrooms.

Jack opened the first door and a small, rusty "ooh" emanated from behind him. His heart skipped a beat at the sound and he felt a surge of hope. Maybe Annalise was right. Maybe this vacation *would* turn Isabella around. Maybe it would even get her talking again. He forced himself to stroll casually into the bedroom, not wanting to betray any sort of reaction to that almost-word, afraid it might alarm her.

Isabella followed him in and made a beeline for a huge wooden structure that was part bunk beds and part tree fort. She vanished into one portion of the fort, climbed through trap doors and along secret tunnels, ending up in a bed cradled in the branches of the manufactured "tree," complete with fabric leaves and stuffed animals hidden in various nooks and crannies. Her vivid green eyes glowed with happiness and Jack realized that nothing had ever given him greater pleasure than the sight of his niece's beaming face.

"Like it?" he asked, striving to keep all trace of emotion from his voice. She nodded eagerly and her blondish-brown ringlets bobbed around her flushed cheeks. "It's good to see her hair growing out," he murmured to Annalise, who came to stand beside him.

"Did they cut it off after the accident?"

He nodded. "According to the pictures I've seen, she had beautiful long hair. But there were so many scalp lacerations, the doctors were forced to cut away large chunks of it. It seemed best to even it up and then let it grow out again. I just never realized how much work it would take to keep it from matting."

Annalise released a chuckle. "The hazards of curly hair, I'm afraid. I can't tell you how many times I've been tempted to go for one of those super-short hairstyles Isabella's sporting."

He studied her bone structure for a long moment. "You'd look good no matter how you wore it."

"Thanks." She actually blushed. "The nice thing is, it'll give me something in common with Isabella. We can do our hair together."

He gave a short laugh. "Good luck. That was one of the battles her former nannies fought on a daily basis. She doesn't like anyone touching her hair."

"Probably because right after the accident it hurt her scalp. That shouldn't be a problem any longer." She spoke with a confidence he hoped would pan out, though he had serious doubts. "I'll work with her on it."

Jack examined the room with a frown. "I didn't realize there would only be children's beds in here. There's no way you'll fit in that tree fort."

She shrugged. "No big deal. I'll sleep on the couch in the living room."

"Let's check out the other bedroom before we decide."

She lifted an eyebrow. "*Your* room? I don't think so."

"Relax. I just thought if it had two beds we could move one of them in here."

Her mouth tilted into a smile. "You sure, Mr. Mason? I could have sworn I saw a distinct green accent coloring that suggestion."

"Not at all, Ms. Stefano. I'm perfectly satisfied with our current relationship." He left her to ponder that while he crossed the hallway to the second bedroom. A huge king bed dominated the room. Annalise came to a stumbling halt behind him. "Puts paid to that idea," he said.

"The couch it is," she agreed. She spared a quick glance at her watch. "We have a couple of hours until lunchtime. I think I'll check out the kitchen and see what supplies I'll need to pick up before then."

"I asked Taye's housekeeper to take care of stocking the shelves and refrigerator. If she overlooked anything you think we'll need, you can call up to the main house and she'll be happy to have it delivered."

"Taye?"

"Taye McClintock. He owns the McMansion we passed on our way here."

Her lips twitched. "And is McClintock a McDreamy, a McSteamy or a McWeeny?"

"McWeeny?" Jack chuckled. Taye had been one of his best friends in college and possessed the face of an angel and the mind of a computer, and was the only man Jack had ever met who could romance a woman into his bed in five minutes flat. "Oh, Taye's definitely a McWeeny, as I'll be sure to inform him the next time I see him."

She stared in horror. "You wouldn't."

"Not only would I, but I will."

A fierce debate raged across her face before she turned on her heel. "I think I'll unpack the car and get organized."

He caught her arm. "The organizing can wait. I'll unpack the car, while you wrestle Isabella into a bathing suit. Then we'll hit the beach before the rays get too intense."

The idea clearly appealed and she nodded. "Sold."

Twenty minutes later, they were out the door and spreading their beach towels on the empty stretch of beach. To his intense interest, Annalise wore a modest two piece in an emerald green that brought out the gold highlights in her eyes. The bottoms were a pair of shorts that skimmed the tops of her thighs and showcased her mile-long legs. The top was equally modest, resembling a cropped tank that left her midriff bare.

If she thought he'd find it less appealing than something scantier, she'd underestimated him. If anything, the outfit teased his senses, whetting his appetite rather than satisfying it. The top fluttered in a flirtatious manner while the bottom clung lovingly to her pert backside and toned thighs. His body clenched and he forced his gaze away. If he was this randy on their first day of vacation, God help him get through the next two weeks.

"I'm going for a quick swim," he informed Annalise. "Will you keep an eye on Isabella?"

"Of course. That's why I'm here."

"For some reason, I'm having trouble remembering that," he muttered.

The ocean had warmed significantly over the past few

weeks of warm, humid weather. He struck out through the gentle swells, working himself hard. By the time he climbed from the water, he'd regained some semblance of control. To his amusement, Annalise and Isabella were busy working on a sand castle. His niece looked up at his approach and waved him over with heartwarming eagerness. She put a plastic shovel in his hands and pointed at the moat they'd started to dig around the castle.

"You want me to help?"

Her broad grin and enthusiastic nod had him setting to the task with a will. Over the next hour they worked diligently, their efforts stymied by the turning tide. The waves crept closer and closer, overflowing the moat and splashing up the sides of the castle ramparts. Isabella shrieked in a combination of protest and laughter, first racing away from the waves then dashing back to prop up the collapsed towers.

Little by little, the sea won the battle. When the final tower toppled, melting into a mere lump of its former glory, Jack gathered up their towels, then scooped his niece into his arms and tossed her over his shoulder, reveling in her laughing squeals of protest. Not even her flailing sandy limbs could curb his pleasure in the changes these few short hours had wrought.

"Time for lunch, munchkin," he announced.

They took advantage of the outdoor shower, rinsing away the sand before entering through the laundry room off the kitchen. While Annalise and Isabella changed, he raided the refrigerator and put together a selection of sandwiches. Then he headed for the bathroom. By the time he returned, he found his niece dressed and seated at the table eating one of the sandwiches, her hair clinging to her head in tidy, damp ringlets.

"I didn't hear any screaming," he murmured to Annalise. "How did you pull that off?"

"I let her help me with mine and then we reversed the process. So far, so good."

"Thank you," he said simply.

He didn't know how else to express his gratitude, except… He hooked her chin with the knuckle of his index finger and started to brush her mouth with his when he suddenly realized what he was doing. He froze and their gazes clashed. Her eyes were wide and startled and her breath escaped her parted lips in a soft gasp.

"I'm sorry," he murmured, inches from her mouth. "I wasn't thinking. I just wanted to thank you."

Everything about her teased his senses—her sweet, sweet fragrance, her silken touch, those glorious eyes—making him want to draw her into his arms and consume her, body and soul.

"Do you thank all your nannies this way?" she demanded.

"Only you." His voice roughened. "I can't explain it."

"You promised not to touch me again."

He deliberately released her and took a step back, amazed at the strength of will it required. "Better?"

For a split second he thought she was about to say, "No." That she'd be the one to take that forbidden step into his arms and finish what he'd started. Then she nodded and deliberately turned away. The next instant acute tension tightened the muscles of her back and shoulders. A single look told him why.

Isabella had stopped eating and stared at them with unmistakable intensity. He couldn't tell whether their embrace had upset his niece or pleased her. Maybe she wasn't sure, either. After an endless moment she smiled, giving her seal of approval. A small dimple winked in her cheek. Until that moment, he didn't even realize she had a dimple, so rare were her smiles. That's what Annalise had managed to accomplish in just one short day.

Jack returned his niece's smile. Whether his dear nanny knew it or not, his niece's smile had just sealed Annalise's fate.

The next several days flew by. Annalise proved to be right on several fronts. Getting away and devoting his full attention to Isabella made a noticeable difference. Of course, it didn't solve all her problems. There was still the occasional tantrum, but to his relief they were few and far between. It also helped that the two adults presented a united front, making it clear that such behavior wouldn't be tolerated.

To Jack, the most telling change came when his niece stopped painting her face in swirls of black, red and violent purple, but switched to more cheerful pastels that reflected her improved outlook on life. Not that the war paint lasted for more than an hour or two each day. Their twice-daily beach visits washed it away almost as soon as she applied it. On the fifth day, she forgot to wear it altogether, and that was when hope took hold.

Maybe, just maybe, there was a pathway out of the darkness.

Jack had to admit that his favorite times were in the evenings when the three of them curled up on the couch together and chose a DVD from the extensive selection stocked on the shelves surrounding the wide-screen TV. There in the darkness, he could relax his guard and simply enjoy this moment out of time.

"I think she's nodded off," Annalise whispered during one of their nightly sessions.

He'd sensed as much ten minutes ago when his niece's breathing had slowed and deepened and her muscles had gone lax against his chest. "I'll take her to bed in a minute."

"You like having her fall asleep on you, don't you?" The lights from the TV flickered, allowing him to catch the brief glitter of compassion reflected in her eyes. "Does it remind you of when you and Joanne were Isabella's age?"

Jack released a harsh laugh, one that had Isabella stirring in his arms. He traced a reassuring hand along his niece's back and forced himself to calmness. With a small, inarticulate murmur Isabella settled. "Not even close," he stated quietly. "My father would have considered this sort of activity a complete waste of time."

"Oh." That single word spoke volumes. "And your mother? Would she have also considered it a waste of time?"

He hoped the darkness concealed his expression, but he could hear the pain creep into his voice. "She was different than my father. Before their divorce she tried not to show her emotions, since he'd use any sign of weakness against her. She changed later on."

"How old were you when they broke up?"

"Eight. Nine, maybe. Joanne was two years older."

"And how did your mother change, afterward?"

"She softened, became more openly affectionate. Of course, it's hard to say if she was like that all the time. I can only base it on the time I saw her."

"What do you mean?" Annalise straightened, and he could feel her attempting to penetrate the darkness in order to read his expression. "Didn't your mother have custody of you?"

"No, only Joanne. My father took me."

He caught Annalise's soft gasp. "They split you up?"

"Yes." A wintry coldness settled over him. With that one single decision, every scrap of love and kindness had been removed from his life. He still felt the loss to this day. "My mother never spoke to me about that time, but Joanne once explained that our father threatened to take both of us and prevent our mother from ever seeing us again if she didn't agree to his terms."

A strobe of brilliance flashed across the screen, allowing him to see that Annalise was visibly shaken. "Could he have done that?"

"Considering I didn't see either my mother or my sister again until I turned thirteen, I'd say not only could he, but he did precisely that."

"How…?" Her voice thickened, betraying her emotional reaction to his response. "Why…?" She shook her head, unable to formulate the questions she clearly wanted to ask.

Jack leaned his head back against the couch cushion and stared blindly at the old *Star Trek* movie that was Isabella's current favorite. "How? With some of the most powerful lawyers money could buy. Why? Because he was—and is—a total bastard who used me to hit out at my mother."

"But you did finally get to see her," Annalise said on a note of urgency.

A smile of satisfaction tugged at his mouth. "That I did."

"I assume he finally relented?" she asked tentatively.

"Not a chance in hell. The summer I turned thirteen, Dad took off overseas on an extended honeymoon with his latest trophy wife. I was supposed to go to camp. Instead, I hitchhiked to Colorado, where my mother was living with her second husband."

"Dear God, Jack!" She reached for him, her hand clutching his arm. "Do you have any idea how dangerous that was? Anything could have happened to you."

He regarded her with a hint of amusement. "That's what my mother said. It was worth it, though. I stayed with them for most of that summer." A summer filled with magic and hope. A summer unlike anything he'd experienced before or since. A summer that had ended in the death of dreams. "Until my father found out, that is. But those couple of months were quite eye-opening."

"In what way?"

His brows tugged together reflecting a hint of the bewilderment he'd experienced during that time period. "They were all so happy. They laughed almost all the time. And when they fought…" He struggled for the right words to explain. "I kept waiting for the other shoe to drop, but it never did."

"You mean when they fought, you weren't worried that they were on the verge of divorce." Her hand shifted, rubbing his arm in a soothing motion. He doubted she was even conscious of her actions. "They were never nasty toward each other."

"Exactly. They were—" he reflected on it for a moment "—casual. As though the way they interacted—the laughter, the tears, the squabbling, the open affection— was a normal, everyday occurrence."

"It probably was." She tilted her head to one side, sending a swath of curls tumbling across her shoulder. "How often did you get to visit after that?"

"I didn't. My disobedience that summer earned me a trip to military school. I didn't see Joanne again until I turned eighteen and my father no longer had any say in where I went or who I saw. Unfortunately, my mother and her husband managed to drive themselves off an icy mountainside a few months beforehand."

"Oh, Jack! How awful." He caught the betraying glitter of tears and felt something shift inside him, something deep and powerful. Something he wanted to protect himself from because it came from a wellspring of emotions he preferred to deny. "What happened to Joanne? Did she move back to Charleston to live with you and your father?"

"No. She was in college by then and flat out refused to have anything to do with our father."

"Or you?" she dared to ask.

He refused to acknowledge the hit. For years he'd believed just that, until Joanne had finally set him straight. But by then he'd found a way to insulate himself from the sort of emotional pain that came from sentiment and familial attachment.

"We managed to revive our relationship, despite my father." His mouth twisted. "Hell, Jo even found it in her heart to forgive him, not that he ever believed he required forgiveness. Ironically, Dad helped her find the lawyer who handled Isabella's adoption." Jack stood then, careful not to wake his niece, while putting an unmistakable period to the conversation. Annalise's hand fell away, leaving behind coldness where once there was warmth. "Time I put our little one to bed. I'll be back in a minute."

He took his time settling his niece, needing those handful of minutes to rebuild his barriers. He'd told Annalise far more than he'd shared with any other woman, opening parts of himself that he'd sealed away for almost two full decades. He didn't ordinarily let people in, didn't dare. That sort of closeness often became messy, risked creating emotions like the ones that had sent his parents' relationship spiraling into vicious arguments and acts of revenge.

He'd made up his mind at a very young age to avoid marriage at all costs. Even when he'd witnessed firsthand his mother's loving relationship with her second husband, he still hadn't trusted that their marriage was anything other than pure dumb luck. The union he contemplated with Annalise wouldn't involve an emotional commitment. When they married it would be carefully scripted with neat, tidy, legal boundaries that specified every aspect of their wedded "bliss" right down to the date of their future divorce. As for any potential romantic entanglements…

That would be determined by contract, as well. He had no objection if she chose to share his bed. But she would enter the affair with her eyes wide open and all the cards on the table. He wouldn't trick her with claims of affection. Theirs would be a mating of body and intellect. A sensible blending rather than an emotional one.

Satisfied that he'd fully regained his self-control, he

turned and found Annalise watching him from the doorway. And that was when he realized he had no self-control when it came to this woman.

None whatsoever.

Five

Jack had no memory of closing the door to Isabella's room. No memory of striding toward Annalise. No memory of backing her against the wall. But from the instant his mouth found hers, it was like a recorder flicked on, burning every tantalizing moment into the pathways of his brain.

He was overwhelmed by the distinctive fragrance of her skin and driven insane by the low, soft moan that reverberated in her throat. The heat of her hands and lips and flesh burned like wildfire, sweeping straight through to the frozen core of him and melting away walls of ice that he'd believed too tall and thick to ever be breached.

"I've tried, Annalise," he said between quick, biting kisses. "I've tried to keep my hands off you. How many times have I promised I would? And yet…"

A husky laugh exploded from her, and she leaned her head back against the wall, exposing her throat. "Somehow it doesn't quite work out that way."

"You don't understand. I always keep my word. Always. It's a point of honor with me. But with you—" Frustration tore through him. "It's like my body and brain are out of sync, or speaking different languages."

"No communication?"

"None." His hand drifted along the golden length of her neck. Then the urge to taste her consumed him and his mouth followed the same pathway his hand had taken. "Well, except for one single urge. On that point, all of the various parts of me are in total agreement."

A line from the movie they'd just watched played through his head: *Resistance is futile.* It described his predicament precisely. Temptation beckoned again and he fought it for all of ten seconds before he tumbled. Unable to help himself, he cupped her breast and traced the rigid peak through the thin cotton of her tank top. The breath exploded from her lungs and her sooty lashes fluttered toward her cheeks in clear surrender.

He used his knee to part her legs and settled into the cradle of her hips, sliding against a body that combined a lean, tensile strength with a sensual softness. He wanted her in his bed, wanted those endless legs wrapped around him. Wanted to sink into her warmth until the last vestige of ice had been driven from his body.

Everything about her propelled him toward a place he'd never been before, never even knew existed. A gentle place. A place of solace. A place of beautiful urgency and endless possibilities. A place where he could safely lose himself in arms that would never let him go, while he basked in the warmth and light of her embrace.

He reached beneath her tank top and found a hint of what that sweet place would hold, and he lingered there while the heat built. Her breasts slipped into his hands, filling them with their silken weight. Her nipples were two hot buds of desire against his palms. He rocked his hips into place between her legs, setting a slow, torturous rhythm that ripped a moan from her throat.

"Sleep with me tonight," he urged.

He watched the struggle play out across her face, a fierce battle waged between common sense and desire. He was intimately familiar with that particular battle. For a brief instant he thought she'd capitulate. But something held her back, something that caused a glimmer of panic to break across the planes of her face and an intense vulnerability to tarnish her eyes. It would seem he wasn't the only one with painful memories.

"I can't. *We*," she corrected, "we can't. Isabella has to come first. And if we do this, we'll be torn between responsibility and desire."

"I'll always put Isabella first."

"Then you won't fight me about this. Because having sex with you isn't putting Isabella first."

She didn't give him room to argue. Besides, she was right. They couldn't afford to be distracted right now. *He* couldn't afford it. He still needed her help. Somehow, someway, he had to find a way to convince Annalise to marry him. And that pathway led through her attachment to Isabella, not through his bedroom door.

As much as he wanted this woman, he couldn't have

her. He reluctantly slid his hands from beneath her top and forced himself to abandon the warmth and softness he'd found for far too brief a time. He took a deliberate step backward. And then another. The want remained in her eyes, along with a hopeless resignation. If she'd uttered a single sound of regret, he'd have swept her into his arms and taken her then and there. But she remained silent. And he gave himself up to duty and responsibility. The familiar cold returned, sweeping into his veins and taking root. How many years had it been his companion? He couldn't remember anymore. Not that it mattered. He'd learned long ago to accept the inevitability of it.

Without a word, he turned and walked away.

Jack jerked awake at the sound of his bedroom door banging open.

"Is Isabella in here?" Annalise demanded. "Is she with you?"

He came off the bed like a shot. "She's missing?"

Annalise nodded rapidly, her breath escaping her lungs in frantic gasps. "When I went in to get her this morning she wasn't there. I thought she was hiding in the tree house. I practically took the thing apart looking for her. I've searched the entire house. She's not here." Undisguised fear glittered in her eyes, shredding her usual control. "I can't find her anywhere."

"Have you checked outside?"

"Oh, God, Jack." She turned a panicked gaze in the direction of the front door. "The ocean."

They both raced for the door. It wasn't locked and he could distinctly remember double-checking it last night to make certain it was. He ripped the door open and erupted onto the front porch. He drew in a deep breath, preparing to shout his niece's name, when suddenly he saw her. She sat halfway between the house and the water, half-buried beneath the largest dog Jack had ever seen.

Behind him, Annalise stumbled against his back. She inhaled sharply and he whipped around and caught hold of her. Sensing the scream building in her lungs, he covered her mouth with his hand.

"Quiet," he ordered in a voice barely above a whisper. "Don't startle them."

At her nod of understanding, he released her. "Jack," she whimpered. "That thing could kill her."

"Don't say it. Don't even think it. Right now, I want you to go back in the house and find my cell. Punch in 911, but don't hit Send until I tell you." She continued to stare at him with glazed, terror-stricken eyes and he gave her a quick shake. "Do you understand?"

She recovered a small semblance of control and nodded. "Yes. Yes, I understand. Dial 911. Don't hit Send until you give the word."

"Then I want you to grab the steaks that are in the fridge and bring them out here to me. Slow and easy, got it? No fast or sudden moves. No loud noises."

"I understand."

Without another word, she slipped back into the house. Jack forced himself to move forward and sit on the porch steps. Then he whistled, low and gentle. Both dog and child jerked to attention, their heads swiveling in unison toward him. To his horror, the dog bristled, emitting a low growl. Even worse, Isabella reached up to pat the animal on the muzzle, her tiny hand inches from a set of lethally bared teeth. He knew Annalise had returned by her soft gasp of reaction at how much more dangerous the situation had become.

"Here." She slipped the raw slabs of meat into his hand. Her fingers trembled against his and her breath warmed the back of his neck in rapid-fire bursts. She was inches from losing it, and yet she spoke with a calmness that washed over him like a gentle balm. "It's going to be all right, Jack. I have my hand on the Send button. Say the word, and I'll place the call."

"Go back inside," he instructed in an undertone. He wouldn't risk her welfare, too. "Be ready to open the door on my signal."

He sensed her silent retreat into the house and fixed his full attention on his niece and the huge animal hovering above her. He didn't dare whistle again. He could only hope that one or the other of them would come to him. Sure enough, Isabella released a gleeful laugh and clambered out from beneath the dog. To Jack's relief, the animal allowed it, though she—at least, he thought it was a female—continued to regard Jack with open suspicion bordering on hostility.

He needed to get the dog away from his niece, and fast. Hoping he wasn't making a hideous mistake, he held up the first steak. "Here you go, girl!"

It was as though someone had thrown a light switch. The hair along the dog's back slicked down and her ears perked up. A huge flirtatious grin spread across her giant square mug. After treating Isabella to a maternal lick of farewell from a tongue big enough to clean his niece's face with one swipe, she galloped toward Jack at top speed. Unfortunately, Isabella released a squeal of annoyance at having their play interrupted and gave chase. The instant the dog reached him, Jack tossed the first of the steaks. It disappeared in one less-than-feminine gulp.

"Sit," he ordered.

To his amazement, the dog sat. She checked him out—particularly the second steak he still held—while he did the same to her, a cautious how-beasty-are-you and who's-the-top-dog exchange of looks. She didn't appear to be in too bad a shape, though her ribs protruded more than he liked. After she'd given him the once-over, she regarded him with a look of unadulterated hope and sweetness. To his relief, he saw that she wore a collar. He didn't see a name tag, but at least there was a shiny new rabies tag dangling from it.

His plan was to toss the second steak as far as he could, snatch up his niece and hightail it into the house. Before he could, Isabella skidded to a halt alongside the dog. He nearly lost it when she wound her twig-thin arms around the animal's massive neck and pressed her face into the short, brindled coat. One miscalculation and the dog would go from chewing on steak to chewing on his niece.

He forced himself to take a calming breath before speaking. "Isabella, go into the house and find Annalise. After you wash your hands, you can show her your new friend. You'll have to do it through the window until I've finished feeding her."

She hesitated, obviously torn between staying with the dog and the pleasure of showing her off to Annalise. He used a tone that didn't brook any argument, one he had never been able to bring himself to use with her. Until today. "Now, miss."

To his intense relief, she obeyed and climbed the steps onto the porch. The door flew open behind him and Annalise snatched her inside. With a whimper of protest, the dog charged forward and mowed all two hundred plus pounds right over top of him, snagging the steak out of his hands as she steamrolled past. Before Annalise could get the door closed, the dog slammed through it and erupted into the house.

Jack lay spread-eagled on his back, struggling just to draw air into his lungs. Getting hit by a Mack truck couldn't have been any more painful. He looked down at himself, half-expecting to discover paw craters denting his body. To his immense relief, he didn't find any. As far as he could tell, all his most vital parts appeared intact and in place.

He rolled over onto his hands and knees. It took three attempts to stand. He staggered through the door to find the dog squatting at Isabella's heels. Even sitting, the animal dwarfed the petite five-year-old, though there was no mistaking the adoration in the dog's brown eyes as she peered down at his niece. Isabella had her arms thrown around the animal's massive neck again. She beamed up at Jack with such undisguised joy it nearly broke his heart.

He closed his eyes with a groan. He knew that look. "We're not keeping her," he stated categorically. "She belongs to somebody and that somebody isn't us."

To his surprise, Isabella didn't throw the expected temper tantrum. She just continued to stare at him with those dewy green eyes and that wide, brilliant grin. Her dimple gave a saucy wink.

"We don't know who owns her, Isabella," Annalise added. "The poor thing is probably lost."

"The 'poor thing' probably got dumped when she grew to the size of a baby elephant and started eating the owners out of house and home," Jack muttered.

It was precisely the wrong thing to say. Annalise turned on him with a horrified expression. "*Dumped?* You think she's been abandoned? Someone left her deliberately?"

Isabella tightened her arms around the dog who responded with a pathetic little whine that rattled every window in the bungalow. God help them if the beast ever cut loose with an actual bark. They'd end up with the roof caving in around their ears.

He spared his niece an uneasy look. "Then again, maybe someone is desperately trying to find her. I'll call Mrs. Westcott and find out if she knows anything about who the owners might be."

"Mrs. Westcott?" Annalise asked.

"Taye's housekeeper." Time to take control of the situation before this went any further. Jack fixed his niece with a steely gaze. "Give it up, sweetheart. We're not keeping the dog. She's wearing a rabies tag, which means she belongs to someone. I'm sure the owners are desperate to get her back."

Annalise intervened by resting a restraining hand on his arm. "She's a gorgeous animal," she commented in a blatant non sequitur. No doubt, it was her way of diffusing the standoff between uncle and niece. "I like all the stripes. She sort of reminds me of a faded tiger."

"It's called a brindle coat," he grudgingly explained.

Annalise continued to eye the dog, no longer betraying

any sign of fear. Not good. "I wonder what her name is." She squatted next to Isabella. "Maybe if she doesn't have any owners we can name her."

Isabella nodded eagerly and the dog put her sly seal of approval on it by licking first his niece and then his nanny/soon-to-be-strangled-wife-to-be.

"No naming the dog!" he protested.

He might as well have saved his breath. Everyone ignored him. Instead, the three females began a timeless bonding ritual that involved the dog positioned on the floor like a sphinx, while Isabella and Annalise petted her from tongue-lolling head to thumping tail. She whimpered in pathetic gratitude at all the attention while rolling her eyes in his direction. He could have sworn he saw smug laughter lurking there. Oh, yeah. Definitely a sly one. Knew just how to tug at the heartstrings.

"You'd think the guy paying the bills would be the one deserving a petting," he muttered. "But hell, no. I get to play bad cop. I know how this story ends—with me in the doghouse, while the dog gets all the attention and affection. Well, not this time, bubba. No way, no how."

"What kind of dog is she?" Annalise asked. "Other than big?"

No one was listening to him, or, at least, they'd developed selective hearing. Caving to the inevitable, he examined the animal with a critical eye. "Definitely Great Dane. And judging by the breadth and shape of her, not to mention the droopy ears, I wouldn't be surprised if she had some mastiff mixed in there somewhere."

"Well, whatever she is, she's a beauty," Annalise replied, rocking back onto her heels.

He bent down and retrieved his cell phone from Annalise and punched in the number to the main house. Mrs. Westcott answered on the first ring. "We have a visitor," he explained after they'd exchanged pleasantries. "She's four-legged, about the size of a Humvee. And half-starved."

"You've seen her? Well, thank goodness for that. Animal Control has been trying to catch her for the past week. She's a clever minx, that one is."

He eyed the ecstatic dog who'd rolled onto her back, enjoying a tummy rub, dinner-plate-sized paws pinwheeling in the air. "Well, your clever minx is currently splayed out in the middle of Taye's bungalow living room floor."

"Oh, Mr. Mason. Aren't you sweet to take her in."

"No! No, I'm not—"

"I've been so worried about her. I was just coming to work when I saw her get dumped. A bunch of college kids tossed her out of the car like so much garbage, poor critter. Thank goodness she'll have a good home."

He gritted his teeth. "Only if someone is insane enough to adopt her. Can you call Animal Control for us?" At the question, three pairs of outraged eyes pinned him to the wall. Mrs. Westcott weighed in with a disapproving *tsk*ing sound. "What?" he asked, a shade defensively.

In response, Isabella threw herself on top of the dog as though to prevent anyone from dragging the animal away. He didn't bother to explain that it would take a crane and bulldozer to move the beast if she turned uncooperative.

Annalise moistened her lips, lips he'd taken great delight in kissing only the night before. If she hadn't chosen such an underhanded distraction, his brain cells would have stayed where they belonged instead of draining out of his ears and puddling on the floor.

"Maybe we should discuss this first, before you make any rash decisions." She didn't phrase it like a suggestion. In fact, it sounded suspiciously like a demand. "I don't see why we can't keep her until you track down the owners."

"Is that your new nanny?" Mrs. Westcott asked. "She sounds like a sensible woman."

With the female-to-male ratio running three-to-one against him—he eyed the dog—no, make that four-to-one—the odds were definitely not in his favor. "I never make rash decisions," he announced in a no-nonsense tone of voice. "And considering I'm the one in charge around here, I believe that makes me best qualified to decide whether or not it's appropriate to call Animal Control."

Mrs. Westcott snorted.

"It would only be for a day," Annalise stated, sounding far too authoritative for an employee. "Two, at most."

"There's a simple way to resolve this," Jack said.

He thanked the housekeeper for her assistance and snapped the phone closed with a decisive *click* before approaching the dog and examining the rabies tag. Sure enough, it listed the address and phone number of the clinic where the shot had been administered. He placed the call and within minutes was handed off to the veterinarian.

"I know the dog you mean. Dane/mastiff mix," the vet said, confirming Jack's guess. "That's Madam. She is— or perhaps more accurately based on what you're telling me—*was* the mascot for a college fraternity. They weren't supposed to have her and were told not to bring her back. Apparently, they played several rounds of beer pong in order to determine who'd be the one taking her home. The boy who lost is the one who brought her in. I gather his parents insisted before she moved in."

"I don't suppose you have a name or phone number?"

"I do, for all the good it'll do you. How does the last name 'Zur,' first name 'Lou,' strike you?"

"Lou Zur?" Jack groaned. "Loser?"

"Hmm. Clever lads, these college boys. It gives me such hope for the future of our country. You can check the home number he gave, but it's probably a local bar or strip joint. My guess is that when the boy showed up at home with Madam his parents changed their mind about keeping her. Dumping the dog must have been his brilliant solution to the problem. I wish I could claim his behavior was the exception, but if you visited an animal shelter, you'd see it isn't."

"Is there anything else you can tell me?" Jack asked.

The sound of rustling papers drifted through the receiver. "I can tell you that Madam is approximately two and a half years old, in excellent health and all her shots are up-to-date."

"Thank you. I appreciate your assistance."

"If you plan on adopting her, I can fax you her medical records."

"I'll let you know." He disconnected the call and swore beneath his breath. Now what? He turned and faced Annalise and Isabella, wincing at the undisguised hope gleaming in their eyes. They must have guessed from what little they'd heard that all had not gone well. Or rather, it had gone extremely well…for them.

"The dog's name is Madam," he stalled.

"What about the owner?" Annalise asked. "Did the vet have any contact information?"

He didn't have a choice. He gave her the facts in short, terse sentences and then handed down his final edict. It was the only logical choice and he made his decision crystal-clear and without exceptions or loopholes, question or qualification. And he used his most intimidating tone of voice, the one that left his employees trembling. The tone that had his various vice presidents and board members scrambling to obey. The tone that no one had dared to openly defy in the decade he'd spent building his empire.

"We are going to turn this dog over to the shelter," he pronounced. "End of discussion."

Annalise didn't so much as quiver, let alone tremble. And there wasn't the slightest inkling of a scramble. Instead she shot a pointed look in Isabella's direction before folding her arms across her chest in open defiance. "I think we should consider keeping Madam. She might help with certain adjustment issues."

Didn't she get it? He didn't argue with employees. He spoke; they obeyed. "Help in what way?" he argued. "By eating us out of house and home? By scaring my neighbors? What if that animal drives off Sara and Brett? I can barely keep a nanny as it is. Now you want to deprive me of my housekeeper and handyman, too?"

"I'm sure they'll both fall in love with Madam." Beside her, Isabella nodded eagerly. "Plus, helping to take care of a dog will teach your niece responsibility." Annalise lowered her voice, knocking the final nail into his coffin with a husky plea. "And maybe it'll help with her grief."

"You... I..." He ground his teeth together. "This isn't a conversation to have in front of Isabella and you damn well know it," he informed Annalise.

"Language."

"Oh, you're going to hear some language, just as soon as I get you alone."

"I don't think it's wise to leave Madam unattended with Isabella," Annalise objected, the wicked twinkle in her eye at direct odds with the demureness of her expression. "Not until we know that it's safe."

"Exactly." He seized on the excuse. He pointed toward Madam. "That animal is too big. She could accidently injure Isabella."

"So far she's been very gentle. Not to mention protective. And if she was raised at a dorm, she's accustomed to being around young people."

"We don't know if the mutt is housebroken. Look at the size of her. In case you're unaware of it, there's a distinct correlation between the size of an animal and the size of its steaming piles of sh—" He broke off at Annalise's warning look. "Chunks of chocolate, not to mention the lakes of pi— Son of a bi—" It was all he could do not to rip his hair out by the roots. "Geysers of ginger ale. Who's going to clean that up?"

Honey-gold eyes brimmed with laughter. "We'll make sure Madam gets frequent walks until we're certain she won't accidentally leave any chocolate treats or ginger-ale geysers around the house."

"And that's another thing," he was quick to point out. "Who's going to walk her? We'll need a private trucking service to pick up all she dumps along the way."

"That's the purpose of pooper scoopers. We'll manage."

"Not only that, but she's a lot of dog to control. We live in the city. If she gets away from you she might break a car or knock over a power pole or mistake a policeman for a chew toy. Or…or eat some tourists—not that that would be so bad."

Isabella began to giggle, the sound the most delicious thing he'd ever heard in his entire life. "She won't fit in the Jag," he added weakly, struggling to steel himself against that sweet, sweet laugh. "She'll knock over the furniture. The house is full of priceless antiques, you know. She'll probably dig holes straight through to China in my backyard, holes Isabella could fall into. Isabella doesn't speak Chinese."

"She doesn't speak at all," Annalise reminded him. "Maybe Madam can help change that."

He couldn't allow the forlorn hope to sway him. "And the barking. Do you know how much it'll cost to replace the windows the creature's barking will break?"

"I have it on excellent authority that you can afford it." She gazed up at him with eyes capable of melting even his heart of stone. "Please, Jack. Please, can we keep her?"

His niece deserted the dog and flung herself against him, wrapping her arms around his legs and squeezing for all she was worth. "Aw, hell," he muttered.

"I take it we have a dog?" Annalise asked.

"That isn't a dog."

"Elephant…dog…chocolate-and-ginger-ale factory…" She shrugged. "Is she ours?"

He blew out a sigh. "I don't see that I have a choice. Looks like we've just adopted a Madam."

Six

Looking back, Jack realized that Madam's arrival in their lives changed everything. Much to his relief, he discovered that she was definitely housebroken. But she was also a total klutz.

"I'm going to owe Taye a fortune in repairs," he complained to Annalise as he swept up the latest Madam mayhem. "That tail of hers should be registered as a deadly weapon."

"You can't fool me, Mason," Annalise replied. She held the dustpan for him, then emptied the remains of the lamp into the trash can. "Admit it. You adore Madam."

He glanced toward the living room where Isabella and the dog were curled up on the couch together. "What I adore is the change in Isabella since Madam arrived."

To his concern, tears welled up in Annalise's eyes. "She's blossomed, hasn't she?"

"Oh, yeah." He wished he'd been able to bring about such a notable change in his niece, but he'd take it however it happened. The important thing was Isabella's recovery. "I've also sicced my PI on the boys who dumped her. When I track them down, I intend to explain the error of their ways in terms they won't ever forget."

"Good." She glared with unexpected ruthlessness. "I don't suppose you have the power to arrange for them to volunteer at their local animal shelter? Maybe that will underscore the lesson."

"Trust me. I'll find a way to make it happen." He grimaced, turning his attention to more immediate matters. "Now all I have to do is figure out how to keep that four-legged disaster from laying waste to my home."

She caught her lip between her teeth, a frown forming between her eyebrows. "What are you going to do?"

"I've already done it." He'd given the matter a lot of thought before reaching a decision and calling his house-keeper with instructions. "I asked Sara to arrange to have most of the furniture and antiques put into storage for the time being."

Annalise gave him an odd look. "Generations of Mason antiques? You'd put them in storage so Isabella can have a dog?"

"Hell, yes. Trust me, it'll make a vast improvement. That place isn't kid friendly, let alone dog friendly. I should have made the change when Isabella first came to live with me." He took the trash can from her and carried it into the kitchen. "I can remember tiptoeing around that mausoleum when my grandmother lived there, afraid if I breathed wrong I might break some Louis the Umpteenth or Early American Irreplaceable. That's no way for a little girl to live."

"No," Annalise agreed softly. A wobbly smile broke across her face. "It's not. Thank you for putting her best interests first."

"Of course I'm putting her best interests first," he retorted, insulted. "Did you think I wouldn't?"

"At first, perhaps." She offered a self-conscious shrug. "You do have a reputation, Jack. And it's not the sort that suggests you'd be indulgent toward the vagaries of a child. I have to admit I was concerned when I read you'd taken custody of your niece."

He stiffened. "Were you?"

She must have realized it wasn't the most tactful remark she could have made because she winced. "You felt duty bound to take her in, didn't you?"

He couldn't deny it. "Yes."

He watched her choose her words with care. "Some in your position might believe that giving Isabella a home fulfilled that duty. A more unfeeling man would turn her over to a nanny with a clear conscience and go back to business as usual."

An arctic wind blew across his soul. "Most who know me would describe me as just that sort of man. It's who my father raised me to be." Why couldn't she see that? Couldn't she sense the coldness in him, the absence of any ability to love? He was driven to ask, needed to see himself through her eyes. "What makes you think I'm not like that?"

She grinned, her eyes full of warm, golden sunshine. "I've had an opportunity to get to know you. Just in the short time we've been together, I can tell you're not that sort of man."

"You're wrong. I'm exactly that sort of man." He couldn't explain why he was driven to argue the point, other than he needed her to face reality, to see him for who and what he was. "That's why I hired you. I wanted someone who could take care of my niece, leaving me free to get back to living my life on my terms."

She waved his confession aside as thought it were of no concern. "Maybe at first. But as soon as you set eyes on your niece, you changed your mind. You're happy to take an active role in Isabella's life."

"I am?"

Her grin widened. "You're here, aren't you? And you've told me you'll do whatever it takes to retain custody of her. Why do you think you're doing that? It's because you're a softy at heart."

"That's a damn lie. You take it back right now."

She swept him a mocking bow. "Of course, Mr. Mason. I absolutely take it back. After all, you're only a man who's taken in his niece when she had no one else, taken a leave of absence from a multi-billion-dollar company in order to spend time with her, adopted a stray dog, stripped his possessions from his house to accommodate said dog and niece. Why, I've never met anyone more deserving of the name Scrooge."

"That's me. Just call me Ebenezer."

Annalise shot him a sparkling look. "So, tell me, Eb. Is there anything you wouldn't do for Isabella?"

"No, there isn't." Time to turn the tables. "But I suspect the eventual question will be... Is there anything *you* wouldn't do?"

Annalise's amusement faded. "What do you mean?"

"One of these days I'm going to ask you for a favor that will help my niece," he warned. "I just wonder how you'll answer when that time comes."

She didn't hesitate. "That's easy." To his surprise, she returned his gaze with one weighted with grim determination. "I'll do whatever it takes, too."

He nodded in satisfaction. "Good answer. And just so you know..." He leaned in. Unable to help himself, he brushed her mouth with his, reveling in the brief flash of heat. "I intend to hold you to that promise."

Their remaining days at the bungalow took on a surreal quality. As Jack had warned, the dog threatened to eat them out of house and home. Within days she put on enough weight to hide her painfully thin rib cage, though Jack suspected that might also have something to do with the treats Annalise and Isabella were sneaking the dog whenever his back was turned.

The days flashed by, exhausting, exhilarating and filled with warmth and laughter and plain, old-fashioned fun. He'd never seen Isabella so carefree, even though she still refused to speak. Between Annalise and Madam she was mothered to within an inch of her life.

Not that he was left out of the mix. As often as his niece could be found in Annalise's arms or sprawled across Madam's back, she spent an equal amount of time curled up in his lap. He hoped their familial connection helped heal her grief the way it helped heal his. Their time together seemed to be making a difference, but he could still sense an undercurrent of sorrow that he had no idea how to reach, let alone assuage. As though sensing his mixed emotions, Madam would rumble over to rest her huge head on his knee and offer licks of reassurance while Annalise watched with her incandescent smile. That smile made him long for something else, something more. Something that would complete their family unit.

But the true breakthrough happened one morning shortly before they were scheduled to leave. The sun had barely broken the plane of the horizon when his bedroom door banged open and the next instant his mattress overflowed with dog, niece, doll and a huge picture book that smacked him square in the jaw as Isabella snuggled down next to him.

"Baby Belle?" he asked sleepily. "What's wrong?"

She shoved the book into his hands and patted it, blinking up at him with absurdly long lashes. Her dimple flashed. Madam settled her huge head on his spare pillow with a wide yawn and promptly went back to sleep.

"You want me to read to you?" Jack asked. She nodded, leaning her head against his chest. Her halo of curls, still pillow-ruffled, were downy soft and seemed to have a mind of their own. A sudden memory came to him. "This is…this is Family Bed, isn't it?" he asked gruffly.

She nodded and patted the book again. Before he could gather himself sufficiently to read, he heard Annalise shuffling in the general direction of his niece's bedroom.

"Isabella? Madam? Hey, where is everyone?"

"She's in here," he called. "We're all in here."

Annalise appeared in the doorway, her curls as tumbled and ruffled as his niece's. She pulled up short at the sight of all of them piled in his bed. "Oh," she said, disconcerted. "There you are. What...what are you doing?"

"It's Family Bed," he offered.

She blinked at him in utter bewilderment. "What's Family Bed?"

And he'd thought he'd been deprived. He wondered why she'd never experienced something so wondrous. What had her childhood been like that she'd never known the pleasure of curling up with her parents and siblings in one big bed? Even he, with his dearth of close family ties had, for one sweet summer, known the joy of Family Bed.

"Every Sunday my mother, stepfather, and Joanne would collect books and newspapers, coffee and juice, and spend the first couple of hours of the day in bed together." He glanced down at his niece, tucked close to his side. "I gather Joanne continued the tradition."

A wistful smile teased at the corners of Annalise's mouth. "It sounds lovely."

"Why don't you join us?"

A sweeping flash of vulnerability betrayed her longing to do just that and made Jack think of a child with her nose pressed to the candy store window, always on the outside looking in. Never allowed a taste of heaven. He'd had close and personal experience with that particular emotion, having iced up his nose on that window on more than one occasion. Then her expression vanished as though it had never been, and he could only marvel at her self-control.

"I don't think it would be appropriate for me to join

you." She edged toward the door. "I'll just get breakfast started while you and Isabella enjoy reading together."

"We can fix breakfast later on. Right now it's time for Family Bed." He nudged his niece. "Isn't that right?"

She nodded eagerly and held out her arms to Annalise, who wavered, clearly torn between a desire to share in something she'd never encountered before and longed to experience, and maintaining a professional distance.

"Come on, Stefano. You're needed here."

He'd said the exact right thing. Her smile nearly blinded him as she approached the bed. He grabbed Madam by her collar and wrestled her toward the end of the mattress in order to give Annalise room. She slid beneath the covers next to Isabella and the three of them reclined side by side, against mounds of pillows. He opened the Mrs. Pennywinkle book and cleared his throat.

"'It was a cold winter day when the magical china doll, Nancy, found her way to the next little girl who needed her…'" he began.

Beside him, his niece patted her doll's back and hugged her closer. "Your doll looks just like the one in the book," Annalise said in surprise. "Is…is she a Nancy doll?" At Isabella's nod, a husky tone entered her voice. "No wonder she's so special. Do you think she's here to help you like the doll in your storybook?"

Again Isabella nodded, this time pointing to the dog. "You think your Nancy doll sent Madam to you?" Jack asked. When his niece nodded a third time, more emphatically, he exchanged an uneasy glance with Annalise. "Is this going to be a problem?"

"I don't think so, not unless she starts to believe that her doll can grant wishes."

"And if that's what she already believes?"

"I don't know," Annalise admitted. "I guess we hope that with the proper amount of love and attention and counseling, she gradually realizes that isn't the case. I have to admit, I'm a little out of my depth on this one."

Isabella gave the book an impatient tap and Jack forced himself to relax and offer an apologetic smile. "Sorry, munchkin. I got distracted there. What do you say we start over?"

The next hour passed on wings, ending too soon as far as Jack was concerned. When his bed emptied out so that everyone could dress, so did the warmth, and he decided then and there that Family Bed would become a weekly ritual from this point forward. His cell phone rang just as Annalise herded Isabella toward the kitchen to whip up a batch of pancakes. He checked caller ID and connected the call.

"Yeah, Derek. What's up?"

"Sorry to call so early in the morning, but the PI's preliminary report just hit my in-box and I knew you'd like the results ASAP."

"And?"

"And Ms. Stefano is clean…for the most part."

Jack spared a quick glance toward the hallway. Girlish laughter slipped out from the direction of the kitchen and he nudged his door closed. "What part isn't so clean?"

"There was a small matter when she was sixteen. Cops raided some kid's birthday bash and issued her a citation for underage drinking. They expunged her record after she completed some court-ordered community service. Since then, she's been so clean she squeaks."

Jack lowered his voice. "If the record was expunged, how did you get the details?"

"I have my sources. I'm not minimizing what she did, Jack, but it was a long time ago. Her mother had died a couple years before that and her father was in the military at the time. After her brush with the law, he took an early discharge and started up a fishing charter service, I'm guessing so he could assume a more hands-on role. He sent her off each summer to stay with an aunt during tourist season. The aunt's a school teacher who lives out near Columbia. She's probably the one who influenced Annalise's career choice."

"Did you find anything that might concern CPS?"

"Nothing. I doubt they'll even dig up as much as I have." There was a brief pause. "So, how's it going at your end? Your marriage project moving right along?" he asked a shade too casually.

"It's coming."

"Coming…as in soon, though, right?"

Jack let out a long sigh. He knew that tone. "Aw, hell. What do you know that I don't?"

"The Locke woman's making noises again. I've done everything I can to have her replaced, but apparently she's irreplaceable."

"How much time do I have?" Jack asked grimly.

"Let's see…. Soon would be good. If you and your charming bride-to-be were to show up at the Judicial Center and fill out a marriage application sometime today, you could be wedded and bedded in twenty-four hours. How does that sound?"

"Hell, Derek. That isn't soon. That's immediate."

"Immediate works for me."

"Well, it doesn't for me. And I guarantee, it won't for Annalise."

"I strongly suggest you find a way for it to work for both of you. Once you're officially married, I can probably hold off CPS for another month or so, convince them the two of you deserve time to settle into connubial bliss. But that's as far as I'll be able to push it. You need to marry now in order for me to insist on any sort of further delay. And then you need to create a loving relationship that's good enough to pass Mrs. Locke's scrutiny."

Jack closed his eyes and ran a hand along the nape of his neck. Damn it to hell. "I'll try."

"I suggest you do more than try."

Jack spent the rest of the day considering and rejecting any number of arguments to present to Annalise, everything from a declaration of undying love—which would leave her laughing herself silly—to the unvarnished truth, which he feared would not only leave him without a bride but without a nanny, as well.

Still… What choice did he have? He couldn't lie to her. He slanted her a calculating look as they put Isabella down for the night. He needed to find a way to convince his nanny to agree to a coldly logical, if highly offensive, proposal of marriage. But, how?

There was only one way. He'd tell her the truth and hope she'd been serious when she had claimed she'd do everything in her power to help Isabella. "We need to talk," he informed her, as soon as they finished tucking in his niece.

Annalise regarded him with a worried frown. "Is something wrong?"

He waited until they'd returned to the living room before explaining. "According to my lawyer, I need to marry immediately in order to retain custody of Isabella."

She stared in shock. "Oh, Jack, is he certain?"

"Very." He gave it to her straight. "Derek's held endless conversations with Mrs. Locke and various officials at CPS. Though they haven't come right out and said I must have a wife, they're extremely concerned that between my work schedule and Isabella's issues I'm not the best person to raise her. There's even been some discussion about placing her in a treatment facility. I won't let that happen, which means I present them with an acceptable wife who can give Isabella the attention she requires when I'm not available."

Annalise stared at him, stunned. "But…who are you going to marry? Does Isabella know her? Does she even like her?"

"She adores her."

That brought her up short. "Oh. Well… Well, that's good. I don't quite know what else to say," she added weakly. "Congratulations?"

"She hasn't accepted my offer yet."

Annalise stilled. "Wait a minute. Is this your way of telling me you no longer need my services?" A look of utter devastation swept across her face. "Is your wife— assuming she accepts your offer—is she going to take care of Isabella full-time?"

"Yes and no. I still need your services." Jack captured an escaped curl, one that tumbled halfway down

Annalise's back, and used it to reel her in. "Just in a slightly different capacity. I hope you'll consider it a promotion."

She was quick to put two and two together and come up with the requisite four. He watched shock etch a path across her elegant features. "You don't mean… You can't possibly think I—"

"Oh, but I can and I do. Ms. Stefano, I would very much appreciate it if you'd consider exchanging your position as nanny for one as my wife."

The couch caught her as her knees gave out. "You can't be serious."

"I'm dead serious. You may recall that I once told you that I'd do whatever it took to retain custody of Isabella. I also seem to remember you saying something quite similar. I know how serious I was when I made that statement. How serious were you?"

Pain burst to life in her eyes, burning with an intensity that seared straight through to his soul. He accepted it, didn't attempt to defend against it. He deserved to burn for what he was about to do. And no doubt he would.

"Oh, Jack," she whispered. "How could you?"

He captured Annalise's hands in his and drew her to her feet again. "As I've informed you more than once, I will do whatever it takes to retain custody of Isabella. But I will also do whatever you ask, give you whatever you demand, in exchange for your agreement to my plan. Please, Annalise. Marry me."

"No." She shook her head, the restlessness of her curls revealing the extent of her distress. "I can't. Anything but that."

"You're not already married?" Surely the PI would have uncovered evidence of a husband.

"No, of course not."

"And you claimed you weren't involved with anyone."

"I'm not."

"Then it's a moral objection."

She gazed at him helplessly. "You don't understand."

He cupped her face, drew her upward so their mouths met, colliding in soft passion, igniting sparks he didn't dare allow to catch fire. "Then explain it to me so I will."

It took her a moment to gather her wits enough to reply. "I adore Isabella, you know that. I'd do anything to ensure her recovery. But it would be wrong for me to agree to this, wrong on so many levels."

"It would be temporary, Annalise. Once CPS signs off, you're free to leave whenever you want. I'll make sure you're provided for."

"You mean money," she said bluntly. "You mean, you'll pay me to be your wife."

He'd never been accused of being a charming man, so he didn't bother trying to act the part. "I believe it's called alimony. But if you'd prefer to consider it wages—just like you're paid wages as Isabella's nanny—that's fine with me."

Her chin quivered. "Well, it's not fine with me."

"Because of the money or because you think it's wrong?"

"I don't know." Her voice broke and she covered her face with her hands. "I just don't know."

"Listen to me. I'm not paying you for sex. If you choose to share my bed, it's because we're attracted to each other physically. Consider this an old-fashioned, arranged marriage. I'm a man with a child in need of a wife and mother. You're a woman who has career goals which can more easily be met as a result of our marriage."

She bowed her head and he waited for endless moments while she weighed her options. Finally, she spoke, her voice whisper-soft. "My father once told me that being a single parent was the most difficult job he'd ever attempted. He never felt he'd done a proper job. The guilt ate him alive."

Jack forced himself to use her admission, hating himself even as he said the words. "I won't have that guilt or those concerns, if you marry me."

Her hands dropped to her sides and he could see tears welling into her eyes. "How long?" she whispered.

"Figure a couple of years, tops."

Pain ripped through her gaze again. "And then you expect me to simply walk away?"

"You were going to walk away regardless, remember?" he reminded her softly. "You agreed to a two-year contract while you pursued your master's, and then you were going to teach."

Her gaze strayed in the direction of Isabella's room and a hint of panic deepened the intense color of her irises, turning them to amber. "This job is just temporary." She said it almost as though reminding herself of that fact. "I know that."

"All I'm suggesting is that you spend those two years as my wife instead of Isabella's nanny."

For once her self-control deserted her, leaving her open and defenseless. "It won't be easy for her when I leave. We'll have grown attached."

"I won't cut you off. I lived that existence, remember?

I wouldn't do that to my niece any more than I'd do that to you. We'll make the transition as slowly and gently as possible. I won't prevent Isabella from seeing you whenever she wants."

To his concern, her tears escaped, streaking down her cheeks. "I wasn't supposed to become attached."

"We'll work it out. You have my word. But all this will be moot if CPS takes Isabella from me."

For some reason, reminding her of that fact got through as nothing else had. She bowed her head and scrubbed the heels of her palms across her cheeks. "She belongs with you," Annalise whispered. "She needs you. I want to do whatever I can to cement your relationship with her. That was the whole point in taking this job."

"Then marry me. I swear you won't regret it."

"Yes, I will." She looked at him. "I'll probably regret it for the rest of my life. But I don't think I have any choice."

The first time he'd seen her, he'd thought her eyes overflowed with ancient wisdom and intense vulnerability. Tonight they also reflected a gut-wrenching devastation. She'd suffered in the past, he sensed, even more than he had. He found he wanted to know her, to dig down through all that pain and uncover her most deeply guarded secrets. As though sensing the direction of his thoughts, shutters snapped closed over her expression and she took a step backward.

"Very well, Jack. I accept your proposal," she said. "I'll marry you and do whatever I can to convince CPS to give you full custody of your niece."

He closed the distance between them, unwilling to allow her to shut him out. They may have chosen to enter their marriage in a cold-blooded fashion, but it wouldn't continue that way. He slid his hands around her waist and tipped her into his arms. She fell against him, all feminine softness and delicious warmth.

"Don't," she pleaded. "It's too much for me to handle."

"Handle?" He lifted an eyebrow. "Or control?"

"Either. Both."

"Then let go. I'll take care of everything."

He lowered his head and took her mouth. It was a simple kiss, yet one that created an intense explosion of pleasure. She struggled for a brief instant, more against herself than him. And then she wrapped her arms around his neck and sank into the heat.

He wished he could claim that he was kissing her for Isabella's sake. But it would have been a lie. Selfishly, he wanted her for himself. Wanted it all. Wanted to right the world for his niece and try to give her some measure of happiness. And he wanted this woman in his bed, to wake beside her each morning. Endless Sundays filled with Family Bed stretched out before him, the mattress over-flowing with child and dog, husband and wife. It was a life he'd never known.

It was a life he'd do whatever was necessary to create.

Seven

The wedding ceremony took place two short days later. It had been a struggle to convince Annalise that a formal wedding gown and tux was an absolute necessity. When he suggested as much, she'd stared at him in horrified disbelief.

"You must be joking."

"Not even a little. Think it through logically, Annalise. This needs to be convincing. The unfortunate fact is, my name is going to generate news. Our marriage is going to generate news. I intend to use that to our advantage. I want every newspaper, rag and media outlet to splash lots of pictures of us in formal wedding gear. I want all the articles to rave about the whirlwind romance between the ruthless tycoon and the adorable nanny who won his heart."

She paled. "My father. He has no idea I even work for you. What am I supposed to tell him about our marriage?"

"Tell him it was love at first sight."

"He'll never believe that."

Jack's eyes narrowed. "Why not?"

"He just won't," she argued. "He knows me. He knows I'm not the type to fall for someone like you."

"Someone like me?" He wondered if he sounded as offended as he felt.

"Rich. Powerful." She regarded him impatiently, refusing to reflect even a modicum of nervousness at his reaction. "It's too fast. I'm a cautious type of person."

"What's really going on, Annalise?"

Her chin shot up. "You once told me your father taught you to do whatever it takes to achieve your goals. Well, mine taught me not to make rash decisions. Just as you've taken your family motto to heart, so have I. My father knows I wouldn't marry someone I've only known for a couple of weeks."

"Then you'll have to find a way to convince him that you've made an exception this one time."

She spun away, turning her back to him so he couldn't read her expression. "Dad agreed to captain a charter into the Caribbean for the summer. It may take a while to track down his boat and get word through to him. This is something that needs to be done in person. When he does get in touch, I'll do my best to convince him it's a love match, but I suggest we come up with an alternative story. Because I guarantee we're going to need one." She faced Jack once again. She'd gathered up her self-control and hid every scrap of emotion behind a calm expression. "How will your father react to our marriage?"

"I guess we'll find out when it hits the newspapers."

Her air of calm evaporated. "You're not going to tell him yourself?"

He bared his teeth in a grin. "Trust me. It'll be more fun if we do it my way."

He didn't give her time to argue the situation. Instead he dropped her and Isabella off at an exclusive little boutique with instructions to the proprietor to dress his bride-to-be in the most romantic gown available, and to make sure that his niece wore something that matched. The blank check he offered to make certain everything was completed on time ensured satisfaction on behalf of both parties. Much to his private amusement, he left Isabella glowing and Annalise glowering.

The next morning Derek had surprised him by showing up on his doorstep with Taye McClintock in tow.

"What the hell…?" Jack greeted his two best friends with a broad grin.

"Fine greeting *that* is," Taye griped. "I fly in all the way from Singapore—"

"I thought you were in Paris."

"That was last month." Taye paused, and his angel's face assumed a wicked expression. "Doesn't really matter, does it? I couldn't miss your wedding, could I?"

Jack spared Derek a brief glance. "You told him?" he asked.

"About the wedding, yes."

"About the reason for it, no," Taye contributed with the comfortable brazenness of an old friend. "But I can make a fairly good guess. And I'm guessing that it has something to do with Isabella and that ongoing fight you're having with CPS. Am I right?"

Jack started to agree, then for reasons he didn't dare analyze, he hesitated. "Isabella's part of the reason," he grudgingly admitted.

He couldn't explain his reluctance to go into the finer points, but suspected it had something to do with Annalise. Even though Derek had drawn up the prenup that spelled out every last detail of their forthcoming marriage, he felt a bone-deep urge to protect his bride from his two best friends, which struck him as vaguely ludicrous. Even so, he didn't want them to think she was marrying him for financial gain, mainly because he knew that wasn't her true reason. Like him, she was simply putting Isabella first, and that fact had to be protected and celebrated.

Derek's eyes narrowed. "Well, well. Who'd have thought?"

"Thought what?" Jack asked defensively.

"That the great Jack Mason has been brought to his knees by his nanny."

"Stuff it, Fletcher. It isn't like that."

"Huh." Taye appeared intrigued. "I think it's exactly like that. I don't doubt Isabella is a big part of the reason for the hasty marriage, but I think you have a thing for your bride-to-be." Before Jack could argue the point, he added, "But, the more interesting question is why the hell would she marry you, Mason?"

Jack felt his anger stir. "If that's the attitude you two are going to adopt, you can support me on my wedding day by taking off."

Taye chuckled. "Oh, yeah. I can definitely see the appeal now."

"You know…" Derek chimed in, "Taye raises an interesting point. I thought she was marrying you for the obvious reasons." He and Taye exchanged a knowing look and chimed in together, "Money."

"You don't think she is?" Taye asked.

"Guys—"

Derek shrugged. "I'm not so sure. When I met with her yesterday, I didn't read 'gold digger,' if you know what I mean."

Jack lost his patience. "That's because she isn't."

"Which brings us back to Taye's point." Derek lifted a sooty eyebrow. "Precisely why *is* she marrying you, Jack? For Isabella's sake? Fast work, that. What in the world would prompt a woman to sacrifice two years of her life for a child she barely knows?"

"Unless it was for money." Taye slipped the suggestion in again with far too much cynicism. But then, he had cause, as Jack knew all too well. A small case of been there/done that. "If it wasn't for the money…" Taye allowed the comment to trail off.

Jack shrugged uneasily. "She cares about Isabella, just as I do. She plans to get her master's over the next two years, and this will provide her with the perfect opportunity to set herself up for the future while helping Isabella."

It sounded weak, even to his ears. As though sensing his concern, his friends exchanged meaningful looks and deliberately changed the subject. Jack listened with half an ear. Now that he stopped to consider the matter, he had to admit that his plan to circumvent CPS had fallen into place with impressive ease. Granted, he'd always had a knack for getting his own way and making things come together to his advantage. This was just one more example of that, right? But he couldn't stop the question from fomenting in the back of his mind.

Why *had* Annalise really agreed to marry him? Was it for Isabella's sake, as she claimed? Or did she have a very different agenda?

The wedding itself took place late that afternoon in the serenity of his backyard, with Taye and Derek at his side. Annalise and Isabella walked together across the lawn toward him, hand in hand, while a string quartet played softly and a photographer worked discreetly in the background. His bride paused halfway to the makeshift altar and stooped to adjust his niece's hat. Dappled sunlight framed them, capturing them within a golden glow. And just like that, his heart stopped.

In that moment, his wife-to-be had to be the most beautiful woman he'd ever seen. Her hair had been pulled back from her face and allowed to tumble in an abandoned riot of curls down her back. Her wispy veil was anchored in place by a circlet of gold and silver, the craftsmanship of the leaf-and-diamond-encrusted piece drawing attention to her vivid eyes. Her ivory gown was perfectly suited to her tall, lean figure, the bodice fitted, the sweeping skirt complemented by a long flowing train. She looked like a fantasy creature from another era, and yet he knew just how real she was.

Isabella also wore an ivory gown with lace insets that matched the trim on Annalise's wedding gown. As far as

Jack was concerned, his niece resembled nothing more than a small angel. Instead of a veil, she wore an adorable wide-brimmed bonnet that framed her apple-cheeked face. Gold-tipped brown ringlets peeked out from the edges and bobbed in the gentle breeze. She beamed with excitement.

Instead of carrying her Nancy doll—something he rarely saw her without—she held a basket full of ivory and blush-pink roses. Then, much to his amusement, he noticed the doll perched at the base of the tree near where he was standing. He grinned. His adorable niece had dressed the doll for the occasion in a gown and bonnet that, even to his untrained eye, appeared identical to the one Isabella wore.

An instant later, the two joined him beneath the weighty fuchsia blossoms of a crape myrtle, and the minister spoke the traditional opening words that would soon join them together as husband and wife. The ceremony took no time at all. One minute he was a man who'd sworn never to take a wife. The next instant he was married to a woman who gazed at him with such a wealth of emotion that it took every ounce of self-control to keep himself from sweeping her into his arms and carrying her off to where they could spend the next twenty-four hours in uninterrupted seclusion.

That wasn't part of the plan, he reminded himself. This marriage had nothing to do with his new bride and everything to do with the child standing at their side. And he'd do well to remember that.

The minister cut across his thoughts, speaking the timeless words to conclude the ceremony. "You may now kiss the bride."

Jack didn't require any further prompting. He cupped Annalise's face and tilted it upward. Her veil fluttered like a flag of surrender, while her curls shivered in protest. But her eyes, those glorious honey-gold eyes, gazed at him with undisguised want. Was she even aware of how much they gave away? He doubted it. If she had the least suspicion, she'd have done everything in her power to tuck the truth away behind that serene facade she clung to with such determination. He hoped Taye and Derek didn't notice her expression. That was his, and his alone, something he refused to share with anyone else.

Slowly he lowered his head and captured her mouth. Her lips were softer than the roses in Isabella's basket and tasted of sunshine and warmth. He filled his hands with the glorious weight of her hair and the silken curls twined around his fingers, anchoring them together. She sighed against his mouth, the sound one of sweet surrender. If he could have gathered up all the various scents and sounds and tastes and preserved them for all time, he would have given his fortune to do so. But moments like this didn't last, and their kiss was no exception.

From the direction of the house a great booming *woof* broke the spell and the ground shook beneath their feet. Madam erupted from the kitchen and spilled onto the patio. Catching sight of the three of them, she gave her widest, most delighted grin and charged across the lawn.

The minister uttered a word that Jack was fairly certain couldn't be found anywhere in the Bible he held and scurried behind the nearest tree. The string quartet grabbed their instruments and made a beeline for the gate exiting from the yard, toppling chairs in their haste to escape. Taking a cue from them, the minister made a speedy departure, as well. Only Taye, Derek and the photographer didn't budge. While his friends burst into shouts of laughter, the photographer simply kept snapping pictures as the beast joined in the festivities.

With a thundering bark of excitement, Madam reared back and lunged at Jack, felling him with one blow. Unfortunately, his hands were still anchored in Annalise's hair. She tumbled onto the grass beside him, in a tangled heap of silk and lace. Isabella launched herself at Madam, attempting to pull the dog off them. It was like watching a kitten attempt to subdue a moose. She ended up riding Madam like a pony, her bonnet turned half sideways, her dainty skirts hitched to her knees.

Beside him he felt Annalise's shoulders tremble and a muffled sound escaped, something that sounded suspiciously like a sob. "Are you hurt?" He tried to find her through all the lace, satin and tulle. "Sweetheart, please don't cry. It'll be all right."

She managed to push aside her veil and a heavy swath of curls, revealing eyes swimming with tears. But they weren't tears of sorrow or anger. She tilted back her head and burst out laughing. His mouth twitched. And then he was laughing, too.

"So much for a traditional, elegant affair," he muttered.

"Considering ours isn't exactly a traditional family to begin with, it seems quite appropriate to me." Annalise attempted to twitch her skirts into place, skirts that had ridden up high enough to reveal—Lord preserve his sanity—a tantalizing glimpse of a sexy lace garter and a hint of creamy thigh. "And, I hate to disappoint you, but I'm not really cut out for elegant."

Jack leaned in and kissed her, a brief, thorough kiss that left her cheeks glowing and her eyes sparkling. "Do I look disappointed?" He shoved at the dog. "You two are now officially forbidden from sneaking Madam any more treats. She's getting so fat, she's practically waddling. And as for you two—" He shot his friends a glare that only served to increase their amusement. "Thanks for your help."

Derek offered a broad grin. "Anytime."

"My pleasure," Taye added.

Jack gained his feet and helped his bride to hers. With one stern command, he had Isabella removed from Madam's back and the dog sitting calmly at his heels. The photographer stepped forward.

"Would you like a few formal shots?" His mouth twitched. "I think all the informal poses are covered."

"But we're a mess," Annalise protested.

Jack shook his head. "You look beautiful."

Her amusement faded, replaced by concern. "You wanted this to look good," she explained in a low voice. "I know how important it is."

"It'll be fine. Here, just a few minor adjustments…"

Gravely, he finger-combed her unruly curls into a semblance of order—but not too orderly. He liked how they rampaged down her back in exuberant disregard. Then he centered the circlet on her brow and straightened her veil. He brushed the bits of grass and debris from her skirts and then nodded in satisfaction.

Isabella tugged at the tails of his tux and regarded him with a worried expression. "Your turn?" he asked gently.

At her solemn nod, he adjusted her bonnet, retying the ribbon beneath her dainty chin. He took his time removing every blade of grass from her skirts and then turned her in a slow circle. He nodded in satisfaction.

"Picture perfect," he said approvingly.

He winked at Annalise, surprised to see tears in her eyes again. This time they weren't from joy. There was bitter-sweet quality to her expression. Forcing a smile to her lips, she stepped forward to join them. The next half hour passed in a flurry of camera shots, some with Madam, some without. By the time they were finished, afternoon had faded into evening. Taye and Derek made their fare-wells, shaking Jack's hand with impressive formality, and kissing the bride with far too much enthusiasm.

"What next?" Annalise asked, once they were alone. She attempted to hide her nervousness with only limited success.

"Sara's prepared a formal dinner for us. I didn't think it wise to go to a hotel in case Isabella has a problem, so we'll be staying here. I've arranged for Mrs. Walters, just in case."

"Oh." To his intense fascination, color came and went in Annalise's face. "Is that really necessary?"

He held her gaze with his. "Without question."

She spared a brief glance in Isabella's direction. His niece was sitting beneath the tree with her Nancy doll. Madam hovered nearby. "I assumed my room would be adjacent to Isabella's and we wouldn't need Mrs. Walters any longer. After all, that's why I'm here."

"You're my wife now. You'll share my room."

Alarm flared to life. "Jack, this isn't a real marriage," she whispered. "We shouldn't be sharing a bedroom."

"This *is* a real marriage and we *will* share a bedroom *and* a bed." He caught her hand in his and drew her closer, keeping his voice low and reassuring. "CPS will notice if we're not living as husband and wife. So will Sara and Mrs. Walters. Even Isabella will sense that something's off. She's too young to understand what, but I want her to feel safe and secure on every level. Having two parents who act like parents will help her do that."

"We never discussed this aspect of our marriage," she protested. "I assumed—"

He smiled. "You assumed wrong."

"How far do you plan to take this?"

"Take what?"

She regarded him with naked apprehension. "Take our relationship."

"As far as you let me," he answered calmly.

"And if it's not as far as you'd like?" she shot back.

"You draw the line, Annalise, wherever you want it. The real question is—" he snatched a quick kiss that had Isabella giggling "—what will you do when one of us steps over it?"

Dinner that night passed on wings, filled with laughter and delicious food, while the conversation flowed with surprising ease. It wasn't until afterward that time slowed and stuttered. Much to Jack's amusement, Annalise did her best to drag the evening out. Still dressed in their wedding finery— at Isabella's insistence—they played games until bedtime, at which point Mrs. Walters came to collect his niece.

There was a moment of concern when she protested being escorted to bed, but Annalise stepped in with surprising firmness, and Isabella gave them a reluctant hug and kiss before retiring. The instant they were alone, Jack scooped his bride into his arms and carried her to their bedroom.

"This isn't necessary," she protested.

"Indulge me. It's not every day a man marries."

"Jack, please."

"I intend to please you."

He shouldered open the door to the master suite and stepped across the threshold before gently setting his bride on her feet. She stood, unmoving, examining her surrounds with a combination of curiosity and nervousness. He tried to see the room through her eyes.

The furnishings were sturdy pieces with clean, simple lines, stained to a deep golden sheen. They weren't overwhelmingly masculine, yet they were a bit stark. The candles helped, giving the room a warm, welcoming glow. Sara had provided a few romantic touches of her own by scattering a pathway of ivory and blush pink rose petals from the doorway to the bed, as well as across the duvet covering the mattress. Two crystal flutes stood at the ready alongside a bottle of champagne that rested in a bucket of ice. He studied the scene with an uncertainty he'd never experienced in the business world, concerned about Annalise's reaction.

For more years than Jack could count, he'd lived in an emotional wasteland. His father had been a cold bastard and still was, and he treated his son as little more than a commodity.

His mother had left him, though he didn't doubt it had been against her will. Not that it had changed those lonely years of his childhood. And Joanne...God, how he missed her. He'd survived her loss, of course. Barely. But ever since his parents' divorce, he'd learned to keep tight control over all aspects of his life. To hold people at a distance. He had no intention of ever being deserted, physically or emotionally, again.

As though sensing the dark direction of his thoughts, Annalise offered him a tentative smile. "This is lovely," she said. "Like something out of a fairy tale."

With the gift of one simple smile, warmth flooded through him and the cold and dark faded. This was his wife. His woman. It didn't matter how or why they'd come to exchange those vows. In this moment, they belonged together and he'd do whatever necessary to make this night one she never forgot.

"I'm glad you like it." He gestured toward the champagne. "Would you care for a glass?"

"I don't drink," she confessed.

He tilted his head to one side. Interesting, considering Derek's report. "Not at all?"

Her mouth twisted. "I had a small run-in with alcohol when I was sixteen. It didn't agree with me."

"This might be a good time to confess that I already know about the incident."

She froze. "How is that possible?" she asked carefully.

"I have an excellent PI. I had you checked out after I hired you. I believe he referred to it as a youthful indiscretion." He attempted to interpret her reaction to his confession with only limited success. "Are you angry that I had you investigated?"

She drew a cautious breath. "I guess that depends on why you did it."

He didn't hesitate. "I did it to make sure you were a safe and trustworthy person to have around Isabella."

She seemed to breathe a little easier. "Yes, of course. Since we're now married, I assume I checked out?"

"With that one exception." He still couldn't get a read on her and it puzzled him. "Did you want to talk about it?"

She shrugged and wandered across the room to the bow window that overlooked the courtyard where they'd been married. Her gown rustled in the silence of the room. She perched on the edge of the window seat, her skirts settling around her in a graceful arc. Moonlight cascaded through the beveled panes and bathed her in silver, while leaving her expression in shadow.

"There's not much to tell. I got drunk."

"It happens to most of us at one point or another. That's when we learn there's a reason for our current drinking laws." He approached her the way he would a wounded animal, slowly and with utmost caution. "Is there more to it than that?"

She sat without moving and simply stared at him. "To be honest, I don't remember a lot about that night."

A hideous suspicion took hold. "Did someone take advantage of you?" he asked sharply. "Were you drugged?"

"Not exactly. At least, I don't think so," she whispered. "But I did lose my virginity."

Fury consumed him. "You were taken advantage of. What sort of bastard—"

She stopped him with a quick shake of her head. "He was no more capable of making rational decisions than I was. Trust me, he paid a steep price for it."

"I gather your father found out?" Jack guessed.

"And his. It…wasn't pretty."

"I can imagine." It explained so much about her, especially her need to keep herself under such tight control. He closed the remaining distance between them and sat beside her, taking her hand in his. Her fingers were like ice. "Why are you telling me all this, Annalise?"

"Because you should know that I haven't had any alcohol since that night." She lifted her chin and met his gaze with a directness that sliced straight through to his soul. "And I haven't been with anyone sexually since then, either."

The air burned in his lungs and he slowly exhaled. "Never?"

"No."

"Because of one youthful mistake?"

She hesitated, as though considering the matter. "It didn't seem…wise. Plus, I've never really been tempted." Her eyes burned in the darkness. "Until now."

He stilled. He hadn't realized until that moment how desperately he wanted her. But he couldn't take her. Not after what she'd told him. He'd been so cold for so long, had looked forward to warming himself in the fiery heat of Annalise's desire. But he couldn't take advantage of her like that callous boy from her youth. He wouldn't.

He fought for control, fought for the cool, calm deliberation that had once come with such ease. "Annalise—"

"You're going to send me away, aren't you?"

"What?" He shook his head. "No, not away. Just to the room next door."

"I was hoping you'd say that."

He froze at her words. A stinging slap couldn't have made a harsher impact.

"Earlier today I was positive that was what I wanted," she went on. "But I realize now that was just fear speaking."

"Fear?"

"Last time I was sixteen," she explained. "I don't even remember the act itself. Now, the pain? That I recall. The embarrassment when it was over is a particularly vivid memory, not to mention the humiliation when the whispers started during the weeks and months afterward."

He regarded her with compassion. "I'm so sorry."

She shrugged. "I'm not sixteen anymore, Jack. My fear isn't logical. It's more of a wispy memory than a rational emotion." Her mouth curved into a smile full of feminine mystery and wry humor. "Don't you think it's past time I changed all that?"

"Are you certain?"

"I'm positive." She shifted to face him. "Please, Jack. Help me replace those other memories with new ones. Better ones. Special ones."

A short, harsh laugh was torn from him. "But no pressure, right?"

"I'm fairly certain most of the pressure is on me." She disengaged her hand from his and slid her fingers along his arm to his neck. She tugged gently. "Like this, for instance."

He bent closer and allowed her to take charge of the kiss. Her mouth slid across his as light as a whisper. She moved in again, a slow, thorough exploration. Then she slipped inward, giving him a taste of such sweetness that it proved headier than the most potent drink. She eased backward, breaking the contact.

"See what I mean? What if I do something wrong?"

He cleared his throat. "Not a chance."

"No? Why don't we test your theory."

She caught the edges of his bow tie and tugged. The scrap of silk slid away and drifted toward the floor, vanishing into the shadows. One by one she removed the studs from his shirt, placing each in turn on the windowsill in a neat line. His shirt parted. Did she have any clue what her slow, deliberate movements were doing to him? It took every ounce of willpower to allow her to take the lead, to follow instead of dictate.

Her hand slid into his and she turned it in order to have access to his cufflinks. First one and then the other joined his shirt studs on the windowsill. He wanted her hands on his skin, to feel them move on him. Warm him. Take him. Instead, she eased his shirt from his shoulders, not once actually touching him.

His breathing grew harsh. "Anna—"

"Shh. It'll be all right."

With a soft rustle of silk, she stood in front of him and gently lifted the circlet and veil from her head. She placed it on the window seat beside him. The tulle and lace flowed over the edge like a waterfall, a silent statement in the moonlit darkness. Never once taking her eyes from his, she lowered the side zip of the gown.

Inch by glorious inch, the beaded silk fell away, revealing skin beautifully gilded by their weeks at the beach. The gown slipped to the floor in a soft cloud of surrender. She stepped free of it, as well as her voluminous petticoats, and stood before him in a lacy bustier. He leaned back against the coolness of the window with a groan. He'd caught a glimpse of her stockings and garter when Madam had knocked them to the ground, but it hadn't prepared him for this.

"Let me do the rest," he demanded.

He didn't wait for her agreement, but erupted from the window seat. Gathering her into his arms, he kissed her. Claimed her. Told her without words how beautiful he found her. And then he journeyed downward, worshipping her with mouth and tongue and teeth.

Turning her so her back was to him, he swept the ebony tumble of curls over her shoulder and unhooked her bustier, exposing the elegant sweep of her spine. He traced his fingertip from the back of her neck down to the dip just above her buttocks. Teasing her with the lightest of caresses, he finished undressing her until she stood before him clad only in the silvery rays pouring in through the window. She lifted her arms and shook her hair free. The heavy ringlets cascaded toward her waist. Then she turned ever so slightly and looked at him over her shoulder. He could just make out the sweet curve of her breast.

"Please, Jack," she whispered. "Make love to me."

Eight

Without a word, Jack swept Annalise into his arms and carried her to the petal-strewn bed. He lowered her to the satin duvet, the rich ruby color a perfect complement to her hair and skin.

"Nudity becomes you, wife."

She laughed softly, just a hint of shyness evident in the deepening color that swept across her cheekbones. "I suspect it would become you, as well." She lifted an eyebrow. "Or were you going to make love to me with your pants on?"

Following her example, he removed his remaining clothing, lingering over the process the same way she had, despite the urgency to simply finish the job and get down to business. He wanted to go slow, to ease toward the moment when they became one. To build the memories one blistering touch at a time.

When he finished stripping, she moistened her lips and lifted up onto her elbows. "Jack...I think I should warn you that I've just started birth control but it's not effective yet. I guess I should have said something sooner."

"I'll take care of everything."

He made short work of the matter and then joined her on the bed. Candlelight flickered across her, gleaming on the sweet, rounded curves of her body and chasing darkness into the dips and valleys. He traced his index finger across the dusky tip of her breast, watching the nipple bead beneath the light caress.

"What should I do?" Annalise asked.

"Whatever you feel like. Nothing you do will be wrong."

"Show me how," she insisted. "Show me what you like."

Jack took her hands in his and guided them to his chest, pressed them there, close to his heart. Her fingertips danced across his flesh. Where once there was ice, each lingering stroke melted the coldness, turned it to warmth. Then to heat. He sank backward and gave himself up to her. Her undisguised pleasure and curiosity were a joy to witness. Little by little her inhibitions fell away and her stroking touch grew bolder.

She cupped him, then measured his length and width with her fingers and he closed his eyes, fighting to retain some vestige of control. This was a first for her, he reminded himself—her first memory of being with a man, of having free rein to indulge the sensuous side of her nature and explore to her heart's content—and he wanted it to be perfect. When she'd driven him as far as he could handle, he gathered her up and flipped her onto her back, caging her within his arms.

"Jack," Annalise whispered, her voice rife with emotion. "Make love to me."

He couldn't help but smile. "I'm working on it."

A soft laugh escaped. "Work faster."

Jack didn't listen. He took his time, not wanting to alarm her or do anything that might remind her of that long-ago event. He needn't have worried. With each touch she loosened, opening more and more of herself, both physically and emotionally. Shards of moonlight caught in her eyes, allowing him to witness her intense pleasure.

He cupped her breasts, filling his hands with the delicious weight of them while he teased the tips into excited buds. Then he tasted, reveling in the unique flavor of her. He felt the pounding of her heart against his cheek and the swift burst of her breath ruffling his hair. Sliding lower, he delved across the tensed muscles of her abdomen to the protected delta below. Cautiously, he drifted inward. Her small gasp of pleasure was all the encouragement he needed. He pleasured her until he felt the early ripples of impending climax. Only then did he pull back and settle himself between her thighs.

Cupping her bottom, he lifted her and slowly surged inward. Her hips shifted to meet his, fighting to find the appropriate rhythm. It took her only a moment to discover it. And then instinct kicked in and she followed the beat. Moved with it. Drove it. Caught within her rapture, she was sheer radiance. She rode them toward a peak, further and higher than anything he'd thought possible. They teetered there for an endless moment before the first tiny convulsions shimmered through them. And then they shattered.

As he flew apart Jack realized that the cold had disappeared, replaced by a raging fire he didn't think could ever be doused. Annalise had done that to him. Had done that *for* him. Somehow, in some strange, unfathomable way, she'd freed him from the arctic wasteland in which he'd been living and brought him into the sun's balmy light.

"Are you all right?" Jack asked much, much later.

Annalise stirred against him. "I think so."

Her tentative comment alarmed him and he rolled over. Cupping her chin, he lifted it just enough so that the moonlight revealed her expression. Her mouth curved in a tremulous smile and a melting softness burnished her gaze. But he could also see a vague bewilderment that tautened her muscles and gave him a worrying sense of uneasiness.

"I'm sorry if it wasn't all you hoped it would be," he said. "It gets better with practice, I promise."

"I can't believe that's possible," she retorted with satisfying speed. She feathered a string of kisses across his chest. "That part was amazing. Incredible. And there's absolutely no comparison between last time and this."

Relief crashed over him. "I would hope not." He gathered up fistfuls of her hair so she had no choice but to look at him. "If that's not the problem, then what is?"

"It's not a problem, exactly."

"But…?"

She caught her lower lip between her teeth. For some reason the small gesture threatened to send him straight over the edge again. He wanted *his* teeth on that lip. Wanted to give it a small nip and tug. And then he wanted to soothe it, kiss it endlessly while he sank into her honeyed mouth. Before he could act, Annalise spoke again.

"Will it be like that every time?"

"Like that...good?" he asked cautiously.

"No, not good." His heart stopped in his chest, until she added, "That was incredible. That was amazing. That was..." She shook her head. "That was beyond belief. I had no idea. None."

"Your previous experience isn't a fair basis for comparison," he explained gently. He waited for her to absorb that. Once she did, his smile turned wicked. "In my opinion, we need more practice in order to improve."

Her eyes widened. "Improve? On *that?*" She lit up. "Are you serious?"

He didn't bother to respond. There was a far more satisfying way to answer her question. He applied himself to the task with all due diligence. He was going to enjoy married life, he decided. He was going to enjoy married life a *lot.*

The next few weeks passed in a blissful haze, overflowing with days of constant laughter, a heartwarmingly joyous Isabella and a fat and sassy Madam. And the nights were even fuller, each moment spent in Annalise's arms richer and more life-affirming than the one before. The changes served to solidify Jack's certainty that he'd done the right thing, both for his niece as well as for himself. Even Mrs. Locke cooperated, delaying her final visit so that the new family had an opportunity to settle into a comfortable routine.

Though Annalise continued to fuss because her father remained out of touch and she'd been unable to tell him about their marriage, Jack's father had given his opinion in no uncertain terms.

"Have you lost your mind?" Jonathan Mason demanded. "You married your nanny? What were you thinking?"

"Wasn't your second wife the au pair of one of your business associates?" Jack shot back. "Or was that wife number three? To be honest, I've lost track."

"I believe she was my third mistake," his father retorted. "I paid through the nose to escape that noose. At least tell me you had that woman sign a prenuptial agreement."

Defensiveness swept through Jack without thought or intention, an instinctive reaction to what he perceived on a gut level as an attack on one of his. His employee. His nanny. *His wife.* He couldn't explain when Annalise had come to mean so much to him, or even why. It wasn't their marriage alone, or the fact that she now shared his bed. It was more than that. Little by little she'd eased past his barriers and infiltrated every aspect of his life. Warmed it. Healed it. She wasn't just his employee, despite what their prenup might say. She was his wife, and he would defend her against everyone and everything, including his father.

"*That woman* has a name. She's Annalise Mason," Jack replied in a hard voice. "And you will treat her with the respect my wife deserves. Are we clear?"

To his surprise, his father apologized. "Call me once the two of you are past the honeymoon period. Suze and I will have you over for dinner. And, Jack…?" He paused, his hesitation out of character for a man so decisive. "One of the few comforts I've had these past few months is knowing that Joanne and I were able to rebuild our relationship before she died. I made a lot of mistakes when you were young. Terrible mistakes that I'd give anything to undo. Would you be willing… Do you think we—" He broke off abruptly.

Jack forced himself to pick up the ball. "Could start over?"

There was another long pause, and then: "I know I don't deserve it," Jonathan said in a rough undertone. "But I want to have my son and granddaughter in my life again. Your wife, as well, if you're willing."

For some reason, picturing Annalise's face stayed Jack's cold refusal. She would want him to take the proffered olive branch, as would Joanne. If his father could humble his pride—something Jack would have once thought an impossibility—so could he. "I'd like that, Dad. We'll call you and set a date."

"Thanks, Jack." Uncharacteristic emotion trembled in Jonathan's voice. "Anytime you're free. Anytime at all will be fine with us."

The weeks flowed by after that, and Family Bed became a Sunday morning staple. Little by little they accumulated furnishings that would better accommodate both a five-year-old and a massive klutz of a dog. Madam, in particular, reveled in her new home, her coat gleaming with health, while the regular nutritional meals kept her nicely filled out.

Or so he thought until Isabella woke them in the early

morning hours with a piercing shriek. He was out of bed a split second before Annalise and raced flat out toward his niece's bedroom. She wasn't there. The covers of her bed were thrown back and Isabella was nowhere to be seen. Jack's heart began to pound in dread.

"Where is she?" Annalise said, slamming into him as she darted into the room. "What's happened?"

Her question was answered by another scream, coming from the direction of the playroom. The two of them flew down the hallway. It took him a minute to find his niece. He finally discovered Isabella and Madam inside the giant playhouse that occupied one end of the room. The dog lay on her side, straining, while his niece frantically petted her. She raised a tear-stained face to Jack and held out her arms. He scooped her up, checking her desperately for any sign of injury.

"What's wrong, Baby Belle?" he murmured. "Where are you hurt?"

"Jack, it's not Isabella. It's Madam. Look." A wet bundle of fur was tucked close to the dog. Madam licked the pup clean and nosed it toward her belly where it latched onto a nipple. Annalise stooped beside Jack and Isabella. "Don't cry, Isabella. Madam isn't hurt. She's having babies."

The change in his niece was instantaneous. Her eyes grew huge and a brilliant smile lit her face. She gave a little bounce that Jack swiftly stilled. "We need to be quiet. It's a lot of hard work to have puppies."

"I guess this explains why she was putting on so much weight," Annalise murmured, as Madam whelped another pup.

"It never occurred to me to ask the vet if she'd been spayed," Jack replied. "We'll get that taken care of as soon as the pups are weaned."

Over the next several hours, six puppies made their way into the world while Isabella looked on, wide-eyed and trembling with happiness.

"What are we going to do with all these dogs?" Annalise asked in dismay. "One Madam is wonderful. But six more…"

"Six more Madam-sized dogs are impossible, especially if these little guys are as klutzy as their mother." He released a gusty sigh. "I'll put the word out. We'll find good homes for them."

Isabella yanked on his arm, shaking her head.

"You want to keep them all, don't you, sweetie?"

She nodded emphatically.

He hesitated, wondering how he could explain it in terms she'd understand. "Do you remember your mommy and daddy telling you about the day they adopted you?" He could tell from her expression that she did. "They adopted you because the lady who gave birth to you…like Madam gave birth to all these puppies…couldn't take care of you, even though I'm sure she wanted to. Your birth mommy did a wonderful thing. She found someone who would love you and give you a safe home because she wasn't able to. In a few weeks, when these puppies are ready to be out on their own, Madam won't be able to take care of so many. It's our job to find good mommies and daddies for all of Madam's puppies, people who will love them and keep them safe. Families with children like you who need their own Madam. Do you understand?"

He could tell Isabella wasn't happy about it, but she nodded reluctantly. He tossed a relieved smile over his shoulder in Annalise's direction, shocked to see the tears streaking down her cheeks.

Fortunately, Isabella was so preoccupied with the puppies, she didn't notice. With an inarticulate murmur, Annalise escaped the intimate circle and distanced herself from them. Jack followed. Some instinct warned that his wife was hanging on by a mere thread, and, without a word, he pulled her into his arms.

"Honey, what's wrong?"

She simply shook her head without responding.

To his relief, Sara and Brett chose that moment to show up. They took in the situation in one glance. "Got a mite worried when no one appeared for breakfast." Sara spoke in an undertone. "Brett had a strong suspicion about what was going on. Mentioned just last night that Madam looked a bit plumper than a few weeks of decent meals could explain."

"I was going to give you the heads-up today," Brett added. "But I see Madam decided to break the news to you herself."

"That she did. Maybe if I'd had more experience with dogs I'd have caught on sooner." Jack spared his wife a swift glance. She continued to cling to him, her face buried in his shoulder. "Would the two of you mind keeping an eye on Isabella? Annalise isn't feeling well and I'd like to take her back to bed."

"Oh, dear," Sara said in concern. "Would it help if I fixed a pot of tea or a bite of toast?"

"I'll let you know," Jack assured. "I suspect Isabella will stay glued to Madam's side for the next few hours, so I don't think she'll be any trouble. Call on the house phone if you need me."

With that, he wrapped an arm around Annalise's waist and ushered her from the room. The second they entered the master suite, she turned and curled into him. His arms closed around her, holding her tight. He felt the shudders ripping through her and caught the small gasping sounds. He waited out the storm, trying to pinpoint what had set her off. Something about the birth of the dogs was all he could come up with.

At long last, she pulled free of his hold. "You can let me go now," she insisted. "I'm sorry to cause such a ridiculous scene."

He tipped up her chin and regarded her in naked concern. "Tell me what's wrong. Is it the puppies? Did they stir old memories of some kind?"

She waved that aside. "Not exactly. I don't know why I reacted in such a silly way. What you told Isabella…" She gave an embarrassed shrug. "I'm sorry. For some reason, it made me cry."

Aw, hell. "You do understand that we can't keep the puppies?" Just the thought of six more dogs as large as Madam rampaging through the house left him weak at the knees. "We can't give that many dogs the time and attention they deserve. We'd be doing them a disservice."

She lifted her tear-streaked face to his. "No, no. I understand that part."

"I'll find good homes for them. The best. I have a lot of contacts in both the local community and the business world. We'll find people whose homes and lifestyles are well suited for a large dog."

"I know you will. It's not that."

Another possibility occurred to him. "Was it what I said about Isabella's adoption?" he asked uneasily. "Joanne and Paul were very open with her about the subject, very matter-of-fact about it. They wanted her to understand the truth from an early age so there wouldn't be any unpleasant shocks later on in life. Not that they were cold-blooded about it," he hastened to add. "They were two of the most loving individuals I've ever known, and their daughter was at the center of that love."

"Everything that's happened to her just seems so unfair."

He hadn't quite gotten to the root of the problem and found himself floundering a bit in his attempt to pin it down. "That won't be an issue for her anymore," he reassured. "Not now that she has the two of us."

"But what about Mrs. Locke and CPS?"

Jack lifted Annalise's face and thumbed the remaining traces of tears from her cheeks. "They don't stand a chance against us."

A smile splashed across her face like sunshine following a cloudburst. It brightened her eyes, banishing the darkness. "How could I forget? You're Jack Mason. No one can stop a Mason once he makes up his mind to accomplish something."

He leaned in until they were almost nose to nose. "In case you've forgotten, you're a Mason now, too."

Her smile faded. "A temporary Mason," she corrected softly.

That did it. He caught hold of the lapels of her robe and reeled her in. Her warmth collided with his, her soft curves locking with stunning perfection against his hard-cut angles. He released her robe and sank his fingers into the mass of inky ringlets spilling down her back. They wrapped around him in joyous abandon, allowing him to anchor her close.

"Did it feel temporary last night when we made love?" he demanded. "Does it feel temporary when you're in my arms like this?"

He could read her uncertainty. "You know that's not what we agreed—" she began.

His mouth tightened. "I'm changing the terms of our agreement."

He didn't give her an opportunity to reply, stopping the incipient argument with a kiss. He kissed her with a passion that had little to do with Isabella and everything to do with his own selfish desires. Her reaction was instantaneous. She returned his embrace with an urgency that stole every thought but one. To lose himself in her. To join them in a way that would defy any and all attempts to force them apart. To bind and blend and mate one unto the other until two became one.

She must have felt something similar because she looked up at him and the longing in her eyes nearly unmanned him. "Please, Jack. Make love to me."

A final rational thought kept him from doing just that. "You're exhausted."

She shook her head. "Not that exhausted. Never that exhausted."

He couldn't resist. In all honesty, he didn't want to. He tugged at the belt anchoring her robe. It parted, revealing the paper-thin nightgown beneath. A brush of his hands sent the robe fluttering around their feet in a pool of vibrant aqua silk. Next he captured the two straps of her night-gown and drew them down her shoulders, baring her desire as he bared her. His clothing followed until all that remained between them was pure desire, a white-hot blaze that drove them toward the bed.

She sank into the mattress and lifted her arms to him, offering herself like some pagan goddess. He didn't hesitate. He claimed what she gave so willingly, branding her with his weight and desperate urgency. He found her breasts and claimed those as well, teasing them to rigid-ness with his teeth and tongue. Her arms enfolded him, pulling him closer still. And he sank into her heat, feeling the lap of it surround him, hearing the roar of it burning in his ears.

"I need this. I don't think I can survive without it. Not anymore."

"I'm here," she whispered in her siren's song. "I'm not going anywhere."

"No, you're not." Somehow it didn't come out as an agreement, but more as a warning. "You're mine now, and I protect and hold what's mine."

Amusement glittered in her witch gold eyes. "We're not possessive, are we?"

"Only with some things." He swept a hand from breast to thigh. *Mine,* his touch seemed to say. He couldn't seem to help it, his need to cleave to her had grown beyond his capacity to control. He tried to explain how he felt, fumbling over the unfamiliar words. "Now that I've found you, I don't want to lose you. Now that I've had you, I don't think I can go back to how it was before you were part of my life."

"Then don't."

There was so much more he longed to say. To explain. But he no longer possessed the ability. So he told her without words. He knew what she liked, what brought her the most pleasure. And he gave it to her. Each caress built, one on the other, and she clung to him as though she'd never let him go.

She trembled beneath his questing hand—the elegant line of her spine, the velveteen swell of her breast, the sweet curve of her thigh. He cupped the downy center of her passion, feeling the gathering tension and delicate quaking of a woman teetering on the verge. He drew her legs around his waist and drove slowly into her, losing himself in the delicious warmth. Her sigh of pleasure slid over him, sank deep inside to the very core of him, to that final place of coldness. With each ebb and flow, they moved ever closer. The eruption came, more powerful and overwhelming than any before.

He took her. Made her his. Let go of the final fragments of his control. When he did, the last sliver of ice melted. And in its place came love, a love he'd never anticipated or asked for. Never even thought possible.

But come it did.

Nine

Naturally, Mrs. Locke chose the worst possible time to arrive on their doorstep, descending six weeks after the birth of the puppies.

The morning started out perfectly, with Annalise in his arms still soft and trembling from the aftermath of their lovemaking. She wrapped him up in a tangle of arms and legs that held him close to the urgent beat of her heart. Though she never actually said the words, every lingering touch, every golden look, every whispered sigh, spoke of love.

Somehow she'd created a magical circle, a bountiful place more comfortable and spacious and exquisite than all the rooms in his family home combined. And in that circle she'd seeded a fertile garden where Isabella thrived. It was a place where he could loosen his grip on the chains of his restraint and reserve and simply let go. In that magical place, Madam romped and Isabella would soon speak and he belonged as he'd never belonged before.

For the first time, Jack felt hope. For the first time in more years than he could count, he'd found his way home, and he had no intention of ever losing his way again. He thrust his fingers deep into Annalise's silken curls and combed them back from her face. She smiled up at him, the words he longed to hear glittering in the brilliance of her eyes and trembling on the rose-petal softness of her lips, hovering so close he could practically hear the whisper of them on each exhalation of her breath. And yet, they remained unspoken.

It was time to take matters into his own hands.

"I want to change the parameters of our agreement," he stated bluntly.

Confusion clouded her gaze and a wariness settled over her. "You what?"

"I want to fire you."

She shoved at his chest and sat up, snatching the sheet to her chest. "Fire me," she repeated in patent disbelief. "Have you lost your mind? What about Isabella? What about CPS?"

His mouth set into a stubborn line. He reached beneath the covers and caught one silken bare leg. He gave it a sharp tug, sending her sliding back under him. "I want our marriage to be real. I want a wife. A permanent one, not a temp who's going to leave us in two years. Isabella needs a mother, and not any mother. She needs you."

For a brief instant she burned with happiness. The next instant it winked out of existence. "I can't promise you that," she stated categorically.

Had he misread her feelings? A rare panic swept through him and he clamped down on it, replacing it with every bit of strength and business acumen that he typically brought to the table whenever a deal threatened to go sour. He could handle Annalise. He'd handle her the same way he handled an unruly business transaction. He'd devastate her defenses with logic, boxing her in until she had nowhere to go other than straight into his arms.

"What's wrong with making our marriage a real one?" he demanded. "Aren't you happy?"

"I'm happier than I've ever been in my life," she conceded. "But our relationship is still new and untested. You don't know everything about me."

He settled on top of her, pressing her into the mattress. "That's the nice part about marriage. You have all those years to spend unwrapping each and every layer."

If anything his comment alarmed her even more. So much for boxing her in. One glimpse of the opening and she shied away. "What if you don't like what you find when all the wrapping paper's off?"

Was she kidding? "That's not possible," he stated quite definitely.

"Yes, Jack. It is." She moistened her lips and he could see her agile mind marshalling her counterarguments. What he didn't understand was why she found it necessary. "What happens if CPS decides to remove Isabella?"

Did she have any doubt? "We fight to get her back," he answered promptly. "To prove to them—no matter how long it takes—that we love her and will do whatever we must to give her the best possible home."

A small frown formed between her brows. "I mean…

What happens to us? The entire reason we married was to provide your niece with a stable home. But what happens to our marriage if Isabella isn't in the picture?"

"Do you think I'll stop wanting you?"

"Yes," she replied bluntly.

He shook his head. "That won't happen."

Her breath caught and she searched his face. "Are you serious? If they took Isabella away, you'd want our marriage to continue?"

"Isn't that what you want, too?"

He could see the naked longing in her gaze, but it was tempered with caution…and something else. Something that had haunted her from the first time they'd met. Before she could reply, the door banged open and Isabella charged into the room with Madam. A tumble of puppies followed close behind. Jack glanced over his shoulder and stopped the entire menagerie in their tracks.

"That is not the proper way to enter a bedroom," he informed her in no uncertain terms. "Please take Madam and the puppies and go outside. Knock on the door and wait until you're invited in before opening the door. Got it?"

His niece stood there, debating whether to turn stubborn or to obey. To his relief, she spun around and shoved at Madam until the dog trotted out of the room. Then she herded the puppies. The instant the door shut behind them, Jack escaped the bed and tossed a nightgown in Annalise's direction while he donned a pair of drawstring pants.

"I believe you still owe me an answer to my question," he reminded his wife.

"There's no time to discuss it right now," she informed him.

"Tonight, then?"

She worried at that for a minute before releasing a gusty sigh and nodding. "Okay, fine. We'll talk about it again tonight."

For some reason, she didn't look happy about it, and a wintry coldness swept through him. He didn't know what secrets she kept, but he refused to lose the world she'd built for all of them. He wouldn't be forced from paradise now that he'd finally found it.

A soft knock sounded at the door of the bedroom, putting an end to the conversation. He opened the door to Isabella who, much to his delight, threw herself into his arms. Madam followed with matronly dignity, which the barking, squabbling puppies spoiled by nipping at her heels and jumping at her tail.

In the six weeks since their birth, they'd put on size and weight at an impressive rate. The vet had been very pleased with their progress during their last checkup and pronounced dame and puppies in excellent health. Jack had already promised three of the pups to eager families of business associates, and he doubted he'd have much difficulty placing the others. He hadn't told Isabella or Annalise, yet, but he'd already decided that they were going to keep the smallest of the six, a male who made up for his status as runt with a personality bigger than the other five combined. This one, in particular, had won all their hearts. He would also make a good companion dog for Madam.

The next hour passed in a rush as everyone pitched in to gather up the puppies and return them to the room in which they remained penned whenever they couldn't be watched. After dressing, he, Annalise and Isabella shared their ritual family breakfast before he headed off to the office. If a hint of stiltedness existed between husband and wife, it couldn't be helped. Whatever the cause, tonight would correct the situation. The instant they finished eating, his niece gave him a farewell kiss then made a beeline for the stairs leading to the bedrooms…and the dogs.

Jack turned to Annalise and held her gaze, forcing himself to use a hint of the ferocity that had helped him turn a small, startup import/export business into a multi-billion-dollar international success story. He aimed it straight in the direction of a lanky, golden-eyed ex-nanny with intoxicating kisses and a heart even larger than his bank account.

"Tonight," he reminded his wife. "Cards on the table." He didn't phrase it as a question.

She gave a steadfast nod. "I told you we would. But, Jack—" Her voice held an unmistakable warning. "You might not like the hand I deal you."

The doorbell sounded in the distance and his mouth twisted. "I may surprise you."

He dropped a swift kiss on his wife's mouth before going to answer the imperious summons. He opened the door, less than pleased to discover the Wicked Witch of all four compass points, plus several in between standing on his welcome mat. Or in her case, his unwelcome mat.

"Mrs. Locke."

"Mr. Mason."

He planted himself between her and his home and eyed the birdlike woman. He'd learned during their first meeting

just how deceptive appearances could be. She barely
reached the middle of his chest and appeared fragile
enough for an errant breeze to snap in two. But that was
as much a lie as the cheerful, robin's-egg-blue eyes that
blinked sweetly from behind the lenses of her rimless
spectacles. She offered a wide, guileless smile that didn't
fool him for one little minute. She was a witch cloaked in
the plumage of an innocent sparrow.

The two squared off against each other and Jack
launched the first volley. "Did we have an appointment
you forgot to arrange?" he asked mildly.

She looked entirely too pleased with herself which put
him on instant alert. "It's called an unannounced home
inspection."

"That's funny. According to my lawyer, you were
supposed to call and arrange a convenient time for a visit."

"That would have defeated the entire point of the 'unannounced' portion of the inspection." She folded her twig
arms across her nonexistent bosom. "Are you going to let
me in, or are you going to continue looming there in that
threatening manner?"

He narrowed his eyes at her phrasing. She narrowed
hers right back at him. He wasn't sure how the stalemate
might have ended if it hadn't been for Isabella charging
toward him with a shriek. Her fingers fluttered in a gesture
she used to alert them to a problem with the puppies. Then
she yanked on his suit coat.

He turned to Mrs. Locke. "You'll have to leave. We
have an emergency on our hands. That takes precedence
over everything else."

She stiffened and yanked out a cell phone from the

purse tucked beneath her arm with impressive speed. "Shall I call 9-1-1?" she asked crisply.

"That won't be necessary. It's a—" he hesitated "—dog emergency."

Mrs. Locke's brows climbed skyward. "A dog emergency is not an emergency I recognize," she informed him in a wintry tone. "The inspection will continue."

Isabella yanked harder at his suit coat and he rested his hand on her head in gentle reassurance. Damn it to hell. Why now, of all days? He regarded Mrs. Locke with a sour expression and gave her two options. "In that case, you may wait here until I'm available, or grace us with your presence at a more convenient time."

"I'll stay," she stated in tones as implacable as his own.

"Jack? Red alert. The puppies are on the loose." Annalise charged into the hallway and skidded to a halt. "Oh, we have guests."

Jack grimaced. This grew more complicated by the minute. He'd wanted time to prep Annalise before the two women met. "Mrs. Locke is *not* a guest. She's here for an inspection."

"Mrs. Locke?" To his disgust a broad, welcoming smile swept across his wife's face. "Isabella's Mrs. Locke?"

The caseworker inclined her head. "And I assume you're Mrs. Mason?"

"Oh, please. Call me Annalise." She held out her hand. "I'm afraid we have a bit of a family emergency going on here."

"So, I understand. Something to do with dogs?"

Isabella made a frantic noise and Jack interrupted. "Which we need to take care of immediately. Annalise, ask

Sara and Brett to scour the first floor. I'll take the bedrooms. You and Isabella see if anyone's found their way to the third level. Since this isn't a scheduled appointment, Mrs. Locke can return at a more convenient time."

His beautiful, sexy, loyal wife fluttered her lashes at him and turned traitor in the blink of an eye. "I'll give Sara and Brett the heads-up while you and Isabella check the bedrooms. Mrs. Locke and I will be having some iced tea out on the patio. Once everyone's rounded up, you can join us there."

"Excellent suggestion," Mrs. Locked concurred. "I wanted some private time with your wife, anyway."

"I— You—"

Annalise smiled in satisfaction. "It's a plan. I'll call your office and warn them you're running behind." She fished her cell phone out of her pocket and hit a preprogrammed button. "Mary, it's Annalise. Jack's going to be late again. What? Oh, yes, of course. The pups on their usual rampage. Expect him when you see him."

Isabella didn't give him an opportunity to argue further. Grabbing his hand, she literally towed him in the direction of the steps. The last view he had of his double-crossing wife was her saucy backside vanishing in the direction of the kitchen, accompanied by the smirking Wicked Witch, her broomstick slung over one shoulder.

This was not good. Not good at all. He'd planned to be there the first time Annalise and Locke spoke, to run interference in case they hit any snags. Based on the smug look the caseworker shot him, she'd known it and took great delight in outmaneuvering him. Not that she'd actually

been the one to make mincemeat of his plan. He could lay
that delightful screwup squarely on his wife.

It took thirty nerve-racking minutes to round up five of
the mischievous puppies and return them to the gated
bedroom that was their "nest." Isabella remained with
them while he went in search of the last one, the runt of
the litter. He found Mister Mayhem, as he'd begun to refer
to the dog, on the verge of sneaking out the kitchen door.
He scooped up the wriggling bundle of energy before the
pup could make good his escape.

From the direction of the patio, he caught the distinctive
sound of feminine laughter. He stood there, literally frozen
in disbelief. That couldn't possibly be Mrs. Locke laughing.
Not the witch herself. He had no idea how Annalise
managed to charm the woman, but he could only thank God
it had happened. Then he immediately shook his head.

He did know how his wife had pulled it off. He'd
watched her do it with him and Isabella, and every other
person she met. She had a knack about her, a natural
charm. No, even that wasn't quite right. She welcomed
people in. Even though she'd been hurt, she hadn't allowed
past events to close her down the way he had. She continued to open herself to others, despite the fact that she
might get hurt again. The vulnerability remained, reflected
in those magnificent eyes of hers. But she gave of herself,
anyway.

The laughter had faded and he heard Mrs. Locke say,
"So, tell me the truth, Annalise. Why did you marry your
husband?"

Jack didn't think he could have moved if Doomsday
itself were unfolding at his feet. Everything within him

strained to hear the answer. But when it came, it was spoken so softly he couldn't catch the words he longed to hear.

He erupted from the kitchen onto the patio, the pup still cradled in his hands. He didn't know what he'd hoped, perhaps to discover Annalise's response still lingering on the summer breeze. Maybe to read it in her expression or glittering like gold dust in her eyes. Instead, her head swiveled in his direction and she simply smiled. Just that. A smile that made his heart stand still and left him more helpless and out of control than he'd ever been in his entire life.

"I assume that's the last straggler? Mayhem?" she asked. "Isn't that what you've dubbed him?"

"Mister Mayhem," he muttered.

"Would you like a glass of sweetened tea?"

The prosaic question ripped him to shreds. It took every ounce of willpower to hold himself in check, when what he wanted more than anything was to tip Locke out of his patio chair and chuck her onto the street so that he could demand his wife repeat to him whatever she'd told the caseworker. He wanted—*needed*—to hear why she'd married him. To know once and for all whether she'd done it just for Isabella or if maybe, just maybe, she'd believed those vows she'd spoken right here in his backyard.

To love, honor and cherish…

Annalise tilted her head to one side and a wealth of curls tumbled across her shoulder. "Tea?" she prompted again in open amusement.

"Thanks, I'd love some." He crossed to her side and dropped a kiss on the top of her head. "Everything okay?"

"Everything's fine."

He took a seat with Mayhem in his lap and tipped the dog onto his back. He rubbed the puppy's plump belly with his index finger. With a wide yawn, Mayhem promptly went to sleep, his head, tail and legs splayed in six different directions.

He glared across the table at Mrs. Locke. "Have you finished interrogating my wife?" he asked.

He knew he sounded defensive, just as he had with his father. But this time he had cause. He had it figured out now. This woman wasn't his niece's nanny any more than she was his employee. Annalise was his wife, a woman who'd given herself to him in marriage. Given herself in every way possible. And he'd do everything within his power to protect her, to fulfill those vows he'd taken mere steps from where they sat.

"I just put away my thumbscrews," she replied in a dry voice. "And now I have one final question before I go visit with Isabella."

He regarded her warily. "Only one?"

"Just one." She leaned forward and set her glass of tea onto the patio table. "I know why Annalise married you. But I'd like you to explain why you married your wife. Is this a love match or is this your clever way of circumventing CPS's objections to your guardianship? Is Annalise here to stay, or here until we go away?"

And there it was, Jack acknowledged. The billion-dollar question.

Before he could reply, Sara stepped onto the patio. "Excuse me, Mr. Mason. There's a gentleman here to see you. He was most insistent—"

Not waiting for either permission or invitation, a tall, lean man in his late thirties, maybe early forties, strode out onto the patio. He carried himself with a military bearing. His curly brown hair was cropped short. A faded cap shaded his deep-set eyes and cast a shadow across his sun-bronzed face. Though he didn't share Annalise's coloring and appeared far too young to have a daughter his wife's age, there was little doubt in Jack's mind that this had to be her father—and his timing couldn't have been worse.

"I'm Robert Stefano," he announced. "And I'm looking for..." He froze, his eyes arrowing in on Annalise. "Leese?"

"Daddy?" Annalise erupted from her chair and threw herself into the man's arms. "Finally! I have been trying to reach you for ages."

He gave his daughter a fierce hug. "Didn't you get my message?"

"About your charter? Yes, yes. Bub passed it on. But—"

He held her at arm's length. "I came as soon as I heard the news. Of course, by the time it reached me, it was long out of date. What the hell have you gone and done?"

He looked over her shoulder toward Jack, who climbed to his feet and set the yawning puppy on the ground beside him. "It's a pleasure to meet you, Mr. Stefano," he said, holding out his hand. "I'm Jack Mason."

To Jack's dismay, his father-in-law swept his daughter behind him in a protective manner. "Not him, Leese. Tell me there's been a mistake and you haven't actually married this man."

"Is there a problem?" Mrs. Locke interrupted.

"No problem at all," Jack replied smoothly. His hand

dropped to his side. "You need to leave. Now. This is a family matter and none of your business."

Of course, she didn't listen. She settled more firmly into her chair. "If this affects Isabella, it most certainly is my business."

"Mr. Stefano?" Jack approached the other man. "I'm Annalise's husband."

"I know who you are." Robert tore off his cap and crushed it between his calloused hands. "What I don't yet know is what sort of game you're playing with my daughter."

Annalise stepped out from behind her father, confronting the situation head-on, just as she had from the moment he'd first met her. "Dad, this isn't a game."

"You're damn right it isn't." Grief tore into the older man's face. "Does he know? Does this supposed husband of yours know the truth?"

To Jack's surprise she faltered, her forthrightness stumbling. "No," she admitted. "He doesn't."

Dread swept through him like the first winter breeze. "Somebody tell me what the *hell* is going on," Jack demanded.

"And then you can explain it to me," Mrs. Locke added.

Robert opened his mouth to reply, but before he could his gaze shifted and locked onto something in the middle of the lawn. Mister Mayhem scampered in that direction and Jack saw why. Isabella had exited into the yard through his study door. She greeted the dog with a crowing laugh.

"Oh, God," Robert whispered. His cap dropped to the patio flagstones. "Is that her?"

He took a step in Isabella's direction, a step that carried

him into the sunlight. The strong summer rays caught in the short brown curls, highlighting them with gold. He stared at Isabella, stared at her with eyes the exact same shade of olive green as those of Jack's niece. Robert clenched his squared jaw, but couldn't seem to keep it from wobbling. And then he broke into a broad grin of incandescent delight. In his cheek a dimple flashed.

Without a word, Jack turned toward Annalise. Tears rained down her cheeks. She caught his look, holding his eyes for an endless moment, hers assuming a defiant slant. He went to her, stepped with her into the shadows of the patio overhang, away from listening ears.

"Isabella looks just like your dad. Is she your sister?" Jack questioned in a hard undertone. "Is Robert Stefano her father?"

"I'm an only child," Annalise stated.

An arctic wind blew through him and he could literally see the life he'd built shattering around him. "Then she's—"

"Mine." Annalise squared her shoulders and lifted tarnished eyes to his. "Isabella is my daughter."

Ten

"It was all a setup, wasn't it?"

"No." Annalise shook her head, speaking with a quiet dignity that cut deep. "No!"

Jack stepped away from her, unable to hide his raw pain and anger. There was no way he could. His fury battered him with all the elemental power of a hurricane, driving emotions he'd always been able to keep under rigid control. They whipped free, exploded from him in a messy, illogical, unmanageable torrent.

"I have to hand it to you. Your plan was absolutely brilliant."

"What plan?" She played the role of the innocent with breathtaking perfection, reflecting just the appropriate amount of bewilderment. "All I ever wanted was to make certain Isabella was safe."

"Safe," he repeated. "I didn't realize my reputation was quite that bad."

She dared to fight back. "You know that's not what I meant."

He ignored that and continued the attack with ruthless precision. "Why did you apply to be Isabella's nanny? You knew she was yours then, didn't you?" He didn't phrase it as a question.

She lifted her chin, refusing to cower. "Yes."

"What then, Annalise? Were you going to use your position to manipulate CPS? To push them that final inch in order to convince them I wasn't an appropriate guardian?"

"Have you lost your mind?" she asked with impressive calm.

He simply shook his head, amazed by her inner fortitude. "I have to hand it to you. Your logic was flawless. As Isabella's nanny you could inveigle yourself into my niece's affections. Maybe drop a word or two of concern in Mrs. Locke's ear."

A spark of anger appeared, at war with her self-control. She folded her arms across her chest. "And then what, Jack? Have Isabella's life upended again when they put her into foster care? Or even worse, stick her into a treatment program?"

He lifted a shoulder in a negligent shrug. "Once she was out of my control you'd have a better shot at getting custody of her."

Fury blossomed, full-throttled and magnificent. "*That's* what you think this is all about? You think I want to take her away from you?"

His anger rose to meet hers. "What am I supposed to think? In all this time, never once did you bother to say, 'Oh, hey, Jack, just so you know, Isabella's my biological daughter.'" He stalked closer. "Did you think I'd never find out?"

"I was going to tell you!"

"Right. Now that we're safely married and you're in an even better position to fight for legal custody."

She went nose to nose with him. "Is that your real opinion of me? After all this time together, you don't know me better than that?"

The ache was almost more than he could bear. "I thought I did," he whispered. "But you lied."

"I never lied. I just didn't tell you all of it." She dared to splay her hand across his chest. Could she still feel his heart beating? It wasn't possible. Not when it had been turned to stone. "Would you have refused to marry me if I'd told you beforehand?"

"I don't know." The confession was ripped from him. "But at least I would have been in a position to make an informed choice."

Her hands dropped to her sides, stealing away the only warmth left to him. She stepped backward. "Then let me make this easy for you." She took another step away from him. "I'll narrow your choices down to two. We can stay married and work through this, or we can divorce."

"And if I want a divorce?"

For the first time, her composure cracked. No, it more than cracked. It shattered. He found that shattering all the more devastating because he'd never seen her lose control to that extent before. She fought the loss for ten full seconds before managing to grind out a reply. "When we first met I had serious doubts about whether or not you were the appropriate person to raise Isabella. I don't have any doubts about that anymore."

He froze. "What the hell does that mean?"

"I think you're an amazing father, Jack," she said. "There's not a single doubt in my mind that she'd not just be safe with you, but that she'll thrive in your care. I won't contest a divorce. Nor will I attempt to take her away from you."

"Annalise—"

She shook her head and her mouth compressed, he suspected to keep her lips from trembling. "If you change your mind about the divorce, you know where to find me." She squared her shoulders and looked him straight in the eye. "But if you decide you want to give our marriage a try, there's only one way I'll return to you. And that's not as Isabella's nanny or your employee. It will be as your partner. As your wife."

With that, Annalise turned and stepped into her father's arms. She clung to him for a long minute while Robert stared at Jack with eyes filled with threat. Without another word, he swept his daughter across the patio and into the house. There they paused, and her gaze clung to an oblivious Isabella a final instant. Not once did she look back at him. Then the door closed behind them with frightening finality.

Jack stood unmoving for an endless moment. How was it possible that in thirty short minutes his life had gone from near perfection, straight to hell? Isabella continued to play with Mister Mayhem, giggling in blissful ignorance at the puppy's ungainly antics. He took a single step toward her when a voice like shards of glass cut into him.

"You, Mr. Mason, are a complete and total idiot," Mrs. Locke announced in ringing tones of disgust.

He spun in his tracks. He'd completely forgotten about the caseworker. She continued to sit beneath the canopied portion of the patio. Without taking her gaze from him, she picked up her glass of iced tea with impressive casualness and took a dainty sip.

She offered a sour smile. "Forgot I was here, didn't you?" He muttered a word that had the woman's carefully stenciled eyebrows climbing. "I certainly hope you don't use that sort of language around Isabella on a regular basis," she said.

"Since she doesn't talk, I didn't think it mattered," he shot back.

To his amazement, Mrs. Locke actually smiled. "I suggest you come and sit down before you fall down." She hefted the pitcher of tea and splashed some into one of the empty glasses. "Here. Drink this."

He reluctantly approached, amazed to find himself taking the proffered glass and obediently downing half the contents in one swallow. The sugar rush hit his system and helped clear his head. "So, how's your morning been so far, Mrs. Locke?" He collapsed into the chair across from the caseworker and stared broodingly at his niece. "Entertaining enough for you?"

"Vastly."

"Glad you enjoyed yourself. Personally, the last time I had a day this bad I was told my sister and her husband had been killed on a flight I was supposed to have been on with them, and that my niece was hanging on to life by a mere thread."

"I'm sorry, Jack." There was no mistaking either her sincerity or her compassion.

He found he couldn't respond. Instead, he traced his finger along a teardrop bead of condensation trickling down the side of his glass. He struggled to gather himself and determine what his next step should be. Having built his business from scratch, he'd learned the importance of flexibility. He'd been an expert at thinking and organizing quickly, and reacting to fluid situations even faster. Logic and ruthless intent had gotten him through many a crisis. But this…

He couldn't think at all, let alone act.

"So, did you marry Annalise because you loved her, or in order to get rid of me?" Mrs. Locke asked.

"To get rid of you." He returned the glass to the table and rubbed at the headache gathering in his temples. "At least, I thought that was the reason."

"Interesting."

His head jerked up. "What's interesting?"

"When I asked Annalise why she'd married you, she said more or less the same thing."

He had a vivid memory of standing in the kitchen, desperate to hear his wife's response to Mrs. Locke's question. The truth came as one more blow. He didn't even attempt to conceal his pain. It cut too deeply. "She told you that?" he murmured.

"No, she told me that's why she'd initially agreed to marry you. She said she married you for one reason and one reason only."

"What?" The word was torn from him before he could prevent it.

Mrs. Locke lifted an eyebrow and pinned him with those bright blue eyes. "Don't you know?" She dismissed her own question with a wave of her hand. "Of course you don't, or you'd never have made those ridiculous accusations."

"Are you going to tell me what she said, or not?" he ground out.

"Not," came the crisp response. "To be honest, it doesn't matter what Annalise said. All that matters is what you have to say. Why did you marry your wife, Mr. Mason? I expect a truthful answer and I expect one now."

The question didn't require any thought. "Because I love her," he answered starkly.

Mrs. Locke pushed back her chair. "I'll give you three days to resolve this situation before rendering my final verdict on Isabella's custody."

He lifted his gaze, feeling the protective predator stirring. No one was going to take his niece from him. "Is that a threat?" he asked softly.

Just like Annalise, Mrs. Locke didn't show the least sign of intimidation. What was it with these women? "Yes, Mr. Mason." She picked up her purse and tucked it under her arm. "That was a threat."

It didn't take three days for Jack to figure out what he intended to do. It didn't even take him three hours. It just took enough time for him to sit quietly and remember. Remember Annalise and how she'd been from the moment they'd first met. From the day she'd stepped foot in his office, she'd lived and breathed her concern for his niece.

No, not just his niece. *Annalise's daughter*.

She hadn't accepted the position of Isabella's nanny

with the intent of attracting a wealthy husband. It hadn't been about him at all. All her attention, all her focus, had been directed toward Isabella and helping her child recover from a hideous trauma that had forever changed her young life.

Even by giving Isabella up for adoption, Annalise had proven that she'd put Isabella first and done what was best for his niece. Marrying him had simply been one more step in that process. He might have wanted her focus to widen enough to include him. But that wasn't her first priority and never would be. Her child was Annalise's priority. He closed his eyes.

Their child.

His gaze drifted to Isabella and he accepted the inescapable truth. She was his niece and he'd always keep her parent's memory alive for her. But at some point, he'd stopped thinking of her as an extension of Joanne and Paul, and begun to think of her as part of himself. A vital part.

As though sensing his attention, Isabella's head jerked up and she looked at him and beamed with happiness. Sweeping Mister Mayhem into her arms, she trotted over to him and climbed into his lap. He hugged her close, inhaling the sweet, baby scent of her. From tragedy had come an existence he'd never believed possible.

It didn't matter what it took. It didn't matter what he had to sacrifice. It didn't even matter that he'd never be first in Annalise's life or heart. He and Isabella needed her and he'd do whatever necessary to bring his wife home. But there was something he had to do first.

He gathered Isabella close and prayed he'd find the

right words. "Do you remember when we talked about finding people to adopt Madam's puppies, like you were adopted?" he asked.

Isabella nodded, though he could tell she still pouted a bit at the thought.

"Do you also remember me telling you about your other mommy? She's the one who gave birth to you before you were adopted?" When Isabella nodded again, he rested his cheek against the soft curls crowning her head. He gathered his self-control and spoke gently. Carefully. Lovingly. "There's something I need to tell you about your birth mommy…"

Jack arrived at the boatyard early that same afternoon. Sun pounded down on him as he walked the weathered planks toward the large charter yacht he'd been informed belonged to Robert Stefano. He saw Annalise's father before the other man caught sight of him. It gave Jack a few seconds to further assess the man and get some sort of handle on him.

Lean and muscular, Robert Stefano wore cutoff shorts and a sleeveless tee, which made him look all the younger and more virile than when he'd first introduced himself. He didn't wear a cap and the sun picked out the burnished streaks that were so similar to Isabella's. He must have realized that he was being watched. His head jerked up and he stiffened, like one predator sensing the presence of another. Slowly, he swung around. Cursing roundly, he stalked down the pier, planting himself square in Jack's path. He folded his well-muscled arms across an equally muscular chest.

"What the hell are you doing here?" he demanded.

Jack assessed his opponent—who also happened to be his father-in-law. He could take the man if he had to. Maybe. He imitated Robert's stance. "I've come for my wife, even if I have to go through you to get to her. But when I leave, it's with Annalise. Now, I can do it with your cooperation, or without. Your choice."

"I vote for 'without.' She's not a real wife to you. She's just a means to an end, and I won't let you use her. So turn around, son." A vicious smile slashed across Robert's face. "You don't stand a chance against me. I eat pencil pushers like you for breakfast."

Jack planted himself, hoping for peace, but prepared for the battle of his life. "Annalise tells me you raised her on your own after her mother died."

"I did." Open grief touched his tanned face before being ruthlessly suppressed. "I let that girl down when she was sixteen. I won't let her down now."

"Sounds like we have ourselves a problem, because I don't want to let Isabella down. She needs Annalise." He drew a deep breath and confessed, "*I* need Annalise."

Suspicion glinted in Robert's green eyes. "For your niece?"

Jack shook his head. "For me. It just took me a while to realize that. Isabella was the excuse I used to bind Annalise to me without admitting why I wanted her."

Robert's arms dropped to his sides and he cocked his head to one side in a gesture eerily similar to Annalise's. "And why is that?"

Jack didn't bother to pull his punches or hide behind his pride. He put it all out there for the other man to rummage through. "Because I love your daughter."

Robert eyed him for a long moment, before nodding in satisfaction. "Then what are you doing wasting your time jawing with me?" He stepped aside. "Go tell my daughter how you feel and put her out of her misery."

"I'll get right on that." Jack didn't hesitate. He passed by the other man and walked toward his future.

"Mason?" Robert waited until Jack turned. "That's two of mine in your care. I will be watching you."

Jack nodded. He could accept that. "I'd be doing the exact same thing if I were in your position." He swung aboard only to have Robert stop him again.

"Oh, and Mason?"

"Yes, sir?"

"You couldn't have taken me."

Jack grinned. "I would have enjoyed trying."

Robert returned the grin. "Yeah. Me, too."

A cursory glance told Jack that Annalise wasn't topside. He crossed the deck to the steps leading to the shadowed interior. His wife stood in the small, efficient galley, her back to him. He paused and allowed himself the luxury of watching her graceful movements as she went about the mundane task of putting a meal together.

She'd swept her hair into a casual ponytail, and the ringlets bounced with each dip and sway of her body. She wore a thin cotton tee that hugged her curves and screeched to a halt a scant couple of inches short of a pair of low-slung shorts that bared her endless legs to his view. He was about to announce his presence when she spoke without turning.

"I have your lunch ready, Dad. Grab a beer out of the fridge if you want one."

"I don't want a beer, thanks."

Her spine went rigid and she carefully returned the plate to the counter with hands that trembled. She drew a careful breath before spinning around. "Jack."

"Annalise."

One look warned that her control was as tenuous as his own. Unfortunately, he still couldn't read her as well as he'd hoped. *Why had she married him?* Was it just for Isabella, or was there more? He'd obsessed over the question ever since his conversation with Mrs. Locke. He wanted to be able to take one look and see the answer in her face. But it wasn't there, and unadulterated fear threatened to bring him to his knees.

"I've been expecting a call from Derek," she said. "I'm surprised you came, instead."

Gathering every shred of composure at his command, Jack leaned his hip against the counter and shrugged. "What's this got to do with Derek? You're *my* wife, not his."

Her chin assumed a combative angle. "For now."

"Forever," he stated decisively.

She shook her head. "Forget it, Jack. I won't live with someone who believes I'm capable of—"

"Stop." He cut her off with that one, quiet word. Perhaps it was the way he said it—naked pain leaking into the single syllable. Whatever the reason, it worked and she stumbled to a halt. "Please, sweetheart. You're killing me."

She gazed at him with a heartbreaking defenselessness that he recognized, mainly because he felt it, too. It was an emotion he'd never experienced before…until now. He'd always been the tough one. He'd always held himself

at a safe distance, refusing to allow himself to feel or show
the vulnerability she displayed so openly. And what had
that gotten him? Money. Success. But what were those in
comparison to an empty heart and a cold bed, and a little
girl waiting for a mother? He'd had a taste of heaven, and
he would do anything and everything to have that back.

Even strip his defenses bare and allow her to cut him
to shreds.

Without a word, he opened his arms to her. Time
seemed to hold its breath as he waited for her decision.
Waited to discover whether he'd know a lifetime of
warmth and joy, or be forced to survive in an arctic wasteland. With an inarticulate cry, she flew to him, and he
breathed in life. He wrapped her up tight and buried his
face against her silken curls and simply inhaled her. The
scent of her. The feel of her. The sound of their hearts
beating as one.

"I love you, Annalise," he murmured against the top of
her head. "And I'm more sorry than I can ever express."

She lifted a glowing face to his. "Sorry you love me?"
she teased.

A rusty laugh escaped. "I'm sorry I believed the worst."

"I should have told you about my relationship to
Isabella. I was going to." She made a gesture that emphasized her bone-deep weariness. "But I should have done
it before we married."

"Tell me now, Annalise. I gather Isabella was the result
of that night you lost your virginity?"

"Yes." She closed her eyes and shuddered. "You have
no idea how terrified I was when I realized I was pregnant."

"What about the boy?"

"He and his family had moved away by then. Dad contacted them, of course. But they wanted nothing to do with me or the baby and were only too happy to sign the adoption papers." She shrugged. "It was just as well. Tommy was no more in a position to raise a baby than I was."

"I remember Joanne saying it was a private adoption, arranged through their lawyer."

Annalise nodded. "Dad met with Joanne and Paul and had them carefully checked out."

He eyed her curiously. "You never considered keeping Isabella?"

It was the wrong question to ask. Her chin wobbled for an instant before she firmed it. "I wanted to keep her with all my heart. I dreamed about it every night. But I was sixteen when I got pregnant. I'd just turned seventeen when I had her." The confession was so soft he barely caught it. "I also know it was the most difficult decision Dad ever made. He'd been a teenage father himself, and he felt he'd done such a poor job of it, that it wouldn't be fair to repeat the cycle for another generation. He was right. I couldn't be selfish." Tears overflowed. "I…I had to do what was best for Isabella, not what was best for me. So I hid my pregnancy until the school year ended and went to stay with my aunt until after Isabella was born. Every summer after that I'd go and stay with her…and remember. Celebrate…and mourn."

He tightened his hold on her, her words tearing him apart. "I'm so sorry."

"I never knew who adopted her, but Dad kept track and would reassure me that she was safe and doing well."

Understanding dawned. "Until the plane crash."

"Yes. It was all over the news. At first, the media reported that everyone onboard perished. I walked in while Dad was listening to the announcement. He was crying. He tried to keep it from me, but it wasn't hard to figure out why he was so upset."

"I gather you read that I'd taken custody of your daughter."

She nodded against his chest. "And that you were having a hard time keeping a nanny. It seemed the perfect opportunity. I'd apply and see if there was anything I could do to help with the transition. I planned to stay just a short time. Neither of you were supposed to discover the truth. I didn't even intend to tell my father I'd taken the job. But then…"

"Then?"

Her sigh rippled through her and into him. "I took one look at her and fell head over heels. I would have stuck to my original plan if it weren't for one other problem."

He stiffened. "What problem?" he managed to ask.

She lifted her head and looked at him, her heart in her eyes. "I fell in love with you. One minute I was trying to build a world for you and Isabella, and the next you became my world."

The inner coldness cracked, splitting apart like chunks of icebergs beneath a spring thaw. He didn't resist any longer. He lowered his head and kissed her. The kiss shouldn't have been any different from all the other ones they'd shared. But it was. He didn't know if it was the absence of secrets or the fact that they'd both allowed the last bastions of their defenses to fall. Maybe the fact that they'd confessed their love altered the elemental nature of the embrace. Whatever the cause, he knew he'd remember this moment for the rest of his life. Remember the heat and the generosity, the certainty and the passion. Most of all, it was the awareness that he'd finally come home. That he'd found what he'd spent most his life searching for— and he held her safely in his arms.

"Come home now," he urged. "We're lost without you."

"I thought I was the one who was lost."

He forked his hands deep into her hair, allowing the curls to bind them together. "The three of us ultimately found each other. That's all that matters now."

He took her mouth in a lingering kiss, sinking into the softness and the warmth. If they'd been anywhere else, he'd have fallen into the nearest bed and spent the next twenty-four hours making her his in every possible sense of the word. Reluctantly, he drew back.

"I never realized how empty my life was until you filled it up," he said.

Her smile was the most radiant he'd ever seen. "Let's go home."

Robert eyed them closely as they left the boat. Whatever he saw must have satisfied him because he simply smiled in satisfaction. "I'd appreciate having an opportunity to get to know my granddaughter," he addressed Jack. "If you're willing."

"Anytime."

The drive to Lover's Folly seemed endless. But they finally arrived. It felt like weeks since he'd last had his wife at home, instead of mere hours. They walked hand in hand from the garage across the backyard. The kitchen door flew open and a half dozen rambunctious puppies spilled out, yipping and squabbling as they came, with Madam close on their heels.

Behind them, Isabella appeared in the doorway and cut loose with a shriek to end all shrieks. She took off at a flat run and arrowed straight for Annalise. His wife released his hand and knelt, cushioning Isabella's landing in a loving embrace.

"Hello, Baby Belle," Annalise greeted her daughter with a tearful laugh.

Isabella twined her twig-thin arms around Annalise's neck and buried her face in the soft crook between neck and shoulder. Jack found he had to swallow hard at the sight. Isabella pulled back and spared him a brief, nervous glance. He gave an encouraging nod, praying for a miracle. And then it happened.

With a shy look, Isabella said, "Hi, Mommy."

* * * * *

BILLION-DOLLAR
BABY BARGAIN

TESSA
RADLEY

Tessa Radley loves travelling, reading and watching the world around her. As a teen Tessa wanted to be an intrepid foreign correspondent. But after completing a bachelor of arts degree and marrying her sweetheart, she became fascinated by law and ended up studying further and practising as an attorney in a city practice. A six-month break travelling through Australia with her family reawoke the yen to write. And life as a writer suits her perfectly: travelling and reading count as research, and as for analysing the world… well, she can think 'what if?' all day long. When she's not reading, travelling or thinking about writing, she's spending time with her husband, her two sons or her zany and wonderful friends. You can contact Tessa through her website, www.tessaradley.com.

For my boys

Prologue

Who would have thought that a baby—cute and gurgly when his mother held him—could be such a demanding little devil? Victoria Sutton sank down onto the couch in the living room of her Auckland town house and gazed at the sleeping baby in the traveling cot with weary disbelief.

Dylan looked utterly angelic as stubby eyelashes rested in dusky crescents against chubby baby cheeks and his mouth moved gently up and down.

Oh, for a shot of caffeine.

Strong, hot Starbucks coffee. Hard to believe the whole weekend had passed without finding time to pick one up. Mandy, her secretary, would laugh herself silly tomorrow when Victoria recounted the events of the past two days.

Had it only been two days?

Propping her elbows on her knees, Victoria rested her chin in her palms, and groaned. Two days, but also two pretty much sleepless nights during which Dylan had turned her normally organized life upside down. Heavens, it seemed like she hadn't drawn a breath since her best friend Suzy had gabbled her last bits of advice on Friday evening as Michael had tugged his wife out the front door, eager to get away for a brief romantic break to celebrate their second wedding anniversary.

Never again would she imagine that babies slept all the time!

Lifting her head from her cupped palms, Victoria scanned the normally immaculate living room and took in the chaotic disarray of toys, diapers and other baby paraphernalia. Another groan escaped. She knew her bedroom looked worse. She needed to get the mess packed up before Dylan's parents arrived to collect him.

Victoria glanced ruefully at the apple puree smears on the winter-white fabric of the couch. And that stain on the carpet hadn't been there before Friday, either. What had possessed her to feed Dylan in the all-white living room this morning? Had she learned nothing over the past two days?

Tomorrow first thing she'd organize to get the marks cleaned.

Tomorrow. Oh, heavens. Victoria's hands shot to her mouth in dismay.

The weekly Monday-morning partners' meeting…

Good grief, she hadn't done any preparation. She thought wildly of how she'd delusionally planned to work while Dylan napped over the weekend.

A glance at the wall clock showed her it was still early. Michael and Suzy would be here within the next two hours to pick up Dylan. The whole evening lay ahead.

If she worked quickly to tidy the apartment, she might even get some work in before the Masons arrived. Grabbing a nappy bag, Victoria started to toss in toys, wet-wipes and unused diapers.

But nothing could take away from the fun she'd had with

her godson. They'd played peekaboo and she'd tickled Dylan's tummy. They'd been to the beach, where she'd dipped Dylan's toes in the shallows while he squealed in ecstasy. They'd even shared an ice-cream cone—granted, most of it had ended up over Dylan's face, plus a few smears down Victoria's favorite Kate Sylvester T-shirt.

So she'd willingly offer to do it again. Her godson was adorable. A memory of his loud, growling screams in the middle of the night made her amend that statement. *Mostly* he was adorable.

The throaty roar of a powerful motor pulling up outside her town house unit made her pause in the act of retrieving a miniature sock from under the coffee table.

She checked the slim gold watch on her wrist. Too early for Michael and Suzy.

The doorbell rang in a long, insistent buzz. Victoria leaped to her feet, a quick glance showing that Dylan hadn't stirred. The bell buzzed again. She shot across the room and, without pausing to look through the peephole, yanked the door open before whoever it was could lean on the doorbell again.

"Connor!"

Connor North, Michael's best man, stood on her doorstep.

To Victoria's annoyance her pulse kicked up, but with practiced ease she avoided Connor's gaze. He wore a white T-shirt that stretched across a broad chest, and a pair of jeans that molded the lean hips.

"I probably should have called."

His voice was gravelly, all male, full of edges with no smooth sweetness. Victoria knew she should reply, should agree that it would have been better for him to have called first—and then hope like blazes that he would go.

Instead, unable to answer him or steel herself to meet his unsettling pale gray eyes, Victoria fixed her gaze on the hard line of his mouth. *Mistake.* It had been two years since he had kissed her at Michael and Suzy's wedding. By rights she should've forgotten all about the texture of his lips against hers, the desire that had spun dizzily within her.

She hadn't.

Victoria swallowed.

The memory of the taste of him, the hardness of his body against hers, was so immediate it could've happened yesterday. Despite her every effort to pretend it had never happened at all.

"Connor…" she croaked, wishing he was a million miles away.

Why had he come? They didn't have the kind of relationship that allowed for casual drop-ins. To be honest they didn't have any kind of relationship at all.

Since the wedding the two of them had developed an unspoken pact of practicing avoidance: when one arrived at the Masons' home, the other departed within minutes. The passage of time had not dulled the hostility that crackled between them. A dislike that they both colluded to conceal from Michael and Suzy—and Dylan.

She tried again. "Connor, what are you doing here?"

Carefully, with immense composure, she raised her gaze from that hard, tight mouth and met his gaze. To her astonishment he didn't look anything like his usual arrogant, assured self. He looked…

She took in his pallor, the dull flatness in his gray eyes. He looked shattered. "Hey, are you okay?"

"Victoria—" He broke off and shoved his hands in his pockets.

At least he seemed to have no difficulty remembering her name these days, Victoria thought wryly. But it wasn't like Connor to be at a loss for words. Usually the sarcastic quips rolled off his tongue. She frowned. "What is it?"

"Can I come in?"

Victoria hesitated. She didn't particularly want him in her home. But he was…he wasn't himself. "Sure."

Leading him into the living room, she felt a flare of embarrassment at what he must see. Toys. Baby blankets. Dirty plates. She would've preferred Connor to see her home as it normally looked. Elegant. Immaculate. "Excuse the mess."

He didn't even glance sideways. "Victoria…" That soulless gaze was focused on her face with an intensity that was awfully disconcerting.

The need to fill the awkward silence made her blurt out, "Can I fix you a cup of coffee? Not that it's anything like Starbucks, but I was about to make myself—" she stopped before she could reveal that one small human had reduced her to a caffeine-craving wreck "—a hot drink."

"No."

"Tea?"

He shook his head.

She moved toward the kitchen, which opened off the living room, flipped the kettle's switch and opened the fridge.

"I don't have beer. Would you like a cola?" she offered with reluctance as his footfalls sounded on the tiles behind her. She wished he'd waited for her in the living room. There wasn't enough space in the kitchen for the two of them.

"Please." He rubbed a hand over the back of his neck and shut his eyes. An instant later they flicked open and she glimpsed…pain?

Victoria swung away and yanked the fridge door open. She stared blindly at the contents before reaching for two cans of cola. Shutting the door, she said more curtly than she'd intended, "So what do you want, Connor?"

His mouth twisted. "Certainly not sympathy."

She flicked him a rapid once-over as she set the cans down on the counter. He made no move toward the drinks. A ring of white that she hadn't noticed before surrounded his lips.

What was wrong with him? "Why on earth would I offer you sympathy?"

It couldn't possibly be about his former girlfriend. That had been over two years ago and no one ever spoke about Dana or Paul Harper, Connor's former business partner who had pinched his live-in lover while Connor had been out of the country on a business trip.

What Victoria had gleaned of the affair had come from a soft-focus women's magazine feature on Dana and Paul not long after Suzy's wedding. Connor's ex had been nominated for a business award, and was quoted gushing about how happy she was, how she'd "come into herself." There'd been an accompanying spread of photos showing the couple at home in a modern Italianate mansion, all glass and marble.

Yet according to stories in business publications, Harper-North Architecture hadn't thrived well under Paul's leadership after Connor had walked out. In fact, Suzy had once told Victoria that Paul Harper still owed Connor money. Victoria had surmised that the only thing keeping Connor from placing Harper-North—and Paul Harper—into receivership must be his intent to squeeze every cent he could out of Paul Harper.

By contrast, there'd been quite a splash in the media about The Phoenix Corporation, the waterfront development company that Connor had floated. Reading between the lines, Victoria had gathered that he'd turned what for a lesser man might have spelled disaster into a multimillion-dollar success story.

Yet a sense that something was not quite right closed in on her, as he rubbed his hands over his face in a manner she could only describe as helpless.

"I shouldn't have made that crack about sympathy," he said. "Oh, hell, let me start over." He dropped his hands to his sides and the eyes that met hers were as expressionless as ever. "I'm sorry, Victoria, I've got bad news."

"Bad news?" Bewilderment set in. "What bad news?"

"Michael—"

"*No,*" she interrupted, as if that might stop her absorbing the reality of the despair that clung to him. "Not Michael!"

Her index finger tapped her watch face with insistent, staccato force. "He'll be here soon. I know it."

Connor was shaking his head and his face was gray, his eyes drained of all vitality. "He won't. He's never coming back."

He had to be.

A sickening fear hollowed out her stomach. She found herself standing right in front of him—closer than she'd ever been, except for that brief disastrous time when they'd danced together at Michael and Suzy's wedding. And when he'd kissed her. "You're wrong."

Because if Michael wasn't coming back that meant…

Seized by desperation, she choked out, "Suzy. Where's Suzy?"

"Victoria…"

This time he didn't have to say anything more. It was all in the way he looked at her with deep sorrow and regret.

"No!" she howled, her throat thickening with grief.

He moved swiftly forward. "Suzy's gone, too."

Victoria fell forward against the broad chest, uncaring of how unyielding Connor's solid frame had become. After a moment of blubbering her arms crept up about his neck.

He grew more rigid still for just a moment until his arms came around her and squeezed. Then he shook off her clinging arms and stepped back, his eyes remote.

"There are arrangements to make. I need to get on to them but I thought you should know…" His voice trailed away.

"That Michael and Suzy are—" she couldn't bring herself to say it "—are not coming home."

A muscle moved high in his cheek. "That's right."

"No, it isn't right. It's wrong!"

The eyes that met hers were full of torment. "Victoria—"

She shook her head. "They're supposed to knock on the door…Suzy will be laughing, she'll call out, 'I'm baaack.'"

He hunched his shoulders.

The lump in her throat finally got too big and her voice broke. Tears welled up from deep within her aching heart. "It's not fair. They should be here."

Backing out of the kitchen, Connor spread his hands, then dropped them to his sides. "Look, there's a lot to be done."

"And you don't have time for good, old-fashioned grief," Victoria said bitterly, as she followed him.

"You're overreacting." He looked hunted. "I'll talk to you later."

"I'm coming with you."

"No, you're not. I work faster alone. And you need to take care of Dylan."

Dylan!

She gaped at Connor in horror. Oh, dear Lord, how could she have forgotten about Dylan?

Dylan had lost his parents.

Connor couldn't leave now. "Connor!"

But Connor was already halfway across the living room. He threw an unreadable glance over his shoulder but didn't slow down. "When I come back we'll talk about Dylan."

One

August, two years ago

The taxi pulled up outside the quaint white church where Suzy and Michael would be getting married tomorrow. Victoria paid the driver and leapt out, tugging her rollaway suitcase behind her.

"Hey, Victoria, over here." Suzy stood in the churchyard, waving madly from behind a white-painted wooden gate, her curly blond hair bubbling about her face. "I'm so glad you made it."

"Me, too."

Opening the gate, Victoria abandoned her suitcase and stretched her arms out wide to give Suzy a fierce hug.

"When my plane was delayed I thought I was going to miss the wedding rehearsal." She'd been away doing an audit for one of her largest clients. The text message from Suzy that she was getting married in five days' time had shaken

Victoria—although in hindsight it shouldn't have. Over the past month, everything Suzy said had been prefaced by "Michael says." But Victoria hadn't expected the romance to escalate so quickly. "You certainly decided to get married in a hurry, didn't you?"

Stepping away, Suzy grabbed Victoria's hand. "Come see what the church committee is doing with the flowers."

"You're changing the subject," Victoria said with fond frustration.

Suzy cast her a grin. "Tory, it's too late to try and talk me out of marrying Michael tomorrow."

Victoria smiled at the woman she'd pulled from more scrapes than she cared to remember. "Well, I hope Michael knows what he's letting himself in for. Is he here yet?"

"He and Connor—his best man—" Suzy tacked on at Victoria's questioning glance, "are on their way. We're taking you both out to dinner tonight to celebrate. I booked a table at Bentley's." She did a little jig. "I can't believe it's the last night we'll spend apart. Michael can't wait for tomorrow, either. Come on."

"Wait, let me grab my bag." With a laugh, Victoria reached for the bag and let Suzy lead her through a courtyard overflowing with ivy and rambling roses, rolling her bag behind her.

The late afternoon sun filtered through the branches of a lofty Norfolk pine, casting shadows across the sundial in the centre of the courtyard.

Victoria came to a halt. Suzy slowed. "What now?"

"Suz, don't you think it might've been better to wait? You've only—"

"Known Michael for a month," interrupted Suzy, finishing the sentence with the familiar ease that came from twenty-four years of friendship, "but I knew after an hour that he was The One."

"But Suz—"

Suzy stamped her foot, managing to look sweet and determined at the same time. "No, don't say anything more. Just be happy for us. Please."

Now, how on earth was she supposed to withstand Suzy's puppy-dog eyes? Truth was she'd never been able to say no to Suzy, despite the fact that Victoria was supposed to be the sensible one.

The sound of footsteps prevented Victoria from responding. She glanced around and her eyes widened.

It wasn't Michael—much as she liked him—who snagged her attention, but rather the dark-haired man who strode into the churchyard beside him. Tall and powerfully built with features that could've been carved from granite—angled cheekbones, a blade of a nose and a hard mouth—he made the hair on the back of her neck stand up.

Victoria recognized the animal. She'd met them, done audits for the super-successful companies.

A tycoon.

Rich. Assured. Ruthless.

And this was Michael's best man? Edging slowly forward, she glanced from one man to the other.

Michael's fair good looks dimmed against the other man's dark strength. They were as different as day from night. Where had Michael found him?

She must have said something because his gaze met hers. That was when her stomach flipped over. In contrast to his swarthy skin his pale-gray eyes held the unnerving translucence of crystal. But they contained utterly no emotion.

Ruthless.

"Connor North."

He spoke in a crisp baritone, and Victoria instantly recognized the name. From its outset Harper-North Architecture had garnered buzz and awards for innovative restoration of

Victorian homesteads and plans for cutting-edge new commercial buildings.

With reluctance Victoria took the hand he held out. A hard hand ridged with calluses clasped hers—hardly the hand of an office-bound paper pusher.

Yet from everything she'd heard, Connor North was very much a corporate animal. Financially astute, frighteningly efficient and with an uncanny talent for picking projects that would become landmarks. There was certainly no need for him to busy himself with the manual labor that the ridges on his palms suggested he did. The man was worth a fortune—and accumulating more. Last she'd heard Harper-North was considering launching a commercial-property venture to develop many of Auckland's old dockside warehouses into exclusive waterfront retail complexes. It would be a feather in her cap to land him as a client—and no doubt he'd be able to introduce her to some of the blue-chip companies he was associated with. One or two more accounts like that and she'd be propelled into the upper echelons of Archer, Cameron & Edge.

He glanced down pointedly at their joined hands. A flare of embarrassment seared her as Victoria realized she still clutched his hand. Daydreaming. She dropped it as if she'd been scorched by a flaming torch.

Even Suzy was staring at her. "Do you two know each other?"

Victoria shook her head, not trusting her voice.

"No." Connor North clearly didn't suffer from the same affliction.

"Connor, meet Suzy's oldest friend, Victoria Sutton." Michael gave her an easy smile. "Despite his reputation, Connor won't bite."

Victoria wasn't so sure. Connor North looked capable of doing a lot worse than biting.

"Victoria is a partner at ACE," Michael informed Connor.

Victoria knew she should be grateful for the punt, because

she should be doing everything she could to land his very lu-
crative account.

Instead, when Connor gave her the opportunity of a lifetime by asking, "The accounting firm?" she could only manage a nod, not trusting her voice. Her stomach, thankfully,
seemed to have recovered from the tumbling sensation that
had shaken her when she had first looked into his eyes.

Bridget Edge, managing partner of Archer, Cameron &
Edge Accounting, would be horrified to see her now. Faced
with the opportunity of a lifetime, Victoria couldn't think of
anything vaguely professional to say. All she could think of was
getting as far away from the man as she could. He made her
feel…the best word she could come up with was…*unsettled*.

Still prickling with a mix of apprehension and a weird
kind of tingling sensation, Victoria allowed Suzy to shepherd
her up the stone stairs into the church while Michael disappeared to put her suitcase in his car.

Inside the church a group of elderly ladies busily arranging white lilies and pristine long-stemmed roses in tall flower
stands greeted Suzy with cries of delight. When Michael
returned there were chirps about how fortunate he was to be
marrying Suzy, and Victoria saw Connor North's mouth turn
down at the corners.

He didn't want Michael to marry Suzy!

The realization rocked Victoria. How could anyone disap-
prove of dear, sweet Suzy?

For the next fifteen minutes Michael smiled indulgently
while Suzy cheerfully ordered everyone around and Connor
grew increasingly remote.

His phone rang six times while Suzy talked nonstop. Each
time, Connor pulled his cell phone out of his pocket, glanced
at it, then let it continue to ring.

Victoria could feel herself growing tenser as Connor's disapproving silence continued, and she was ready to scream by

the time Suzy called a halt, finally satisfied that the groom, the groomsman and the maid of honor knew what was expected of them.

"I want tomorrow to be perfect." Suzy dimpled a smile at Victoria and moved on to include Connor, too. "Michael and I just want to thank the church ladies for the wonderful job they've done with the flowers, then we'll meet you outside."

"We've been dismissed." Connor gave a grimace that Victoria supposed passed for a smile and stood aside for her to walk ahead of him up the aisle.

Conscious of him stalking behind her, Victoria increased her pace.

As they neared the vestibule his phone rang again. He checked it and this time said, "Excuse me, Verity, I have to take this call."

Victoria pursed her lips. "Victoria."

Connor North stared at her blankly with all the interest of someone examining a moth on the wall. It did nothing to endear him to her. She'd been away on an audit all week. She was hot, tired and he had her in such a tizz, while he barely knew she existed.

"Victoria," she repeated tersely. "My name is Victoria."

His gaze raked her and Victoria became aware that her white blouse was creased from the flight, that her long, straight black skirt clung to her hips and must make her look like a scrawny scarecrow. She ran her fingers past her ears, through her hair, and was relieved to find that the shoulder-length bob was as sleek as ever.

"Sure." Connor shrugged dismissively, and turned away to answer his cell phone.

Victoria followed slowly as he strode out of the church, knowing she ought to care that he'd seen her annoyance. After all, he would be an A-list client. But did she want to deal with him?

No, she decided.

In fact, she could think of nothing worse.

Verity, indeed! Clearly all women were interchangeable in his mind. Like gray cats in the night….

Startled, she pulled her thoughts up short. Where had that come from? There was no chance she would ever be one of Connor North's gray cats. Although his women would be far from gray. No doubt he was the kind of man who went for decorative, desirable D-cups.

A rueful downward glance reminded her that she would be no contender.

Skinny. Beanstalk. Swot. Four-eyes. She had to remind herself that the ugly labels were no longer true, and that only Suzy knew that pathetic creature had ever existed. It was ancient history. In the past. Now she held a partnership in a well-respected accounting firm. No one could take that away from her. She'd fought for it, not allowing cruel, childish taunts or her neglectful parents to roadblock her journey to success…and independence.

Forcing herself not to dwell on the old, self-destructive memories, Victoria fixed a bright smile to her face as she stepped through the carved church doors to the vestibule where Connor paced, his cell phone glued to his ear. She let the scent of lavender hedges in the courtyard outside swirl around her, and slowly serenity returned.

"Michael and Suzy have booked a table to take us to dinner," she told Connor when his call ended, in case he planned to bolt off on a hot date, forgetting all about the bridal couple.

His mouth flattened. "I'm quite sure Michael and Suzy would prefer to spend a quiet evening together before the rush of tomorrow's wedding."

Why hadn't she thought of that?

As they started down the stone steps that led to the courtyard, Victoria noticed with surprise that Connor dwarfed her. It wasn't often that a man made her feel downright dainty.

In the courtyard Suzy and Michael caught up to them. After tomorrow Victoria knew their friendship would never be the same again. A sense of loss filled her, yet she'd never seen Suzy look happier.

She remembered Connor's clever suggestion. "Wouldn't the two of you prefer to have dinner alone tonight?"

Suzy dumped a basket of hymn books into Victoria's arms. "Here, you'll need to give these to the ushers to hand out tomorrow at the door. And of course we want to take the two of you out—we'll have the rest of our lives to spend alone together." Suzy gave Michael a bittersweet smile and Victoria wondered if he, too, had seen the shadows in Suzy's eyes as she spoke…or knew the reason for them.

The way he put an arm across Suzy's shoulders and pulled her close suggested he did. "Victoria, you're Suzy's oldest friend, and Connor's the closest thing I've got to a brother. It will be great for the four of us to have dinner together."

Michael was so nice, Victoria decided. Maybe Suzy hadn't made a mistake. About to give Michael a grateful smile for setting to rest the doubts that Connor had raised, Victoria paused as she intercepted the glacial look Connor shot Michael.

What was that about?

Yet Michael, bless him, smiled in the face of Connor's icy disapproval. He clapped a hand on his best man's shoulder and leant forward to murmur something that caused Connor's pale eyes to flare with suppressed emotion as he shot Victoria a look of intense dislike.

What had she done to deserve *that?* The unexpected unease he'd already roused in her coalesced into a hard ball of antipathy.

As Michael went to fetch his car, Suzy added, "After dinner I'm going home—alone." She winked suggestively at

Victoria. "I told Michael it's unlucky for him to see the bride before the wedding and I'm determined not to do anything that might tip the scales against us."

"You shouldn't be getting married if you need superstitious hocus-pocus to make it last," Connor said from behind them, causing both women to start.

As surprise—followed swiftly by hurt—flashed in Suzy's eyes, Victoria swung around and saw no levity in the man's strange eyes.

Outraged that he'd attacked sweet, effervescent Suzy the moment Michael had vanished, she forgot her own reservations about the hasty marriage. Coldly she pointed out, "But Suzy and Michael *are* getting married. They love each other. And there's not a thing you can do about it."

"Love?" Connor's eyes glittered in the dwindling sunlight and his sharp bark of laughter caused Victoria to bristle defensively. "Is that what women call it?"

"It's what Michael calls it, too." A chill enveloped Victoria. She must be mad to challenge this man. "And what gives you the right to sit judgment on what Michael and Suzy feel for each other, anyway?"

He stared down his nose at her. "Love is overrated."

Hoisting the basket of hymn books to stop them falling, she said, "If you're that cynical then perhaps you shouldn't have agreed to be Michael's best man."

"Victoria—"

"No, Suzy." She broke free of the bride-to-be's restraining arm. "What he said was rude and uncalled for."

Suzy looked decidedly uncomfortable.

"Can I take those for you?" Connor had the basket before she could object.

"Thanks," she said ungraciously.

"It looked like you were about to drop them."

The superior tone annoyed her afresh. Victoria wondered

if the hard, handsome man in front of her had ever apologized to anyone. He would, she vowed. "Are you proud of yourself?"

"For helping relieve you of the basket?" He tilted his head sideways. "I suppose I am."

"That's not what I mean." And he knew it. Splaying her hands on her skinny hips, Victoria faced Connor down. She was taller than Suzy by a head, yet Connor still loomed over her. For a moment her resolve wavered; then she stiffened her spine. "Is that what you wanted?" She nodded to Suzy where she stood, her shoulders sagging. "You're going to ruin her day if you carry on like this."

There was a long, brooding silence.

"Sorry." But he didn't sound sorry in the least.

"That's the best you can do?" demanded Victoria.

"I accept his apology," Suzy said quickly. "I understand why he's upset."

"I'm not *upset*," he growled, and gave Victoria a killing how-dare-you stare before stalking off in Michael's wake, the basket swinging incongruously at his side.

"Jerk!" Victoria fumed. To her astonishment she found that her hands were trembling. She brushed them over her hair, more to regain her composure than to smooth the style. She was too tired to be tactful. "What does Michael see in the man?"

"Make allowances for him." Suzy put a hand on her arm. "His girlfriend just dumped him for his business partner. It can't be a good time for him."

Victoria gave a derisive laugh. "I don't blame her one bit. No sane woman could live with a jerk like him."

"He's hurting," Suzy protested.

"Didn't you hear the way he said 'love'? Like it was something foreign to him. Connor North feels as much emotion as a slab of granite."

"Michael says he doesn't share much, so maybe he did love her. He's been very good about it, even letting her keep the house."

"I'm sure she deserved it."

"Shh." Suzy's grip on her arm tightened. "He might hear you."

"I don't care."

"Well, I do. C'mon, Tory, Michael and I were seriously hoping the two of you would become…well…friends."

Friends with Connor North? Friendship implied affection, warmth and loyalty. Victoria couldn't imagine Rock-Face ever exhibiting any of those qualities. She stared down at the person who knew her better than anyone in the world and gave a snort of disbelief. "You're dreaming, Suz."

Had Michael and Suzy been planning to match-make?

"Okay." Suzy held up her hands. "I'm not going to argue, so let's change the subject. I've been meaning to ask you, Tory, if you wouldn't mind popping past the cottage to water the potted plants while we're on honeymoon. Connor might forget."

Victoria frowned suspiciously. "What do you mean 'Connor might forget?'"

"He's been staying with Michael this past week and the two of them have been working like dogs every evening to get the house all painted inside. And Connor will look after it while we're on honeymoon—Michael dotes on that house."

"I suppose I can drop round in my lunch hour—that way I won't bump into him." Then Victoria clicked her tongue. "Suzy, you're not intending to start off your marriage with a houseguest, are you?"

"Oh, no, he's not the type to be a third wheel—though he's helped Michael heaps with the house. Michael could never have done as much alone. No, Connor will find a place while we're on honeymoon. Michael just felt he needed a few days to get over the shock of losing his woman, his home and his business in one shot."

Victoria steeled herself against a sneaky twinge of sympathy. However hard a time he'd had, it was no reason to attack Suzy. "I'm sure he'll recover."

"Please be nice to him, Tory." Suzy stretched her blue eyes wide. "I don't want the wedding photos ruined because the maid of honor and best man have a fistfight."

No sane woman could live with a jerk like him.

Telling himself that the dislike was mutual didn't stop the maid of honor's words from rankling as Connor marched across the car park tucked away behind the church hall. He came to a stop where Michael Mason rummaged in the trunk of a modest Toyota parked in the dark shade of two tall pines.

"That woman is a menace." Connor dropped the basket filled with hymn books into the trunk next to the black rollaway bag.

The groom's head came up, and the brown eyes of a man Connor met twice weekly for a killer game of squash grew cool as Michael said with deceptive mildness, "Suzy is going to be my wife, Connor. Watch what you say."

Connor did a double take. "Wow. You've got it bad." His mouth slanted as Michael tensed. "Steady on, I was talking about the maid of honor."

"Victoria?" Michael slammed the trunk shut. "She's been friends with Suzy for decades. In fact—"

The sudden gleam in Michael's eyes had Connor bringing his hands up in front of him to ward off the inevitable. "Don't go there—she's not my type."

The woman was way too opinionated.

Michael ignored the warning. "Maybe you need a change from blonds. In fact, Suzy and I thought she might be the perfect antidote to Dana."

Fresh annoyance surged through Connor at the memory of overhearing Suzy telling her friend that he'd been dumped by his girlfriend. And the sympathy in her eyes when she'd said she understood why he was upset.

Upset? Hell, he wasn't upset. He was damned mad.

Mad at Dana. Mad at Paul Harper. Mad at Michael for divulging a confidence. And mad at the irritating, interfering witch who'd forced an apology out of him.

Breathing deeply, he said, "I gather you told Suzy all about Dana?"

Michael extracted a set of car keys from his pants pocket and activated the remote to unlock the doors. "How could I not? She would've found out anyway."

"My business partner and my girlfriend…and I was the last to know." Connor tried to laugh as he went around to the passenger side. "Soap opera stuff, huh?"

The raw hurt and betrayal that two days earlier had scorched all the way to his soul resurfaced. He hated the thought of people picking over the details of his devastated life.

"What Paul did was unforgivable." Michael's mouth was firm as he settled in the seat beside Connor. "And Dana was more than your girlfriend. The woman's been living with you for nearly two years. Hell, you even made her a director of Harper-North."

How Connor regretted Wednesday's drunken bout of self-pity. He'd been away, laying the groundwork to open Harper-North's first Australian office. On his return from Sydney, Dana had hit him with the news that their relationship was over. She had a new lover—the man he'd gone to university with, the man he'd founded a business with. His best friend. His *former* best friend.

Connor had gone to Michael's house, gotten drunk, and blurted it all out. Dumb.

"The whole world shifted on its axis in the three weeks I

was gone." Connor raked his hands through his hair. It needed a cut. The mundane thought steadied him. "Came back to find my life in uproar and you planning marriage." He shook his head. "Crazy."

"Not that crazy. I've know Suzy a while, even though we only started dating about a month ago."

"A month?" Connor raised his brows. "After two years I didn't know what kind of treachery Dana was capable of. You should've taken more time."

"A month. A year. Two years. It's not going to make a difference to how I feel about Suzy."

"So what makes you so sure Suzy isn't after a lifelong meal ticket?"

A chuckle filled the car. "Mate, I'm not the billionaire here. I don't wear thousand-dollar suits—" Michael gave Connor's Armani a mocking inspection "—drive a Maserati, or live in a marble mansion."

"I don't live there anymore."

This week's showdown came back to haunt Connor. Paul had already moved into *his* house with Dana. But he'd wring every cent that he could from the pair of them in exchange for the mansion that Dana had craved…and the share of Harper-North that Connor had walked away from. They weren't going to get off scott-free.

"Sorry." The laughter faded from Michael's eyes. "But trust me, Suzy's not marrying me for money. She's a teacher, just like me, so our incomes are pretty equal."

Dana had been trying to wheedle an engagement ring out of Connor for ages. His thoughts came to a grinding halt. Had Suzy tricked Michael into a proposal with the oldest trick in the book?

"What about children?" Connor prodded. Dana had begged for a child. But Connor had resisted. He hadn't wanted marriage—which he suspected was the real reason for Dana's desperate desire for a child. A child would've been a mistake. They were both too busy for kids, he'd told her.

Michael turned the key in the ignition. His jaw had firmed and his hands gripped the steering wheel.

"I'm not asking if this woman's already pregnant," Connor lied hastily as the motor took. "Just wondering if she views you as a father figure for any children she has." A high school guidance counselor, Michael would make the perfect mark for a solo mother wanting financial and emotional support.

"She doesn't have any." The reply was clipped.

"That's a relief. I was worried she might be a desperate divorcée." Connor paused as they rolled down a narrow lane lined with clipped hedges that hid the church from view.

"She's divorced but she's not desperate." Michael's jaw jutted out, a sign of the stubborn streak that usually remained hidden beneath his affable, calm exterior. "You'll like Suzy, Connor—if you let yourself. There's no catch."

Connor stared at Michael's profile, aware he wasn't getting anywhere. The strange notion that his orderly life had spun out of control increased. He shook his head. "You're not listening. There's always a catch."

"Of course I'm listening."

"But?" Something about the set of Michael's jaw told Connor this was one of the rare times that none of his arguments were going to succeed.

In the years he'd been playing squash with Michael he'd come to value the calm, unconditional friendship they'd forged. Connor often offered Michael financial advice, and only twice had Michael disregarded it. The first time Michael had lost thousands on a development that went belly up. The second time Connor had advised him to steer clear of a derelict Edwardian cottage on a busy road. Michael had wanted to use an unexpected legacy from a great-aunt as a deposit. Connor had warned him the restoration would devour money faster than a hungry loan shark.

But Michael had bought the place anyway and spent every weekend working on it. Connor had taken to dropping by on Sunday afternoons to lend Michael a hand—much to Dana's disgust—and the manual labor involved in stripping old paintwork and restoring the cottage had proved extremely rewarding. As the house took shape Connor finally admitted he'd been wrong. Despite the exorbitant amount of time and money it consumed, Michael's home was special.

It had reminded him of the days when he and Paul had first started out, fired by dreams of preserving as many forgotten buildings as they could.

When had they lost that idealism? When had it all become about the next million?

Yet just because Michael had been right about that old place of his didn't mean this madly rushed marriage would work out, Connor decided as they waited for a break in the traffic.

"But…Suzy's nothing like Dana."

Connor bristled at the mention of Dana's name. "I never said she was."

Michael threw him a disbelieving look. "Don't let what Dana did embitter you. I think you're well rid of her. I never liked her, you know. You deserve someone better."

"Right now I'm hardly in the mood to play dating games," Connor growled.

"You'll get over it." Michael nosed the Toyota onto the road that ran past the front of the church. "We'll find someone to kiss your broken heart better at the wedding tomorrow."

Connor gave him a baleful glare. "My heart isn't broken."

"No," Michael agreed. "It's your pride that's battered."

"Thanks, mate, I really needed to hear that!"

Michael was still laughing as they pulled up in front of the church gate where the bride and her maid of honor waited.

Despite Suzy's blonde prettiness, Connor found his gaze drawn to her friend. A patina of reserve clung to her. There was not a hint of feminine flounce in the straight black skirt, black stockings or the tailored white shirt. Yet when she moved toward the car, she carried herself with an easy, swinging grace that contrasted sharply with her coolly composed features.

"Best therapy right now would be another woman. Victoria—"

"*No.*" Connor looked away from the termagant and directed a stony stare at Michael. "I definitely don't need another hard-boiled career woman with her eye on the main chance. So don't try any matchmaking tonight or you'll be looking for a new best man for your wedding tomorrow."

Two

Connor barely noticed the radiant beauty of the stained-glass window backlit by the afternoon sun. Or how the kaleidoscopic light fell onto the faces of bride and groom, giving them an otherworldly quality. Instead he stood stiffly next to *her* behind the bridal pair as they exchanged vows, Michael's voice deep and serious, Suzy sounding much breathier.

His anger at *her* had driven away his annoyance that Michael had dared to discuss Connor's abortive personal affairs with Suzy. He couldn't bear the thought of being pitied by anyone.

Although he could hardly accuse *her* of pitying him.

Unwillingly Connor slanted a sideways look at the maid of honor. He'd planned to ignore her today. She'd said little at dinner last night. Despite his threats to Michael, his and Suzy's matchmaking efforts had been irritatingly obvious, and Connor had no intention of giving the argumentative woman any encouragement. The next woman he dated would be pure entertainment…no strings and plenty of hot sex. Not another high-flyer married to her career.

Her pallor last night had suggested she'd be more prone to headaches than hot sex. So had her attitude—she'd excused herself just after eleven, pleading exhaustion, but when he'd offered her a ride home she'd given him a look that suggested she'd rather eat slugs, and insisted on calling a taxi.

He had to admit she looked much better today. Suzy's doing, no doubt. He almost hadn't recognized her at the church door. Only her height—she was tall, her head coming up to his chin—her slender body and those wary hazel eyes had identified her.

Yet she was impossible to ignore.

Yesterday's rumpled white shirt and black sacklike skirt had given way to an ultrafeminine dress of some pale, gauzy fabric that turned what he could see of her skin to the delicious luminescence of pearl. She'd done something different with her hair, too, twisting the dark strands up so it exposed the soft, pale skin of her neck, and a couple of loose tendrils brushed the slope of her shoulders.

And all that bare, feminine skin tempted him to touch, to stroke.

What the hell was he thinking? One week without a woman to call his own and even this plain, uptight female was starting to look attractive.

Despite Michael's advice, the last thing he needed in his life was a woman. Even if he did, this one didn't qualify—she was way too intense. And, as Suzy's best friend, too complicated.

A hush fell over the church and he turned his head to watch Michael slip a plain gold band onto Suzy's finger. There was a moment where the world seemed to hold its breath, and Michael looked positively bewitched.

Connor let out the breath he was holding.

He should've advised Michael on the wedding band. Women

liked diamonds. Dana would've demanded a humdinger—for investment purposes of course. Michael should at least have had a row of diamonds channel set.

The priest was giving Michael permission to kiss the bride. Connor blanked out the sighs from the congregation and his awareness of the woman standing beside him, and found himself hoping Suzy would be more trustworthy than Dana had been.

Then, thankfully, the service was over. As they filed out of the church Connor pulled out his BlackBerry and made a note to himself about a meeting with a Realtor to look at new offices that he'd remembered he was supposed to attend on Monday.

The maid of honor—he really should remember her name—was glaring at him. Guiltily he stuck the BlackBerry back in his pocket.

"Wait," she ordered as he headed for the stairs. "Michael and Suzy will want a photo at the church door."

Violet? Was that her name? "There's a wedding photographer to do that." He gestured to where the man stood. "I didn't bring a camera."

"They might want us to be in the photo with them. We should smile. Look happy."

"Sure."

She shot him a narrow look; clearly she hadn't missed his sarcasm. Not Violet, but it had been something equally old-fashioned. Edith? No, that wasn't right, either.

He was saved from the need to reply by Michael and Suzy's emergence from the church, their faces alight with what even he could recognize was joy. Envy speared him. Then he suppressed it. He was done with love and romance… from now on his relationships would be based purely on sex. No emotion. No tenderness.

That way there would be no betrayal.

The bridal couple paused under the arched church door

beneath a flurry of pink-and-white rose petals, and the photographer leapt into action.

The damn woman had been right.

Unbidden, his eyes landed on her. She was smiling, and Connor had to admit it transformed her face. At least she wasn't gloating. His gaze lingered on her curved lips and he couldn't help noticing that her mouth was very pretty when it wasn't screwed up in disapproval.

"Connor, Victoria, over here!" called Suzy.

Victoria. Of course! "We're being summoned." He placed a hand under her elbow. Her skin was silky beneath his fingertips. Out of nowhere a totally unexpected surge of lust hit him. Perhaps the wedding reception wouldn't be such an ordeal after all…

Suzy was beckoning impatiently. "Come on, we need a photo with the two of you."

"I told you so," muttered Victoria.

Connor shot her a look of dislike. Okay, so he'd been wrong on two counts. Firstly, the reception was going to be every bit as bad as he'd imagined and, secondly, she *had* been gloating. She'd simply concealed it under that sweetly deceptive smile.

All desire waned. It didn't need Michael's grin—nor the pointed look to Connor's hand where it rested—for his hand to drop away from her arm.

The further he stayed away from Queen we-are-not-amused Victoria, the better.

On entering the ballroom, Connor discovered—much to his horror—that rather than the two of them flanking the bridal pair, he and Victoria had been seated beside each other.

"Give the two of you a chance to talk, seeing that all my attention will be on my bride," Michael murmured sotto voce, holding a chair out for Suzy, who glanced up and gave Connor a little wave, her eyes glittering with mischief.

Irritation swarmed through Connor and he glared at the smug groom.

Connor survived the first round of speeches by ignoring Victoria completely, although if he'd been honest he'd have had to admit that the subtly seductive scent she wore didn't make that easy. By the time he had to propose a toast to the bride and groom he'd downed three glasses of too-sweet wedding wine. When the first notes of the wedding waltz struck up he looked vainly around for a waiter to order a double whiskey.

"Come on," an unwelcome voice beside him prompted. "We should join them."

"I'm not dancing," he said flatly, settling for another glass of sweet champagne with a grimace.

Her gaze landed on the glass and her straight eyebrows drew together in a frown. "Surely you're not going to use Suzy and Michael's wedding as an excuse to get drunk?"

Deliberately provocative, he raised the tulip-glass in a mocking toast. "I'm celebrating the love that you believe in."

"Don't be so flippant." Her disapproval deepened. "This is the happiest day of Suzy and Michael's life and you're going to ruin it for them if you carry on. And all because you're too busy feeling sorry for yourself."

Connor blinked in disbelief. "*What* did you say?" He couldn't have heard right. Everyone had been pussyfooting around the subject of Dana and Paul's affair. Surely she wouldn't dare…

Their eyes locked. Hers were more green than brown, flashing little flecks of gold. It wasn't pity he read there but disdain.

He'd heard perfectly. And grew convinced this woman would dare anything.

Anger knotted in his chest.

"Snap out of it. Think of someone except yourself for a

change. It's only a couple more hours." Her gaze dropped to the glass in front of him. "And I suggest you slow down on the alcohol."

"I don't know who you think you are—" he lowered his voice to a lethal rasp "—but you are way out of line."

"I'm Victoria." A grim smile accompanied the words. "In case you've forgotten, I'm the bride's best friend—" she emphasized *best* "—but I don't understand how Michael can call you a friend at all. I certainly haven't seen you do anything to deserve it."

Her words stung. He was on his feet before he could think. "I don't have to listen to this!"

Startled dismay flitted across her face. She cast a quick glance to where the bride was nestled in the groom's arms. Michael chose that moment to glance at them over the top of Suzy's curls. Victoria muttered something that sounded suspiciously like an expletive, pushed her chair back and grabbed his hand.

"Great." The beaming smile she turned on him transformed her face. "Let's get dancing."

Connor stared at her, poleaxed by the wattage of her smile. It made her look almost beautiful.

He blurted out, "You should smile more often," and in a daze followed her onto the dance floor.

Michael slowed to a shuffle and mouthed, "Everything okay?"

Crap, she was right. Again. He *was* being selfish. Forcing a smile, Connor gave Michael the thumbs-up.

Everything was great.

Right.

Somehow the maid of honor was in his arms, swaying into the wedding waltz, her dress soft and silky under the hands he hadn't even realized he'd placed on her waist.

"How did you meet Michael?" she asked, still smiling up at him.

He again noticed how lovely her mouth was and forgot the sheer fury she aroused in him. It was, after all, a very distracting mouth. One taste…it would surely rid his tongue of the aftertaste of that awful champagne.

"We're members of the same squash club. When our original partners stopped playing—" Paul had preferred the gym "—we were both at a loose end, so we teamed up." That had been six years ago. Despite seeing his business partner every day of his life, Connor realized Michael had proved to be the better friend. He switched off that train of thought before the bleakness that had hovered over him for the past three days descended again.

No Paul or Dana today.

Not even dreaming up grisly plans for revenge.

"Do you work with Suzy?" he asked, determined to get his mind out of the rut it kept drifting back to. Maybe Michael was right and a date with Victoria would be a good distraction.

The smile faded and her eyes turned cool. "I'm an accountant—Michael told you that, remember?"

"That's right." No, a date with Victoria would be a very bad idea. "But should you have reminded me? Isn't that rude?" He gave her a sharklike smile that held no humor.

"Not as impolite as your evident disinterest—you can't even remember my name."

Touché. He took in the flare of rosy color on her cheeks, the sparkle of spirit in her eyes. How had he ever thought she was dreary? "Your name is Victoria. And I can't think why I thought you were a teacher."

"Perhaps because I know Suzy?"

No, it was that silent reserve, and the way she didn't hesitate to correct him. He wasn't accustomed to that—except from his assistant Iris. And that was different; Iris was a friend of his mother's and had known him for three decades.

"It's the way you told me off."

She slanted him an upward glance. "Yesterday or just now? Either way, you deserved it."

Connor tried to convince himself that yesterday's scene had been her fault, but he couldn't shrug off the discomfort that lingered at the memory of the expression in Suzy's eyes. Telling himself that *Victoria* had provoked him didn't wash. He was accountable for his own actions, and the fact that his life was in chaos was irrelevant.

Instead of responding, he simply shrugged.

"I think you need people to stand up to you more often."

She pursed that luscious mouth again and Connor had a wild desire to shake her out of her righteous complacency.

"Everyone seems to know what I need." Her lips parted and Connor got the impression she, too, was about to tell him exactly what she thought he needed. Wickedly determined to silence her, he drew her closer into his arms, bent his head and murmured in her ear, "Michael thinks I need a woman."

Alone with Suzy in the hotel's honeymoon suite where they'd retreated to mend the flounce of Suzy's wedding dress, Victoria couldn't forget the heady excitement that dancing with Connor had aroused—or the words he'd whispered in her ear.

Michael thinks I need a woman.

His touch on her waist…the way he made her feel so fragile and feminine in his arms…the glorious male scent of him that had surrounded her. She shivered.

Heavens, it had been too long since she'd dated if a man she despised could reduce her to quivering desire, she decided acerbically. Victoria pulled the final stitch tight and savagely snapped off the thread. "There, that should hold as long as you don't put a heel through the hem again."

"Victoria, I need a favor."

Glancing up from where she knelt beside Suzy, Victoria

met Suzy's eyes in the floor-to-ceiling mirrored closet doors. "What's the favor?"

"Don't feel you have to agree."

"How bad can it be? Come on, spit it out."

There was a pause as Victoria arranged the skirts around Suzy's legs, waiting. Then, "It's harder than I thought it would be."

At the hesitant note in Suzy's voice, Victoria's attention sharpened. She rocked back on her heels—no easy task given the close-fitting sheath dress she'd chosen to wear. "You can ask me anything—you know that."

"This is different…it's difficult. And I'm going to swear you to secrecy if you agree. You can never, ever tell anyone about it."

Curiouser and curiouser. "Can it be more difficult than asking me to tell your mother you'd driven over her rose-bushes? Did I refuse then?" Victoria raised an eyebrow, inviting Suzy to smile with her. "Granted, you didn't swear me to secrecy that time."

But Suzy didn't laugh.

"You can't be having second thoughts about your wedding?" Victoria's heart sank at the thought. "You're not about to run out on Michael, are you?"

Suzy's blue eyes grew round. "Oh, no! I'd never do that. How could you even think that, Tory? Michael's everything I ever dreamed of finding."

The certainty in Suzy's voice caused a sudden flare of envy. Pushing herself up off the carpet, Victoria suppressed it. She'd made her choices. After a string of disastrous relationships had ended in accusations that she was too ambitious, she'd decided there were more rewarding ways to fill her life.

She had her job. A fantastic job where she'd built up an impressive client list. And she had Suzy, the best and most loyal friend anyone could wish for.

She didn't need a man…or a wedding.

So why on earth was she envying Suzy?

And realistically what chance did she have of finding the kind of man she wanted? A man who would let her keep the independence she craved, and love her for it? The memory of a pair of hard hands at her waist, a harsh whisper in her ear, stole over her. Certainly not a man like Connor North. Arrogant. Demanding. A man who didn't even believe in love.

Drawing a shaky breath, Victoria forced herself to focus on Suzy, on the issue at hand rather than on the illusion of finding someone who would love her forever. "I just thought you might've belatedly remembered your vow never to marry again."

"That was years ago." Suzy waved a dismissive hand and turned to the mirror to study herself. "I'd just come from the lawyer's office and a horrible fight about the divorce settlement with Thomas. Of course I was feeling a little sore about marriage."

A *little* sore? Victoria almost laughed at the understatement but the tension in her friend's shoulders warned against it. Suzy had studiously avoided weddings for a year after that first disastrous attempt at matrimony.

"I love Michael. I want…*need*…this time to work." Suzy spun back, her dress whirling around in a froth of white, and slanted Victoria an imploring look. "You of all people must know that I want what Mum and Dad had."

How had Suzy unerringly known to pick on the one thing that would silence Victoria?

Suzy's parents had adored each other—and they'd been loving and incredibly kind. Whenever Victoria's father had been overcome by a bout of wanderlust, her mother had retreated into a sobbing self-pity. It had been Suzy's parents who had offered Victoria a bed for the night, cooked meals for her and ensured that she made it to school with her clothes clean and her homework done.

When they'd drowned in a boating accident, Suzy and Victoria had been at university and Victoria felt the double loss almost as acutely as her friend. She would never forget the sanctuary that Suzy's home had become during her adolescent years. It had saved her, creating a debt she could never repay. Without Suzy and her parents, who knew how she would've turned out?

Victoria held her best friend's gaze. "I hope you find the same happiness your parents had. I think it's wonderful that you've found someone—I just don't want you to be hurt again."

Suzy threw her arms around Victoria. "Relax, Michael is nothing like Thomas."

Clumsily hugging Suzy back, Victoria stared over her friend's shoulder at their reflection in the mirror, Suzy so beautiful in her high-necked lacy wedding gown, the hem no longer dragging on the ground.

She wanted Suzy to stay happy forever. She'd hated how Thomas had made bright, bubbly Suzy so miserable. Just like her own father had killed all the joy in her mother...

How she'd resented her mother for allowing it. How she'd wished that her mother had stood up and told her father to leave, never to return—and to stop neglecting them both—rather than weeping pathetically and sinking into depression every time he vanished. If only her mother had been stronger, not so emotionally dependent on the handsome but feckless man she'd married.

Suzy's arms dropped away. "Stop frowning, Tory. It's my wedding day, remember?"

Victoria blinked. "How could I forget?" she said wryly, gesturing to their reflections in the mirror. "Your gorgeous dress...the flowers...the suite."

"Connor arranged the suite—and our honeymoon to Hawaii. It's his wedding present to us. Wasn't that generous?"

Victoria had no intention of acknowledging any redeeming

qualities in the man. "All this talk of secrets had me concerned. But if you're truly happy then I have no cause to worry."

There was an expression in Suzy's eyes that Victoria had never seen before. A mixture of trepidation and yearning. The sinking feeling returned. "There is something! What is it, Suz? Are you in trouble?"

"Michael knows the reason my marriage to Thomas fell apart was because I couldn't—" Suzy swallowed visibly "—have a baby."

"Oh, Suzy." Victoria took Suzy's hands in hers. Despite the heating in the honeymoon suite, her friend's fingers were cold.

"He knows that Thomas and I tried IVF and that it was unsuccessful. So we talked to a specialist. From my medical records, she thinks there's still a chance I could get pregnant."

"That's wonderful!"

"But only if we can find an egg donor," Suzy finished in a rush, pulling her hands free and, after a quick glance at Victoria, turning away to retrieve her bridal bouquet off the bed behind them.

"You want me to be your donor?" For a moment Victoria wondered what would be involved. Pain. Expense. All sorts of stuff she'd never had to contemplate before. Victoria took in Suzy's tense figure, the way she hunched over her wedding bouquet as she waited for Victoria's reply. What was some physical discomfort compared to Suzy's pain? Suzy had already lost one husband because of her inability to conceive, and while Michael loved her, it would be understandable that she feared his love would diminish as time passed and other couples they knew started to conceive.

Suzy was more than a friend. She was the sister Victoria had never had. Her only family. The person she owed more than she could ever give back. "Of course I'll do it. Consider it a gift. My wedding gift to you and Michael." To help this marriage hold together. To bring Suzy the happiness she richly deserved.

Instantly she was enfolded in a fierce hug, and the fragrance from the posy of white roses and gardenias Suzy clutched wafted around them.

"Thank you!" Suzy's eyes brimmed with tears as she pulled back. "That's the best gift ever…even if it doesn't work out and there's no baby, I'll never forget this."

"Miracles have been known to happen. And no one deserves this miracle more than you, Suz." Victoria felt her own throat clogging up. "Help, now you're making me cry."

Suzy gave her a radiant smile. "It's okay to cry at weddings—so long as it's the happy kind of crying. Now let's get back downstairs—I intend to dance the night away."

Connor wasn't at the wedding table.

Michael thinks I need a woman. Victoria couldn't get his mocking words out of her head. Maybe he'd decided to follow the groom's advice and find a willing female. There would be no shortage of them among the guests.

Searching the dance floor, Victoria couldn't pick out his dark hair and tall figure, which should have towered above everyone else. She drifted around the edge of the polished wooden floor and finally spotted him standing near the open glass doors that led out onto a wide veranda.

He turned his head as if he knew she was watching him and met her gaze. Without a word, he headed for the doors and Victoria followed automatically, drawn against all good sense.

"So do you want to dance out here in the starlight?" He stood in the shadows of the balcony, leaning against the railing, moonlight casting a strange silver-and-black glow over his face.

Her breath caught in her throat. The music spilled through the doors, a slow, sweet, seductive beat. It would take only two steps to bring her into his arms, to feel the heat of his body close to hers again. No. Madness! "The moon's too bright tonight to speak of starlight."

His white teeth glittered as he grinned. "You're probably right—but then I'm sure you make a career of being right."

He pushed away from the railing and moved toward her. "So do you concur with Michael, that the warmth of a woman's body is what I need?" The words cut through the night.

Victoria swallowed, her mouth suddenly dry. Why hadn't she just minded her own business? He wasn't the kind of man to play with.

"If you don't want to dance, what are you looking for? Are you here to offer yourself?" he murmured huskily. "It's supposed to be one of the delights of being the best man, hooking up with the maid of honor. What fun."

Victoria found nothing amusing in his biting tone. "No." She backed up but, before she could retreat, his arms came around her and he lowered his head.

"Don't—" she managed, and then his mouth ground down on hers.

It wasn't a gentle kiss. Full of whiskey and force and anger, it was unlike anything she'd ever experienced.

Victoria struggled but his grip was tight, pinning her arms at her sides. He moved closer, his thighs thrusting against her softness, making it clear he was aroused.

God.

She fought herself free. "What the hell was that about?"

"I don't like being manipulated." He was breathing hard. "I don't want a woman, understand?"

"You're insane." She resisted the urge to retort that he was fooling himself—he was desperate for a woman. For her.

"You're saying you didn't come out for exactly that? Conspiring with your friend, hoping to catch me on the rebound?"

"You are such a jerk." She swung her back on him, determined to leave him out here alone.

He grabbed her and yanked her back. "Not nice."

This time when his lips descended she knew what was coming—and tensed.

But it was different.

Soft, seductive. His tongue stroked the corners of her mouth until she parted her lips, granting him access. This time he kissed her with a dark desire that stirred wants that had never been woken. Dark, traitorous desires. And when his hands swept up over her arms, down her back, she edged closer, craving more—wishing he'd sweep her off to someplace private where they could spend hours together exploring naked skin and sweet sensations.

By the time he ended the kiss she was ready to do whatever he asked.

Connor North set her away from him with shaking hands. "Now, tell me that wasn't what you wanted."

She lifted a hand to her mouth, the fullness of her lips tingling. Damn Connor North. He must surely be aware of his effect on her. Sucking in a shuddering breath, she said, "Don't try it again or I'll slap you so hard it'll leave marks on your face."

He laughed. "Here—" he thrust a pristine, folded white handkerchief at her "—use this for that other dramatic gesture B-grade girls love. Wipe it across your mouth and make the necessary sounds of disgust." His eyes glittered wildly in the half light.

Ignoring the shaky feeling inside, Victoria quirked one expressive, dark eyebrow. "Girls do that to you often?"

"No…but then the women I know don't threaten to slap me, either." His not-so-subtle emphasis of the word *women* caused color to flame in her face.

She balled the handkerchief in a fist, and he flinched as she raised it to his mouth.

"Stand still." Her voice was tight. "Better I wipe my lipstick off *your* mouth."

The curves of his mouth felt full and sensual under the fabric. "There, I'm done."

Connor stared down at the red stain on the white cloth and his lips twisted. "You should have left your mark on my mouth."

He raised his head and Victoria felt the force of his reckless attraction hit her like a surge of current. "Why would I want to do that?" She injected scorn into her voice.

He shrugged carelessly. "It would have given all the gossips something to talk about other than my scurrilous split from Dana."

"I don't want to be linked to you." Victoria was appalled at the idea. "So we're going to go back to the table and smile like crazy—for Suzy and Michael's sake. But after today I intend to take great pains to keep as far away from you as possible."

"That won't be necessary. You're hardly my type…" he paused, then added tauntingly "…Elizabeth."

Victoria spun away and stalked inside and quite spoilt the moment by failing to remind him that her name was Victoria.

Three

August, present day, two years later

Late on Monday afternoon, Connor walked out of the morgue in the small Northland town where the bodies had been taken and gulped in a lungful of crisp, fresh air. *Michael.* The face he'd known so well in life had been unrecognizable in death. And all the dazzling laughter had left Suzy forever. Connor craved the deep, cleansing peace of tears.

But grown men didn't cry.

Nor did he have time to grieve. Picking up his pace, he jogged across the car park to where the Maserati waited.

But once inside, he sat motionless, staring blindly through the windshield.

He should call Victoria. The thought came from nowhere. He sighed. What the hell was the purpose? Except to upset her further.

Pulling out of the car park, he headed for the highway.

Not far from the exit to the town he saw again the sickening skid marks, and the white symbols the police had painted on the tarmac.

Driven by a nameless, senseless urge Connor pulled over and got out.

The grass verge was peppered with glass, and he stepped over the deep furrows Michael's tires had gouged out of the turf. A light country breeze blew across his face and cars whizzed past. There was none of the sense that Michael's spirit still lingered—as Connor realized he'd hoped for when he'd pulled over.

It's not fair. They should be here! Victoria's words rang in his ears.

Balling his fists against his eyes, he faced the fact that he would never again see the slight smile that changed Michael's expression from intellectual to human. He would never again play squash against that killer competitive drive that few people knew Michael possessed.

A tidal wave of sorrow swept over him, and a moment later the aftershock of loneliness set in, paralyzing him.

Even after the fiasco with his ex-girlfriend and his business partner, he'd been able to act. He hadn't even missed Dana—he'd kept himself too busy. Working like a fiend to get the Phoenix Corporation up. Going to the gym. Squash and beers with Michael. Dating a string of women who entertained but didn't enthrall. While all the time Michael watched him with that quiet smile and offered advice that Connor hadn't taken.

And now he'd never see Michael again.

Even fighting with Victoria had to be better than this miserable emptiness. Then he remembered her face as he'd last seen it yesterday. Devastated by the loss of Suzy. Again the compulsion to call Victoria nagged him.

Michael…

Hell.

He dropped his balled fists to his side, blinked rapidly and swallowed, furious at the hot tightness in his chest. Never was a long time. And right now it stretched before him endlessly.

He wasn't accustomed to being powerless.

The only things left for him to do for Michael were so final—so futile. Arranging the funeral. Carrying the coffin. Executing his will. Ensuring that Dylan was protected.

A car swept by in a rush of air, the driver hooting, jerking him out of his trance of grief.

Dylan.

Connor raked both his hands through his wind-ruffled hair. Michael had loved Dylan; he loved Dylan, too.

No doubt about it, Dylan was special. Never had a baby been more loved. And that's the way it had always been meant to be.

When, shortly after his wedding, Michael had confessed to Connor that he was sterile as a result of contracting mumps as a boy, Connor had agreed to donate sperm to allow the Masons a chance at a baby. It hadn't been a hard decision for him to make. Anyone who knew Suzy and Michael could see that they were made to be parents. Perfect parents. Yet they'd worried about how their baby might one day react if he discovered Conner was his biological father.

Michael and Suzy had wanted the truth about his biological father to stay forever secret—and Connor had acquiesced to their request. The baby had always been intended to be theirs. Not his.

But now Michael and Suzy were dead.

Connor flinched at the finality of the word. But he would not break his vow to the Masons. At least not until Dylan was old enough to understand why he'd been created from his father's friend's seed.

The foggy lethargy that had clung to him for most of the day started to lift. Connor strode back to the Maserati.

At last he had something to do. Something worthwhile. He

had a duty—one he would not fail in. He would bring Dylan up to remember the fine man that Michael had been. And someday, when Dylan was older, he would explain how much his parents had loved him—and wanted him. That would be the time to tell Dylan—and the world—the truth.

Victoria reached for the shrilling phone and Dylan's eyes, which had been growing heavier, popped open. He again started to suck greedily on the bottle she'd been feeding him.

Juggling the handset and the bottle, she waited for him to settle again in the crook of her arm before saying, "Hello?"

"I'll be there in under an hour."

Her heart started to knock against her ribs. "Who is this speaking, please?"

"Don't play games, Victoria," growled Connor. "It's been a hell of a day."

Victoria fell silent. Her day had been pretty awful, too. First thing this morning she'd called Bridget Edge, the managing partner at work, to let her know she wouldn't be in, that she was taking compassionate leave because her best friend had died.

There had been a short silence. Then, after uttering per-functory condolences, Bridget had asked when she would be back at work.

Victoria had known in that moment it wouldn't be wise to say anything about Dylan. Yet.

Bridget would never understand. She wasn't married and had no children. How could Victoria have confessed that Dylan needed her right now? Or that she needed Dylan more than anything in the world? Bridget would've thought she'd lost her marbles. Finally Victoria said she would be back as soon as the funeral had been held.

Suzy had placed Dylan in a day care center a month ago. So far he'd only been going for half a day as Suzy eased herself back into teaching part-time. But if Dylan returned, it would save her from needing to make other arrangements—and keep his routine normal. Tomorrow she'd call the supervisor, let her know to expect Dylan back.

Tomorrow—when she'd gotten a handle on her grief and could talk without her throat tightening up.

Oh, Suzy!

She certainly didn't feel like facing Connor in less than an hour. Her emotions were too raw, her heart too sore. "I've just gotten Dylan to sleep and I'm about to take a bath. Perhaps we can talk tomorrow?"

"I thought you might want a copy of Michael and Suzy's will."

"Michael and Suzy's will?" Good grief, she hadn't even given a thought to a will. Most unlike her. Her gaze dropped to Dylan, whose mouth was now just twitching on the teat. Emotion overwhelmed her in a hot, poignant wave. The baby had kept her mercifully busy most of the day. He'd been querulous, almost as if he knew….

Except that wasn't possible.

Connor was speaking again. She forced herself to concentrate.

"Yes, a joint will. I've just dropped the original at my solicitor's so they can start winding up the estate."

"I could've done that. It's not going to be a complicated estate."

"You're too busy. Besides I'm the executor."

Hurt blasted her. She'd been the executor of Suzy's will before Suzy had gotten married.

Dylan grunted uneasily.

Cuddling the baby closer, she rocked him in a slow rhythm. "I didn't know Suzy and Michael had a joint will."

She'd nagged Suzy a couple of times to update her will when she was pregnant, but after Dylan was born, Victoria had forgotten all about it in the hectic pace of everyday work. That would have been around the time she'd taken over two new, big accounts on top of her already crippling workload. She'd finally built the practice she'd always wanted, but not without sacrifice.

"My solicitor updated it for them about a year ago." Connor's voice was clipped. "There's not a great deal in the estate."

"They both worked for state schools. They had expenses...." Victoria broke off, then added lamely, "And debts." She'd promised never to reveal her part in Dylan's conception. It certainly wasn't for her to reveal the staggering costs involved—she'd contributed a large sum despite Suzy and Michael's resistance.

"Not surprising," Connor concurred, "given they had a mortgage, too. But Michael took out life insurance to cover that."

Victoria knew Connor had spent hours helping Michael renovate the Masons's home. He'd even organized grants from a historic trust for assistance.

A sense of guilt filled her. Connor had clearly sorted out Michael's money matters, whereas she, an accountant, had failed to protect Dylan and Suzy's interests, leaving it to her new husband to look after her. And would his life insurance cover the IVF debts?

I'll make it up to you, Dylan.

She stroked the baby's soft head. He would want for nothing that was in her power to give him.

She'd contributed to Dylan's coming into the world, given Michael and Suzy the precious eggs they'd needed.

Dylan was a part of her.

"Are you still there?" The impatience in Connor's voice jerked her back.

"Yes. I was just thinking." The baby had just fallen asleep with the suddenness that still took Victoria by surprise. "Once the estate's been wound up I can invest the proceeds for Dylan."

There was a deafening silence.

Then Connor said, "I've always looked after Michael's business affairs."

And she'd always helped Suzy. Except when she'd become too busy. Discomfort filled Victoria.

This was not a time for a power struggle. She had to do her best to accommodate Connor; already he'd done a better job of looking after Suzy—and Dylan—when she'd been remiss.

But it will never happen again, she silently promised the baby in her arms. She was nothing like her parents. She would never neglect Dylan.

"Connor, as executor of the estate, of course you'd need to approve the investments. I'm sure we'll be able to work together in Dylan's best interests." She might not like him but they were both grown adults.

"I'm sure we will." Connor didn't sound nearly as convinced. "As Dylan's—" he broke off "—*guardian* you can bet your bottom dollar I will be very interested."

Her heart stopped. "Guardian?" she croaked. Her mind raced. Had Michael decided to appoint Connor North the baby's guardian? "*You* are Dylan's guardian?" Oh, Suzy, how could you let this happen?

Connor's voice, terse and cool, came over the line. "That's what I want to talk to you about. I'll be there in half an hour."

By the time Connor arrived, Victoria had laid Dylan down in his traveling cot, showered and changed into a simple long-sleeved dress, and had just poured herself a cup of tea.

Rushing across the living room to open the front door before Connor could ring the doorbell, she pressed her finger to her lips and motioned him into the kitchen. "I just got him to sleep."

In the kitchen, Victoria honed in on the subject that had

been eating at her since their telephone conversation. "I'd like to see the will." She did her best to keep the hostility out of her voice, to keep it level and professional.

Connor drew a leather document holder from under his arm and eyed the counter, which was covered with dirty dishes.

Embarrassment spread through Victoria. But then he hadn't been looking after a baby all day.

A surreptitious glance revealed lines of tiredness etched deep into his face, though they failed to mute the impact of his hard, handsome features.

Only the loosened tie and undone top button of his white shirt hinted at the turmoil he must be going through.

The will could wait—whatever it held would not change now. And Connor looked like a train wreck.

"Would you like a cup of coffee?"

"God, I don't know if I need more stimulants," Connor muttered, leaning against the counter.

She gestured to the crowded countertop. "I've just made tea for myself. Would you like a cup?"

She took his grunt as assent, poured him a cup of tea from the little white teapot and topped the brew up with boiling water.

He glared into the cup she passed him. "What the hell is this?"

"Chamomile tea," she said sweetly. "Lots of antioxidants. Good for you in times of stress."

"I doubt it will help." His startlingly pale eyes clashed with hers but the opacity in them caused Victoria's heart to bump and her throat to contract with painful emotion. She wanted to offer him the same comfort she craved—an embrace that went beyond words—but she knew he wouldn't accept it. Not from her.

And to be truthful she didn't care much for him, either. But she felt empathy for him—in the same way she felt pity for herself. She'd lost the person she'd been most deeply bonded to in the world. And, hard as it was to imagine Rock-Man bonded to anyone, Michael had been fond of him. Judging by the emptiness in Connor's eyes, somewhere in that cold heart he'd been fond of Michael, too.

The sadness—the futility of it all—made her want to weep.

But she couldn't let herself forget that he was Dylan's guardian now. Please God, he hadn't been granted custody, too.

Connor wasn't the right person to bring up Dylan—he was too hard. Yet, given the animosity between them, it would be no easy task convincing him *she* was the right person. But failure to do so was not an option.

Because even though she hadn't carried him in her womb, Dylan had been conceived from her egg—he was her baby.

"Come and sit out here." Picking up the two cups and saucers she led him to the small deck that opened off the living room, edged with planter boxes filled with primulas and purple pansies.

Without a word, Connor followed.

Once seated, he placed the leather document holder on the white wrought-iron table where she often ate breakfast, and zipped it open.

Unable to restrain herself, Victoria snatched up the will, scanning the headings as she flicked through the pages. And found the clause that spelled out guardianship and custody.

Four

Fury bubbled up inside Victoria. She threw the papers down on the table and her chair scraped back against the deck. "You told me you were Dylan's guardian," she accused.

"Coguardian." Connor shrugged. "And we share custody, too. We need to discuss it."

The coldhearted bastard had nearly given her heart failure. She'd thought she'd have to *beg* to be allowed a say in Dylan's upbringing. All her unspoken reservations about her ability to be the kind of mother that Dylan needed came crashing in on her.

A gust of chilly wind cut through the fabric of her dress. She shivered. Crossing her arms, she rubbed her hands absently up and down her body. She couldn't allow her insecurities to take hold. She had to believe in herself. Because she was the only parent Dylan had.

Joint custody and coguardianship. How on earth was that going to work? Damn, what had Suzy been thinking?

Or not thinking.

Clearly Suzy had not imagined dying. Suzy would not have thought how impractical it all was to juggle such a young baby between two households.

Sure, it had been done before. But Connor had no motive to cooperate—it wasn't as if he was the baby's father. Still, as a single man who ran a large business, he probably wouldn't want to be hamstrung with a baby. Her heart lifted a little at the realization. In fact, he'd be glad to be rid of the burden.

Connor moved his chair a little nearer and Victoria tensed as she always did when he invaded her space. He stopped, too close now, and leaned toward her. Protectively she tightened her arms around herself. She could smell the crisp, lemony scent of his aftershave, which still lingered after the long day.

The light-gray eyes held her captive. "Victoria, if you don't mind keeping Dylan for another day or so while I get a room ready and painted out for him, I'll take him as soon as I can. Certainly by Thursday."

The spell snapped. Don't mind keeping Dylan? Then give him up to Connor in a day or two? That wasn't happening!

Pushing her chair back, she leapt to her feet. "Dylan will live with me," she cut in, desperate to get this settled as quickly as possible.

"With you?" Connor tilted his head back and gave her a raking glance. He looked unnervingly assured. "No way!"

"What do you mean, no way?" For one awful moment she thought he'd seen all the way to her soul. Read her doubts about her mothering abilities. Then she pulled herself together. She would learn. She would ask the caregivers at the day-care center a thousand questions. There was no way she could do a worse job than her own parents. "How will you cope with a baby? You don't even have a home!" At the blaze of fury in his eyes Victoria wished she'd left the last rash bit unsaid. Heck, she didn't even know if it was still true. "I mean, your ex took your home."

"And I bought another," he said very softly, his eyes glinting dangerously.

So he thought a home could simply be bought?

Something of her skepticism must have shown, because he added, "I have a house with a garden to play ball in and a swimming pool to splash around in—not a shoebox like this." Connor cast a disparaging look around the small deck, his gaze pointedly resting on the pale-cream couches and white carpets visible through the glass sliders. "At least Dylan will be able to grow up a boy in my home. What kind of life would he have here?"

"I'll buy a suburban house with a garden," she said, thinking back to the warmth and love that had filled Suzy's parents' home. "I haven't needed more than this until now."

She could afford to do it. Her savings were in a healthy state. Despite the lump sum she'd insisted on giving Suzy to help with the IVF expenses, which had been worth every cent. The outcome had been Dylan.

"And that'll mean your commute to work will increase." He gave her that sharklike smile. "Or did you intend to stop working?"

"Of course not!"

She needed to carry on working, otherwise how would she be able to give Dylan everything he deserved? Good day care and private schooling were expensive. And Dylan would get the best. She had no intention of leaving Dylan to the mercy of her own ignorance. And besides, it wasn't only for Dylan. She loved her job. It gave her a sense of self-worth. And it paid pretty damn well, too. She couldn't imagine giving up the client base she'd worked so hard to build. Nor would she ever throw away the independence she'd strived all her adult life to secure.

"Don't try telling me you would give up work if Dylan lived with you," she challenged, "because I won't swallow it."

"But I can take as much time off as I want to spend with

Dylan—I'm the boss. And I have a full-time housekeeper. Dylan would be well cared for. It has nothing to do with double standards." His bleak gaze settled on her. "Unlike you, I can devote as much time to Dylan as he needs."

The emptiness that lay behind his eyes was the very reason she could *never* surrender Dylan into his care. He would never be able to convince her he could give Dylan more love than she could. If her parenting skills were in doubt, Connor's were even more so.

A strong surge of maternal yearning took her by surprise. She swallowed. She would not lose Dylan to the block of rock who stood in front of her.

The baby was hers.

Hers.

And she would fight with everything she possessed, every weapon at her disposal, to make sure Dylan stayed with her. She, at least, was capable of giving him love.

"He's not leaving here." She realized her voice had risen.

"Victoria, be sensible—"

"I'm being perfectly sensible."

He gave a snort. "With the hours you work you don't have time for a baby. Suzy told me—me and Michael," he amended as her brows drew together. "She was worried about you. She thought you'd buried yourself alive. All you lived for was building a practice that would lead to more status."

"Buried myself alive?" The idea that Suzy had discussed her with Connor hurt. "What about you? You started a new company—and not just any company, the Phoenix Corporation is a huge venture."

"Yes, but I employ a large staff, I delegate—I don't do everything myself. I still found time to visit Michael and Suzy—"

"You pig!" Victoria couldn't believe she'd heard right. "How can you say that? You cruel—"

"Oh, God, I'm sorry, Victoria." His chair crashed backward and he came toward her, his hands outstretched. "I didn't mean it that—"

She slapped his hands away. "You meant it exactly that way." Her fingers stung. She stared down at her reddening palms. The tears she'd stanched so fiercely for the past two days leaked out.

"Victoria, I'm sorry." His arms closed around her.

She fought him off, elbowing him fiercely. "Let go of me, damn you!"

He dropped his arms and stepped back, breathing heavily.

She stormed past him through the glass sliders. Half a dozen strides carried her across the living room and she yanked the front door open, her clammy hands clutching the door handle to keep her trembling knees from giving out. She'd wanted him to hold her, to share the grief…but never like this. "Get out."

"We need to talk about Dy—"

"I have nothing to say to you. Go."

"Victoria—"

She kept her gaze averted, horribly conscious of the soundless tears streaming down her face and the nausea rising in the back of her throat. "Please, just go."

He stumbled past her. At the last moment he turned. "If you need—"

Hot, blinding anger surged, and she said, "I don't need anything you can give me."

Without another word Connor left.

The funeral was finally over. Mourners huddled in groups in the church hall sipping coffee from white cups.

Connor glanced to where Victoria stood in silence beside three women who he assumed must've been friends of Suzy's. The scooped neckline of the fitted black dress she wore accentuated her collar bones and the delicate line of her throat, and her tall, slender body moved to-and-fro as she rocked

Dylan. But she didn't spare him a glance. She'd barely spoken to him today.

Guilt gnawed at him. How had he managed to screw up so royally two nights ago? Judging by the dark rings around her eyes, she hadn't slept since. She was hurting. He could feel it. Hell, she'd made him so mad, but that was no excuse. Nor did the knowledge that he'd never intended to wound her so deeply ease his guilt.

He was worse than the pig she'd called him.

She'd loved Suzy. She would never forgive him for implying that she'd neglected Suzy before her tragic death. And how could he blame her?

The baby's head was nestled close against her shoulder, and Dylan's eyes widened with interest as Connor came closer.

"Here, let me take the baby."

He saw her stiffen, her hold tighten around the baby, as she became aware of him. "No!"

Did she think he was going to rip the baby away from her?

"Please?" Couldn't she see his remorse? "Dylan must be heavy."

She edged away from the group she'd been standing with, but not before one of them gave him a strange look. He didn't care. It was Victoria that concerned him right now.

"We're fine."

Her pallor, her reddened eyes, the way her fingers dug into the blanket that swaddled Dylan gave lie to that. She so wasn't fine. But he wasn't about to argue with her here for everyone to see.

"Victoria…" Connor searched for the words that would mend everything between them, that would put them back into the state of almost-truce that had existed before his insensitive accusation. And came up dry.

"Go away," she hissed. "You're *not* taking the baby from me."

"Victoria—" An elegant woman with short hair wearing a black-and-white houndstooth suit came up beside them eyeing Connor with curiosity. "I wanted to say how sorry I am for the loss of your friend."

"Thank you, Bridget."

"And who is this fellow?" Bridget studied Dylan with decidedly wary eyes, causing Connor to suppress his first grin in days.

"This is Dylan, Suzy's baby."

"Oh." Bridget exchanged long looks with Victoria. "How dreadful. Is her family looking after him?"

"Suzy doesn't have any close family—her parents are dead, and she was an only child. Dylan's been staying with me."

His smile fading, Connor watched Bridget—whoever the hell she was—process that information silently. Victoria must have seen her doubts, too, because her arms tightened around the baby, causing Dylan to squawk in protest.

Connor reached for the wriggling baby. "I'll hold him for you." Dylan lurched toward him with a gurgle before Victoria could argue.

Bridget examined him with interest.

Connor nodded politely.

With visible reluctance Victoria performed the introductions. "Bridget, this is Connor North, a friend of the Masons. Connor, Bridget Edge is managing partner at Archer, Cameron and Edge."

"Connor North? Of the Phoenix Corporation?" Bridget's gaze sharpened. Connor could see her mentally tallying up his assets. "I didn't know you were connected to Phoenix, Victoria."

Victoria looked trapped.

Connor couldn't resist saying wickedly, "We've been friends for years. We met at Suzy and Michael's wedding—I was best man and Victoria was maid of honor."

"How romantic." Bridget gave him a thin smile before her

gaze settled back on Dylan. "This arrangement of looking after the baby isn't going to be permanent, is it?"

"No," said Connor.

"Yes," said Victoria, her color high.

Dylan blew a raspberry.

"Well, it sounds like you two have matters to sort out." Bridget's carefully plucked eyebrows were nearly up to her hairline. "Please call me at the office later, Victoria. I think we should talk."

The tension in Victoria's slim figure only increased with her boss's departure. As the last of the stragglers drifted out, leaving Connor alone with Victoria…and a sleeping Dylan in his car seat, he said, "Come, it's been a long day. Time for me to take the two of you home."

"You know I'm going to have to call the office," said Victoria.

Work. The funeral barely over and already she was fretting about work.

"All Frigid wants is for you to confirm that the baby won't interfere with your billable hours." Connor knew his cynicism was showing.

"Bridget. Her name is Bridget."

He kept his face deadpan. "I've always had a problem with names—you know that."

"Let it go, Connor." But her lips twitched.

So she did have a sense of humor. If he hadn't been watching her carefully he'd have missed that barely perceptible movement.

Outside the sky had turned gray and ominous, promising rain. As they headed toward the row of pines where the Maserati was parked, Connor said, "If Dylan comes to stay with me that will solve all her concerns."

"No."

So Victoria was digging in her heels. Connor knew the only way he was going to make her see sense was to be brutal.

"You'll never be able to raise a boy." Pausing beside the car, he set the infant seat down and opened the rear door. After securing the infant seat without waking Dylan, he turned back to Victoria and raked his gaze over her, telling her without words that he considered her wanting. "I give you two weeks tops before you surrender."

For a moment, he thought he'd shaken her. Then she narrowed her pinkened eyes. "You don't think I can do this? *I'm* the one who was watching him in the first place!"

Victoria had backbone, he had to give her that. But then, given her career he would've expected it. The question was: would she be able to cope all alone with a demanding job and a baby? He doubted it.

Connor took in her hands clenched in front of her breasts, and the way her mouth trembled. Her crushed-rose lips only emphasized her pallor. She looked too damned fragile.

For a moment he considered sweeping her into his arms, holding her close...

Then he shook the impulse away.

This was Victoria, not some frail butterfly. And she didn't need anything from him—she'd told him so herself.

He stepped closer to her. "That wasn't a dare. You don't need to prove anything to me. All I want is Dylan." And dammit, that was the truth of it. "Make it easy on yourself, let him stay with me." That's what he wanted desperately—what Michael would've wanted—his son to stay with him. But he couldn't say that. He'd already hurt her enough. "You can come and visit as often as you want."

The gold-green eyes that clashed with his were full of tur-bulence. "You think I haven't thought of letting him go to you? But I can't!"

"Why not?" he challenged.

"Because..." She gnawed at her lip.

"Because?" he prompted, forcing his gaze not to linger on her mouth.

"Don't ask this of me." There were shadows in her eyes that went way beyond grief. "I can't do it."

"It would be the easy solution."

She hesitated, clenching and unclenching her hands. "Easy solutions aren't always right. Suzy and I had been inseparable since we were five. I met her on our first day of school. Did you know that?"

He shook his head.

"She was tiny, like a beautiful, blue-eyed doll. She had blond curls, whereas I had dead straight, mousy hair. I felt so thin and tall next to her—she made me want to look after her."

Victoria's eyes had glazed over, and Connor knew she'd forgotten about him, about where they were, about the approaching storm. She was in a place he could not reach.

"We seemed like such opposites. Suzy so social, me so quiet."

"You were fortunate that your friendship endured for all those years."

"She was so much more than a friend. More than a sister, even. She was my confidante. My family. The person I trusted more than anyone else in the world when my family let me down." Her gaze cleared. "I can't give Dylan up. Don't ask it of me."

Connor's sigh went all the way to his soul. He'd already hurt her beyond belief with his swipe that she hadn't had time for Suzy before she died. How could he take her last link with her friend away from her? Even though he knew that Michael would've wanted Dylan to be with him.

The provision for sharing of guardianship and custody in the will had startled him. Victoria was a working woman who clearly didn't have time for bringing up a child. What had the Masons been thinking? Suzy must've insisted on it, never believing the will would have to be acted on long before Dylan grew to adulthood.

But whatever the will provided for, it was absolutely irrefutable that Suzy's death had left a vast chasm in Victoria's life.

Connor drew a deep breath and made the biggest concession of his life. Despite what he believed was the right thing for Dylan—and him, he would go along with the provisions of the will. "Then we'll have to split the custody—work out which of us gets which days."

Emotion flashed in her eyes. "How can you even suggest that? It took Dylan almost the whole weekend to settle with me. He's missing his parents, and now you're suggesting ripping him away from me."

"Not ripping," said Connor firmly. "We'll share him."

"And he's going to know what's happening?" She shook her head so hard the silken mass of her hair whipped from side to side. "No, he's not going to understand the terms of a custody arrangement. His parents are gone. Right now everything in his little life is in upheaval. I'm his only constant. How can you yank up the few roots he has left and take him away from me?"

She had a point. He remembered how Dylan had snuggled against her earlier.

"And you can't take Dylan away from my home. That's all that's familiar to him right now. Another change of place is going to unsettle him all over again."

He tilted his head to one side and replayed her words through his mind—*Another change of place is going to unsettle him all over again.* "That's it!"

At his exclamation Victoria stared at him as though he'd taken leave of his senses.

He hit a hand against his forehead. "The answer is simple."

Five

"Come on." Connor held open the door.

Victoria hesitated only for a second. No way was she abandoning Dylan to Connor and the powerful Maserati.

She stepped past Connor, catching a whiff of lemon and male, and settled into the passenger seat. The acreage of leather was seductively plush, and before she could protest Connor had leaned across her and clicked the seat restraint into place, strapping her in.

She'd barely recovered from the jolt to her senses of having him so close when he joined her in the intimacy of the cockpit.

"Ready?"

Victoria nodded, unsure what she was letting herself in for.

The motor roared, and the rich, husky voice of Nina Simone poured from the surround-sound system, silencing even Dylan. Connor's hands slid over the steering wheel with such tactile pleasure that Victoria had to suppress a groan. A moment later he swung the vehicle out of the churchyard.

The journey passed in a flash. As Connor throttled back the surging engine, Victoria glimpsed through the side window a familiar oak with wide, spreading branches.

What were they doing outside Suzy and Michael's home?

She struggled impotently to unlock the car door, until—to her immense frustration—Connor strode around and freed her.

Clambering out, she slung her tote over her shoulder and asked, "Why have you brought us here, Connor?"

"Let me get Dylan first."

Nostalgia welled up as she stared at the Edwardian cottage that had been Suzy and Michael's home since their marriage—and where she had spent so many happy hours.

She wandered across the sidewalk to the low, white wooden gate.

Dylan had been baptized in this garden. Right there in the arbor tucked into the east side, under the canopy of girly, pale-pink roses. It had been one of the few times she and Connor had visited the house at the same time. As the baby's godparents they'd been forced to put on a façade of friendship for Michael and Suzy's sakes.

The gate swung open under her touch. As she stepped onto the winding garden path a gigantic wave of sadness drowned her. The ghosts of Suzy's laughter and Michael's slow smiles lurked everywhere. In the pretty pansies that brightened the pots lining the pathway, in the fresh coat of lily-white paint on the shutters and in the shriek of a gull overhead, its wings icy-pale against the darkening sky.

She started as Connor came up beside her.

"Connor, I'm not sure that I'm ready to do this. I don't think I can even go into the cottage yet." A tempest of grief was imminent. Only Connor's presence held the tears in check. "I need time."

"Look." Connor swung the baby seat forward. "I think Dylan knows he's home."

The baby was cricking his neck, and making gurgling sounds of pleasure.

Sorrow tasted bitter in the back of her mouth. What did poor Dylan know? "It's not his home anymore," she choked. "Michael and Suzy are gone."

And she and Connor were going to have to decide—and agree—what to do with the house.

Michael had done a marvelous job restoring the old cottage—with Suzy and Connor's help. But the maintenance would be a nightmare. Best to sell it and invest the proceeds for Dylan.

Moisture escaped from the corner of one eye and she quickly brushed it away before Connor could notice.

He swung around. "I've been thinking…"

She gave a surreptitious sniff. "What?"

"One of the reasons you felt that Dylan should live with you was because he's grown accustomed to his surroundings in the past few days."

"Well, yes…" It looked like she'd gotten through to him. Finally. The first thread of relief started to unwind. She glanced up at him, grateful for his understanding. "It'll be much better for him than going to your home, which he doesn't know."

"I wouldn't say he doesn't know it," Connor objected. "He has been there with his parents. But as you pointed out, it would be much better for him to be in familiar surroundings— like here."

"*Here?*" Dismay filled her.

Connor nodded. "This is, after all, his home."

In the distance thunder growled. Victoria decided that even the weather gods disagreed with Connor.

"Oh, no, I couldn't live here." The comforting sense of relief had vanished. There were far too many memories of Suzy and Michael. In every piece of painted wood, every flower. It would kill her to have to live here. "Don't ask me to do that."

"I'm not asking you to—I'll move in. Can't you see?" He was looking at her as if he expected her to applaud his perspicacity. "You were right, Victoria. And this way I won't be displacing the baby. He'll be in familiar surroundings."

Her own arguments had caused him to come to this conclusion? Her heart started to thud in fear. She was going to lose Dylan after all. "You can't do this!"

He thrust his hand into his pants pocket and brought out a bunch of keys. "Why not?"

Because Dylan is mine, she thought. But she couldn't tell him that. She'd promised Suzy she wouldn't reveal her part in Dylan's birth.

Oh, dear God.

She tried to get her thoughts straight. Surely Suzy's death released her from that promise.

Or did it?

She rubbed her fingertips against the sides of her nose. Finally she said thinly, "It's macabre that you're thinking of moving into their home when we only buried them today." Her head started to ache. "Tell me you don't mean this?"

But Connor was already striding up the path that wound to the wooden front door, keys jangling between his fingers, the handle of the infant seat hooked over his arm.

A splatter of moisture landed on her arm. Victoria glanced up, startled at how dark the sky had grown. She hurried after Connor and grabbed his arm.

He swung around. "Careful, you'll awaken—"

"I'm not going in there. I'm not." Barely conscious of the wetness on her cheeks, Victoria tipped her head back and glared at him defiantly.

Connor grew still. His free hand came up and touched her cheek with gentle fingers. "You're crying."

She ducked her head sideways, dislodging his touch. "I'm not crying. It's the rain." It seemed important to convince him of that. To reveal no weakness. Victoria pointed to the sky. "Look how low the clouds are."

But his gaze didn't waver from her face, and his eyes softened to the color of mist. "Okay, it's the rain."

"It's going to get worse." She wiped her eyes with the back of her hand. "We can't stay out here. Dylan will get drenched." Hunching her shoulders, she threw a haunted glance toward the cottage.

"I'll take the two of you home." Connor put an arm around her shoulder and turned her toward the gate, the infant seat swinging gently from his other hand.

The warmth of his body against hers flooded Victoria with a rush of emotion. She blinked frantically as he held the garden gate open for her, determined not to cry any more. This was Connor, why was he being so darned gentle? It made her want to cry all the more.

The rain began to fall in stinging drops. Connor dropped his arm from her shoulders and hurried to get Dylan into the back of the Maserati.

Victoria stood on the sidewalk, unmindful as the drops turned to sheets of water. She'd won. She could hardly believe it. He wasn't going to force her—or Dylan—to go into the cottage. Conner was taking them both home.

So why didn't she feel a thrill of victory? Why did she feel so terribly lost?

"You need to get out of that wet dress."

Connor jerked his gaze away from the sodden material that clung to Victoria's skin, blatantly revealing the gentle curves and the tight tips of her breasts as she shivered.

"But Dylan—"

"Is perfectly dry. I got him into the car before the heavens opened." Connor's attention fell onto the baby still sleeping in his infant seat.

"He's exhausted."

He knew without looking that she'd followed his gaze. Victoria must be exhausted, too. After all, she'd been holding the baby for most of the day. But if he said anything more, she'd only deny it. So Connor settled himself down onto a couch and propped his feet up on the coffee table. "Why don't you go have a hot shower. I'll watch the baby for a while."

Edging forward, she said, "Why don't you make yourself at home?"

"Not now, Victoria." Weariness crept into his voice. He'd had enough of all the sniping between them.

She stared at him for a long moment, then bowed her head. "I'm sorry."

Connor nodded and closed his eyes. Hearing so sound of movement, he cracked them open. She hadn't moved. She stood in front of him, looking every bit as drained as he felt.

"You'll feel better after a shower."

"Maybe." Her hazel eyes remained fixed on him. "But right not I don't really want to be alone."

"Oh, Victoria!"

Her reluctant admission moved him. She was so fiercely independent. Connor knew for her to reveal any weakness at all meant she must be feeling utterly empty. Dropping his legs down, he reached forward and scooped her off her feet. She landed across his lap with a squeak, a struggling mass of arms and legs.

"I'm wet!" she wailed. "I'm going to soak you, too."

"Shh." He bent his head over hers. "Just relax."

Her body softened instantly. For long minutes he held her, not speaking, not thinking, simply savoring the scent of her, the softness of her body under his soothing palm that rubbed along her back in long strokes.

At last she shifted. "I must be heavy."

Connor almost groaned as her bottom moved in his lap. Heat shot through his spine and he fought the urge to shudder in reaction. If she'd only stayed still...

Victoria froze. Her head came up, and startled golden-green eyes met his. Connor knew she'd felt his unmistakable reaction. He waited for her to pull away. She didn't.

"Victoria...?"

With a groan he pulled her toward him. Her parted lips met his, and he sucked in the whisper of her breath. It was a hungry kiss, full of pent-up emotion, of passion long resisted. Connor licked the soft sweetness of her bottom lip, tasting her deeply, and she wriggled closer.

His fingers found the zipper of her dress, and he broke off the kiss. The rasp of the sliding zipper cut across the sound of their ragged breathing. Connor peeled the wet fabric off her shoulders and slid the dress over her hips, down her legs, his gaze all the time holding hers, watching as a flush of passion flooded her pale cheeks.

When the dress was off, he pulled her atop him so that her bare legs straddled his hips. Her naked skin shimmered in the evening light, as pale as pearl against the seductive black satin bra and panties. Connor's breath caught at the sheer grace of her long limbs and sweet curves.

With shaking fingers she reached forward and undid the buttons of his shirt. "Your shirt is damp, too."

"Just a little." He'd gotten wet holding the car door open for her.

Pulling the edges apart, she murmured, "Then it will also have to come off."

Connor leaned forward and shrugged his arms out of the sleeves. "Anything you say."

A glint lit her eyes, and her lips curved into a delicious smile. "You should always be so amenable."

"I'm at your mercy." He stared at her rosy lush mouth.

She laughed. Driven by an impulse he could not resist, Connor reached out a shaky finger and outlined the full, wide, laughing curse. Her mirth died away, and the pink tip of her tongue came out and touched his finger.

"You undo me, woman," he said hoarsely, "with one little flick of your tongue."

"Then what about this?" She trailed a tantalizing finger down his chest, across his stomach, before halting an inch above his belt.

"Tease," he groaned.

"Your skin is so silken," whispered Victoria.

His erection leapt. "That's my line," he growled, yanking her to him and bending his head forward to ravenously plant a row of kisses along the tempting arch of her throat. Under his lips he felt her throat contract as she gasped. His mouth opened, and he tongued the silky skin. His open mouth slid down, over the narrow slip of black satin that joined the cups of her bra covering her breasts…down farther…savoring the sweetness of her flesh.

Grasping her hips between his hands, he lifted her up and kissed the smooth skin of her belly.

"Connor!" The sound was guttural, full of need and desire.

"Be patient." His erection strained again his pants, rigid with desperation. He wasn't so sure that he was capable of following his own command.

She pulled away and settled back astride his lap.

Connor's back arched instinctively at the contact. "My God, woman."

He felt the buckle of his belt give under the persuasion of her nimble fingers. His heart skipped a beat as she undid the button below. The sound of his breathing filled the room, hoarse and jagged.

Light danced across his eyelids as he squeezed his eyes shut. Sliding his hands up her sleek back, he reached the catch of her bra and fumbled, his fingers suddenly clumsy.

A cry filled the air.

Victoria's hands stilled. "Dylan."

She scrambled off his lap, tugging the clinging black dress over her breasts, and ran to the other side of the room. Lifting the baby out of the infant seat, she turned her head, and Connor's throat closed up as he read the turbulent confusion in her eyes.

Bewilderment. Guilt. Shame.

And, underneath it all, the heat of desire, too.

Connor rose slowly to his feet.

"Put your shirt back on." Her voice was a thready croak.

"It's damp."

"Please," she implored.

"Okay." He pulled it on and watched as she tried to juggle the baby while trying to push her arms back into the wet sleeves of her dress. "Give Dylan here—I'll entertain him while you change."

Without meeting his gaze, she thrust the baby into his arms and fled.

How could he have allowed—no, encouraged—that to happen?

Victoria couldn't believe that she'd almost ended up having sex with Connor. She fastened her jeans and reached for a lambs wool sweater. If Dylan hadn't woken up…

Oh, God!

How could she have been so foolish? And now she had to leave her bedroom to go back downstairs. She groaned in dismay. It would take all her courage to face Connor after what had happened. And to demand that he never touch her again. They both had a duty to Dylan. As his guardians. Passion couldn't be allowed to interfere with their respon- sibilities.

As Dylan's mother, she couldn't afford to risk alienating

Connor. It would be the height of irresponsibility to let passion rule her—and make her no better than her parents had been.

By the time she entered the living room, she'd pulled herself together, making sure that none of her trepidation showed. The man who'd kissed her to distraction was sitting on the carpet, and the contents of the baby's diaper bag were strewn around the room.

Connor looked up at her entrance and gave her a sheepish grin. "I figured out how to change his diaper."

Victoria yanked her gaze away from the chest she'd run her fingers over. Thankfully he'd covered the glorious muscles up with a shirt as she'd requested.

"Congratulations," she managed and searched for the words to tell him that she did not want him to ever kiss her again— that it was a dereliction of their duties as Dylan's guardians.

Dylan chose that moment to flap his arms and, gazing at her accusingly, he started to cry. Victoria picked him up, taking care not to brush against Connor's legs.

"He's hungry." Forcing herself to glance at Connor, she said, "There's a bottle ready in the fridge. Won't you fetch it please?"

To Victoria's surprise, Connor went without demur.

As the minutes passed, Dylan grew increasingly fractious. Victoria jiggled him up and down, hushing him, but to no avail, so she started to sing.

When Connor came back, Dylan's cries intensified at the sight of the bottle.

"Give me a second, Dyl." As Dylan protested she removed the plastic seal and replaced the top of the bottle, then sank onto the plump cushions of the couch and positioned him in the crook of her arm. "There you go," she murmured, giving him the bottle.

She resumed humming a snatch of "Big Rock Candy Mountain," then ceased as she became aware of Connor watching her, a smile lurking around his mouth.

"Don't stop."

Flushing, and terribly self-conscious under his intense scrutiny, she said, "I don't hum—or sing—very well."

"It sounded fine to me, and more importantly Dylan liked it. Look, he's complaining because you've stopped."

Victoria glanced down to see Dylan's mouth working frantically, his tongue clearly visible as he prepared to let out a loud bellow.

"That's not my humming he's missing—it's the teat." Victoria offered the dislodged teat to him and the baby latched on with gusto.

She slanted a faint smile up at Connor. "But thanks for saying he was missing it, even if it was the tallest tale I've ever heard."

"It wasn't that bad."

"It was worse, but we'll keep that our secret, okay?"

He gave her a long look. "Our secret."

Suddenly feeling as if her skin had grown too tight, Victoria pulled Dylan closer. The silence surrounding the three of them seemed to quiver.

What in heaven's name was happening to her? Victoria started to hum again. Anything to break that seething quiet. After a while she switched over to "Old MacDonald Had a Farm" and Connor joined in.

Dylan sucked the last dregs out of the bottle and his eyelids started to droop.

"I've been thinking…"

Instantly Connor had all her attention. "What?"

"Dylan should stay here."

Euphoria swept Victoria along. She'd gotten what she'd wanted. Now she had to make it work, prove to Connor it was the right thing for Dylan. "I'm so glad you realized I was right."

His gaze narrowed to cool slits and all the easygoing camaraderie evaporated. "Hang on, we're not changing the custody arrangement of the will. He stays with you for now, but we'll review the arrangement in a month."

No, that wasn't what she'd intended.

She considered arguing that his solution only meant unsettling Dylan later down the line, then decided to quit while she was still ahead. When the time came, she was sure she'd be able to convince him that Dylan would be better off staying with her. As for her resolve to tell Connor that she wanted to keep their relationship formal as Dylan's guardians, it appeared that would not be necessary. Connor was all business. He certainly showed no signs of being a man overwhelmed by desire. She suppressed a ridiculous stab of something suspiciously like disappointment.

He was speaking again. "Dylan needs you. I can't deny it—you're so good with him."

Victoria stared at him, astonished. Connor thought she was good with Dylan? He wasn't the kind of man to give false praise. A surge of happiness swept her. So much for all her fears that she'd be terrible at the mothering stuff.

He was still talking. "But it's going to slow down your career track."

"I know, and I've come to terms with that." She would have to speak to Bridget and tell her that she wouldn't be working late into the evenings anymore. She gave Connor a bright smile that faded a little as his gaze intensified in a way that made her shiver inside.

"So you'll need to take leave for a couple of weeks."

Take leave? Averting her face, Victoria placed the empty bottle on the coffee table. How could she take leave? Especially now when everyone at ACE was working to full capacity. She'd tell him later that she had no intention of taking leave. Now was not a good time. He might renege on his decision to leave Dylan with her.

When she was sure she had her emotions under control,

she raised her head—and clashed with Connor's intense gaze. Her stomach rolled over.

Victoria drew a steadying breath. Now was not the time to be sucked in by Connor's lethal charisma. She wasn't looking for a man. And he was the last one on earth that she'd pick. Surely she hadn't forgotten that?

He was all wrong for her—he'd just proved it beyond a shadow of a doubt. He'd never let her retain the financial and emotional independence she'd fought so hard to attain. He'd want a woman who he could control and command. A woman who would give up work at his demand. And that would never be her.

She would never risk being at the mercy of a man's whims. Like her mother had been. It wasn't only the woman who suffered, but her children too. She had first-hand experience of what happened when children paid the price of impulsive passion.

But she wasn't about to lose custody of the only son she'd ever have. So Victoria said carefully, "Yes. And I'm going to take a leaf out of your book and delegate more—hire a junior to assist me. That's just one more thing I need to discuss with Bridget."

Six

After Connor had gone, Victoria called Bridget Edge.

The assurance that Victoria would be at work the following day was met with a sigh of undisguised relief. And after a small pause Bridget had agreed to Victoria's suggestion that hiring a junior accountant would be a good idea—provided, of course, that Victoria's client base kept growing.

Victoria set the phone down and closed her eyes. For the first time since learning of Michael and Suzy's deaths her sense of optimism blossomed again.

Everything was going to work out.

She quashed the growing apprehension that Connor would not be happy with the outcome.

The next day, Victoria dropped Dylan at the day care center that Suzy had enrolled Dylan in. Leaving him was a terrible wrench, but she assuaged her guilt by slipping out during lunch time to check on him. One of the young day care em-

ployees murmured that the baby hadn't settled and appeared
to be fretting.

Of course Dylan was fretting.

Poor baby! Victoria picked him up, inhaling the scent of
powder and baby. Dylan was missing Suzy and Michael. And
she'd left him in this unfamiliar place. Guilt overwhelmed her.
She'd added to his sense of dislocation—but what other
choice did she have?

Connor, a little voice said, she could have called Connor
for help. He'd offered to take the baby. But if she called him
he would crow in victory—and claim Dylan.

She would lose her baby.

And Connor wouldn't look after the baby personally,
either. He'd simply hire a nanny, which was no different from
what she was doing. Dylan wriggled in her arms. Victoria
kissed his head apologetically and loosened her grip.

But what if she confided in Connor that she was Dylan's
biological mother? Would he understand…would he be
prepared to compromise? She nuzzled Dylan's soft baby hair
and thought of the Connor North she knew.…

Hard. Decisive. Ruthless. There wasn't a compromising
bone in that strong, too-male body.

No. She couldn't tell him.

She would have to get through this by herself.

The rest of the day passed in a rush. And Victoria, who'd
intended to leave not long after lunch for the first time in her
life, left work far later than she'd intended.

Dylan still hadn't settled by the Victoria went to collect
him. But the staff were sure Monday would be better.

The weekend went by in a blur of sleepless exhaustion.
Victoria missed a call from Connor while she and Dylan
napped, and after listening to the recording of his deep, provocative voice saying, "Just wanted to see if you're coping,"
decided against phoning him back.

So he thought she wasn't coping?

Well, she certainly wasn't going to cry for help.

By the following Tuesday Dylan was visibly querulous, and one of the day care workers called to say he was running a slight temperature.

Panic flooded Victoria and she wasted no time getting to the day care center.

"He didn't drink his last bottle." The day care attendant looked concerned. "If his temperature rises further you may want to take him to the doctor."

By the time Victoria got Dylan home, after an hour in peak-hour traffic, he was hot and flushed. Pausing only to take his temperature, which had rocketed alarmingly, she faced the fact that this was more than grief and dislocation. Dylan was ill.

A call to her doctor garnered his pager. Victoria swore. But within minutes a doctor on call had phoned and told her to take the baby to the nearest medical center. Berating herself for leaving it so long, she hoisted Dylan into the baby seat, secured him and hurried to the front door.

Connor had been waiting all week for Victoria to phone and beg him to take Dylan, to admit defeat. But she hadn't. To his annoyance she hadn't even responded to the message he'd left on her answering service. And Connor was left wishing he'd never allowed the hollowness in her eyes to persuade him to leave Dylan in her care. What had he been thinking? Dylan was the most important person in his life.

Five days had passed since the funeral, and he couldn't wait any longer. The driving urge to see Dylan—a primal, deeply-rooted need to reassure himself that his baby was happy—dominated him. Yet as the Maserati ate up the now-familiar route Connor admitted it wasn't only Dylan he'd been missing—he wanted to see Victoria, too.

It was perfectly normal, this desire to spend time with her.

Right. It was perfectly normal to crave the presence of someone who drove you crazy?

Connor's mouth slanted.

They'd each lost someone they loved—an aching loss that the other understood better than anyone else in existence. That made sense. But it wasn't convincing. It sure didn't explain why the shape of her wide mouth haunted him when he should've been thinking about work. Or why the memory of her slender body bending over Dylan's car seat could wake him in the middle of the night, even though he'd always preferred blondes with hourglass curves. Or why he kept fantasizing about the silken softness of her skin under his fingertips.

Hell, he'd even wondered how she'd coped with telling Bridget she was taking more time off work to look after the baby. He'd actually considered calling earlier in the week to see if she needed support.

But he'd managed to hold out.

Until now.

As he lifted his hand to ring her doorbell the front door flew open.

"Oh, you startled me."

His first thought was that he must have been blind. Victoria was beautiful. How had he ever missed it? How had he ever thought her plain?

Her long hair swirled about a face that was simply perfect. Straight, uncompromising brows, direct hazel eyes and a wide mouth of such delicious rosy-red that he fought the urge to kiss it.

Then he saw that she was upset.

His gaze dropped to the infant seat. "Are you going out?"

"Dylan isn't well. I'm taking him to the medical center."

Connor didn't ask questions. "We'll go in my car."

When she looked like she wanted to protest, he added, "If I drive you can look after Dylan."

She nodded.

Once he'd made sure she and Dylan were comfortably ensconced in the back seat of the Maserati, Connor pulled out his cell phone and made a call, before climbing into the driver's seat.

"This isn't the medical center I meant," Victoria said sharply fifteen minutes later.

Connor felt the impact of her accusing gaze on the back of his head, but he didn't shift his eyes from the road ahead. "I called a friend who's a pediatrician. He's meeting us at his rooms—he understands the background."

Chuck had known Michael, and knew Connor had been named guardian of his child. Chuck even knew the truth about Dylan's paternity. "If it's necessary Chuck will admit Dylan to Starship," he said, referring to the well-known children's hospital.

"Chuck?" She sounded doubtful. "How do you know him?"

"His name is Charles Drysdale, if that's any better. We play squash at the same club." A stab of pain pierced Connor at the thought of visiting the courts without Michael. "And he's one of the best pediatricians in town. You'll be charmed—most women are."

Charles—or Chuck—Drysdale had twinkling eyes and a way of putting patients at ease within minutes of meeting him. Victoria liked him at once.

"Tell me what you noticed, Victoria," he asked when she'd taken Dylan out of the infant seat and sat down with him on her lap.

Victoria shifted guiltily in the chair, all too conscious of Connor hovering anxiously behind her. "Dylan has been a little crabby for a couple of days."

Connor came closer and scowled. "You never let me know."

"I thought he was missing his parents," she said defensively.

"He'd certainly notice that," Chuck said. "So two days? That's how long he's been crabby?"

Victoria thought back to how demanding the baby had been over the weekend, how only holding him had settled him. "Maybe a little longer—from Friday perhaps. The funeral was on Thursday and he seemed fine then. But I can't say for sure."

Chuck made a note on the pad in front of him. "Did you notice anything else?"

"Li called me at work earlier. Dylan had a temperature and—"

"Who is Li?" Connor paced closer.

Victoria shrank into the chair. "She's one of the caregivers in the day care center."

"Day care center? What's Dylan doing in a day care center?" Connor's eyes glittered with the kind of rage she'd never seen. "We've *never* discussed putting Dylan in a day care center."

Chuck held up a hand. "Connor, save it for later. Let's see what's wrong with the baby first." The doctor rose to his feet and crossed the room to an examining couch. He gave Victoria a sympathetic smile. "Why don't you bring Dylan here?"

Victoria felt totally wretched as she laid Dylan down on the bed. Every doubt she'd ever had about mothering crashed in on her. "I'm not doing a good job, am I?"

"You're doing just fine. Most new mothers feel a little frazzled and uncertain when their baby becomes ill."

He asked some more questions while he examined Dylan. Finally he said, "Have you ever had chicken pox, Victoria?"

"Chicken pox? That's what Dylan has?"

"Certainly looks like it. It's not common for such young babies to get chicken pox, but it does happen, and the symptoms fit—the temperature, not drinking…and see here?"

She stared down to where he pointed to a small pink dot on Dylan's chest. "And here." He indicated another spot, this one with a small scab.

"I saw that—I thought it was an insect bite. But shouldn't there be more spots?"

"Not necessarily. Some cases only have a few spots here and there."

Lifting her head, she said, "But I thought chicken pox spots were watery blisters."

"That one," he gestured to the pink dot, "will blister soon. Then it will scab over."

Victoria stared at Chuck, conscious of an overwhelming sense of relief. Dylan wasn't going to die. It wasn't scarlet fever or convulsions or some incurable disease. "He'll be all right, won't he?"

"Plenty of fluids, calamine lotion and cool baths. I'll prescribe some acetaminophen for Dylan and a mild sedative for you. Is there anyone to help you with the baby? He'll need to stay home for a week. And you need some rest."

Oh, no. She gave a groan. "I need to go to work."

"I'll give you a note."

What would Bridget and the rest of the partners say? "I can't, I've taken too much time off already."

"Your body needs rest if you've been up the kind of hours I suspect this young man has been keeping." Chuck drew a card from a holder on the nearby table. "This is for a nursing service. They'll be able to assist you over the next week, although he can go back to the day care center once he's better."

"That must be where he picked this up," Connor growled from behind her.

Victoria felt awful, and remorse set in afresh.

"He could've come into contact with the virus anywhere." Chuck shrugged. "But the incubation period is ten to twenty days, so given the time he's been at the day care center it's highly unlikely he contracted chicken pox there."

Victoria could've kissed Chuck. *It wasn't her fault.* But the feeling of relief that numbed her knees turned to horror as she heard Chuck ask Connor, "Have you had chicken pox?"

Connor nodded.

"Good, then you can help Victoria."

Connor's angry gaze bored into her. "Don't worry, I intend to."

Misery sank like a dark cloud over Victoria. He would take Dylan away from her. She really didn't need the only kind of help Connor was prepared to give.

"Thanks so much for taking us to Charles Drysdale. He's such a nice doctor."

Connor listened to Victoria's polite babble as she whipped the sleeping Dylan through the front door, set the infant seat down on the white carpet and swung the door closed in Connor's face.

Before it could click shut he threw his full weight forward against the wood. "Not so fast," he growled, sticking a foot in the crack.

Folding her arms, she blocked the gap he'd leveraged open. "If you don't mind I need to see to the baby."

"I mind very much," he said with slow menace that caused her hazel eyes to turn gold in startled fear.

"It's late, Connor. Can't this wait until tomorrow?"

"No!" He'd done with compromise. Now they would do things his way.

He shouldered the door open. She shrank back. Damn right she should be scared. Right now he was too furious to pay much attention to her fears.

"What are you going to do tomorrow? Take more leave?"

"I can't—I'm in the middle of…" Her voice trailed away

as his frown deepened. Then she drew a deep breath and ran her fingers through her hair. "To be honest, I haven't had a chance to think what I'm going to do. Perhaps I'll hire a nurse."

"And leave the baby with someone you've never met?" The anger that had been smoldering since he'd first discovered she'd lied to him about taking leave and had taken Dylan to a center full of other babies reignited.

"I'll make sure I get someone with good references."

"You won't need to."

Fear shadowed the gold-green eyes. "What do you mean?"

"We agreed that you would take leave!"

"*You* demanded that I take leave—I never agreed."

Connor ran his hands through his hair and tried to remember back to what had been said. "Well, you certainly never objected. You know I'd assumed you'd agreed."

"Did I?" But her gaze flickered away.

"You lied to me by omission, Victoria." He bore down on her. "How dare you take the baby to day care without consulting me? We hold joint custody, remember…or are you trying to get me angry enough to apply to court to have that revoked?"

She looked shaken. "You can't do that."

"I can—and I will if you persist in this stupidity. What's important here is Dylan's well-being."

"Everything I've done has been in Dylan's interests."

"No, it isn't." His rage boiled over. "You're only looking after your interests—your damned career that's so important to you. Not caring for a grieving baby!" He shook his head. "God, but you make me sick!"

She went white. "I—"

He couldn't let that air of deceptive feminine fragility sway him. "Spare me from ambitious women who walk over everyone to get what they want."

A sprinkling of freckles he'd never noticed before stood

out in sharp relief against her pallor. "I would never jeopardize Dylan for my career—"

"Never?" he said softly. "That's why you took a young baby to a nursery full of other children where he could pick up viruses?"

"Chuck said—"

"That it was unlikely, not that it was impossible." He leaned closer until his nose was up against hers. "Do you think that's what Suzy wanted for her baby?"

She stumbled back. "Suzy enrolled Dylan in that center. I've done nothing Suzy would not have done herself."

That caused him to hesitate, but only for an instant. Dylan was his son. When he thought what might have happened... Damn, he'd never be able to trust her with Dylan again. "Why the hell didn't you call me?" he snarled.

She remained mute.

Of everything, it was the not calling that enraged him most. She was so pigheaded, so stubborn she would've let the baby come to harm before she called him.

His baby.

What had once been a favor to a devastated friend, a random donation of sperm, had turned into the most important thing in his life. Dylan was more precious than anything in the world. And she hadn't bothered to tell him that his baby was sick. The baby he'd entrusted her with against his own better judgment.

A surge of sheer instinctive paternal possessiveness shook him as he stalked closer. "It was an unforgivable mistake not to call me."

Pinned against the wall, she faced him. The glaze of shock had receded and her eyes shot sparks at him. "You would've taken Dylan away from me."

"Oh, for..." He broke off before the force of the crude curse erupted.

She squeezed her eyes shut.

Recognizing how real her dread was, Connor stepped back and leashed the anger that vibrated through his large frame. "This has gone far enough. I'm taking the baby with me."

"No." There was raw pain in the sound. "You can't!"

"You'll find that I can."

Victoria's head came up. Her cheeks were stained with hectic color, a vivid contrast to her previous bleached paleness. "No. Michael and Suzy wanted us to share custody. I can only see one way that this can work."

"What's that?"

"I'm coming to live with you, too."

Connor gave her an incredulous stare. The silence reverberated with tension. Then he said, "Fine. You can come, too!"

Seven

Victoria walked into Connor's palatial home for the first time the next evening, not sure of what she would find.

What she didn't expect was to see Connor lying on his back on the thick carpet in the living room, bouncing above him a bathed, ecstatic Dylan. She hesitated in the doorway and watched as Dylan squealed in delight and Connor whooped.

A long-forgotten sense of being the outsider swept her, of being the kid with the mother who slept all day while her father blew in and out of town like tumbleweed.

Then Connor caught sight of her, and flashed her a dizzying smile. "Look, Dylan, there's Victoria."

She dropped her leather laptop case and took a step forward. Dylan stretched his arms toward her. She swung him up and buried her nose against his neck. He smelled clean, of baby powder and calamine lotion. He made soft snuffling sounds and her heart melted.

"How was your day?" Connor had sat up, the laughter fading from his face as his eyes became watchful.

She let out a deep breath. "A lot better than yesterday." Knowing that Dylan was being looked after by Connor's housekeeper had lifted a great weight off her shoulders.

"How's Dylan been?" She set the baby down on the floor and, dropping down beside him, she tugged his T-shirt up.

"Ratty a little earlier. But he had a good sleep."

"The spots are looking better, not so red."

"He was fussing so I bathed him…and the cool water seemed to settle him."

"He loves his bath." Victoria searched Connor's chest for signs that Dylan had splashed with his usual abandon but he looked as immaculate as ever. Typical. If it had been her, her shirt would be clinging to her.

"I think you can handle bath time from now on. You must do a far better job."

His grin flashed back. "I've changed—both my jeans and shirt looked like candidates for the wettest wet."

"Oh." Victoria instantly felt better. "I've arranged for some of my things to be delivered tomorrow. I'll put the rest into storage and let the town house."

"I've made some calls," Connor said. "I'll be interviewing for an au pair for Dylan tomorrow during the morning."

"But I thought we'd do that together." He was doing it again—taking over, marginalizing her involvement. And underlining her own insecurities. "I want to have input into the person that we hire."

Connor frowned. "I've already arranged the interviews, and I'll be working from home until I employ an au pair. It's not fair to leave Moni with the house and Dylan."

"Moni?"

"My housekeeper. I'll introduce you shortly."

"Thanks," she said brusquely. "But I'd appreciate it if you would rearrange the interviews for when I come home. We've got joint guardianship—and that means we're partners, we consult each other and make joint decisions." That would be hard for him. Connor North didn't have a compromising bone in that powerful, autocratic body.

Her gaze dwelled for a moment on the strong shoulders, the determined jaw, then locked with his unreadable gray gaze. A shivery awareness caused her to shift her attention back to the baby wriggling on the carpet.

"I want to satisfy myself that the person looking after Dylan is the best candidate we can get."

"And you don't trust me to find that person?"

She thought of his track record. He hadn't done a great job picking trustworthy people to surround himself with in the past. Dana Fisher and Paul Harper had turned out to be faithless. But she couldn't very well remind him of that.

Instead she said stubbornly, "I'm coguardian, I have a right to be involved."

"You're determined to make this as difficult as possible, aren't you?"

Victoria shook her head. "I just want to make sure you choose the right person."

So the next day, in consultation with Victoria, Connor rescheduled the interviews. Two were set for that night and one for Friday evening. The first candidate, a young woman with impeccable qualifications, had already arrived by the time Victoria came home from work, late and flustered.

After ten minutes' easy conversation with Anne Greenside, Connor had decided she was the perfect choice.

But Victoria clearly had other ideas. "I see most of your jobs have involved older children," she quizzed Anne.

"I love babies," Anne said with a sincerity Connor found convincing.

"But you can't stay late?"

Connor had known that would be a stumbling block the moment he'd seen the woman's resume. Despite her devotion to Dylan, Victoria was ambitious. Work would always come first. She would want a nanny who could work late. On a regular basis. He didn't have to cast his mind back far to remember the kind of hours Dana had worked.

"I live with my invalid mother—she needs me at night. But I can start tomorrow, if that makes it easier for you and your husband."

"We're not married—Dylan's not even our baby," Victoria blurted out.

"I'm sorry. I wasn't aware of that." But Anne looked curiously from one to the other.

"My fault," said Connor easily, "I should've explained the situation to the agency." He quickly filled her in.

"Poor baby." Anne looked stricken. "He's fortunate to have the two of you. But it's not going to be easy for him as he grows up."

"What do you mean?" Victoria asked first.

"He'll always have questions—he's not like other children now. His parents' death has seen to that."

"He'll have us."

Connor could feel Victoria's growing tension.

"Yes, but you're not his parents. You aren't planning to adopt him—" She looked at them enquiringly.

Connor shook his head slowly.

"We haven't discussed it," Victoria said repressively.

After Anne had left, Connor said. "I like her. She's perfect. We should offer her the position before someone else snaps her up."

Victoria shook her head. "I don't agree. And she's very opinionated."

But Anne had said spoken the truth. It was in Dylan's interests for them to consider all points of view. But Connor bit his tongue. He should've expected this. When had Victoria ever agreed with him? Yet, instead of accusing her of merely trying to frustrate him, he drew a deep breath. "Her references are fantastic."

"I still need to call and verify them. I can only do that tomorrow." She glanced at him. "Anyway, we have to see the others. I'd like you to keep an open mind while we interview them."

Before he could respond the next candidate had arrived. It didn't take long for Connor to catch Victoria's eye. She looked equally dubious.

He relaxed a little. His concerns that Victoria might oppose him simply for the hell of it evaporated.

They thanked the woman for coming and Connor saw her out.

When he returned to the study Victoria said, "She was awful."

"Agreed." That must be a first. He started to grin and Victoria smiled back, her mouth wide and luscious. Instantly, heat spread through him.

"I want someone older. Steadier."

Connor forced his gaze away from her mouth and tried to focus on what she was saying. "Not too old."

Victoria stuck her bottom lip out in that infuriating way that he'd come to recognize meant trouble.

"I can see you've already decided on Anne," she said. "You should've waited until I came before you started the interview."

The warmth and desire that had filled him evaporated. "Don't be unreasonable. I didn't start it alone by design. You were late."

"Something came up." But she looked abashed. "It won't happen tomorrow."

* * *

But when Victoria rushed home on Friday evening, it was to find that the third prospect had cancelled. And Connor had gone ahead and employed Anne.

"I called. You were in a meeting," he said to her intense fury.

"You should've waited."

"I didn't want to mess around and lose Anne," he said with patient logic that infuriated her further.

After giving Dylan his bottle that night, Victoria headed downstairs in her nightgown and dressing gown to make herself a cup of tea in the state-of-the-art kitchen, still annoyed at his take-charge actions.

She drank the hot tea, and thought how lovely it had been to come home to a hot meal that Connor's housekeeper had prepared. Usually she was too tired at night to make much more than a sandwich for dinner.

When she'd finished her tea and rinsed out the cup, she felt much better, and wearily wound her way up the stairs to her room—suite of rooms, she amended. A large bathroom and two bedrooms led off the sitting room. The smaller of the bedrooms had been converted into a nursery—complete with pale-blue walls and bright-yellow ducks stenciled as a border.

She pushed open the nursery door. As her eyes adjusted to the dimness from the night-light she made out a big, bulky shadow beside the cot where the baby slept.

Connor.

She stilled. She hadn't expected to find him here. Stupid. Of course he'd want to say good-night to the baby. Her anger at him was overtaken by the slow pound of her heart that was suddenly loud in her ears.

Connor turned his head. "The big guy is fast asleep."

"I know, I put him down." Victoria felt the smile tug at the corner of her lips. "Tonight was a struggle, he fought so hard against sleep."

"Tough fellow."

Stopping beside Connor, she said softly, "He's so little."

"And amazingly resilient."

"And we're responsible for him."

"I still find it tough to believe that we're now standing in loco parentis." Connor gazed down at the baby with an expression Victoria could not decipher.

In the place of his parents.

It brought home the reality of the responsibility facing them. And how permanent the arrangement was. It was vital for her and Connor to work together. For all intents and purposes they were now Dylan's parents. The only difference between them was that she really was Dylan's mother.

Her baby lay so still in the crib that she leant forward to touch him.

"He's sleeping—I checked, too." Connor gave her a slight smile. Then his gaze dropped and grew warm.

Victoria glanced down, to find that her dressing gown tie had come undone and fallen open to reveal the white lace, diaphanous nightgowns that she favored.

She flushed. "I think I'll call it a night."

And when Connor responded, "That's a very good idea." She had no idea what to make of his reply.

Eight

"Truce?" Connor offered at breakfast on Saturday.

After a moment Victoria took the hand he held out. This was the closest Connor would come to an apology for employing Anne without her input. "Truce," she agreed.

For Dylan's sake.

And for her own. She had to learn to get on with Connor better. But it wasn't easy—he could be so dominating.

"Anne's very good with Dylan," she conceded. She felt the day brighten when Connor grinned at her.

"Let's take Dylan out today to celebrate his recovery," he suggested as he reached for a slice of toast.

"Today?"

Dismayed, Victoria stared at him. She'd intended to wash her hair while Dylan had his morning nap. The week had sped past, and between work and Dylan she'd hardly had a moment to call her own. She hadn't even had an opportunity to try out the large bath with jets in the guest en suite bathroom.

Connor's face hardened. "I'll take him to the zoo alone—and you can go to work."

Annoyance ignited within her. This was his idea of a truce? "I had no intention of working this weekend. And the zoo sounds fantastic. I just wanted an hour to—" washing her hair sounded so self-indulgent and would no doubt unleash more contempt "—to take a shower."

"How about I feed Dylan and keep him out of your hair for an hour and we leave a little later?"

"That would be wonderful." She beamed at Connor, her heart lighter than it had been for weeks. "Thank you."

Two lionesses lolled about on their backs like giant kittens on a grassy hillock, revealing creamy tummies to the delighted crowd that had taken advantage of the sunny day to visit the zoo.

Dylan gurgled in his pushchair and several children shrieked as one of the lionesses rolled over lithely and rose to her feet, before padding to the edge of the moat that divided the big cats from the spectators.

After the giant feline had finished drinking and had flopped down on a sunny rock, Connor and Victoria meandered farther along the path, Connor pushing the baby's loaded buggy, to where two elephants picked at a hay net with their trunks.

Connor glanced over at Victoria. Since they'd gotten to the zoo she'd attracted a fair amount of second looks. With her hair as sleek and shiny in the sunlight as polished mahogany and her hazel eyes alight with excitement, she looked happier than he'd ever seen her.

And, dammit, she was downright gorgeous.

To get his attention off the way her white denim skirt clung to her posterior, Connor swept Dylan out of his pushchair and held him high.

"See the elephants, Dylan?" Victoria pointed and her buttoned yellow cardigan pulled taut across her breasts.

Connor stifled a groan and his hands involuntarily tightened on the baby, who muttered a protest and wriggled in Connor's arms.

"Sorry, mate."

But Dylan had already stilled at the sight of the huge pachyderms as the nearest elephant flapped its ears. A chortle escaped—the sound of baby delight.

Connor laughed aloud and his eyes caught Victoria's over Dylan's head. For a second they shared a pure joy. Then Dylan began to bump up and down in Connor's arms in excitement.

"Whoa, that's an elephant, Dyl. He's too big to pick a fight with."

"Size doesn't matter," said Victoria.

Connor shot her a glance. Nope, she wouldn't hold back against a bigger opponent.

High color flagged her cheeks. "Sorry, that came out wrong. What I meant to say was that Dylan should never let himself be intimidated."

His mouth twitching, Connor cocked his head to one side and considered her. "So you're conceding size does count?"

She gave him a quick up-down look and Connor waited for the acid comeback. Instead he encountered eyes filled with flustered nervousness.

He'd unsettled her. Score to him.

Connor grinned inwardly.

She blinked rapidly. "I'm just saying the giant doesn't always win—remember David and Goliath."

He swept his gaze slowly over her. "You don't look like any David I've ever met."

She made a sound of mock disgust. Connor threw back his head and laughed, and a moment later, to his astonishment, Victoria joined in.

He held out a hand to her. "Let's go see the otters."

To his surprise she reached for his hand, her fingers linking through his, the pushchair trailing in her other hand. Heat bolted through him and all laughter vanished as he looked at her—*really* looked at her—with a shaken sense of never having seen her before.

Then Dylan butted him, claiming his attention, and Connor came back to reality with a thump.

Later Victoria helped Connor lay a rug down on the freshly mown grass in front of an empty bandstand near a lake with ducks and swans. Connor rolled on his back, pulling Dylan onto his chest while Victoria knelt beside him and reached for the picnic basket they'd brought along.

It was all so domestic.

And most amazing of all, she and Connor hadn't argued once.

He was holding Dylan above him on outstretched arms, making airplane noises. Laughter lines crinkled his cheeks. God, he was gorgeous.

An unwanted echo of that moment when their eyes had locked—of the scintillating awareness that had sizzled earlier—sent a frisson through her.

No.

She was not falling into that trap. Connor was her coguardian, not a prospective date. She daren't start finding him attractive.

Looking away, she rummaged into the basket and pulled out a container of sandwiches that Moni had prepared.

The thud on her back took her breath away. Her eyes shot open in time to see a football rolling along the blanket and a pair of sneakers following in swift pursuit. Boyish hands scooped the ball up.

"Jordan, apologize at once!"

"Sorry." A sheepish grin appeared from beneath a baseball cap. "Won't do it again." A singsong note of overuse underlay the words.

Her breath back, Victoria suppressed the urge to call him a name—or worse, grin at him and condone the carelessness. "Perhaps kick the ball the other way."

Connor sat up beside her, perching Dylan on his knee, and gave the boy a level stare.

"No, I've already told Jordan that he's not to lose a fifty-dollar ball in the tiger's cage." A harried-looking woman with red hair standing up in spikes had appeared. "You have to be more careful, boy."

But Jordan was already gone, zigzagging over the lawn, dribbling the ball ahead of him.

"Kids." The woman rolled her eyes. Then she added, "At least yours is still harmless. Enjoy him while you can. It gets worse."

Victoria started to correct the redhead, to tell her that Dylan wasn't their baby. Then she stopped herself. It was just too hard to explain.

So she smiled instead. "We will."

"Your baby's very cute."

Dylan gurgled and blew a raspberry on cue.

"Thanks."

Jordan's mother shifted her attention to Connor. "He's going to have his mother's goldy-brown eyes and his father's dimples."

"I'm sure you're right," Connor said politely.

Victoria could've kissed him for silently standing by her decision to say as little as possible.

Victoria had laughed with Suzy in the past when complete strangers had told short, blonde, bubbly Suzy how much the newborn Dylan looked like her—not realizing he didn't possess any of Suzy's DNA. Now the memory made her ache with loneliness.

"I'd better find Jordan before he wrecks the place." The redhead scanned the surroundings until she found her son. "Or lands in the pond with the goldfish!" She gave them a rueful smile. "I made the mistake of having only one—so when he doesn't have a friend, guess who has to play with him?" She thrust a thumb at her chest. "Me. Don't do what I did. Make sure you have another kid to keep yours company."

Victoria fidgeted, uncomfortably hot at the too-tempting idea of creating a baby with Connor. Thankfully, Jordan's mother didn't seem to expect a reply; she simply wiggled her fingers at Dylan before vanishing in Jordan's wake.

After what seemed an age Victoria couldn't bear the tingling silence any longer. Unable to help herself, she turned her head. And instantly wished she'd resisted the lure.

Connor was staring at her with predatory speculation, and the normally cool eyes simmered with heat.

Her heart skipped a beat.

Victoria pulled herself together. It was up to her to defuse this sexual tension, and as rapidly as possible.

She chose to do so with humor. "Poor Jordan. What on earth is his mother going to tell his girlfriends one day?"

Connor flung his head back and laughed. And the strange, heavy ache below her heart expanded, filling her with a yearning she'd never expected.

The day ended all too soon.

After securing Dylan in the backseat, Connor held the Maserati's passenger door open for Victoria. And found himself staring at her legs with all the frustrated hunger of a university student eager for his first lay.

They were nice legs. Encased in opaque winter stockings, they were shapely, too. So why the hell hadn't he noticed them before?

Probably because he'd never seen them. She usually wore

black trousers, or long skirts in neutral colors. Black, navy or gray. She never wore a denim skirt that rode up.

Like now.

But he shouldn't feel this…desperate…about stroking them.

She cleared her throat. "You can shut the door."

Caught.

"Sorry." He shook his head sheepishly. "Don't know what I was thinking."

She gave him an old-fashioned look. He shrugged and decided to try for some damage control. He didn't need her knowing how she'd tied him into damned Gordian knots. "So I've always been a bit of a leg man—blame a male's basic instincts."

"Control those instincts." But she laughed, flushing a little. "You've spent too long around the animals today, I think."

"Perhaps," he conceded.

If she only knew how much testosterone her spontaneous smile and slender body had unleashed, she'd be running for the hills—with him in hot pursuit.

He closed the door with a snap and strode around to the driver's side.

A stolen sideways glance revealed that despite Dylan's inquisitive fingers her hair was still sleek. Yet sometime during the day she'd lost the faint tension that always seemed to cling to her. It must be the fact that a smile had never been far from her lips.

It wasn't something she did often enough.

He fired up the Maserati and pulled out onto the road. "Tired?" he asked as he stopped for a red light.

"Exhausted."

He pushed the gearshift into neutral and turned his head. "At least I'm not alone in that."

The smile she gave him caused his groin to tighten.

"But it was worth it," she said. "Thanks. It was a great idea."

Connor told himself to keep it light. "Zoos were created for adults."

She tilted her head. "Why do you say that?"

"Didn't you notice the amount of newborns and young babies? All those parents have been waiting years to legitimately get back into a zoo, bitterly regretting the day they told their parents that thirteen made them too cool for kiddie outings."

She laughed.

Then she ruined his pleasure by pointing out, "The lights have changed."

"Thanks." Connor put the car into gear and accelerated smoothly away.

"You could be right. I think most of the parents there today were having more fun than the kids." She leaned her head back on the headrest. "Dylan certainly slept through a good part of the day."

And it had been during those spells that he'd been tempted to give in to the devilish urge to kiss her. Hot memories of the last time he'd kissed her—when she'd almost ended up totally naked on his lap—had kept him awake more than one night since she'd moved in. But he'd resisted it, fearing he might destroy the delicate truce that had developed between them.

"I had fun," he murmured finally.

"Me, too."

Her voice was smiling. Connor wished he could take his eyes from the road to study her, to see if the corners of her mouth had tipped up into that irresistible curve.

Okay, he wanted her. There. He'd admitted it. He wanted to soak himself in the scent of her, wanted to sate himself in her body.

So where did that leave him?

Connor started through the options with relentless efficiency. He would have to invest time in this—Victoria wouldn't accept anything less, he was certain of that.

Yet he couldn't possibly have an affair with Dylan's co-guardian. Somewhere down the line it would all turn to custard, and Dylan would be the one to suffer.

He thought back to earlier in the afternoon when Jordan's mother had mistaken them for a couple. And Dylan for his baby…

It didn't mean a thing.

Because she'd also assumed Victoria was Dylan's mother.

A glance in the rearview mirror showed Dylan snoozing in the backseat of the Maserati, his dark-gray eyes closed, his cheeks pink and his mouth open in an O.

Goldy-brown eyes. The woman was a kook.

Victoria bore no resemblance to Dylan at all. They weren't even related. But they could be…if he married her.

Because then she'd be the wife of Dylan's sperm-donor father.

He tightened his hands around the steering wheel. God, how had this gotten so complicated? It made his head go numb.

But not nearly as badly as the desire that made him crave to get Victoria into his bed, under his body—

"We should do it again sometime."

"What?" His voice went rough with want. Could she have read his carnal thoughts?

"Visit the zoo again."

Of course she couldn't read his thoughts. He blew out in relief. "Yes, yes, we must."

He could marry her—the crazy thought leapt back into his mind and just as quickly he banished it. He didn't want to marry the woman. Hell, he hadn't wanted to marry Dana, either. Victoria was just as career-minded—nothing like the kind of woman he wanted to live with for the rest of his life.

Except his libido refused to agree.

* * *

After putting the baby into his night suit on Sunday night, Victoria settled down to feed him his bottle in the spacious rocking chair that had been delivered to the nursery yesterday while they'd been out at the zoo.

Yesterday.

She glanced across to Connor where he sat perched on the love seat opposite her, riffling through a pile of picture books on the floor in front of him.

Yesterday she'd discovered a side to Connor that she'd never known existed. A warm, fun, *funny* side. But as soon as they'd gotten home Connor had disappeared, and today she'd barely seen him. She was starting to think he must be avoiding her.

Yet here he was acting as though everything was normal.

Victoria decided she'd never fathom the man out.

He seemed impervious to her disquiet as he picked up a picture book and held it up, saying, "This one, don't you think, big guy?"

Dylan sucked more fiercely on the bottle.

"Good taste, son."

Connor flipped open the first page. Despite his deep voice, he read with a soft, easy rhythm that was curiously soothing. By the time he'd reached the end of the board book, Dylan's eyelids had fallen and Victoria was feeling easier…almost sleepy.

Setting the book on the pile beside the love seat, Connor stretched his arms above his head. "I've been thinking."

The warm, fuzzy feeling receded. Victoria opened her eyes in time to see him rise to his feet. She regarded him warily as tension zapped through her. "About?"

He looked remote, powerful and somewhat alien, standing across from her with his hands on his hips. Was he about to tell her that he'd reconsidered their unconventional custody arrangement—that she should go home? Or was he going to demand she give up work to stay home with Dylan? She'd been dreading that.

She told herself Connor couldn't force her to do anything she didn't want to do.

But imperceptibly her muscles grew taut.

He hesitated only for an instant. "I think we should get married."

"What?"

Dylan stirred in her arms and she rocked him hurriedly. "Where did that come from?" she whispered fiercely to Connor.

"It will make it much easier for Dylan," he said in a low voice, crossing the space between them and staring down at the baby who slept so peacefully in the crook of her arm. "And do away with the constant need for explanations."

"This is because of the woman at the zoo yesterday?"

He spread his hands out wide. "Her mistake was understandable and it's going to happen more and more, particularly if we're living together."

Victoria couldn't believe she hadn't blurted out *no* to his proposal straight away. Until a few days ago there'd always been hostile tension between them. They'd never gotten along, and she'd spent two years actively avoiding him while Suzy and Michael were alive.

So why hadn't she simply said *no?*

One word.

No…no…no!

Easy.

But she didn't say it.

Because of Dylan.

She tilted her head back and studied Connor critically. He was tall. Strong. Deep in her belly, heat stirred. She suppressed it ruthlessly. She knew he was good at sport. He'd be able to pass those skills on to Dylan.

Dylan was the only reason she could ever marry Connor….

A glance down at the baby revealed his smooth, round face, untroubled by the demons chasing her. If she married Connor then Dylan would have a family again. A mother and a father. A world away from merely living with his guardians.

How could she deprive him of that?

A real family.

But Victoria couldn't lie to herself. There was another, much more selfish reason to marry Connor. If she did her place in Dylan's life would be secure.

She would be able to relax, to stop worrying that he'd get rid of her as soon as Dylan settled down. As his wife, it would be a lot harder for Connor to evict her from Dylan's life.

Uncannily, Connor echoed her thoughts: "If we were married we could provide a stable home for Dylan."

A shivery awareness filled her. How far did he intend to take this idea of giving Dylan a stable home? She thought about the frank woman at the zoo. *Don't do what I did. Make sure you have another kid to keep yours company.* Would Connor want to provide Dylan with siblings? Would he expect her to make love with him? Past experience had proved that he only had to touch her for desire to ignite into burning heat.

She turned her attention away from the baby and back to the man who'd taken over her thoughts, her life. "Connor—"

He held up a hand. "Wait. Before you reject the idea, you need to know that I'm committed to this. I won't pull out in a year or two and want a divorce."

She tried to read the expression in his eyes, but the night-light was too dim.

To put a little distance between them she rose to her feet and gently deposited the snoozing Dylan in his cot. Tugging at the cord that hung near the baby's cot, she flooded the room with soft light and turned to face the man who had put her world into uproar.

"How can you possibly be so sure? You might fall in love

and want a real marriage." Would she be any good at marriage? Her parents had married because she was already on the way. Would marrying for Dylan's sake be any different?

"I'm not looking for love." He gave her a crooked smile. "Let's just say that Dana forever killed any desire I had for a 'real' marriage."

Sadness unexpectedly seeped through Victoria. No woman would be able to steal that cold, shriveled heart. He'd shut himself up behind high, impenetrable walls.

Deeply disappointed for some reason she couldn't fathom, she found herself shaking her head. "I can't marry you."

He seemed to take root and a stillness overtook his large frame. "You don't think it would be a good idea for Dylan?"

What was she supposed to say to that? Tell him about her own parents' failures? And let him realize how poor a mother she might be? Definitely not! "Of course, Dylan would benefit."

"So why not marry me?"

She shifted restlessly. She thought of her father…ever drifting, never home. Of her mother's unhappiness. "There's more to marriage than Dylan."

His eyes gleamed. "Are you referring to sex?"

Her skin went all tight.

"You don't want to have sex with me? Is that it?"

Oh, dear God. He'd misunderstood. But sex…

She couldn't stop staring at him. At the depth of his chest. The large, capable hands. The hard mouth that could smile so gorgeously. Her skin grew tighter. "No…no, I don't."

He smiled. It wasn't a very nice smile. "May I ask why not?"

Damn him.

She wriggled like a bug on a stick. "Because I don't make love with every conceited, arrogant jerk who comes along."

He shook his head and laughed. "That puts me in my place."

"And I don't like you," she said, seized by a burst of unreasonable anger, "and I'm quite sure you don't like me much either."

"Liking has nothing whatsoever to do with sex, Victoria." He drawled her name out slowly, deliberately, making her feel utterly *Victorian* and positively puritanical.

At the pale-silver gleam in those dangerous eyes she grew itchy, but forced herself to sit unmoving. "I need to actually *like* a man to make love with him."

"So naive. You can't have liked a great many men then."

The implication took her breath away. "I'm not a misanthrope—I'm discerning. And it's only you I've never liked. I've made love to enough men to know that I don't do casual encounters."

She'd even dated a guy for two years before breaking it off when he'd asked her to marry him. She'd gotten scared. It would never have worked—not even if she'd been more confident—he'd been easygoing and fun loving. A tumbleweed. He'd constantly nagged her to relax, to slow down, unable to understand that she was driven for reasons of her own to make a success of her life. Whatever the cost.

At least that was one thing she had in common with Connor—he'd worked hard to get where he was. Even though he'd expected her to take extended leave at the drop of a hat.

Shadows flickered in the silvery depths. "There will be nothing casual about our encounter. I can promise you that."

She shivered deep inside. "You make it sound dangerous."

He stalked closer. "We've always struck sparks off each other, and this will be no different." He stared into her eyes, searching for something she was equally determined never to concede. "It will blow your world apart."

It was so tempting....

"I know there's no one out there waiting for you. Just say yes, Victoria."

Too tempting.

And the emptiness would be forever filled by Connor…
and Dylan. A family. A chance to have what Suzy had had.
What she'd never dared hope for.

Before she could think better of it, she leaned forward and
placed her lips against his.

He froze.

She parted her lips. Lightly, delicately she traced her
tongue tip over his mouth. His chest lifted against her, rising,
pressing against breasts that were suddenly tender.

She tasted him, sipped at him, until his breath escaped in
short, jerky gasps. His arms came around her, engulfing her,
holding her close. He was hard, all male. The snug fit of his
jeans couldn't hide the erection that had sprung to life, a
rock-like ridge against her lower belly.

He cupped her bottom, pulled her up against him and took
her mouth. It was her turn to shudder with desire. He thrust
his tongue deep, and the act of possession sent a primitive
thrill through her.

Stroking the inside of her mouth, his tongue searched out the
smooth skin inside her cheeks, the highly sensitized roof-arch.

She groaned, a hoarse, wanting sound.

No longer aware of where they were—barely aware of
how long it had been since the kiss began—she focused on
the hunger that raged between them.

He moved closer, his leg pushing between hers, the
harsh fabric of his jeans rough against her skin. But that
was sexy, too.

Until Dylan mumbled in the cot behind her and she leapt
away from Connor as if she'd been scalded.

Connor stood rigid. His eyes were wide and, for the first
time since the night he'd come to tell her of Michael's death,
she recognized the emotion in his eyes.

Shock.

Her heart hammering, she balled her hands at her sides to

stop them from reaching for him. "See what you made me do? That was monumentally stupid."

He swallowed, and she fixed her gaze on his Adam's apple, watched it bob up and down, avoiding his too-astute eyes. Hurriedly she added, "*You* irritated *me*." And flicked her gaze up.

Then wished she hadn't.

White-hot. That's what his eyes were. Enough to incinerate her.

"I overreacted—and so did you." Silence. "Don't you agree?" More silence. "I don't want to make love without it meaning anything," she protested, more to convince herself than him, wishing she wasn't having this wretched one-sided conversation with a man she simply didn't understand.

"I'm not asking you to." He sounded so reasonable. "I only asked you to marry me."

Her heart sank. "So you're proposing a marriage in name only? Absolutely no sex?" She risked a look at him. His expression was indecipherable.

"Do I understand you correctly?" He drew a deep, audible breath. "If we take sex out of the equation you'd marry me?"

"Maybe…" It was a croak of sound. But her body was urging *more, more, more*.

"This is no time for maybe, Victoria. Yes or no?"

They weren't touching. Yet over the gap that separated them she could feel the heat of his body, the force of his power.

Victoria started to tremble. She was ready to say anything to stop the sizzle.

"Yes," she sighed.

Nine

Connor discovered over the next few days that getting married solely for Dylan's sake wasn't what he wanted. He wasn't that noble. He wanted more.

She was driving him crazy. Once or twice as she sashayed past he considered yanking her off her feet, into his lap, and repeating the experiment.

Their no-sex agreement had to be the most idiotic thing he'd ever done. Hell, she was going to wear his ring. That would brand her his for the world to see. Yet he wouldn't be allowed to touch. Sooner or later something was going to have to give—and it would be Victoria. He was quite confident that he would achieve that. She would come around. He'd see to it because he sure as hell had no intention of sticking to their stupid pact.

In the meantime, he made up for it by looking. Surreptitiously, carefully and at every opportunity he got.

It was torture.

Several times each day he would call Victoria at work—ostensibly to talk about Dylan. But he found himself looking forward to those segments of time when her husky voice came over the line, especially when he managed to get her to laugh.

Lust had turned him into something pathetic.

It was a sign of how entangled he'd become with his new life that, when Iris came into his spacious corner office with his coffee and announced that she'd heard Dana and Paul were getting married, Connor felt one brief flare of resentment and then…nothing.

The lack of turmoil and emotion was liberating. He stood staring at Iris until she said, "Connor, are you okay?"

He gave his assistant an unabashed grin. "I'm better than okay—I'm great."

She snorted. "Because Dana and Paul are getting married?"

"Yep." His grin widened. "Makes me feel much better than I thought."

A wave of relief crashed over him that there was no need for anger, or to exact further revenge. That phase of his life was over.

What he had now was so much better.

Iris straightened the papers on his desk into a neat pile. "There's a rumor that Dana's pregnant."

Even that didn't disturb him. He grinned at her over the top of the coffee mug. "I should've anticipated that. Poor Paul."

"You had a lucky escape."

"I certainly did." Setting the mug down on a wooden coaster, he tipped his head sideways and studied Iris as she slit his correspondence with a letter opener. "You never indicated you didn't like Dana."

"Wasn't my place—you seemed happy enough with her."

His gaze paused on her pursed mouth. "You're not the only one. Michael never liked her, either, nor did Brett." His brother had been open in his reservations about Dana after their first meeting. Of course, Dana hadn't cared for Brett either—she'd been relieved that he lived in London.

There was a scrape as Iris shredded the empty envelopes. "Dana was always good at her job, and she knew who to impress. But she'd clamber over anyone in her way to get what she wanted." Iris turned back to face him.

Leaning back in his executive chair, Connor folded his arms behind his head. "It wasn't easy for her. People are always harder on women who are successful in business." He thought of Victoria. "Even me." He couldn't help wondering what Iris would make of Victoria.

"It had nothing to do with Dana's successes, just the way she went about achieving them." Disapproval came off Iris in waves. "And you shouldn't be defending her." With that, she bustled out of his office, pausing at the doorway to say, "Don't forget you have a meeting at noon."

Connor nodded, then swiveled his chair to look out the window at the knot of gum trees that flourished beside a pond. A pair of ungainly blue-and-black pukekos minced on orange webbed feet along the bank of the pond, picking for food.

His motherly assistant thought Dana had used him as a way to get what she'd wanted, but to be honest, he'd used Dana, too. He was starting to realize that what he liked about Dana was that she *didn't* affect him—he could stay heart whole and devoted to work. He didn't think about her all day long. He hadn't felt the same compulsion to talk to her as he did with Victoria. Dana hadn't been a constant distraction from his work. Sure, she'd been a very decorative diversion, and of course he'd gotten a kick out the covetous looks other men had given her. And she could be as feral as a sex-starved mink in bed.

Yet her infidelity still left a bitter taste.

But Michael had hit the nail on the head. It had been his

pride—rather than his heart—that had been bleeding when she'd walked out.

He'd never thought he'd land himself in a similar position.

Yet Victoria was even sexier to him, and her beauty was more subtle but no less captivating…and he had a suspicion that Victoria could make him never want to go to work again.

And she was even smarter than Dana.

Just look how she'd gotten him to agree to a marriage without sex—only minutes after kissing him stupid. She'd reduced him to a quivering lump.

Masterly.

And he'd been the fool who'd agreed to it! Even though he was certain he'd be able to convince her otherwise. Given time.

As the pukekos disappeared into the reeds on the waterline, an inner voice whispered, Dana would never have done that. She'd have used sex as another weapon in her arsenal.

But then he couldn't remember ever wanting, yearning, going mad with desire for Dana in quite the same way.…

Out of respect for Suzy and Michael it was decided the wedding would be a small one with no frills and flounces—and definitely no fairy-tale white dress.

The following night after they'd put Dylan to bed Connor came to the small sitting room upstairs that Victoria had claimed as her own, where he hadn't invaded until now. He paused at the threshold, and she watched him survey the changes she'd made to the elegant cream-and-dull-gold décor. The addition of a wall hanging in muted colors that she'd brought from her town house. A large fern she'd called Audrey, which was draping enthusiastic fronds over the back of the couch where she sat holding a wineglass.

"I don't want to disturb you," he said at last.

Didn't the man know by now that he always disturbed

her? Even wearing only a T-shirt and black jeans he managed to make her pulse pick up.

Of course she'd never admit it.

"Would you like a glass of burgundy?" she asked, setting her glass down and reaching for a clean one from the butler's tray on the side of the couch. "A client gave it to me—and it's rather good." Relaxing, too—which she needed now that the realization she and Connor were actually getting married was starting to sink in.

Connor looked taken aback for a moment, then nodded. "Just half a glass. I'm not staying long."

Once she'd poured, he moved farther into the room. Taking the glass from her, he raised it to his nose before sniffing and saying, "Mmm…nice." Then he glanced down at her. "I came to ask for a list of friends and family you're inviting to the wedding. Iris—my PA—will send out invitations if you give me details. She's a whiz."

"No."

That caused his eyebrows to leap to his hairline. "Aren't you a little busy to be doing it yourself?"

"There isn't anyone I want to invite." Victoria took a sip of her wine. "Have a taste, it's very smooth."

Settling himself against the antique writing desk across from her, he sipped. "Very smooth. No friends at all?"

She shook her head slowly, supremely conscious of the weight of his stare.

With the exception of Suzy, she'd lost contact with most of her friends over the past ten years, too busy with work. Occasionally she'd gone out with Suzy and her teacher friends to a movie, or to dinner with a group from Archer, Cameron & Edge. But she wasn't close to any of them.

"What about family?" He shifted, crossing one ankle over the other where he leaned, the rustle of denim loud in the intimacy of the sitting room. "My brother's coming."

"I don't have brothers or sisters." Victoria dropped her gaze away. "My mom's dead, and I haven't spoken to my father in years."

"Then this might be the time to invite him and mend some fences. Both my parents are dead—at least you still have a father who could be there for you."

She played with the stem of her glass. Connor couldn't know what he was asking of her. "I thought the purpose of the day was to get married and provide a family for Dylan."

"Nothing wrong with using the opportunity for reconciliation, Victoria."

Connor's arrogant assumption that inviting her tumbleweed father to her wedding would make amends for decades of irresponsibility and selfish neglect rubbed her the wrong way. "So I take it you'll be inviting Dana and Paul?"

There was a horrible pause. Then he said, "Okay, maybe we should just focus on the wedding."

"Good idea." In an effort to restore the peace she said brightly, "I didn't know you had a brother."

He drained his glass and set it down on the desk behind him. "Brett's been living it up in London for the past few years."

"And he's coming all the way out to New Zealand?"

Straightening, Connor gave her a grim smile. "It's my wedding—probably the only one he'll ever see me celebrate. Of course he's coming."

Less than a week after Connor had asked Victoria to marry him, the wedding took place.

In sharp contrast to Suzy and Michael's wedding, it was a small affair with no bouquets, flower girls or white lacy bridal dress in sight. In fact, Victoria decided that *celebrate* was a far too strong word for the civil ceremony that they rushed through in an anonymous Queen Street government building.

Afterward, accompanied by Connor's brother and Anne—who'd come to take care of Dylan but ended up acting as a witness—they went to a lovely restaurant set in the rolling, parklike gardens of Auckland's domain. Sitting at a table on a verandah that overlooked a series of lakes shaded by budding willows and frequented by swans, Victoria's gaze settled on Dylan perched in the high chair beside Anne, and she finally relaxed.

Married.

Her place in Dylan's life was secure now.

"Congratulations!" Connor's brother waved a glass of champagne. "Welcome to our family."

Victoria smiled and raised her glass. Brett's personality had come as a surprise. Younger than Connor, he had a boyish flirtatiousness that made her laugh.

"Connor needs to be married," he told her while Connor discussed their meal with the restaurant owner. "Even though I would rather you'd had a very unequivocal, big, splashy wedding instead of this hole-in-the-corner affair."

"*Needs* to be married?" Victoria raised one brow skeptically and carefully ignored the rest of his explosive statement.

"Oh, yes. He likes domesticity."

"*Connor?*"

She glanced at the man whose commanding presence had conjured up the owner and a trio of waiters in minutes. His baby brother was mistaken—Connor was as domesticated as a Bengal tiger.

Brett nodded emphatically. "Oh, yes. He's suffering from empty nest syndrome."

She must have looked blank, because Brett elaborated. "Since I left home." His eyes widened. "He never told you that he raised me?"

"No."

Victoria started to feel ridiculous. She knew nothing

about the man she was marrying—except that he'd been dumped by his girlfriend and betrayed by his partner two years ago, and had built a multimillion dollar corporation out of the ruins of those relationships. She'd been crazy to think that was enough. "Until last week I didn't even know he had a brother."

"What mischief are you whispering to my bride?"

The owner had departed, wearing a very satisfied smile. But Connor's eyes narrowed alarmingly as he focused on Victoria and his brother.

"No mischief…yet. I'm still trying to impress her with how upstanding we are. I'll get to the skeletons in the closet later."

Connor's eyes crinkled into a smile. "Those are all yours, brother."

After that lunch became a noisy, happy affair—where even Dylan contributed much gurgling. The food was sublime and the pale-golden sunshine gave the occasion luster. After listening to the brothers bantering, Victoria met Anne's eyes and both women collapsed in paroxysms of laughter.

Dylan finally decided he'd had enough sitting.

"I'll show him the swans," Anne said, rising to free the baby from the high chair. "And it's probably time for a change, too."

"I'll get a travel rug from the car—" Connor was on his feet "—for you to lay him on."

"You may have noticed that Connor doesn't talk much about himself," Brett said to Victoria once Connor had disappeared around the corner of the building.

Now, that was an understatement. She flashed Brett a wry glance.

"Our parents are dead—did you know that?"

She nodded. "He mentioned it, but he didn't give any details." And she hadn't asked because the last thing she'd wanted was Connor asking questions about her estrangement from her father.

"A train crash." Brett paused. "That's why he was so upset about Michael. Brought back old memories."

She hadn't even known; Connor had hidden the old, festering wound so well under that icy exterior.

Brett leaned closer. "Has he told you about Dana?"

"His ex?"

"The viper."

A giggle escaped despite Victoria's attempts to look disapproving. "Brett!"

"She kicked him out of his own home, but in a way it was a relief when I heard. I was scared shitless Connor would marry her—she was angling for it."

"Should you be telling the new wife all this stuff?"

"It's on a need-to-know basis." He dipped down close and lowered his voice conspiratorially. "Dana is poison. She told Connor she wanted children, but he didn't believe her."

Despite her qualms, Victoria couldn't resist probing for more information. It was unlikely to be forthcoming from Connor. "Why?"

"He thought her work meant too much for her to take time out for kids."

Uh-oh. That went some way toward explaining his attitude in relation to Dylan with her. "How do you know all this?"

He sat back in his chair and selected a toothpick. "I watched…and they sniped at each other sometimes. And after they split up Connor came to London and I took him on a pub crawl."

Victoria frowned.

"Think of it as therapy—it was the only way I could get him to talk."

"You're devious."

"Very," he said with immense satisfaction. "And you'd better remember that, because I'm counting on you to feather Connor's nest and keep him happy."

Victoria laughed at the outrageous comment. But the sound dried in her throat when a hand landed on her waist. "Be careful of my baby brother."

Connor's husky growl close to her right ear caused her to shiver with delight.

"He's just been warning me of how dangerous he is." She slanted a mirthful look up at Connor.

Resting his arms across the back of her chair, he leaned closer, his body warm and his male scent familiar. Shuddery sensations of awareness tingled over her nape as her new groom said, "Unfortunately, it's all true."

"Right."

"See, I told you to be careful of me." Brett looked as innocent as an angel. "Now I'm off to whisper some secrets to Dylan."

"More like flirt with Anne," Connor murmured as Brett took off down to the water. He slid into the chair that Brett's desertion had freed.

The latent tension in Victoria wound a notch tighter. No longer laughing, she pivoted on her seat to face Connor. "Brett tells me you brought him up."

"He exaggerates."

"So how old was he when your parents died?"

"You mean he didn't get around to telling you everything?" The humor vanished, and his eyes cooled, becoming remote.

"He ran out of time. But I deserve to know—I'm your wife, remember?"

"In name only."

The terse retort came like a slap in the face and she looked down, determined he shouldn't see how he had wounded her.

"Brett was fifteen."

Victoria snatched up the olive branch. Driven by an overwhelming need to know more about him, she lifted her chin and asked, "And you were?"

"Twenty-two."

"Twenty-two! That would have been a demanding time of your life."

Connor didn't say anything.

"It was good of you to look after him," she persisted.

"Anyone would have done it."

"No, they wouldn't." Her father had shown next to no responsibility for his wife and child. Yet Connor had single-handedly raised his brother. She studied his guarded features, admiring the purpose and determination in the rocklike jaw, the sweep of the wide cheekbones and the dark hair that the late August wind had ruffled, giving him a sexy, rumpled look. "And now you're doing it again. For Dylan."

He shrugged. "Michael was my friend—my best friend, as it turned out."

Without the irony, she might never have asked, "Tell me about your business partner."

"Brett talk about Paul, too?"

"No."

"So what brought on this bout of curiosity?"

His gaze was unnerving. Victoria gave a careless shrug and reached for her sunglasses. "Perhaps I'm just trying to understand what would drive a man's friend to behave like that."

"You think I drove him to do it?"

"I didn't say that!" She blew out a breath in frustration. "I think what he did to you was despicable."

"And what do you think of Dana's behavior?"

She met his gaze squarely. "I thought that was pretty shabby, too."

He nodded slowly as though her answer had satisfied a question deep inside him. Then, pinning her with his intimidating gaze, he said, "I once heard you tell Suzy that you didn't blame Dana one bit."

Victoria slipped her sunglasses on, and frowned. "I said that? When?"

"The day that we first met. You called me a jerk."

Her eyes went around behind the dark lenses. "You *heard* that?"

"So you remember."

"Yes, I was furious with you for attacking Suzy." And it would have knifed him when he was already down. "So that's why you were so hostile to me at the wedding."

"Partly."

She'd thought he'd taken an unreasonable dislike to her, and that had hurt. To learn that her own behavior had been a major part of the problem made her want to groan in dismay. "I'd found out while I was away on a grueling weeklong audit that Suzy was getting married. I was concerned about Suzy." She paused, then decided he deserved the whole truth. "I was dog tired and your in-your-face arrogance was more than I could stomach." Of course she'd bristled in return and the whole sorry situation had snowballed.

"And the other part of your hostility? Where did that come from," she asked, curious now.

"It's complicated."

He was a complicated man. She decided to humor him, make him laugh. She shifted her chair back a little. "Come on, how complicated can it be? You're a male, men are supposed to be easy."

"I am definitely easy," he deadpanned.

Victoria rolled her eyes. "You're not getting out of this conversation by relying on sexual innuendo."

"I wanted to see you blush so deliciously again."

"I don't blush." She felt the rush of color even as he quirked a dark brow at her.

"That was so much easier than I thought," he murmured, his eyes full of lazy humor.

"Oh, stop it!" She didn't know where to look. He was altogether overwhelming in this mood. "Tell me the other reason you disliked me."

"You reminded me of Dana."

Her breath caught. Ouch. All relaxation and lazy desire fled. "I would *never* do what she did to you."

She turned as Brett and Anne came up the grassy back toward them, Dylan happily squealing in Brett's arms. "Don't confuse me with Dana, Connor—I'm nothing like her."

"Sure," said Connor from behind her.

But he sounded far from convinced.

Silence fell over the house.

Victoria had discarded the pale-ivory suit she'd worn for the wedding, and showered. Anne had long since left for home, and Brett had taken off to meet the old friends he was staying with. Victoria set the empty baby bottle on a table beside her, Dylan having been lulled to sleep by Connor's reading. She looked over the baby's sleeping head to where Connor lay sprawled on the dark-blue carpet at the foot of the rocker, his head propped up on his elbow…watching her.

She shifted, and the nursing chair rocked in a gentle motion.

"Is the baby getting heavy?"

"A little," Victoria prevaricated, taking the easy excuse he offered for her sudden restlessness.

Connor pushed himself to his feet in one lithe movement. "I'll put him to bed." His eyes sought hers. "Then we can go downstairs and share a toast to our marriage."

Butterflies fluttered in her stomach at the thought of being alone with Connor. "Oh, he's fine—"

But it was too late. Connor had already swept Dylan up. For an instant the emptiness in her arms roused an ache of separation and she felt a flare of anxiety that she might never hold Dylan again.

She shook off the foolish fancy.

There would be lots of time to spend with her baby. She would be here for every day of his life—she could watch him grow, reach out to the world, become a real, rounded person.

Marriage to Connor had ensured that.

And, in spite of their differences in the past, both of them were committed to making this unlikely marriage work.

It had to.

Not only for Dylan, but for them, too.

Pulling her dressing gown more tightly around her, Victoria crossed the room to the oak crib where Connor stood, his broad shoulders accentuated by the white dress shirt, his hips lean in dark pants. She leaned forward as he tucked Dylan in.

"He's getting big. Must be devouring rubber bands." Maternal pride filled her as she studied the length of the oblivious baby. "He's going to be tall one day."

Connor pulled up the patchwork Peter Rabbit quilt. "He's still just a baby. So many hopes and dreams tied up in one little person."

The words moved her. "You feel that way, too?"

He turned his head, and in the dim glow of the nursery lamp part of his face remained in shadow. "I love him."

She hadn't imagined Connor capable of love. He'd always seemed too remote, too self-sufficient. Yet clearly he loved Brett, and now he was telling her that he loved Dylan, too. The tender expression he wore as he glanced down at Dylan made Victoria feel all soft and molten inside.

Connor doesn't talk much about himself, Brett had said earlier. Well, she'd just have to learn how to draw him out, Victoria decided. The man she'd just glimpsed would be worth finding.

* * *

Downstairs the overhead lights in the living room blazed, illuminating the sculpted lines of the wide deck outside and reflecting off the glistening surface of the swimming pool under the night sky beyond.

"What about a glass of champagne?" Connor offered, and Victoria nodded.

He pushed some buttons in a wall panel and the brightness in the room dimmed, immediately transforming the mood from stark sophistication to shadowed intimacy. Victoria came to a dead standstill in the middle of an exquisite kelim and cast him a wary glance.

The invitation had been for a toast, she'd thought—not a seduction.

He extracted a bottle of champagne from a fridge concealed in a mahogany wall unit and two long-stemmed glasses from a cubbyhole above, and came toward Victoria where she stood dithering. Giving her a glass, he took her free hand.

Immediately, conflicting sensations rushed through Victoria. Trepidation. Nerves. And something far too close to desire for her comfort. But instead of fighting to free her hand she let him lead her to the black leather couch, her heartbeat loud in her ears.

"I prefer to sit on the deck outside at night, but it's a little fresh out there tonight." Connor increased her confusion by sinking down beside her instead of choosing the matching couch on the other side of the Murano-glass coffee table. After he'd filled both glasses, he said, "We're paying the price for those open blue skies earlier."

Determined to keep the conversation neutral, she said, "I'm not surprised you spend a lot of time on the deck—the view of the bay is simply stunning."

It had been one of the first things about the house to capture her attention—right then she'd seen what Connor had meant.

With its hardwood floors, big spaces, wide lawns and spar-kling pool, this was the ideal place for a boy to grow up.

"And we were fortunate with the glorious weather today," she added when he made no move to touch her. Get a grip, she told herself. They had a deal. She relaxed enough to take a sip of her bubbly wine.

"To my bride."

Victoria couldn't read his expression. The subtle tension notched upward. She decided to take the toast at face value and raised her glass in return. "My groom."

He scooted closer and clinked his glass to hers. A sharp ting rang out. They sipped...and over the rims of the glasses their eyes held.

A bolt of electricity sizzled between them.

Victoria tore her gaze from his.

His hand came up and wrenched the black bow tie from his throat, peeled open the top button of his shirt. Victoria's breath caught as her attention honed in on the ripple of a pulse under the swarthy skin. She didn't dare raise her eyes lest she meet his and be scorched by more shudders of desire.

He shifted beside her. Aware of every inch of his long body, of the coiling muscle of his thighs under his dark, formal pants, Victoria stayed absolutely immobile. He leaned closer, and her breath dried up.

God.

"I should—"

"I think I should—"

They both stopped. Victoria gave an awkward laugh, and fluttered a quick sideways glance at him. "I was going to say I should go to bed...it's been a long day."

"And I was going to say I should kiss my bride," said Connor with wry humor.

"Oh."

She knew he'd seen her alarm because one side of his mouth kicked up.

"I still think I should." He leaned nearer and, when she did nothing, he pressed his lips to hers.

For a long moment there was no sound.

Then he lifted his head. "Not so scary, was it?"

"I wasn't scared," she objected, all too conscious of the hard-edged features and his unblinking silver-gray gaze.

His hand reached out and his fingertips traced her brow bone. "Then why the wide eyes?"

Okay, so maybe she had been scared. Not of him, but of responding too enthusiastically to anything he might try, taking the kiss far beyond the kind of intimacy he intended. Like she did every time he kissed her.

Connor had a knack of making her want…more.

"We agreed no sex. You took me by surprise," she sputtered.

He laughed. "A kiss is a long way from sex."

Now he thought she was prissy. Damn. But she wasn't going to let him roll her over. "It's a darn good start along the road. Our bargain was that I marry you to give Dylan a stable home. No sex involved."

"The billion-dollar baby bargain," he said sardonically, his fingers sliding along her jawline.

"Hey—" the implication annoyed her, and his caress was unsettling "—I'm not doing this for money, you know that. I wouldn't take a cent from you."

But despite her heated words her bones were turning to fluid under his tantalizing touch. The citrus and male scent of him surrounded her. And the assault on her senses conspired to make her give a little shiver.

His fingertips came to rest under her chin. "Perhaps I should've offered you a million dollars to walk away from your custody and guardian responsibilities?"

Could he be serious? She wasn't sure. But she decided to rid him of that notion once and for all. "You're insane. I would never've taken it. Dylan is worth more than any amount of money to me."

"And me, too." He moved his thumb along her throat until it rested in the soft hollow beneath her ear. "Stalemate. So we're stuck with each other."

"But we're not going to have sex." She sounded ridiculously breathless.

He smiled, a slow, wolfish smile. "If you're certain, then why is your pulse beating so fast?"

"It's not my pulse—it's yours you're feeling through your thumb," she said in a strangled voice.

Connor laughed. And her toes curled up at the sound.

"We're going to have sex," he said. "And like I promised, it will be far from casual."

"You're so arrogant," she accused him.

"Think so?"

He moved and she squealed.

"Too late." His arms were around her shoulders. "I'm not going to let you go."

"But we agreed—"

"The idea of being married and not making love is…" His voice trailed away as he placed a kiss against her neck.

"Is what?" He'd taken her breath away again—along with her ability to think.

"It's stupid." His mouth opened hungrily against her silken skin. "Whose idea was it, anyway?"

"I don't know." Her voice was hoarse.

He blew softly, and shivers broke over her skin.

"Million-dollar question—what do you want me to do now, Victoria?"

Was he asking permission? Did Connor really care what she wanted? Or would he just take what he wanted and tumble away, like every man she'd ever known?

Ten

Connor felt her stiffen.

Not giving her time to gather her defenses, he licked the hollow at the base of her throat.

She jumped.

He repeated the caress. This time she groaned, and her body went soft, pliable—no sign of resistance remaining.

Her dressing gown opened with one tug of the sash that she'd tied in a bow. Underneath she wore a white, lacy confection that was likely to drive him insane.

Three buttons teased him.

It took him less than thirty seconds to unfasten them all. He brushed the neckline open, exposing the sweetly scented dip between her breasts. The slopes of her breasts glowed, pale and luminescent. Like a pair of priceless pearls.

Dana had always sported a tan. He forced his thoughts away from Dana, and stroked his hand across the rise of pale skin.

"Beautiful."

He peeled the lace of the tab away, baring her breasts and covered her with his hands. "See? You fit inside my palms like you were made for them. Why would you want more?"

He could feel himself growing hard.

Releasing her, he unbuttoned his shirt and shrugged it off. Her hands came up and touched the bare skin of his stomach. His muscles pulled taut, and he fought back a groan of delight.

He wanted to murmur, "Touch me, touch me". But it was too soon.

Instead he lowered his head and kissed the tips of her exposed breasts.

She arched her back, coming off the couch.

Connor opened his mouth, covering her whole nipple and used his tongue.

Victoria moaned, her eyelashes falling against her cheeks. Her head moved restlessly from side to side.

He moved across and sucked on the other nipple, until she shifted and moaned again.

"Like that?"

All he heard was a guttural sound of pure desire.

Connor blew on both nipples, and watched as they hardened and gooseflesh rippled across her breasts and belly. The hunger that took him was raw and primal in its intensity.

Lifting his own head, Connor slipped his hands under the hem of her skimpy nightgown, and stripped it off over her head.

His fingers trembled with want. And his heart was racing, the beat of it pounding in his ears.

He rose to his feet and dropped his pants and boxers.

"Don't stop," she remonstrated, opening her eyes. They grew wide as they took in his nakedness, his readiness for her.

He waited for her to back out.

But she didn't.

Instead she sat up and stroked the length of his erection

with her delicate fingers. Connor saw stars. He fell back against the couch and pulled her over him.

"Now," he whispered.

She straddled him. Before he could shift himself nearer, she'd surrounded him with her hands and drawn him to the entrance of her body. In one swift movement she sank down on him.

Her body was hot and wet and wild around his.

When she started to move, he moved, too. The rhythm that built was full of passion and power. As he thrust upward, Connor felt the heat take him.

He met her gaze, the green-gold eyes wild with emotion. He'd never seen anything…felt anything…so absolutely, perfectly exquisite.

"I can't hold—" He gasped.

Then pleasure surrounded him as her orgasm hurled her over the edge and the feminine shivers trembled around him.

Victoria awakened to the sound of clinking china. She opened her eyes to the unfamiliar surroundings of Connor's bedroom. And the domestic picture of Connor clasping Dylan—clad in only a diaper—against his hip, while he carefully poured tea. The dark liquid spilled into two delicate, rose-patterned tea cups arranged on a tray on the chest at the bottom of the bed, much to Dylan's wide-eyed fascination.

Connor should've looked incongruous—he didn't.

In fact he'd never looked more gorgeous. Wearing only a pair of boxers—and an almost naked baby—he'd never appeared more male. Her gaze lingered on the broad chest on which she'd rested her head before falling asleep in the early hours of the morning.

Images of the intimacies they'd shared last night flashed through her mind.

It had been wonderful. And, as Connor had promised, there had been nothing casual about the experience. Victoria stretched, languorously, slowly becoming aware of all the hidden places where she ached.

"You're awake," Connor greeted her as she moved.

She gave a soft groan. He raised a dark eyebrow with interest and she felt her cheeks grow hot.

Before he could say anything—anything at all, however innocent—she said, "Oh, I'm dying for a cup of tea."

At his slow grin she realized she'd given him an opening for any number of risqué comments, so she simply cooed at Dylan to break the growing hush.

A moment later Connor asked blandly, "Do you want sugar in your tea?"

The incongruity of it all struck her. She'd slept with a man who knew barely anything about her, who didn't even know how she took her tea. Yet he was her husband—and now he knew exactly what intimacies made her go wild with delight.

As for herself, she suspected she was falling headlong in love with her handsome husband. The thought of being at a man's mercy was what she'd always dreaded. But it was proving to be the most sensual, most emotional experience of her life. Nothing like what her mother had experienced.

"One spoon, please."

He stirred it in. Hitching Dylan higher, he picked up the cup and saucer and came around the bed end.

As Connor put the tea down on the bed stand, Dylan grunted in protest and wriggled in his arms, clearly intent on diving into the covers. Laughing, Victoria hoisted the baby into her arms and buried her nose in his soft neck, making snuffling sounds that caused him to wriggle more wildly. Happiness soared through her.

Dylan grabbed at her hair.

"Ow." Victoria carefully freed his fingers from the silky

strands. Connor stooped forward to help. Dylan, finally spying an opening, dived under Connor's arm in search of the tea cup.

"Hot," Victoria said. Dylan reared away, already recognizing the warning.

A pile of newspapers landed on the bed beside her. "Why don't you take it easy. Drink your tea, and take the opportunity to read the paper?"

She laughed. "Opportunity? With Dylan to help?"

"I'd planned to take Dylan to shower with me."

"Ooh, he'll love that." And she gave Connor a glowing smile. "Thank you. I can't remember when last I relaxed and simply lazed in bed."

Shadows darkened the eyes that looked down into hers. Her heart contracted. They both knew the last time for either of them to relax without a care had been before that watershed weekend when Michael and Suzy had been killed.

Her throat tightened…her happiness, this dizzy emotional roller coaster, had followed the worst tragedy of her life. The terrible, wrenching loss that had taken Suzy from her had given her Dylan—and brought Connor into her life. He was far from being the total jerk she'd always thought he was— she'd discovered a side of him she liked…loved…that she wanted to get to know better.

It was insane.

Connor bent forward and kissed her forehead. "Take it easy, Tory. Dylan and I will make breakfast after our shower." He swept the baby off the covers and jiggled Dylan up and down. "Won't we, big guy?"

At the familiar name, she gave him a misty smile, then settled herself against the pillows and listened to Dylan's crowing with glee.

"Thanks, Connor. It sounds like heaven."

He hesitated. "I seem to remember Suzy calling you Tory. Everyone else calls you Victoria?"

"Well, yes, it's my name, after all."

"Don't get smart," he growled, swotting her bottom.

"I've never liked being called Vicki."

"What about Tory? Do you like that?"

A pang shot through her. "Only Suzy and her parents ever called me that. It made it very special. Now they're all gone."

A brief silence fell.

At last Connor said gruffly, "Tory suits you. Makes me think of the toffee-gold in your eyes. It's much less of a mouthful than Victoria."

"You can call me Tory if you want," she offered.

"I think I will." He looked down at the baby curled against him. "Don't you think so, Dyl?"

Dylan gooed.

Grinning at her, Connor said, "He agrees I should call you Tory."

Still smiling, as Connor disappeared with the baby into the en suite, Victoria thought about the unexpected turn her life had taken.

And the Connor she'd discovered last night had blown her mind. Gentle. Passionate. She'd never intended to sleep with him, but it had been so right. She couldn't bring herself to regret the annihilation of their no-sex pact, even though she suspected last night was going to change everything between them.

For the better.

From the bathroom she could hear the rumble of her lover's deep voice and Dylan's squeals.

He'd assured her he wouldn't leave her high and dry. They had a chance to be the family she'd never dared dream of.

Despite her reservations about herself, about Connor's ability to give her the independence she needed, they really could make this marriage work. At least they both knew exactly where they stood. There were no pretenses. For a brief moment she thought about the fact that she's never told Connor that her eggs had helped Suzy to fall pregnant. That Dylan was part of her. Then she pushed it away. That wasn't really a pretense—she'd kept it secret for Suzy's sake. And she'd never considered herself Dylan's mother—not until Suzy had been killed. But she knew she would have to tell Connor the truth—the sooner the better.

Contentment spread over her as she picked up the paper. The headlines were too depressing; she pulled her face. Her usual favorite, the financial pages didn't draw her as they normally did. She flipped to the middle of the paper, to the personality features. An inset photo drew her eye.

Connor...

In the gossip pages?

The larger surrounding photo was of a laughing couple in wedding dress. She glanced at the caption. "Business as usual?" Dana and Paul had gotten married?

Did Connor know?

She quickly scanned further. The story salaciously rehashed the fact that Dana had been Connor's live-in lover and that her defection to Paul's bed had caused a split in the company.

But it was the concluding paragraph of the story that disturbed Victoria most. The reporter's sly insinuation, that Connor's same-day, low-key wedding had been his way of beating the wedding couple to the church door was given credence by Connor's apparent refusal to comment.

Unmindful of the hiss of the shower and the sounds of glee in the en suite, Victoria set down the paper and stared blindly out of the bedroom window. She didn't even see the first pair of tuis of the spring whistling in the giant pohutukawa in the garden—which would normally have delighted her.

Connor had known that Dana and Paul were getting married yesterday.

Nothing could dislodge that earth-shattering discovery.

Connor had clearly known about the wedding—he'd even been tackily asked to comment. Had last night been about Dana marrying Paul?

A feeling of violation shrouded Victoria. Was it possible that in some twisted way she'd become Connor's instrument of revenge against the couple who'd betrayed him?

No, it wasn't possible. Because *she* had made the choice to move in with him. Not Connor.

But Connor had come up with the idea of marriage....

And deep in her heart she suspected this was the reason why.

He was hurting. Two years on and still he couldn't let it go. Underneath his bitterness at their betrayal must lie an immensely profound love for Dana....

She gave a groan and rolled onto her stomach to bury her face in the soft down pillows.

She needed time to come to terms with this Sunday-morning bombshell. Once she'd recovered from the searing hurt, she'd confront Connor.

But not yet. Not while she felt wounded, raw...and so horribly exposed.

Connor juggled the slippery baby in his arms as water sluiced over them, rinsing off the suds.

Dylan was in heaven, if his squeals and frantic wiggles were anything to go by. Connor had a feeling today's shower was going to become a weekly Sunday-morning ritual.

And damned if he hadn't had fun, too.

He hiked the baby up and gave his sodden head a quick kiss. Soft warmth expanded in his chest.

A part of him.

Dylan was his.

And, God willing, they would have years together. He would watch Dylan grow up and he'd always be looking for parts of himself. Would Dylan's dark-gray baby eyes lighten to the clarity of his? Or would they change to match Suzy's angelic blues?

He was Dylan's daddy. He could hardly wait for Dylan to utter the word. He'd teach it to the baby. But it would take nothing away from Michael.

In asking for his help Michael had given him the greatest gift of all. He'd agreed to be a sperm donor so that the bout of mumps Michael had suffered as a child wouldn't deprive him and Suzy of the child they so desperately wanted.

He would make sure that Dylan grew up knowing everything about Michael. And his mother, too.

Although there were no signs of Suzy in Dylan yet, they would come. With luck the baby had inherited his own height.

"Never fear, you won't be short," he murmured to Dylan who was inquisitively playing with the stream of water that drenched them. "My genes won't allow it."

He grinned. Victoria would claim it was his arrogant gene showing through.

Victoria…

Intertwined with thinking about her sleepy eyes and tousled hair this morning came memories of last night. Her heat, her generosity, her gentle love for his son that contrasted so sharply with her blowtorch sensuality, which had forever altered his perceptions of her.

Dreary?

Not a damn.

Last night he'd gotten a very good feeling about the future. And today he intended to solidify what they already had.

"Ouch," he exclaimed as Dylan grabbed at a sprinkling of chest hair. The baby gave him a grin that was all gums. Connor laughed back, then pinning Dylan securely to his right side, he used his free hand to turn off the faucet.

Dylan protested vocally.

"C'mon, Dylan, time to get Victoria—" He broke off. That

wasn't right. It should be Tory. Come to think of it, he was Dylan's father…his daddy…and he wanted to make that fact public.

Yet according to Dylan's birth certificate his father was listed as Michael.

God, this was getting complicated.…

Dylan's squawks of complaint grew louder.

And as he drew a breath for the next burst, Connor hastily turned the water back on. "Okay, you win, big fella." Connor rather suspected he was creating a problem for next time. "Just a few minutes, right?"

Dylan gurgled with satisfaction.

A bolt of love for the bundle of determination in his arms surged through him. Guardianship and custody were only a part of the complicated ties that bound him to Dylan. Fatherhood was so much more.

A sudden thought startled him. Victoria was more than Dylan's guardian, too. She was also his wife. But not Dylan's mommy.

Yet, although she might not share a biological bond with the baby like he did, Connor knew she loved Dylan.

And he really had no right to the title of Daddy until he'd formalized his relationship with Dylan by adopting him.

It was possible Victoria would want to adopt the baby, too…that way she would become Dylan's mother in fact. Dylan would have a mummy and a daddy.

He bounced Dylan up and down until the baby squealed with laughter. That was something else for them to discuss today. He had great plans for a day on the beach. Building sand castles. A picnic. Paddling in the shallows. And he was determined that he and Victoria would enjoy the day every bit as much as Dylan.

Today. The first day of the rest of their lives. Such a cliché, but so true.

He could barely wait.

* * *

By the time Connor had gotten a now screaming-in-protest Dylan out of the shower and switched off the faucets, Victoria was no longer in the bedroom.

He frowned as he took in the neatly made bed. He'd expected to find her languishing amongst the covers, reading the papers and perhaps sipping a second cup of tea.

But the room was empty.

And only a hint of Victoria's subtle fragrance lingered.

No matter. He'd find her as soon as he'd dressed Dylan, and he'd share what he had planned for the day.

Fifteen minutes later Connor had dressed himself and the baby and come downstairs to find Victoria in the kitchen, buttering a piece of toast. She started as he entered, Dylan riding on his right hip.

He halted in the doorway. "I was going to make breakfast in bed for you."

"I can't stay. Sorry." She gave a rueful shrug. "I need to go to work."

"*Work?*" For the first time he noticed she was wearing black trousers and a crisp white shirt with pin tucks down the front. "Today?"

Her eyes slid away from his. "Bridget called. I need to go into the office."

Disappointment flooded Connor. He'd planned—

The hell with it. It didn't matter a toss what he'd planned. His plans didn't fit with Victoria's goals for her life.

Resentment tasted bitter on his tongue. Last night had given him a false sense of wonder. He'd hoped...

Blast what he'd hoped. Victoria's career would always come first. He'd married her knowing that, so why the hell was he so disappointed?

Because of last night. Because of the way she'd touched

him and responded so sweetly and because of the wonder he'd thought he'd seen in her eyes.

He'd been here before. Yet this time, despite knowing exactly what Victoria's priorities were, despite being armored against her, he'd begun to believe that this time it would be different.

That what they shared was special.

That Victoria was nothing like Dana.

And she was different—he knew she genuinely cared for Dylan, whereas Dana had only ever raised the topic of children as a precursor to a discussion about marriage.

Victoria wasn't manipulative…she wouldn't sleep with him to get a partnership, or beg for a baby when all she wanted was a ring on her finger.

But she did share the same ruthless, single-minded ambition that had driven his ex-lover. And he couldn't help resenting the fact that Victoria would always put work first.

He'd been a victim of—and survived—that vicious circle once. He had no intention of being devastated a second time. And this time it wasn't only his heart at risk. This time there was Dylan—his own son—to consider, too.

He wouldn't—couldn't—allow Victoria to be so cavalier about her responsibility to his baby. *His* baby.

But now was not the time to get into that. Let her go to work. He wasn't about to blurt it all out in a moment of anger. He'd held off telling her that Dylan was his baby this long because she'd been so worried that he intended to take Dylan away from her. He could wait a little longer. Once he'd cooled down he would confront her with his relationship to Dylan— and with what he'd decided to do about it.

It was time for Victoria to learn who called the shots.

"Do what you want," he bit out and swung away.

She shifted from one foot to the other, clearly uneasy. "What are you going to do?"

"What I'd planned." He gave her a look of scorching contempt. "I'm taking Connor to the beach. We'll spend a day doing what families do."

He watched as her eyes darkened and a not-very-nice sense of victory swelled him. She'd made her choice.

And so had he.

Eleven

Over the next week and a half Victoria avoided Connor.

The tightening tension gave her a sense of sitting on the lip of a volcano about to erupt.

Outwardly Connor was civil, and he still read to Dylan every night while she fed the baby his final bottle of the day. But they'd barely spoken since that fateful Sunday morning.

When she met his eyes she could glimpse the gathering turbulence in the darkening storm of gray. There was a confrontation coming and, like the coward she was, she avoided him by using the best excuse she had—work.

As soon as Dylan had eaten breakfast she kissed him goodbye and left him in Anne's capable hands. She came home after a work day and desperately avoided Connor in the evenings—with the exception of Dylan's bedtime. Afterward she retreated to her room—and her laptop.

The crumbling of their truce did little to ease the tension that was building day by day between them.

It all came to a head when Victoria arrived home late one night to find Dylan already asleep—and a glowering Connor waiting for her in the living room, every light blazing.

She came to a halt and set her laptop bag down on one of the leather couches.

Standing there, his legs apart, in a beautifully tailored black business suit and pale-blue shirt sans tie, with his shoes still an impossibly glossy black at the end of a day, he looked formidable. Unreachable. It was impossible to tell whether he felt anything for her at all. Except the anger and annoyance that the harsh overhead lighting revealed so clearly.

"Dylan needs a mother."

Startled by his words, she continued to stare at him.

What did he mean? Anxiety—never far away where Dylan was concerned—pooled in her stomach. Dylan already had a mother.

But she'd never told him....

Had she been too reticent? Was the omission intended to protect Suzy's memory going to cost her dearly?

"Nothing to say?"

The glare he directed at her held anger and frustration and something that was dark and dangerous.

"I had to stay later than—"

"I have a business. I work long hours—but I still have time for Dylan. This is the third time you're late this week—and it's only Wednesday. And last week you were late almost every night, too."

He'd been counting. But instead of making her feel like she was winning this battle of wills between them, a wretched anguish speared her. He didn't think her fit to be a mother.

Her shoulders sagged. Served her right, she supposed. Tonight had been a genuine emergency—the rest of the time she'd been avoiding Connor. She'd been stopping for dinner on the way home so that she didn't have to eat with him and endure the awful estrangement between them, arriving home in time for Dylan's bath and bedtime story. She'd desperately missed out on the extra time with Dylan. But what choice did she have?

Right now she couldn't bear to be anywhere near Connor. It simply hurt too much.

She was trapped between her need to be with Dylan and her desperation to avoid Connor—and protect her breaking heart.

The memory of their night together…of what they might have had…was eating her alive.

Connor was speaking again, the words sharp and cold as hailstones. She pulled herself out of her misery.

"Victoria, if you can't be available for Dylan, if you can't be relied on to be here for the child, then its better you move out."

"*What?*"

Shock caused the blood to drain from her face. She collapsed onto the nearest of the two long, black leather couches, suddenly chilled and weak. "What are you *talking* about?"

"I think you know."

Divorce. He was talking about divorce. "But you promised."

"What?"

"That you wouldn't end it between us." Victoria placed her fingers against her temples, hunching over where she sat as she struggled to gather her thoughts.

She heard his footfalls across the carpet as he moved closer. Those perfectly shiny shoes came into her line of vision. "Things have changed, Victoria."

Dana and Paul had gotten married.

Connor had realized that this fake marriage was never going to be enough for him.

And now he wanted out.

She spoke at his shoes. "You can't do thi—"

"You've hardly been home for Dylan over the past ten days." The words were as harsh as a whip. "You spent last Sunday and most of this past weekend at work."

To avoid him. Because she'd been unable to bear the tension, the antagonism between them. She looked up, her gaze unconsciously pleading with him. "I'll make sure—"

He shook his head. "I'm sorry, Victoria. I have to end this. For Dylan's sake."

His words cut deep into her heart.

If she'd thought the pain unbearable before, she now bled pure grief. This was what she'd feared all along. Marriage to Connor was supposed to have roadblocked this outcome.

The first burst of angry determination fired up. *No.* She wasn't going to let Connor shove her out of Dylan's life because he hadn't gotten the woman he'd really wanted.

She put out of her mind those glorious hours when they'd managed to live together only too well…that magical wedding night that had changed everything between them…that had made it impossible for her to live under the same roof when she knew Connor still loved Dana.

It was unbearable that Dana's wedding had triggered that night of ecstatic passion and incredible emotion. It was worse that he was going to end their arrangement because of a woman who didn't deserve him.

She swallowed the thick ache that misery had lodged in her throat.

"This is all about Dana."

Her voice came out all wrong. Instead of sounding cool and composed, it was an accusatory croak.

"Dana?" He did a wonderful job of looking totally blank.

"Yes, Dana." So he was going to make her spell it out. "Dana, who used to work with you, who used to share your bed—"

"I know who Dana is," he cut in impatiently, putting his hands on his hips and managing to look even more intimidating than ever. "But I fail to see what she has to do with this discussion."

"Everything!" Couldn't he see it? It was so obvious. "She got married last week."

"Yes, I know Dana got married. So what?"

Somehow Victoria didn't think he'd appreciate her telling him he was still hung up on his ex. Especially if he was desperately denying that truth to himself.

Denial was a terrible thing. Ask her, she knew all about that. She'd been telling herself for two years that she disliked Connor, despised him, that he was the most arrogant jerk she'd ever met. When the truth was so much more shameful. She wanted him, she craved him, she'd been wanting to crawl into his bed and do exactly what they had the night of Dana's wedding.

And she'd reveled in every minute of it.

But she wasn't telling him her sordid little secret. "You only married me to get back at Dana."

"That's utter rubbish." His eyes had started to blaze with unfamiliar emotion.

She drew a shaky breath. "It's not rubbish—"

"It's crap." He glared down at her. "We got married because of Dylan. You're making it sound like I'm still hung up on Dana—I'm not."

Maybe she was over-reacting.

According to the newspaper article, he had known Dana and Paul were getting married. No argument there. Victoria tried desperately to regroup her thoughts.

His eyes snapped with fury, and it took all Victoria's determination to carry on with him towering above her like a dark lord full of fury and wrath. But she had to—if she wanted any chance at keeping Dylan.

"But *knowing* that they were getting married is different from living with the *reality* of Dana wedded to Paul." If his love for Dana was anything like the unfurling love she'd discovered for him, that would have been terribly painful. "It took her out of your life permanently. I can understand—"

He edged closer, knee to knee with her now.

"You understand nothing!"

"I can understand," Victoria continued as though he'd never interrupted so rudely, "that you wanted to get back at her. And what better way than by going through with our wedding?"

To Victoria's dismay, he didn't deny it.

After a long moment, she said, "Clearly you've since decided that our marriage isn't what you want." Because Connor loved Dana.

When he finally spoke again his voice was icier than she'd ever heard it. "Spare me the psychobabble. The issue here is not Dana, it's your commitment to Dylan."

Her commitment to Dylan was not in question; he was her child, for heaven's sake. And it was time Connor learned that.

"You don't want to be married to me because I'm not Dana. I can understand that. But you need to understand that I'm not giving Dylan up. He's—"

"I'm not going to give you a choice, Victoria."

"You have to," she said with grim satisfaction. "I'm co-guardian, joint custodian, and I'm—"

"And I am Dylan's biological father!"

Horror struck, she leaped to her feet. They stood face-to-face, both breathing raggedly.

"*You're* Dylan's father?"

He nodded.

"You can't be! *Michael* is his father."

She wanted to howl. It wasn't supposed to be like this. Dylan couldn't be Connor's baby.

Not with everything the way it was between them. The way it had always been, right from that very first meeting when she'd wanted him after one look and he couldn't even remember her darn name. They could not possibly have created together the perfect being that was Dylan.

It was too cruel to be true.

"I'm his biological father. It's my seed that gave him life. And I will do whatever I can to protect him. He's my son."

Just the sound of that possessive claim knocked the bottom out of her world.

Victoria put her fingers to her throbbing temples.

She wasn't giving up her baby. Connor was going to have a fight on his hands like he'd never seen before. The fight for his company against Dana and Paul would be nothing compared to the war she would wage.

She flung her head back, and their gazes locked. "Even if that means throwing out his mother? Yes, I donated the egg that Suzy carried in her body. That makes him part of me. What do you think Dylan will think when he learns about that when he's older?"

Connor's eyes had turned to slits of dark ice. "I don't believe you."

"Why should I lie? It wouldn't get me anywhere." She stood toe-to-toe with him. If she let him win this battle it would be over. She had to convince him. "I can produce the donor agreement to prove that I'm his mother. And you're not kicking me out of my son's life because you've realized you can't get over your worthless lover."

Under her shock and the growing anger there was hurt that he thought her so unworthy of motherhood. But she was dammed if she would let him see how much she cared.

"I'm not in love with Dana," he said into the hush that had fallen.

She studied him, looking for signs of subterfuge. "You don't need to pretend with me."

He grimaced. "I'm not pretending. I got over her a while ago. And it's been surprising to learn how many people think I've had a lucky escape."

A feeling of immense relief fell over her. If he wasn't in

love with Dana, and if they were both Dylan's parents, then there was no reason for him to push her away.

Except that he felt she hadn't been a very good mother....

Victoria sank back onto the couch and dropped her head in her hands. "Dylan is more important to me than anything in the world." Half-fearful of what expression she'd find, she parted her fingers and gazed up at Connor through the gaps.

The cushion lowered as he dropped down beside her. "But what about your job? That's always been your number-one priority." His face was stern, but at least he was listening.

"I love my work, Connor."

How could she explain to him that her work was her security blanket? The thing in life that made her feel worthwhile. He'd think her a total nut.

So instead, she said, "Don't push me out of Dylan's life. He's all I have left of Suzy and he's the only child I'll ever have."

"You should have told me sooner."

"I considered it. But I promised Suzy that I wouldn't tell anyone. I finally convinced myself that you should know. But I couldn't find a way to tell you. What stopped you telling me?"

He shook his head. "At first there was just so much to cope with, I honestly never considered it. Then once you moved in I thought that you were already so stressed that I might take Dylan away from you, that if you knew he was my son you would become even more anxious. I wanted you to settle down a bit before I told you."

"I suppose that's why you're kicking me out now," she said sarcastically.

Connor's expression changed. "Tory—"

Her mobile rang.

"Leave it," he ordered as she dropped onto her knees and rummaged in the side pocket of her laptop bag.

Prickling at the return of his high-handed tone, she said, "I can't. It might be important."

"Work, you mean."

She forced herself to ignore the icily sarcastic jibe and squinted at the face of her cell phone. The number was unfamiliar. And so was the voice that introduced itself as Juliet after she'd said hello.

Listening in absolute silence and in growing guilt to what Juliet had to say, Victoria heard the silent screaming in her head. *Please not this.*

She terminated the call and raised her gaze to Connor's bleak visage.

"My father has had a heart attack."

Connor insisted on accompanying Victoria to the hospital after waking Moni to look after Dylan. It didn't take him long to bundle a rigid Victoria into the Maserati and head for the hospital.

"I haven't seen my father for three years—and I haven't spoken to him in months."

Connor shot a look to Victoria where she sat curled in the passenger seat, her hair tousled and wild against the leather seat back, her eyes dull and staring.

"The conversation ended badly the last time he called."

Her voice was flat and lifeless—nothing like the decisive Victoria he knew. Guilt etched deeply into her pale, drawn features. Empathy for her overwhelmed him. And he wished he could absorb the pain she must be feeling. Coming on top of the crushing shock of Suzy's death, the news of her father's heart attack must be a heavy blow.

He nosed the car into the hospital's underground car park and came around to help her out before putting a hand under her elbow and escorting her into the elevator.

Frank Sutton was still undergoing an emergency angioplasty to open the blocked coronary artery, they were advised by an efficient nurse who sent them to the visitor's waiting room.

As they came through the double doors a woman with a round face and laugh lines leaped to her feet and directed a shaky, uncertain smile at them. "Victoria?"

Victoria moved forward. "Juliet?" At the older woman's nod she said, "Thank you for calling me."

"I tried your home number first, but a disconnect message gave me your cell number." There was a hint of curiosity as Juliet's gaze flickered from Victoria to Connor.

"This is Connor North." Victoria linked her hand through his elbow as she introduced him. Drawing a deep, audible breath, she added in a rush, "My husband."

She hadn't found that easy to admit, Connor realized with grim humor.

"Oh, Frank didn't mention…" Juliet's voice trailed away.

"My father doesn't know yet," Victoria said brusquely. "Do you have any idea when I'll be able to see him?"

"The nurses said it would be a while." After an uncomfortable pause Juliet said, "Frank's been talking about you a lot over the past few weeks."

Tears welled up in Juliet's eyes, and Connor read the discomfort in Victoria's expression. She had no idea of Juliet's role in her father's life, he realized suddenly.

Stepping forward, he said, "There's a coffee dispenser in the corner. What would you each like?"

Both women turned to him with expressions of identical relief. Thank God for coffee. It fixed everything.

"I'll come over and make my own." He should've known that Victoria would be her usual, independent self—even in a time of crisis.

"I'll come, too. Oh, good, there's hot chocolate." Juliet rubbed her hands up and down her arms as though her skin was already too tight. "I don't think I could face caffeine right now."

So he was wrong—and coffee wasn't always the answer.

Especially where human relationships were involved. Connor could only hope that the outcome this time would be happier than it had been for Michael and Suzy. For Victoria's sake, he offered up a desperate prayer for her father to make it safely through without any further complications.

It was three hours before they were allowed to see Frank Sutton. Although the angioplasty had been a success, Victoria was shocked at how much her father had aged since she'd last seen him.

"You came, Victoria!" His eyes lit up as she halted beside his hospital cot.

"Yes, I came," she said lamely. "Juliet called me."

"Ah, Juliet. She's my guardian angel."

"How did you meet her?"

"I started going to church," he replied. "She was one of the first to welcome me." He must've seen her shock because he added, "Hard to believe, I know."

His skin held a yellow cast marred with liver spots that she'd never noticed. He looked old and tired. A broken man. Nothing like the feckless, handsome man who'd ruined her mother's life and made her childhood a battlefield. A sliver of pity pierced her heart.

Whatever he'd done, however enraged and disappointed she'd been with him in the past for failing her, he didn't deserve this.

His hand inched out and closed over hers, the tightening fingers telling her without words of his fear and desperation.

"Frank, this is Victoria's husband, Connor North," Juliet said from the foot of the bed.

Frank lifted his head with a struggle. "You're married?"

And she'd never told him.

It hung between them, yet another recrimination.

Victoria nodded miserably. Connor had been right. She should have invited her father to the wedding, despite their differences.

"Remember my friend Suzy?"

"Of course I remember Suzy. I was sometimes home through the years." His mouth twisted. "Even though you and your mother probably wouldn't believe that, not that I blame either of you," he added as she clenched her fingers under his grip.

"Suzy died in a car accident. Her husband was killed, too." How to explain it? "They had a baby—"

"Oh, poor mite," exclaimed Juliet.

"His name is Dylan…Connor and I were appointed his guardians—"

"And you fell in love." Juliet wore a dreamy expression, and Victoria didn't have the heart to disillusion her.

She searched for something to say that wouldn't make their marriage sound like a cold, convenient arrangement.

Juliet took Frank's other hand. "Your father has been wanting to call you. He's got something to ask you." A smile lit up her cheerful round face, and Victoria found herself warming more and more to the other woman. She had a brisk lightheartedness that was contagious.

"Juliet wants us to get married." Her father's eyes were oddly anxious as he waited for her response.

What did he expect her to do? Refuse permission? She would never do that. Even though she believed Juliet ought to be warned what she was getting herself into.

But it wasn't apprehension that lurked in his eyes. It was something infinitely more basic….

Her father wanted her approval.

Deep within her something gave. He'd never sought her approval before.

"That's wonderful," she said. "When will the wedding be?"

The lines around his eyes eased fractionally. "I've still got to propose. Maybe Juliet won't have me."

"It's been difficult enough to get you to this point, so I'm hardly likely to bolt now." Despite her tart tone, Juliet's eyes overflowed with emotion, tears not far away. "You silly, stubborn man. You had to almost die before you saw sense. Now you'd better hurry up and ask."

"Worried I might croak?"

"Don't joke about dying." Juliet gave a visible shiver then leaned across the bed and brushed her lips across his furrowed brow. "There's nothing remotely funny about it."

"You could do so much better, my dear," Frank whispered and Victoria's own eyes grew dewy.

"Don't sell yourself short, honey." Juliet straightened. "Now hurry up, before the nurse comes back and chases us all out. I've got witnesses now, so you won't be able to back out later."

Victoria exchanged looks with Connor—his eyes were gleaming with humor.

"Juliet, my dear, I've wasted a lot of time because I was afraid I'd let you down. I'm certainly no Romeo, but you will bring light to my life if you marry me."

A funny sensation shot through Victoria.

Juliet loved her father. The emotion in her glowing eyes was unmistakable as she gazed at Frank. But Victoria's stomach hollowed out at the certainty that Juliet was heading for heartbreak.

Her father wasn't capable of living up to anyone's love. He'd even admitted that he hadn't wanted to propose because he knew he would let Juliet down.

Yet before she could protest she heard Juliet reply, "Of course I'll marry you, Frank. Tomorrow if you wish. You only ever had to ask."

Twelve

It was midnight by the time Connor pushed open the front door. The coolness of the night had already settled like a blanket over the house. As they crossed the darkened entrance hall, Victoria finally broke the silence that had clung to her like a heavy pall on the way home.

"You were right," she said listlessly, "I should've invited him—them—to the wedding."

"Victoria, you couldn't have known—"

"He called me. He wanted to see me more often. I told him I didn't believe we could sustain a relationship." She glanced at Connor. "I was afraid, in case he walked away like he'd always done."

"You think he's going to let Juliet down, too, don't you?"

She spread her hands. "I hope not. But I don't know. He doesn't have a good track record at staying—or being responsible. But to be fair, my mother didn't try very hard either.

She just gave up. I thought that was what loving someone meant. Pain and unhappiness."

"Don't underestimate Juliet. There's toughness under that merry cheerfulness."

"She'd better be made of steel to survive my father."

There was no bitterness. It was what she genuinely believed. He considered her. "Frank was a bad father."

"Yes. Between him and my mother, I was determined never to have to rely on someone for money or love. But I don't think they ever loved each other—they got married because of me."

Was that why she was so desperate to be successful? Connor wondered. Or was it independence rather than success that she craved? That rang more true. If she could take care of herself, she wouldn't need to be reliant on a father…or a husband. Suddenly a lot made sense.

It was possible, too, that she saw Dylan as the opportunity to relive her own upbringing. This time with a happy ending.

In a moment of clarity Connor recognized that Victoria had never anticipated a happy ending for herself—her parents had seen to that. Yet she'd married him. He ached for her. She'd chosen to move in with a man she despised rather than leave Dylan vulnerable.

She had backbone all right, this wife of his.

He opened his arms. "Your father is going to be okay. Come, let me hold you."

"I don't know whether my father and I can ever find common ground. But I won't close this door on him again." She came into his arms without hesitation.

Connor started off intending to give comfort, and found instead that by holding her close, her warmth and softness filled a chasm that he hadn't even been aware of having.

Last time she'd asked to be held, he hadn't been ready. He'd been too full of grief.

But now he was ready.

Slowly he inhaled her sweet, feminine scent and realized that he never wanted to let her go. That she had crept into his life, into his heart. That she had become a part of him.

By the time she pulled away, Connor knew that the healing had finally begun.

Victoria stepped into Bridget Edge's office the following morning and shut the door behind her with a gentle thud. She'd given much thought to what she was about to do. After the shock of her father's heart attack and Connor's surprising tenderness in the aftermath, she'd come to the conclusion it was the only option open to her.

Entering the large office that was the domain of the managing partner made her feel a little like a schoolgirl appearing in front of the head mistress. And the steely look in Bridget's gaze did little to ease the butterflies already fluttering in Victoria's stomach.

Taking a deep breath, she said, "Bridget, I've come to give you my resignation."

"Have a seat." Bridget waved to the chair opposite her, barely glancing at the white envelope Victoria set down on the desk. "You're very valuable to us. Why do you want to leave?"

With a sigh, Victoria settled into the chair. "I need some time to straighten my life out. We'll also need to sort out what's to be done about my share in the partnership."

The older woman took off her stylish, dark-rimmed glasses and set them down on her gleaming cherrywood desk. "You've been under a great deal of emotional stress—and your role here at Archer, Cameron & Edge is very demanding."

Victoria nodded, relieved that Bridget understood her position. "I'm failing Dylan, too."

"And Connor North?" Bridget's brows rose. "Where does he fit in?"

That was the most difficult question of all. Victoria wasn't sure of the answer herself.

Oh, Connor. Closing her eyes, she said, "He thinks I'm a terrible mother."

And not the wife he wanted. What was going to happen to their marriage still needed to be resolved, and Victoria wasn't looking forward to that discussion, either. Connor had been tiptoeing around her sensibilities since the news of her father's heart attack, and hadn't raised the subject again. But despite his gentleness, it would have to be dealt with.

Victoria hoped that her resignation from ACE would make Connor reconsider, that it would convince him how seriously she took her commitment to mothering Dylan.

"It's far from easy juggling a demanding career and being the perfect wife and mother. We women have such high expectations of ourselves."

Victoria gave a tired laugh, and opened her eyes. "You can say that again. I had such grand intentions."

"Don't be too hard on yourself, Victoria." Bridget sat forward in her tall leather chair. "It's been a traumatic time for you—inheriting a baby, acquiring a husband and keeping up with your workload. I'm quite a fan of yours, you know."

Staring at Bridget in disbelief, she said slowly, "No, I didn't know. I thought I'd disappointed you, too."

"Not at all." Bridget gave her a smile. "I admired you two years ago when you told me that you were going to be an egg donor so that your best friend could have a baby. You were worried that I would be unhappy because the process would take time from your work."

"Yes." She'd been very concerned. Being a donor had been physically and emotionally taxing and had taken up time that had cut into her workday. "But you never objected once—aside from suggesting that I have counseling to make sure that I would be able to separate myself from the baby once it was born."

"At the time I thought it unlikely that you would ever have children—you didn't seem to have much of a life outside work. I thought that the baby might be your only one."

Victoria watched as Bridget glanced at a photo on her desk, then back at her.

"You probably don't know I was engaged once."

"No, I didn't." Victoria had perceived Bridget as having no life away from ACE Accounting. She couldn't help wondering what had gone wrong with the engagement.

Bridget must have seen the questions in her eyes. "We were touring, on a motorcycle. He drove, I rode pillion. There was an accident—an oncoming driver overtaking recklessly. They told me I was lucky. I broke my back—he died."

The image of Bridget young, on holiday and riding a motorcycle with her lover shifted Victoria's entire perception of her. "I'm so sorry."

"It was almost twenty-five years ago." Bridget gave her a small smile. "I got over it. But, as you may realize, what I have isn't the life I imagined for myself. I pictured myself at fifty-five with a happy marriage, children all grown up and a successful career. I thought I would have it all."

Sadness for the other woman filled Victoria. "Thank you for sharing this."

"I want you to know that I understand a little of what you may be feeling. Loss and emptiness are terrible things. You lost your friend. But you have a baby—and a husband. Enjoy them. Resign if you must. But if your husband knows you as he should, he won't want you to give up your career for him, or even for the baby. If he loves you, he'd want you to find a solution that lets you have it all, without stressing you to death in the process." Another smile softened the words. "But I'll accept your resignation, if that's what you decide *you* really want."

Victoria felt infinitely lighter, as though a load of expectation had been taken from her shoulders. She started to thank Bridget but the other woman interrupted her.

"Of course, there is another option that may bear thinking about. Why don't we rearrange your hours? Perhaps you can come in three days a week? Or five mornings? It'll be easy to organize, now that you've hired a junior accountant to help you."

"But partners have to work full time—it's in my contract," Victoria protested.

"Archer, Cameron & Edge wouldn't want to lose you, Victoria." Bridget gave her a wink. "Particularly when there's a chance that we might secure the account of the Phoenix Corporation. Reducing hours wouldn't even impact on your profit share—I'd make sure of that."

Victoria couldn't help it, she laughed.

"You didn't think this was all about philanthropy, did you?"

But Victoria had seen under the frigid exterior. A bond had been forged between them today that she knew would endure. A peculiar friendship. Bridget was not the hard-nosed harridan she always appeared to be.

Rising to her feet, Victoria picked up the envelope that still lay unopened on the desk. "I'll think about cutting back my hours. It might be a solution." If she could convince Connor that it would give her more time to spend with Dylan, and lessen her office load, there was a possibility that if could work.

Was there a chance that she could truly have it all?

"Good." Bridget picked up her glasses and put them back on. "It will give you a chance to get through this time—and through the next few years." She peered over the rims of her glasses. "I take it you will be having another child or two?"

Victoria gaped. "I—we—haven't talked about that." Connor had been determined to get her out of his life…not pregnant with his baby. That dampened her newly discovered optimism.

Bridget raised her brows. "Well, perhaps it's time you did."

Victoria left work early the next afternoon and dropped by the hospital to be greeted by the news that her father would be discharged the following day.

Both Frank and Juliet were thrilled.

"It's a cause for celebration," said Juliet. "And not the only celebration today, I believe. Surprise!"

Juliet whipped a bunch of wildflowers brightly wrapped in colored cellophane out of the bathroom.

Her father started to sing an off-key "Happy Birthday" and Victoria stared at them both in stunned disbelief.

"How did you…? You remembered," she said, when she found her voice.

"I have a lot to make up for, Victoria. I forgot too many birthdays when you were growing up. Never again." Frank met her eyes squarely. "Sometimes I wasn't even…there."

Victoria didn't want to think back to those days.

Juliet had fallen silent, busying herself in the corner of the room, and Victoria felt a wave of gratitude for the other woman's tact.

"Will you give me a chance to make it up to you?" Frank's expression was uncertain.

He expected her to refuse.

She placed a hand over his. "Of course I will, Dad." It was the first time she'd called him that in years. "A girl can't refuse the chance to be spoilt to death by her father."

"You're worth it, Victoria."

When her father turned away to take a sip of water from the glass on his bedside table, Victoria looked across to Juliet where she stood watching them both, a pleased smile on her face, and mouthed, "Thanks."

She knew exactly who had bought the flowers and made sure that she and her father got the best shot at a reconciliation.

By the time Victoria got home she found Connor dressed in a long-sleeved white shirt that hung out over a pair of well-tailored dark pants. He'd recently shaved and his dark hair was still damp from a shower. He looked utterly divine.

And her heart sank at the realization that he was on his way out.

The only out-of-place note was the baby perched on his arm. Dylan flapped his arms and screeched when he saw her. A tidal wave of love crashed over Victoria.

She crossed the floor in three strides. "It's good to see you, too, sweetie."

He held out his arms and she took him, covering his face with little kisses. "Is that ticklish?" she asked as he giggled and squirmed in her arms. "You and I are going to play this evening."

"Don't make promises you can't keep," said Connor in that deep voice that did illegal things to her heartbeat. "I'm taking you out for dinner."

Victoria lifted her head from the baby's face. "That would be nice."

Nice?

Who was she kidding?

She couldn't wait.

When last had she been out on a date? Usually she used work as an excuse to put men off. She was too busy. She had to be at an audit early the next morning. She had a meeting. She'd used them all.

Work had become her excuse to avoid relationships with men.

Until Suzy and Michael's death had forced her into a building relationship with Connor.

The last time she'd been out to dinner had been with Suzy

and two of her teacher friends, Victoria remembered. A crazy night at an Italian restaurant eating slices of pizza and sipping Chianti and filled with gales of riotous laughter.

For the first time she didn't ache at the memory of Suzy. There was only nostalgia and warmth and a glow of love. The terrible, yawning sense of loss had eased a little. She could think of the good times—there had been so many—without her throat knotting and tears catching her breath.

But she knew going out for dinner with Connor would be nothing like that hilarity-filled evening with Suzy and her friends. Dark excitement curled in her stomach.

"What about Dylan?"

"I've arranged for Anne to come in."

"But doesn't her mother need her in the evenings?"

"I booked a nurse to look after her mother."

"Oh." It was flattering that he'd gone to so much trouble. And that left her with no room for protest. "It looks like you've got everything covered."

"I have." He tossed her a knee-weakening grin. "Give Dylan to me and go shower and get dressed."

Victoria obeyed, feeling like she was stepping into a void.

In the soft glow of the candlelight that gave the restaurant an intimate ambience, Connor studied Victoria. She was wearing a yellow, sleeveless dress with a scooped neck-line that left her shoulders and elegant neck exposed. The golden flame reflected in her eyes, giving them a mysterious sparkle.

He shifted, and keys jingled in his pocket. He wanted to tell her how beautiful she was…how much she meant to him. He didn't know where to start.

"I offered Bridget Edge my resignation today."

Her words shocked him. "You didn't."

She nodded.

"But why?"

For an instant uncertainty glimmered in those lovely eyes. "So that I can spend more time with Dylan. So that you don't divorce me, and take him away."

"Tory!"

"Are you pleased?" She looked worried.

He tried to figure out what he felt. After Michael and Suzy's deaths, he'd hoped that she'd resign and spend all her time with Dylan—like his mother had with him and Brett. Yet now there was only relief at the thought that the terrible pressure that had been on Victoria would ease. What with Suzy and Michael's death, minding a baby, doing a demanding job and now her father's heart attack…something had to give. And he didn't want it to be Victoria who suffered.

But he knew she loved her work—and the independence it gave her—something he hadn't understood when he'd met her two years ago.

"It's not about whether I'm pleased—it's what you want." He chose his words carefully. "If you want to stay home all day with Dylan, you must do so. But if you want to work, then don't feel you need to resign." Had she resigned because she thought that was what he expected? Had he put that much fear into her?

God, he hoped not. That was the last reason in the world he wanted her to do it.

"Bridget was surprised, too."

The waiter chose that moment to bring their meals—Tory's steamed salmon and his steak. Connor waited impatiently for the waiter to finish tending them and leave.

"What did Frigid say?" he asked as he cut his steak.

"Don't call her that," she admonished, "she was very understanding. She suggested that I cut my hours back."

"How do you feel about that?"

Victoria paused to swallow a mouthful of fish. "I think it might be a solution. If I go in the mornings it will give me all afternoon with Dylan."

"Sounds feasible." Already she was looking more at ease. And Connor was delighted.

"I had an interesting day, too." He told her about the visit he'd gotten from the chairman of an infertility support group to whom Suzy and Michael had left a modest legacy. "Turned out that's where they met."

"It was driving me nuts—no one seemed to know."

"They didn't want people to know about what they saw as a humiliating flaw."

"Neither of them were flawed," said Victoria with some heat.

"I couldn't agree more." Connor finished the last bit of steak as Victoria down put her knife and fork. "I thought we might have some dessert."

"That sounds lovely."

But before he could signal to the waiter to bring the dessert menus, he heard someone call his name.

"Connor."

He looked up. Dana was standing next to their table.

"It *is* you. I thought it must be, from the shape of your head." Her gaze went past him and settled on Victoria. "I heard you'd gotten married."

"Dana, our table is ready." Paul came up behind her, and he didn't meet Connor's eyes. "We need to go through."

She pouted prettily. "Soon, darling." And turned back to Connor. "I didn't think you'd ever marry."

"The right woman came along."

Annoyance flared in the dark-blue eyes. "How romantic, darling. I want to hear everything." She shifted into the booth beside him, her black dress hiking up, and a stockinged thigh brushed his.

Instead of desire, all he felt was distaste.

By contrast, Victoria was smiling up at Paul and shaking hands as they introduced themselves. Elegant, gracious Victoria.

His wife.

Connor moved away from Dana imperceptibly.

Her hand landed on his thigh, high enough for her intent to be obvious. His distaste grew more pronounced.

"We came out to celebrate tonight," said Paul. "Dana's pregnant—she had a scan today."

"A baby? How lovely." But Victoria was looking at him, her hazel eyes velvety with concern.

"I always wanted a baby. Didn't I, Connor darling?"

A wedding ring, more like. Threaded through his nose. Marriage to a wealthy man and a generous prenuptial contract had figured heavily in Dana's goals. Her own success had not been enough. She had craved more. More money. More status. More power.

He met Paul's gaze. "I wish you both every happiness."

The tension in Victoria's shoulders eased a little.

She'd obviously been worried he might create a scene. He wanted to reassure her, tell her that Dana truly meant nothing to him.

He smiled at her instead, a slow, sensual smile, and watched as awareness flared in her eyes. Heat spread through him. He suppressed a silent groan. What had he started?

"Does Victoria know you don't intend to have children?" Dana's comment was as unwelcome as a bucket of cold water.

But Victoria only arched a well-shaped brow. "I don't think it's true that Connor never wanted children. Otherwise, why did he choose to become a sperm donor?"

Connor tried very hard not to laugh. It made him sound like he'd done it for a living. Victoria was outrageous.

Dana's mouth had fallen open. Even Paul looked startled.

"Connor donated sperm?"

"You didn't know?" Victoria did great work of looking amazed. "Connor and I donated so that friends of ours could have the child of their dreams, didn't we, Connor darling?" She drawled *darling* in a wicked imitation of Dana's use of the endearment, and Connor bit down on the fierce urge to laugh.

"That was very generous—of both of you."

"Suzy was my best friend. That's what you do for friends, help make their dreams come true." She gave an angelic smile as she encountered Connor's arrested gaze. He wondered if only he knew that she was actually chastising Paul.

"Do you often see the child?" Paul looked sheepish.

"His parents were killed and—"

"—we decided to adopt him, didn't we, Victoria?" He knew it was wrong to railroad her into something they hadn't even discussed. But the last thing in the world he wanted was a divorce. He'd be foolish to let Victoria slip away.

"Er…yes." Her eyes lit up with joy.

"So you only got married because of the child?" Dana had been silent, obviously thinking it through. Now her features relaxed in relief.

"Isn't that why many couples get married?" Connor gave the other couple a narrow stare. Paul glanced away first. "But at least I wasn't trapped into a marriage I didn't want." In spite of the fury that glittered in Dana's eyes, Connor didn't feel the satisfaction he'd expected as he made the comment. He had no need to pay either of them back further for what they'd done to him—they'd landed in a hell of their own making. With its huge mortgage that house would be a noose around their necks, and no doubt Paul was still struggling to service the interest on the loan he'd taken to pay Connor out for his share of Harper-North.

"Marrying Victoria is the best decision I've ever made," he continued softly, reaching over to stroke Victoria's hand.

Dana rose to her feet with an angry rustle of taffeta. "We should be on our way."

Paul's expression was far from happy. "Nice meeting you,"

he said to Victoria, and she smiled back at him as Paul sidled out of the booth.

Connor couldn't help thinking that even Paul knew who had gotten the better deal. And it wasn't Paul.

Thirteen

When they arrived home it was late, and Dylan was asleep. After seeing Anne out, Connor locked the front door and Victoria headed for the stairs.

"Victoria…"

She froze on the first step as Connor's deep voice cut into the night. He came up behind her, his breath warm on her bare shoulders. "I forgot to give you your birthday gift."

Swinging around, she saw with a shock that he was very close. Standing on the step put her directly at eye level with him. She took the flat parcel that he offered.

"Thank you—you didn't need to do it." She gave him a bright smile. "But it's very much appreciated." Turning, she ran lightly up the stairs, through the sitting room that adjoined her room with the nursery, into her bedroom.

"Aren't you going to open it?"

She hadn't heard him come up behind her. Drawing a deep

breath, she hoped that he wouldn't hear the thunder in her heart as she turned around.

"Yes, yes, of course."

Her fingers were trembling as she untied the ribbons. The gay wrapping paper fell away to reveal a picture frame. She turned it over and found herself looking into four smiling faces under the arch of a church door.

"You remember that photo, don't you?" Connor was much too close. "You even told me to smile."

"I remember." A soft ache welled up as Victoria stared into Suzy's beloved face...and then moved on to Michael's grin. Flanking Michael, even Connor's hard face wore a smile.

"We all look so happy."

"That's how Suzy and Michael would want us to remember them," he said.

She swung around to face him. "Thank you for this. You couldn't have given me a better present." She flung her arms around his neck, the frame dangling over his shoulder, and kissed him.

After a moment he kissed her back.

"Tory!"

She pulled away and looked into the face that had become as familiar as her own. The hewn cheekbones, the bladed nose and those penetrating eyes.

Connor wasn't her father.

There wasn't a neglectful, irresponsible bone in his body. He'd done everything he could to give Dylan a future that would be secure. And he'd always been there for her.

She owed him an apology. "I'm sorry for believing that you were a jerk."

"Oh, Tory." His hands tightened on her bare arms. "And I'm sorry for believing you were dull and dreary."

"*What?*"

His eyes laughed down into hers.

"I know. I don't know how I came up with that." This time the kiss was deep and very, very hot. By the time it was over they were both breathless.

He took the photo frame from her and set it down carefully on the dressing table.

Then he returned to her.

"We're going to make love," he told her. "No casual encounter. And this time you're going to stay—no rushing off before I let you go."

"Never again," she vowed.

"Oh, God, Tory."

She curved into him, her body so close that she could feel the outline of his chest muscles against her. "I'm staying right here."

"Forever."

"If you want."

"I want."

His fingers pulled down the zipper at the back of her dress. She shimmied out of it and it fell in a pool on the carpet.

He'd trodden out his shoes and unbuttoned the top two buttons of his shirt, and now he pulled the white shirt over his head. He stepped out of his pants a moment later. He wore only close-fitting boxers, and the sight of his hard, muscled body gave her a secret thrill.

Victoria kicked off her heels.

And trembled a little with anticipation as his arms came around her and he undid the hooks of the white lacy bra that she wore. He skimmed his hands over her hips, sweeping the brief bits of lace down her legs, leaving her naked to his ravenous gaze.

A moment later he was naked, too.

The hard ridge of his erection revealed how much he desired her. And he swept her into his arms and lowered her onto the queen bed.

"This is going to be over way too fast," he murmured into her ear. "I want you so badly."

He licked the shell-like shape of her ear and Victoria shivered with delight.

But despite his forecast he stretched the pleasure forever. He used his hands, and his lips, and his tongue to bring Victoria to heights that she'd never experienced.

When he finally parted her legs, she was on fire for him.

Connor positioned himself over her and drove deep.

She closed her eyes and let the passion take her. Her fingertips dug into his shoulders. He gasped and drove again.

Arching beneath him, Victoria found the rhythm. And then they were moving in unison, as one.

The pleasure rose in a bright, blinding arc. And as the light exploded behind her eyes, she heard Connor whisper, "I love you, Tory. How I love you."

The words tilted her into a dizzying whirl of color and ecstasy that seemed to go on forever. And she found herself gasping, "I love you, too."

Afterward they lay on their backs on the bed, their hunger for each other temporarily sated.

"Did you mean what you said?" she asked, turning her head to meet his warm eyes.

"That I love you?"

She nodded.

"Of course I did."

She gave him a slow, dreamy smile. "I love you, too. I've been thinking, Connor. That billion-dollar baby bargain of yours? I got the best bargain of all—as well as Dylan, I got you."

"Nah." He shook his head. "I definitely did better out of it. I got you, when I might have ended up with Dana in the greatest mistake of my life. My guardian angel must've been looking out for me."

"You believe in angels?"

He nodded solemnly. "Falling in love did that for me."

"I like the idea of Suzy as an angel." Victoria glanced at the photo on her dressing table. "I can see her wearing a halo on her curls, smiling that sweet smile of hers."

"With Michael beside her, holding her hand."

"Of course."

"They'd be happy for us, you know."

Victoria nodded. "I think so, too."

"They tried to match-make us two years ago—I was furious about it."

"I'm not surprised! You'd just been through a bad experience with Dana. It wasn't the right time."

"And you didn't like me," he said righteously. "You thought I was a jerk that no sane woman could live with. Yet look at you now."

"I didn't know you!" she corrected, laughing at him.

He bent forward and placed a kiss on the tip of her nose. "So you think you know me now?"

Victoria nodded. "To know you is to love you."

"Oh, Tory." He pulled her into his arms and kissed her. "I'll never tire of hearing that, of kissing you, of making love to you."

"I suppose that means that there will have to be a little brother or sister for Dylan one day." Her eyes turned a wicked gold.

"That sounds like a great idea." Connor laughed silently, happiness and joy filling him. "But we'll need to practice."

"So what are we waiting for?" his wife asked, pulling his head down to hers.

Epilogue

Frank and Juliet's wedding took place at Victoria and Connor's home.

And Victoria disgraced herself by crying buckets. But she didn't care. Nor did the man who stood proudly beside her, holding her hand.

They were both happy.

And so were the bridal couple.

"Just know that it's not that I don't adore you. I do," she sobbingly assured a radiant Juliet.

"It's true," Connor assured her.

Juliet laughed and patted her on the shoulder.

On the pretext of fetching a tissue, Victoria rushed upstairs and washed her face with cool water. She returned to the large deck onto which the reception rooms had been flung open, where a trio of musicians played festive songs. The evening was clear, and the first stars were starting to show. Lights flickered romantically in the trees while candles floated on the swimming pool.

Victoria couldn't suppress a smile at the sight of Anne restraining Dylan as he leaned toward the flames on the water's surface, gurgling with pleasure.

"Okay?" Connor asked her, coming up behind her and placing an arm around her shoulder.

She gave one last sniff. "I'm fine. I always cry at weddings."

"I remember. You cried at Suzy and Michael's wedding. But you didn't cry at ours." He placed a finger under her chin and gave her a searching glance. "Any reason for that?"

"Because I was terrified that once I started I wouldn't be able to stop."

He opened his arms and she stepped into them. "I'm still here."

"Don't," she whispered, "you'll set me off all over again."

He shuffled his feet and she followed his lead. It looked to all the world as if they were dancing.

"I love your happy tears. Don't store them up, you should release them."

"I'd drown you." She gave him a weak smile.

He smiled back. "Do your worst, I don't scare easily."

Oh, Connor.

This was when he turned her heart to mush. Wordlessly, she snuggled up to him and let the music take her to a quiet place where only she and Connor, with his arms around her and his body close to hers, existed.

When the song came to an end they made their way to the pool. Dylan saw them approaching and shrieked happily.

This was her family, her home. As the next melody started to play, Victoria knew that her life was complete, she had it all.

* * * * *

THE PRINCE DEMANDS AN HEIR...
AND WHAT HE WANTS, HE GETS!

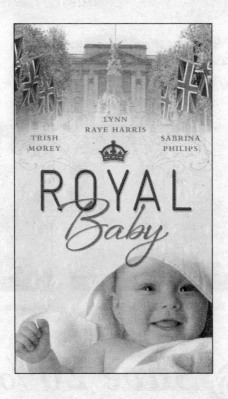

Let us treat you like a queen—relax and enjoy three glamorous, passionate stories about privileged royal life, love affairs...and scandalous pregnancies!

www.millsandboon.co.uk

0613/MB420

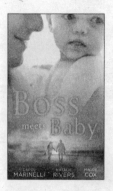

The World of Mills & Boon®

There's a Mills & Boon® series that's perfect for you. We publish ten series and, with new titles every month, you never have to wait long for your favourite to come along.

Blaze.
Scorching hot, sexy reads
4 new stories every month

By Request
Relive the romance with the best of the best
9 new stories every month

Cherish™
Romance to melt the heart every time
12 new stories every month

Desire™
Passionate and dramatic love stories
8 new stories every month